ACKNOWLEDGEMENTS

Writing a novel always seems like a solitary endeavour, until you get to this part and realise what a great number of people aided you along the way.

I would first like to thank the experts I turned to, from the authors of the many books I plundered for knowledge to the guides and curators at scores of historical sites I visited during my months of research, whose enthusiasm helped bring these places to life.

A special thank you goes to historian Marc Morris for reading the manuscript – his red pen once again helping spare me from too red a face. I'm also indebted to Edward J. Cowan for the memorable walk in Glen Trool, to Fiona Watson for granting me invaluable access to her report on the Battle of Bannockburn, to Scott McMaster at the Bannockburn Heritage Centre for the incredible tour of the battle site, to Duncan Thomson, Sarah Crome and all at the Robert the Bruce Heritage Centre for the warm welcome, and to Robert Low for the information on Viking boat burnings.

In this dawning digital age I feel it's especially important to thank the host of people who contributed to this novel behind the scenes – for their passion, their skill and their support.

A huge thank you first of all goes to my assistant, Becky Smith, for keeping everything running so smoothly. My gratitude goes to my agent, Rupert Heath, to Camilla Ferrier and everyone at the Marsh Agency, to Dan Conaway at Writers' House, Meg Davis at Ki Agency and Roberta Oliva. A heartfelt thank you also to all my editors, translators and publishing teams overseas, whose hard work is very much appreciated.

I am hugely grateful, as always, to the fantastic team at Hodder

& Stoughton, with special thanks to my editor, Nick Sayers, for his patience and insight, to Laura Macdougall, Kerry Hood, Lucy Hale, Catherine Worsley, Ben Gutcher, Lucy Upton, Auriol Bishop, Alexandra Percy, Laura del Vescovo and Jamie Hodder-Williams, as well as to everyone in publicity, sales, marketing, foreign rights and art and production, with a huge round of applause to Lee Wilson for the fabulous cover!

Thank you to my copy-editor Morag Lyall, proofreader Barbara Westmore and to the reps, especially Jack and Gillian for looking after me in Scotland. My sincere appreciation as well to all the book-sellers, without whom this book wouldn't reach you, with a special thank you to David, Daniel and the staff at Goldsboro Books for helping me to launch the trilogy in style.

Finally, my thanks and love to all my friends for their support and their friendship, with an extra special shout out to my fellow witches for the light in dark places. And, lastly, to Lee, for everything – thank you, my love.

ROBYN
YOUNG
KINGDOM

HODDER

First published in Great Britain in 2014 by Hodder & Stoughton
An Hachette UK company

First published in paperback in 2015

1

A CIP catalogue record for this title is available from the British Library.

ISBN 978 0 340 96372 2

Map drawn by Sandra Oakins

Typeset in Perpetua by Hewer Text UK Ltd, Edinburgh

Printed and bound by CPI Group (UK) Ltd, Croydon, CR0 4YY

Hodder & Stoughton policy is to use papers that are natural, renewable and recyclable
products and made from wood grown in sustainable forests. The logging and manufacturing
processes are expected to conform to the environmental regulations of the country of origin.

Hodder & Stoughton Ltd
338 Euston Road
London NW1 3BH

www.hodder.co.uk

CONTENTS

For we fight not for glory nor riches nor honours, but for freedom alone, which no good man gives up except with his life.

The Declaration of Arbroath, 1320 AD

PROLOGUE

1292 AD

After this shall succeed two dragons, whereof one shall be killed with the sting of envy, but the other shall return under the shadow of a name.

The History of the Kings of Britain, *Geoffrey of Monmouth*

Lochmaben, Scotland

1292 AD

*T*hey were leaving, while dusk stole the last of the light. In the November gloom the men's faces were pale patches in the shadows of their hoods. Few spoke as they worked, porters hefting chests on to the wagons, squires checking harnesses on the carthorses and moving between those knights already mounted on their palfreys, tugging at girths and adjusting stirrups, their frozen fingers struggling with buckles. The air was misty with rain, which darkened the thatch on the timber buildings that crowded the bailey and turned the courtyard to a slick of horse dung, earth and mouldering leaves.

Robert watched the preparations, Uathach's leash looped around his fist. A week ago the place had been teeming with lords and their retinues arriving for the feast, the bailey echoing with voices and laughter, music and firelight spilling from his grandfather's hall. A week ago he had crossed this yard with Eva, her skirts rustling as she moved at his side, the flush of wine leached from his face by the frosty dark. But then the tidings had come, heralded by the iron ring of hooves and borne in the mouths of the messengers; five words that had changed everything.

John Balliol will be king.

Only a week? It seemed much longer.

Robert looked round as two servants struggled out of the building behind him, bearing a wicker basket from which items of clothing trailed, packed in haste. Uathach sprang towards them barking, but fell back at a rough jerk of the leash. Settling against his boot, the pup looked questioningly up at his unsmiling face. As the servants headed for the wagons, Robert saw a scrap of material had fallen from the basket, a white wrinkle on the dark ground. Crossing to it, he picked it up. It was one of his mother's veils, now stained with mud. Hearing a soft voice behind him, barely audible over the thud and scrape of the chests being loaded, he turned.

Countess Marjorie smiled as she reached him, placing a cool hand over his, which held the soiled veil. 'Agnes will deal with that.'

Over the past year, Robert had grown tall, the sudden surge raising him above his once formidable mother, who in the same time had seemed to shrink. Looking down on her now, swamped by her fur-trimmed travel cloak, he felt like a giant; his hands, calloused from his sword, dwarfing hers, his arms, corded with muscle, capable of crushing her thin frame. He thought of the watery bloodstains on the sheets he had seen Agnes, her laundress, carrying from the chamber earlier that afternoon. 'This is madness,' he murmured. 'Stay. At least for the night.'

Marjorie's smile faded. Her brow furrowed as she looked away. 'Your father has arranged to lodge with one of your grandfather's vassals tonight. His hall is on our road home.'

'Then you stay. Grandfather can have you escorted safe to Turnberry when you are well.'

'He has made his decision.' Marjorie's eyes flicked back to him, harder now and set, something of her old strength within them. 'My place is with him.'

Robert wondered if he heard accusation in his mother's tone. Did she too blame him for his grandfather's decision?

She seemed to sense his question, for she squeezed his hand. 'Your father has accepted the lord's judgement. Carrick is yours, by his seal. Now he must return home to set his affairs in order. Give him time, Robert. He will come to accept it in his heart.'

He wanted to tell her they both knew this wasn't true, but then his sisters emerged from their lodgings, Isabel calling to the countess.

'Our chambers are empty, Mother. We are ready to leave.' She glanced at Robert as she spoke.

Marjorie nodded to her eldest daughter. 'Get your sisters settled.'

Dutifully, Isabel Bruce led her three younger siblings across the mud-slick courtyard, pulling her hood up against the rain. It was falling harder now, drumming on the waxed canvas covering the wagons. Christian walked at Isabel's side, looking over at Robert as she passed. He gave his fair-haired sister a reassuring smile, which she returned only briefly, worry plain in her face. Their governess followed, holding the hand of Matilda, who traipsed along reluctantly, eyes red from crying. Seven-year-old Mary came last, arms folded tightly across her chest, refusing to be led. They were all subdued, the younger two ignorant of the circumstances, but sensing the tension in the adults, the older girls aware that this flight from Lochmaben signified more than just the bitter end of a long battle for the Bruce family; that it was perhaps the ending of their family itself.

A harsh voice cut across the murmurs of the men making ready to depart. Robert saw his father had appeared and was ordering the servants to bring torches. His hulking frame was made even larger by a heavy black cloak that swung from his shoulders as he gestured brusquely for his squire to bring his horse. For Robert, the absence of his white mantle, emblazoned with the red chevron of Carrick, was strange. He looked like a different person. The cloak's hood was pushed back and his father's thin hair was dripping with rain. At his side was Edward Bruce, his youthful face pensive. With Niall and Thomas in fosterage in Antrim and Alexander training for the priesthood, Edward was the only one of Robert's brothers present for this.

Catching sight of his wife, the elder Bruce strode over. 'It is time,' he said gruffly, keeping his gaze on the countess.

Marjorie turned to Robert. 'Farewell,' she murmured, cradling his cheek with her hand. 'I will pray for you tomorrow, when you receive the sword and spurs.'

Slipping from him, she paused to kiss Edward, before moving to the wagon her daughters had climbed into. The carriage wasn't fit for a countess, but she was now too weak to ride. While the porters helped her inside, servants passed torches up to the mounted squires, the flames guttering and hissing in the wet.

Robert faced his father. He wanted to demand why he was dragging his wife and daughters out on the road in the rain and dark, but the look on his father's face stopped the words in his mouth. That rigid expression was answer enough. Robert felt a surge of anger, not towards his father, but his grandfather, whose actions this day had caused the rift between them to widen, perhaps to a point that could not now be bridged. The old man wasn't even here to witness it.

'I will do right by the people of Carrick, Father,' Robert said suddenly, feeling the need to justify himself. 'I will govern them by your example.'

His father flinched. His face, mottled by the wine that had soured his breath, flushed a deeper shade of red. 'When your mother is well enough, I will take Isabel to Norway. King Eric has been without a queen long past mourning. Your sister will offer a decent prospect. You rule your new earldom as you see fit, Robert. But be assured, I will not stay to see it.'

With that, he strode to his horse.

Robert had seen disappointment in his father's glacial eyes, anger and frustration, but never had he seen such cold resentment. It shook him.

As the knights and squires formed up, their horses jostling, Edward came to stand at Robert's side. Together, the brothers watched the wagons roll towards the castle gates, which stood in the shadow of the motte that rose above the bailey, crowned by its stone keep. The guards at the palisade hauled open the barriers and the company funnelled through, the gusting light of the torches fading with the thudding hooves.

Glancing down as Uathach strained at her leash, Robert realised his mother's veil was still crumpled in his hand. 'Where is he?'

Edward looked round at the sharp question. He studied his brother's face. 'Down by the loch with Scáthach, I think.'

Stuffing the veil into Edward's hand, Robert set off between the buildings. Passing the chapel and kitchens, he headed for a smaller gate in the palisade.

The last light was vanishing as he took the boggy path through the trees that led down to Kirk Loch. Uathach, off her leash now the horses were gone, trotted at his side as he quickened his pace. The patter of rain striking the webbed canopy of branches was loud. After a short distance, the trees opened out on a bank that sloped down to the shore of the small loch. It stretched before him, a pale mirror of the rain-drenched sky. Standing on the reed-fringed banks, looking out over the water, was a tall man in a hooded cloak.

As Robert walked towards him, there was a low growl and a sinewy shape came slinking out of the gloom. He paused for Scáthach to get his scent, then made his way down the bank, leaving Uathach to greet her mother with a volley of barks.

The Lord of Annandale didn't turn at the sound, nor did he look round as Robert came to stand beside him. 'They have gone?'

Robert stared at his grandfather, whose face was half hidden by his hood, only his hawk-like nose visible in profile. Despite his seventy years he was still broad-shouldered and erect. Robert felt a new emotion as he studied the man who had raised him as a son, taught him to hunt and to fight, and had forged in him an iron pride in his family's heritage. It was distrust. Unfamiliar and unwelcome, it tightened in his chest as he thought of how he had become a chess piece, pushed on to the board by his grandfather in a move against his father. He stood now alone, a pawn between two men who wanted to be king.

'You have something to say, Robert?' Now the lord did turn, fixing him with his gaze. His mane of hair, trapped by his hood, clouded white on the edges of his hard, lined face.

Robert met the challenge in those dark eyes. 'He blames me.'

'I know.'

Robert gritted his teeth and looked out over the loch. Rain peppered the surface. He thought of Affraig, whose appearance that afternoon had been the harbinger for the events that followed. He wondered if the witch was still in Lochmaben or whether she had already left for her home in Turnberry, on the same road his family had taken. He thought of her withered hand touching his *grandfather's face with affection; the same hands that brought him into the world eighteen years ago and wove men's destinies out of herbs, twigs and bones to be strung like webs in the tree outside her hovel. 'Did you do it because Affraig asked it of you? Was it revenge against my father? For what his man did to her?'*

'Revenge? No, boy, I bestowed this honour upon you because I think you worthy. Affraig came because she believes, as I, that the strength of my line lies in you — not in my son. His time is passing, as is mine. We tried to uphold our claim. We failed.'

Robert listened, unable to reconcile these words with the optimism a week ago at the feast, when they were all still confident King Edward of England would choose the old lord to sit upon the throne of Scotland, empty since the tragic death of King Alexander. This past year, during the trial to choose Alexander's successor, Robert had watched proudly as his grandfather, an illustrious player on the stage of Britain for almost sixty years, garnered the full-throated support of some of the greatest barons of the realm, in the hope of accepting that accolade. Now, the lion of a man beside him, who had fought the infidel on the sands of Palestine and served four kings, had been pushed aside and he, Robert, had been thrust into his place. Tomorrow, he would be knighted and, taking Carrick from his father, would become one of the thirteen earls of Scotland.

'On the feast of St Andrew, John Balliol will be seated on the Stone of Destiny.' The lord closed his eyes and inhaled, his chest expanding under the sodden folds of his cloak. 'They will already be preparing the Moot Hill. The men of the realm will soon make their way to Scone.' His face drew in, his brow knotting. 'The Comyns will no doubt be first among them, crowing about their victory. Balliol will give his allies whatever offices they desire. Our days in the royal court are over.' When he spoke again his voice was low. 'But the wheel turns. Always it turns.'

'Wheel?' When there was no answer, Robert pressed him. 'Grandfather?'

'On the Wheel of Fortune a man may rise from nothing to the very height of greatness, but tomorrow, when the same wheel turns, he will be brought tumbling back to earth.' The lord's eyes narrowed as he stared out over the loch. 'It turns for all of us.'

'Are our lands safe?' Robert asked him, after a pause. 'Will Balliol and the Comyns retaliate for our attack on their strongholds? For the deaths at Buittle Castle?'

'I do not believe so. But it is another reason to pass our family's claim to you. You were not part of that campaign. The blood of their people is not on

*your hands.' He studied Robert. 'You swore that you accepted the charge – to
uphold our family's claim to the throne of Scotland, no matter the pretenders
who sit upon it in defiance of our right. Your face now tells a different story.'*

Robert felt rain threading coldly down his neck. That afternoon, when his
grandfather told him he would inherit both the earldom of Carrick and the
Bruce claim to the throne, he had been so stunned that he had sworn the oath
his grandfather demanded of him without question. Now, he felt all the hopes
of the Bruce line – from his father and grandfather back to his ancestors of the
royal house of Canmore – settling on his shoulders. As the eldest son, he had
known this time would come; had been in training for it since he was a boy, but
he hadn't expected to assume the office of earl until his father's death. Now it
was before him he faltered, reluctant to reach out and grasp the burden, knowing the weight of it would crush the last freedom of his youth. 'Am I ready?' he
wondered out loud.

'I was your age when King Alexander named me heir presumptive. Did I fear
to live up to the expectation? Of course. Only the proud and the foolish do not
doubt themselves. Do not fear to question your readiness, Robert. The wise man
studies the way ahead and makes certain he is prepared. The fool rushes in.'

Robert's mind filled with the memory of his father and grandfather returning from the campaign in Galloway, six years ago. On discovering John Balliol
aimed at the throne, left empty on Alexander's death, they had swept down into
his lordship with the aid of their vassals, burning estates and razing castles.
Managing to halt Balliol's first attempt at kingship, his family had returned
to Turnberry Castle victorious, but not without cost. He thought of the cart
that had followed his grandfather and father home, filled with wounded men.
He chose his next words carefully, not wanting his grandfather to think him a
coward. 'I am ready to take the oath of knighthood and to accept the earldom.
But to fight John Balliol, as you and Father did? I don't know how I——'

'Fight?' The lord turned. His face was a craggy landscape of shadows. The rain
was easing, turning to mist. 'I do not mean for you to fight them, Robert. This
battle will not now be won by the sword. That time has passed. I – and all the
claimants – submitted to King Edward's judgement in order to avoid further
bloodshed. Balliol was chosen with the agreement of the court of the realm. Our
people have spoken. To challenge that could tear apart our kingdom.'

Robert shook his head. 'But to uphold our claim? How will I do that without challenging him? When John Balliol dies his son and heir will be king. The
bloodline is set. If we cannot remove him by force, then how will——'

'You uphold it in your words and in your bearing. You keep it alive in you
and in your allies. Our claim is a torch. I have held it aloft for years, drawn

men to me by it and lit a path for my heirs. Now, it is your turn to keep that flame alight. Just as, one day, it will be the burden of your sons. It may take a hundred years, but, God willing, if we keep that flame alive a Bruce may yet sit upon the throne of Scotland.'

Robert felt the tension leave his body in a shuddery rush. He almost laughed. 'I thought you meant for me to lead an army against him.'

'These are not the dark days of our ancestors. We will not take the throne by civil war.' His grandfather grasped his shoulder. 'The first duty of a king is to hold the kingdom together, Robert. Always remember that.'

PART 1

1306 AD

'I, to keep faith with God, will endeavour to revenge the blood of my countrymen this day upon them. To arms, soldiers, to arms, and courageously fall upon the perfidious wretches, over whom we shall, with Christ assisting us, undoubtedly obtain the victory.'

The History of the Kings of Britain, *Geoffrey of Monmouth*

I

Perth, Scotland, 1306 AD
(14 years later)

It was noon when the army entered the town. Over two thousand strong, they filled the wide main street heading for the market square, the hooves of the knights' destriers scuffing up dirty clouds of dust. Foot soldiers marched in their wake, boots crunching on the road, and the wheels of supply wagons groaned round under the weight of their loads. Torches, held by infantry, were pale spectres of fire in the midday sun.

Beneath the richly brocaded folds of mantles and surcoats mail gleamed like fish-scales. Raised lances made a forest of spears, adorned with streaming pennons that fluttered against the great plains of colour borne aloft by the banner-bearers. Across the swathes of cloth, dyed crimson and purple, gold and azure, were black-winged eagles, snarling leopards and square-headed bulls. Broadswords hung in decorated scabbards at the hips of knights, while squires and foot soldiers brandished cleaver-like falchions, spiked axes and hammers: all the instruments of war, honed for the splitting of flesh.

The men and women of Perth clustered in the doorways of houses and workshops, watching the procession pass. Wives clutched the arms of husbands, or pushed curious children back behind them, while blacksmiths and leatherworkers hefted tools uneasily in their hands, wondering if they would need to use them to defend their families.

Perth's citizens were no strangers to the terror of an English army. Since the war began ten years ago, the royal burgh had been sacked, invaded and occupied. They had seen the ships coming up the Tay carrying timber for siege engines and carts laden with meat and grain to feed the army rolling in through their streets, and they had been evicted from their homes to make room for the king's men, who raided their cellars and ruined crop-fields for the sport of their tournaments. But on this cool day in early June, with the salt-sour breeze drifting in from the North Sea, the mood of the invaders seemed different – less arrogant and aggressive, more grim and purposeful. At the head of the host was raised a great standard that the people of Perth had never seen before. Larger than the other banners, the material faded with age and patched in places, it was blood scarlet with a golden dragon rearing at its centre, wreathed in fire.

Aymer de Valence, Earl of Pembroke and cousin to King Edward of England, rode beneath the red shadow of the standard, his nostrils filled with the acrid stink of Perth's tanneries and abattoirs, the hides and blood of which had fattened the town with a thriving trade in leather and wool to the Low Countries. The earl's muscular frame was augmented by the coat-of-plates and the mail hauberk he wore beneath his surcoat and mantle, both of which were striped blue and white, and decorated with red birds. The Pembroke arms were mirrored in his shield and the silk trapper of his horse. His helm, the visor of which was raised, was crested with a spray of goose feathers dyed blue.

From the height of his destrier, Aymer scanned the frightened townsfolk, crowded like rabbits in the dark openings of their wattle and daub homes. The bell of St John's Church was clanging madly above the rumble of hooves and wagon wheels, but it sounded a warning rather than a call to arms, sending those out in the streets scuttling into the perceived safety of their houses. The townsfolk weren't putting up any defence. Nor should they, for despite the events of recent months Scotland remained under the dominion of King Edward, as it had since the nobles of the realm submitted to his authority two years ago at St Andrews. Still, Aymer remained watchful, well aware that the fires of rebellion had inflamed the hearts of many Scots and that within these tightly packed dwellings, interlinked by a confusion of rigs and alleys, could be those ready and willing to fight and die for their new-crowned rebel king.

'You believe he will come?'

Aymer glanced at the man riding beside him, several hands shorter on a shaggy white palfrey. It took him a moment to discern what the man had said, the clamour of hooves making the captain's French, heavily accented by his native Gaelic, harder to understand. 'He will come.' Aymer glanced over his shoulder at the six men who jolted and jerked in the midst of the company, dragged on ropes behind the horses of his knights, their hands bound and their clothes shredded by the grit that peppered the packed-down refuse of the street. 'I'll give him no choice.'

Aymer flicked his tongue over the cold threads of silver wire that bound in place his front teeth, taken from another man's mouth. The deeper he and his men had moved into Scotland, the more his mind had seethed with thoughts of his enemy and the revenge he would finally be able to exact. Here, barely miles from Scone where Robert Bruce had crowned himself king three months ago, Aymer could almost feel the bastard's presence.

Ahead, the main street opened on to a market square, green with gardens and lined with wooden stalls. It was surrounded by the stone halls of the town's wealthiest occupants. Some of the buildings had a second storey of timber with ceramic tiles cladding the roofs. The steel plates on Aymer's gauntlets flexed as he brought his horse to a stop. 'This will suit us.' He turned to his knights and gestured to the halls where faces could be seen at the windows. 'Move in.'

As orders were shouted and men hastened to obey, the rest of the army continued to pour into the square, wagon wheels churning up the soil of the market gardens, soldiers using the empty stalls to dump bags and gear. Once he and his knights were settled, Aymer would have the infantry camp outside the walls, but for now he wanted them with him; a display of might.

'What can I do?'

Aymer glanced at the captain, his eyes flicking to the blue standard hoisted above him. The white lion at its centre was replicated in the shields of the mass of men, over five hundred strong, now moving in around their commander. They were a rough band, clad in scraps of armour stripped from battlegrounds. Most of their shields, from small bucklers to the large kite-shaped shields favoured by English knights, had been crudely daubed with the lion over the original arms, the old colours bleeding through the paint. Aymer wondered how many had been taken from dead and dying comrades of his. So far, he had hesitated to use their strength, cautious to trust their pledge of loyalty, made on the border in the spring. His gaze moved back to the captain, who held the reins of his palfrey looped in his gloved right hand. His left arm ended at the wrist, the scarred bulb of flesh jutting from beneath the sleeve of his gambeson. The captain might be a hated Scot, but they shared the same enemy. Aymer tongued the wire that bound his front teeth. Bruce had taken something from them both. 'Do your men know the lands about here?'

'One of my master's estates isn't far. Some of them know this region well.'

'Pick a trusted few who know it best. I have a task for them. For now, have the rest patrol the streets and stop any trouble before it's started. Make sure they are forceful, Captain. I want the people of Perth to know who their master is.'

As the captain moved to relay the command to his motley company, Aymer noticed three men approaching from one of the halls, outside which a crowd was starting to gather. Better dressed than most of the townsfolk he had seen, with jewelled brooches pinning their cloaks, he took them for burgesses or town officials. A few of his knights were eyeing them, hands on the pommels of their swords. With a jab of his knee, Aymer turned his destrier. The beast snorted deeply and struck the ground with its iron-shod hoof.

The three men came to a halt, faced by the warhorse's armoured head. Beneath its silk trapper swung a heavy skirt of mail. Such horses were trained to kill.

One of the men stepped forward uneasily. 'Sir Aymer, I am the sheriff here. It is an honour to welcome you, but might I ask what business brings you to Perth?'

Aymer's eyes narrowed. 'You know full well, Sheriff, what brings me to this godforsaken hole. I have come for the traitor, Robert Bruce, and all who support him.' His imperious tone was loud enough for the crowd of Scots gathered beyond to hear. 'My men and I will occupy your town until the knave appears before me to accept his judgement.'

As English knights, swords drawn, began entering the halls and roughly ushering out women, children and servants, one of the burgesses with the sheriff started forward. His comrade clutched his arm to stop him.

The sheriff went to protest, then halted as his gaze alighted on the six men tethered like dogs to the cruppers of the knights' horses. Two were lying prone on the ground. One was groaning, his arm pulled from its socket during the brutal drawing through the street. The others had struggled to their knees, bound hands clasped as if in prayer. 'My men!'

'Your men, Sheriff, were caught tracking us as we approached the city. When pressed they confessed to being Bruce's spies.'

'That's a lie, sir!' shouted one of the tethered men. He was silenced by the mailed fist of one of the knights.

The sheriff paled. He turned to Aymer, raising his hands. 'I swear, Sir Aymer, these are my men, not Robert Bruce's! I can vouch for them personally. When we heard rumour of your approach I simply sent them to seek word of your arrival. They aren't spies!'

'We should not have to remind you people of the price of rebellion,' Aymer continued, his dark eyes not leaving the sheriff's. 'When the rotten limb of that treasonous whoreson, William Wallace, still dangles from your gatehouse tower. But, clearly, another lesson is needed.' He turned, motioning to his knights. 'Hang them up. Use the stalls.'

The six men began to shout and struggle as Aymer's knights hauled them to their feet. The one with the injured arm screamed to the sky. Those who fought their captors were punched in the stomach. Doubled over, choking, they were dragged to the stalls, feet scuffing lines through the dust.

'Do not do this! I beg you!' The sheriff moved towards his men, but found his way barred by the swords of English knights. He turned to Aymer. 'Have mercy, for Christ's sake!'

'There is no escaping justice for any who defy King Edward,' Aymer said, as his knights flung the ropes that had hauled the sheriff's men through the town over the beams of the stalls, which would support covers on market days. 'The dragon has been raised. Tell your people under its shadow no mercy will be shown.'

The sheriff stared up at the standard, emblazoned with the fierce winged serpent surrounded by flames that glittered gold in the sunlight. He went to speak, but faltered into impotent silence.

Aymer watched his men twist the ends of the ropes into nooses, pulling on them to test the knots. All around the market square, more townsfolk were appearing, hounded from their houses and corralled like sheep. Aymer scanned their stricken faces, satisfied. He needed an audience for this.

A harsh cry sounded and a woman burst out of the crowd, racing towards the condemned men. '*Alan!*' she was screaming, '*Dear God, my son!*'

One of the younger men, his chin bloodied from the street, jerked towards her. His face contorted, his mouth working, trying to form words, as the noose was tugged down over his head. Two of Aymer's knights grabbed the woman before she could reach her son. She fought them bitterly, flailing and scratching, but was no match. The young man closed his eyes, his mouth still moving silently.

One of his companions, an older man with a rough red face, was cursing his executioners, spittle flying from his mouth as he promised them hell and damnation. He bucked away as they drew the noose tight at his neck, but with his hands still bound his attempts were in vain. He continued to resist as the knights heaved on the rope, which sawed slowly over the stall's beam until he was lifted from the ground. He seemed to hold his breath for a long moment, then let it out in a rush. His Adam's apple bobbed wildly beneath the constricting rope. One by one, the other five men were hoisted into the air, two begging for their lives until their words were snatched away by the noose. The young man kicked and twisted in silence, the ragged screams of his mother giving voice to his dying.

Aymer turned his horse from the men, who would take some time to strangle to death. He had no interest in watching their drawn-out expiration, the final throes of which would see each man foul himself. The deed was done and already over as far as he was concerned. The bait was set; now to lure the wolf. Riding in a wide circle, he addressed the townsfolk, his voice rising over the noise of the army. 'This, here, is the price you pay for the treason of your false king. Spread the word among your countrymen that until Robert Bruce appears before me to accept his judgement, I will kill more. All who value their lives and the lives of those they love will make certain this message is delivered far and wide, lest you be next at the end of the rope.'

Methven Wood, Scotland, 1306 AD

Beyond the barley fields and meadows the walls of Perth, rising over the dark defile of a moat, were stained crimson with the last rays of sun. Several miles to the west, from the high vantage of a mossy slab of rock that jutted from the hillside, Robert Bruce scanned the distant town.

At first glance, Perth, corralled by its defences into a tight labyrinth of streets and houses dominated by the tower of St John's, appeared tranquil in the summer evening. Streams of smoke from cooking fires formed gauzy banners over the rooftops and three fishing boats inched up the broad waters of the Tay, circled by gulls. Looking towards the walls, the illusion of peace was shattered by the large encampment that crowded outside the west gate, close to a meadow where scores of horses were paddocked. Robert's keen eyes picked out the figures of men moving among the sprawl of tents and wagons, scattered with the amber constellations of campfires. High above the camp a trebuchet squatted on top of the gatehouse tower, one of four siege engines positioned around the town's ramparts. There were more men on patrol along Perth's walls.

Robert had been deep in Galloway, hunting the last supporters of John Balliol, when word reached him that Aymer de Valence had taken the town. Rumours, flying from person to person, growing more disparate the further they travelled, were livid with tales of rape and torture, and of townsmen hanged in the market square left to bloat in the heat. The Galloway campaign had proven fruitless, the lands of his enemies filled only with brooding silence, and Robert had been forced to busy himself razing minor strongholds belonging to the Balliol and Comyn families, acutely aware that these were petty victories. In some ways the challenge posed by the English occupation of Perth had been a welcome one and it was with a renewed sense of determination that he had turned his army north to face it.

Hearing a footfall scuff the rock, Robert turned to see Edward climbing up behind him, the hem of his mail coat skimming the stone. The rest of the company remained on the hillside, their eyes on the distant town. Among the dozen knights from Carrick and Annandale were Earl John of Atholl and his son, David. They talked quietly among themselves, sharing around wine skins and flexing muscles sore from the day's ride. Beyond, on the fringes of a wood, through the branches of which bled the fire of the setting sun, squires waited with the horses.

'Any sign of them?' asked Edward, coming to stand beside Robert on the crown of the rock.

'Not yet.'

'So close,' Edward murmured.

Robert glanced at his brother. In youth, Edward, who was only a year younger, had been as a mirror to him – the same strong features framed by the same cropped black hair – but over the past ten years the war had etched a different story in each of them, altering them from one another. Now, at thirty-one, Edward's face was leaner, harder. Battle scars carved new lines in his expression, stubble shadowed his jaw and dust tracked dark along the creases at the corners of his pale blue eyes. Those eyes filled with a keen hunger as he studied the English camp.

'Does their force seem smaller than we expected?'

Robert had thought as much himself, but didn't want to build false hope. 'It is hard to tell. Let us wait for word.'

'More waiting?' Edward forced a smile as he looked at Robert. 'Christ knows we have had enough practice at that.' He gripped the hilt of his sword, which hung down in its scabbard, the leather embossed with white enamel crosses. His smile faded. 'Soon, God willing, it will be time for action.'

In Edward's face, Robert saw the bitter memory of the years spent living among the English in the service of their king, pretending loyalty, while waiting for the moment they could break its hated shackles. Since their return to Scotland in the autumn, fleeing before the wrath of the king, who had discovered Robert's secret intent to take the throne, his brother had spoken often of the bloody butchery of William Wallace, which, as a knight of the prince's household, he had been forced to watch. Robert, too, found the memory of the rebel leader's death still vivid, acute in its horror despite all the blood he had seen spilled over the years. He wanted a victory over Wallace's executioners as much as his brother did, but it was need more than retribution that had brought him to this hillside in pursuit of that.

The words Elizabeth had spoken at his coronation three months ago, when the weight of the crown was new upon his head, echoed in his mind.

'You aren't here by right. You are here by revolution and murder. Do you think the rest of the realm will follow you when they know what you've done?'

He had assured his wife and queen they would, if they wanted to survive the conflict that would be coming, but his forces, although increased since his enthronement, were still not enough to face the iron might of England. Aymer de Valence's company, sighted in the spring, was only the vanguard. The main body of the English army was yet to come. But come it would, and soon. Robert knew a victory here in Perth would convince more men to follow him; would prove to them his strength and conviction. Only then, with the realm united behind him, could he stand against the English king and drive him and his men from Scotland, once and for all.

'There,' said Edward, pointing down the hillside.

Robert followed his finger to see two figures scrabbling their way up. Behind him the rasps of swords being drawn from scabbards sounded as his men were alerted by the snap of undergrowth. 'It's them,' he called, jumping down from the rock to join the company, quickly followed by his brother.

Moments later the two figures appeared, clambering up to the ridge. One was short and wiry, the other tall and broad. Both wore threadbare cloaks over tunics and hose, covered with dust from the barley fields. They looked like a couple of beggars. As Robert went to meet them, John of Atholl moved into step beside him. The ventail attached to the earl's coif of mail hung free, revealing the tight-lipped line of his mouth. Robert noticed his brother-in-law had his hand on the pommel of his sword. John only relaxed when the figures pushed back the hoods of their cloaks, revealing their faces. Both men were panting hard from the climb.

Neil Campbell nodded to Robert. 'My lord,' greeted the Argyll knight, between breaths.

Gilbert de la Hay also bowed, but his large form remained bent for some moments more, his hands on his thighs and sweat dripping from his nose. Robert was used to seeing the powerfully built Lord of Erroll clad in mail and surcoat. Gilbert looked rather comical in the ill-fitting peasant garb, borrowed from one of the drovers in the army.

'What did you find out?' Robert pressed, gesturing to David of Atholl, who was holding a wine skin.

The young man stepped forward and handed the skin to Neil, who gulped gratefully at the wine, before passing it to Gilbert.

'Those are Valence's men down there all right.'

'You saw Valence himself?' Robert asked sharply.

Neil shook his head. 'But his standard was raised in the camp and several men we saw were wearing his colours. Most of the others had the cross of St George on bands of cloth. Here,' he added, clasping his upper arm.

'Like Falkirk,' said John of Atholl darkly. 'Infantry,' he said, glancing at Robert.

'How large is the force by your reckoning?' Robert questioned.

'Maybe as many as a thousand.'

'Our scouts put the company they saw crossing the border in April at two thousand,' ventured Edward, at Robert's side. 'Where are the rest?'

'Inside,' answered Neil.

Robert's brow furrowed. 'You were able to enter the town?'

'No, my lord,' said Gilbert, straightening and pushing a hand through his sweat-soaked mop of blond hair. 'The gates were closed for curfew and the few people we saw on the road outside were being questioned by English soldiers. We couldn't risk getting too close.'

'We spoke to a cowherd out in the pastures,' explained Neil. 'He told us the English have more men inside Perth. They've taken over the houses of the burgesses.'

'Could he say how many?'

'Couldn't even count his cows, my lord,' responded Neil wryly.

'But he confirmed the stories of townsfolk being put to death,' said Gilbert. 'Valence is letting it be known far and wide that he'll hang more each day until you appear before him to accept judgement for – in his words, my lord – your treason and the murder of his dear brother.'

'Dear brother?' Robert's harsh laugh was devoid of humour. Aymer de Valence and John Comyn had been brothers by marriage alone. The two men had been close for a time in youth, mostly, he thought, because they shared a dislike of him, but that early friendship hadn't survived the war. 'Did you learn anything else?'

'Just one thing.' Neil's scarred face was grave. 'The cowherd mentioned a banner raised in the market square. He said it was decorated with a golden dragon.'

Robert's mind filled with the image of a great standard, blood scarlet in colour, with a fierce winged serpent at its centre, shrouded in flames. It was an emblem as familiar as his own coat of arms and one he had loved and come to loathe by turns. In youth he had seen it lifted over tournament grounds, a mark of pomp and pride. Later, he had seen it hoisted above battlegrounds like a fist; a symbol of terror. It was the dragon banner of King Edward of England and to raise it was to declare no mercy.

The men around him looked grim. They all knew the meaning of the banner. Chivalry flew in the face of it. Robert's gaze drifted to

Perth's ramparts, where the campfires of the English were glowing brighter with the approach of dusk. Despite the fact he had been expecting it for months, and preparing for it as best he could, the coming conflict had still seemed distant, unreal almost. Now it was before him, evident in that sprawling encampment, and all too real with the red menace of that standard.

War was finally upon him.

2

Methven Wood, Scotland, 1306 AD

Robert rode through the woods at the head of the company, dead branches and sprays of pine cones splintering under the hooves of his grey palfrey, Ghost. The trees that cloaked the hill thinned to the right where the land fell sharply into the valley cut by the River Almond. Beyond, in the distance, the mountains of Breadalbane were stark against the wine-dark sky.

While he had been spying on Perth, the greater part of his army had spread out among the trees on the other side of the ridge. Almost one thousand strong, they were a diverse assembly of drovers, shepherds, farmers and tradesmen armed with spears and clubs, young squires girded with keen-bladed swords and archers from Selkirk Forest in green woollen hukes. There were also a number of Highlanders bearing long-handled axes and clad in their customary short tunics, their bare legs covered with bites from insects that came as a plague on the midsummer winds. Among these commoners were some of the highest-born men of the realm, garbed in surcoats and mail, surrounded by retinues of knights and servants. Many rested on the grass, helms and shields beside them. The amber glow of torches highlighted their faces, full of question and expectation as their king rode in, his gold mantle cascading over the rump of his horse, emblazoned with the red lion of Scotland.

Ordering John of Atholl to summon the rest of his commanders to a war council, Robert urged Ghost into a clearing where Nes was overseeing two servants erecting a tent. A small campfire was burning and an iron pot had been strung up over it. The rich smell of meat mingled with the tang of smoke and pine sap.

'I had Patrick make camp, sire,' Nes said, taking the palfrey's reins. Although recently knighted, Nes had been Robert's squire for years before that and the gesture was automatic.

The tent was small, with room for just one man, but it was shelter enough on a balmy night like this. Buckets, blankets and other supplies had been stacked on the ground, removed from the packhorses. The raid on Galloway had called for the army to travel light from Aberdeen, forgoing carts and wagons. Robert didn't even have the royal standard with him, only his old banner that displayed the Carrick arms. The standard, the only item of Scottish regalia hidden from King Edward after the first conquest, had been presented before his coronation by Robert Wishart, Bishop of Glasgow, but after the ceremony, he had asked the bishop to keep it safe until his reign was secured.

This simple forest camp wasn't much fit for a king, but there was comfort in its familiarity. In the early years of the war Robert had spent more nights with moss and bracken for a bed than silk and feathers.

Feeling something brush his leg, he looked down to see his hound had come to greet him. Fionn, the last of Uathach's brood, named after the Irish warrior whose legends he had learned in the hall of his foster-father in Antrim, was tall, almost at his hip, with a coarse grey coat. A fearsome hunter who could bring down a fully grown buck, Fionn wore a thick leather collar studded with spikes. Robert ruffled his ears.

Nes handed Ghost's reins to one of the grooms, who led the palfrey away, avoiding Hunter, cropping the grass nearby. As Robert's gaze moved over the muscular rump of his warhorse he realised the leather bag Hunter had carried since the coronation was gone. He looked to the pile of gear outside the tent. It wasn't there. 'Nes, where is my pack?'

'In your tent. Safe, my lord.'

Robert's concern dissipated slowly. 'Have Patrick bring wine and food for me and my men.'

As the order to make camp went round, the army fanned out across the ridge. Men gathered wood and hacked at the undergrowth to clear pitches for blankets. As Robert crossed to the fire his servants had set, he worried for a moment whether the smoke would be seen from Perth, but the town was miles away and the high point of the ridge and the dense cover of trees shrouded them from enemy eyes. Scouts had already been sent to patrol the boundary of the woods. As he stood, watching the flames, going over in his mind what he had seen of the English camp, Fionn settled down beside him, his great head resting on outstretched paws. One by one, Robert's commanders joined him there.

His brother, Edward, was first, with Neil Campbell and Christopher Seton. Neil, who had discarded the peasant disguise and was back in his mail and surcoat, took the goblet of wine offered by Patrick. The knotted scar on Neil's cheek was highlighted by the yellow bloom of the fire; an ugly legacy from the skirmish outside Glasgow a year ago, which had seen the capture of William Wallace. Robert knew deeper scars of that battle lay below the surface, the knight blaming himself for not saving Wallace, in whose company he had found a home and a purpose after the loss of his lands to the MacDougall lords of Argyll. Christopher Seton declined the proffered wine. There was a time when the amiable Yorkshireman would have brought cheer to any gathering, but that fateful night five months ago in Dumfries had wrought its darkness in him and he remained sombre and unspeaking as he crouched beside Neil, his fair hair hanging in his eyes as he stared into the flames.

Gilbert de la Hay arrived, taking a slab of bread and a bowl of the meat stew Patrick was dishing out. At his side was Malcolm, Earl of Lennox, a full foot shorter, wearing a black velvet cloak over his surcoat which showed his livery: a red saltire and four roses on white. Malcolm's handsome face was pensive as he accepted the wine, his eyes on Robert. Following them were Earl John of Atholl and his son David. Robert at once felt fortified by his brother-in-law's presence. John, a good friend of his grandfather's, had become one of his most trusted companions. The older man exuded a reassuring authority that Robert had grown to welcome more and more these turbulent past months. Privately, he envied David having such a man for a father.

James Douglas emerged from the shadows beyond the pool of firelight, his hair crow-black against his white skin, strangely untouched by the summer sun. James, who had lost his lands and his father to the English, had recently turned twenty-one. The softness of youth had all but faded from his face, his features hardening into those of a determined, intense young man. With him was Niall Bruce, the youngest of Robert's four brothers, as tall and dark as James yet lighter in manner, with a smile for his brother as he approached. Robert frowned, seeing a third figure behind them – a sandy-haired youth with narrow-set eyes. His nephew, Thomas Randolph, hadn't been invited to the council. Robert thought to dismiss him, but stopped himself. Thomas, who had recently inherited his father's lands in Roxburgh, had brought a good number of men to his company. He didn't have to like the youth, but he ought to give him a chance to prove himself. Besides, he had promised his half-sister, Margaret, he would look after her son on the campaign.

As these young squires sat by the fire, Thomas looking around self-importantly, the last men arrived – James Stewart, Simon Fraser and Alexander Seton. Alexander took the goblet that was handed to him, without thanks. Not meeting Robert's eye, the lord from East Lothian stood apart from the others.

Robert surveyed the thirteen men, whose faces were bruised by the firelight. There were notable absences in the form of his brothers, Thomas and Alexander, and the bishops of St Andrews and Glasgow, but in the main those here present were, through trust, need or circumstance, his closest advisers. Together they formed a disparate council: great magnates like John of Atholl and James Stewart who had served King Alexander and remembered well the days of peace before the war with England, and hard-bitten warriors like Neil Campbell, Simon Fraser and Gilbert de la Hay, who had cultivated reputations for violence under William Wallace and been lords of the Forest in the glory days of the insurrection. All listened, silent to a man, while their king spoke, the thud of axe-blades and the splintering of trees rising all around as the army laid claim to the woods.

Malcolm was the first to break the silence when Robert had finished. 'So there's maybe a thousand in their camp, most of them infantry – but what of Valence and his knights, my lord? Do we have any idea of the numbers within the town?'

Robert looked over at him. Long before Malcolm inherited the earldom of Lennox, with the blue jewel of Loch Lomond at its heart, he had been among the force of Scots who had attacked him and his father at Carlisle, where the Bruce had been governor under King Edward. Later, when Robert joined the rebellion against the English, he and Malcolm had fought alongside one another, but it wasn't until five months ago, when the man pledged his sword to him in the shadow of Dumbarton Rock, that Robert had come to know him. That knowledge had since deepened into trust and the beginnings of friendship. 'Based on the numbers seen in the spring by my scouts there could be up to a thousand within Perth's walls.'

'What of the reports we've had since?' questioned Niall Bruce. 'In Galloway we heard tell of many thousands terrorising the city.'

'I think we can judge those accounts to be exaggerations swelled by fear,' Robert assured his younger brother. 'We believe they have two thousand. No more.'

'Any sign of sentries on the outskirts?' asked Simon Fraser, looking between Gilbert de la Hay and Neil Campbell.

'No,' answered Neil, after a thoughtful pause. 'But then with Perth's strong defences and such large numbers in their camp I suppose the arrogant sons of bitches feel secure enough without them.'

'We did see soldiers questioning people outside the town,' Gilbert reminded him, swallowing down the last of his bread. 'They are on the alert at least.'

'As is to be expected,' said John of Atholl, his eyes flicking to Robert. 'Valence wanted you to come here. That much was clear from the reports.'

'The lack of sentries plays to our advantage,' Robert told his men, ready to set out the plan he'd been mulling over. 'It will allow us to mount an assault on their camp.' Picking up one of the sticks his servants had set aside for kindling, he used it to sketch a line on the ground. 'The English camp is here, just outside the west gate.' With his boot he nudged a pine cone into the place. 'The road leading to it has good cover of trees and we would be hidden for some distance as we approach.' He flicked the tip of the stick in a long line towards the cone. 'Using a strong force of cavalry we would attack at dawn from the west, doing as much damage as possible, before retreating to our position here.' He scanned their faces. 'I know Valence. He will ride out in pursuit – him and all his knights. That will be our chance.'

'For an ambush?' said John of Atholl, nodding in contemplation.

'Yes. By the main body of our army, that will be lying in wait.'

'Forgive me, my lord,' said Christopher Seton, 'but if the English outnumber us two to one how can we be sure of victory?'

'The majority of their horses appear to be paddocked outside the walls. In the raid we will target the animals as well as the foot soldiers, limiting the number of cavalry that can pursue us. I believe we can create better odds with the initial attack.'

'Who will lead the raid, my lord?' James Douglas wanted to know, his blue eyes glinting in the flame-light.

'Sir Neil and Sir Gilbert.' Robert glanced at the two men, who nodded. 'But they will need strong riders with them, Master James.' As the young man gave a keen smile, Robert noticed James Stewart staring at him. Disapproval at the role assigned to his nephew and godson was plain in the high steward's face.

'One armoured knight is worth ten foot soldiers, my lord. You can be sure Valence has several hundred heavy cavalry under his command. They will still outmatch us considerably.'

Robert studied their expressions, seeing approval in some, but uncertainty in others now the high steward had expressed his doubts. 'Valence drew me to him with the blood of Perth's people. I will do the same with the blood of his men. We will have the high ground, the cover of the woods and surprise on our side. We have the advantage.'

'Valence drew you knowing full well you would not surrender yourself willingly.' Alexander Seton's eyes were on Robert as he stepped from the shadows. 'Those being hanged in Perth are casualties of a war that has seen too much Scots' blood spilled for any of us to falter now through pity. Do you not think he will have made plans of his own? I say again what I have said since we left Galloway: I believe you are walking into a trap.'

Robert's jaw tightened. It was a long time since the lord, who had fought in his company the longest of any here, had trusted his judgement. 'Valence lured me because he didn't want to waste weeks searching for me. Sir Neil is right – he is an arrogant son of a bitch. I expect he thinks I will come, we will fight and he will beat me.' He kept his tone confident despite the unease that crept into his mind at Alexander's warning.

Even when they were brothers-in-arms, bound by the same oaths, Aymer de Valence had hated him. Robert thought of Llanfaes: the town burning and streams of blood in the icy streets as he and Aymer went at one another in that hovel, fuelled by bitter rivalry, their blades still slick with Welsh blood. He recalled the violent joy he'd felt slamming his mailed fist into the knight's mouth; the crunch and give of the bastard's teeth. When he first broke his oaths to King Edward to fight for Scotland, Aymer's hatred of him had been vindicated. Years later, when he returned to Edward's peace, kneeling before the king in Westminster Hall to beg his forgiveness, Aymer continued to believe him a traitor. His obsession with proving it eventually lost him all respect in the royal court. The irony was he had been the only one who was right.

An image flashed in Robert's mind: William Wallace being taken down from the gallows while still alive to be opened on the executioner's table, his naked, ruined body finally beheaded and dismembered in accordance with Edward's orders for the gratification of the mob. Robert knew Aymer didn't want to deliver him to King Edward simply for the sake of justice. The earl hoped to witness first-hand his suffering, degradation and death.

'This is a great risk,' Alexander continued into Robert's silence. 'Whatever men we lose in a raid or a battle will mean fewer in our lines when we face the full strength of England. We lost ten thousand on the field at Falkirk,' he reminded them all. 'We have less than a tenth of that number now. King Edward's cavalry will cut through us like we are corn.'

'What do you suggest we do, Alexander?' demanded Edward Bruce. 'Lay down our arms and give ourselves up?'

Robert raised his hand as Neil Campbell and Gilbert de la Hay began speaking. 'It is true. I cannot face King Edward's army on the field of battle. Not yet. But what I can do,' he finished, locking eyes with Alexander, 'by liberating Perth, is inspire more loyal men to join me.'

Silence followed.

'Agreed,' said John of Atholl, breaking the tension.

When the earl's accord was added to by most of the others, Robert drained his goblet and tossed the dregs into the fire. 'Get some sleep, all of you. We make our preparations at dawn.'

As he headed for his tent, James Stewart followed, calling his name.

Robert turned with a rough exhalation. 'I am tired, James. Let us speak in the morning.'

'Your campaign in Galloway failed to vanquish those of your countrymen still against you, my lord. The whereabouts of MacDouall and the Disinherited remains unknown. But we do know the Black Comyn is raising his kinsmen in Argyll against you. The English are not the only threat you face.'

'I cannot change what happened in Dumfries, however much you will it.' Robert kept his voice low as the men began to disperse, heading for their own campfires. He saw Christopher Seton try to catch Alexander's arm, but the older man shrugged off his cousin's attempt to talk and moved off alone.

'But you can make reparation,' insisted James. 'The Comyns may not forgive your crime, but their family has always responded to the lure of power. Grant the Black Comyn a position of authority in your court and he may relent.'

Robert caught something imploring in the steward's brown eyes, creased at the corners with age and worry. He felt a pang of regret for the dissolution of their friendship, but banished it forcefully, weary of trying to appease his detractors – he had enough of them outside this circle. 'My grandfather once tried to reason with the Comyns and they left him to rot in a cell in Lewes. There is no reparation.'

'More than anything, your grandfather wanted you to break that cycle of hatred,' the high steward called after him.

'You're wrong, James,' said Robert, turning as he reached his tent. 'What my grandfather wanted, more than anything, was for me to be king.'

Ignoring the troubled glances from Nes and his servants, Robert pushed into the tent. Fionn followed him in, flopping down on the blankets. Light danced around the interior as the flame of a candle guttered in the disturbed air. Robert shrugged off his gold cloak, the red lion crumpling in on itself as it fell to the floor. He unbuckled his belt and removed his broadsword. The high steward had presented him with the blade on the night of his enthronement. It was a beautiful weapon: forty inches of steel with an eight-inch grip made of horn and a tear-drop pommel of gold, a fine replacement for his grandfather's old sword, broken at Dumfries. Robert tossed it on to the blankets and sat, pulling off his coif of mail and the padded arming cap beneath. His scalp, dampened by sweat, prickled as the air dried his skin.

Lying back, his muscles stretched and sore, he listened to the sounds of the army settling down across the ridge. He closed his eyes, craving sleep, but was unable to stop James's words repeating in his mind.

More than anything, your grandfather wanted you to break that cycle of hatred.

It was three months, almost to the day, since he'd been crowned on the Moot Hill and there, at the ancient place of enthronement, heard the names of Scotland's kings read aloud and his own – *Robert Bruce, Earl of Carrick, Lord of Annandale* – added to their number. Three months. John Comyn's body would be rotted under the soil. Worms might still be sucking on the remnants of his flesh, his organs liquid, bones bared to the earth. Robert imagined the poisons seeping up from his remains to infect the ground above, fragments of him collected by the soles of men and carried far and wide.

His mind replayed the moment the deed had been done: his dirk rising as Comyn came at him, the brief resistance of flesh, before it yielded to a firm shove of the dagger, steel grazing bone as it slid between ribs. Blood flowed hot over his hand and spattered on the tiled floor of the Greyfriars Church. Comyn staggered back, grasping the high altar, the hilt of the dirk protruding obscenely from his side. It was Christopher Seton who had ended the man's life with a desperate thrust of his sword, but Robert knew that first strike had been a mortal one.

As he opened his eyes the images in his mind vanished like smoke on the wind. Candlelight flooded his vision and the world returned to the solid present. He looked over at the pack Nes had stowed safely in the tent. The leather had sagged and he could see the outline of the box inside. He thought of the moment it had jolted from his fingers to crack on the jewelled floor of Westminster Abbey, the moment he had seen, through the split in its side, that its black lacquered interior contained no ancient prophecy; empty of anything except its own reflection. He thought of the man who tried to kill him in Ireland, his corpse laid out in the cellar of Dunluce Castle, and James Stewart's shock when he recognised King Alexander's squire, the last man to see the king alive, all the disparate threads of a tapestry joining to make a dark, disturbing scene.

Robert's hand moved up to his throat, his finger trailing over the leather thong on which was bound the fragment of the crossbow bolt that had been pulled from his shoulder. James, more than anyone, should know he could not falter now, despite what had happened in Dumfries. There was a time when he would have done whatever the high steward commanded, but he was no longer a youth marching to the drums of his elders.

He was king.

A moth tilted at the candle, then fluttered away, burned by the heat. Its shadow played huge across the canvas, black wings beating the air. Gradually, Robert's breaths evened out and his limbs, still stiffly encased in layers of mail and padding, yielded to the heaviness that weighed on them.

He was almost asleep when the night was filled with screaming.

3

Robert wrenched his broadsword from its jewelled scabbard. The cries outside had been joined by the clash of swords, tearing undergrowth and the shrill screams of horses: a dense wave of sound that seemed to crash in at him from everywhere at once. Fionn had gone, barking frantically. Robert plunged after him, out into the night.

It was midsummer and the sky wasn't fully dark. By the pale twilight that filtered through the canopy, punctuated by the bright flare of campfires, Robert saw men running. Many were shouting, their voices high with panic and fear. Others, who had been asleep on the mossy ground, were staggering up. Robert's servants were already on their feet, Nes with them, staring through the trees to the east.

'*Attack!*' came a harsh cry.

A surge of blood fired Robert's limbs. Diving back into the tent, he grabbed his leather pack. Emerging, he shouted at Nes. The knight jerked round and caught the pack as Robert tossed it at him.

'Saddle Hunter,' Robert shouted to one of his grooms, who hastened to obey, as Edward Bruce and Neil Campbell burst into the clearing.

'English!' Edward yelled, seeing his brother. 'Valence's forces!'

Before Robert could respond, the rapid throb of hooves filled the air and six horsemen plunged into their midst, shields painted with the white and blue stripes of Pembroke.

Edward threw himself back as one swung a sword at him. Neil Campbell reacted quickly, dropping and hacking his blade, two-handed, into the front legs of one of the horses. The animal pitched forward, its leg buckling beneath it. There was a heavy crunch as it ploughed into the forest floor, hurling its rider over the high pommel of the saddle. Neil swooped as the knight crashed to the ground. Crushing his boot into the man's throat, he shoved his sword, wet with horse blood, through the eye-slit in the helm. Blood burst from the visor. The knight's body convulsed as Neil wrenched the blade out of his brain.

Robert caught all this as a series of brief images, broken by the legs and trappers of the horses as the rest of the knights galloped on through. One horse vaulted the campfire, its hoof clipping a burning log and causing the fire to burst apart in a billow of sparks. Closer, just in front of him, his servants were falling back from the swords of the enemy. There was a flash as a blade reflected the firelight. Robert felt something hot spray across his cheek. Patrick spun towards him, hands rising to his face, which had been split diagonally. The white of bone and teeth gleamed briefly in the bloody furrow that separated his lips, nose and right eye, before the servant collapsed.

'Sire!' His groom was pulling Hunter through the undergrowth. The warhorse was rearing, teeth bared.

Grabbing hold of the reins, Robert hollered for his brother and Neil to mount up. He hauled himself into the saddle, and shortened the reins in one hand, the other still gripping his broadsword. Hunter wheeled and stamped beneath him. Where, for Christ's sake, were the scouts? Alexander Seton's voice echoed in his mind, filling him with icy truth. *I say again – I believe you are walking into a trap.* Dear God, he had ordered his men to make camp and they had dutifully spread out across the hillside. He had made them lambs in a field. Now, the wolves had come.

Nes reappeared at his side, mounted on a palfrey, the leather bag over his shoulder. He was carrying a helm and a shield, the chevron of Carrick a bold red arrow on the curved white surface. 'Here, my lord!'

As Robert forced his hand through the iron grips, securing the shield against his arm, John and David of Atholl and Malcolm of Lennox came riding into the clearing at the head of several score men, Niall Bruce, Simon Fraser and the Setons among them. Not all were fully prepared for battle, a distinct lack of helms among their number, but they were armed and determination was livid in their faces. '*With me!*' Robert roared, snapping down his visor and urging Hunter into a charge.

As his men rode around him, their battle cries a fierce clamour, Robert glimpsed a grey shape streaking through the undergrowth. Fionn. A twig shattered on his helm, pulling his attention forward. A larger branch loomed in the narrow slit of his vision and he cuffed it away with his shield. There was a smell of smoke in the air and a ruddy haze of fire somewhere ahead. Suddenly, men appeared out of the gloom, dozens of them, running towards him. Robert raised his sword, then realised they were his own soldiers, most of them commoners clutching spears, confused and leaderless. As they scattered before the oncoming horses, Robert caught faces filled with fear.

John of Atholl bellowed at them over the thunder of the charge — switching from French into Scots. 'Fight in the name of your king! On the English dogs! *On them!*'

David rode beside him, lips peeled back as he echoed his father's cry.

Many of the peasants heeded the command. Panic changing to purpose, they hefted their spears and made after their king, sprinting in the wake of the cavalry.

Ahead, through the trees, a fire was spreading — some device of the enemy, or a campfire burning out of control. It had been a dry June and the flames leapt through the brushwood, smoke curling thickly. Silhouetted by the blaze, men and horses made a grotesque shadow-play of rearing heads, thrusting swords and arching bodies. Agonised shrieks juddered through their mass.

Valence's knights had fallen hard upon the infantry on the edges of the camp. Those who survived the first moments of the attack had gathered together and were fighting furiously, but peasants in woollen cloaks were no match for armoured knights, who had trapped them in a killing ground, ringed by slicing blades. Other knights were already breaking off to penetrate deeper into the woods, cutting down Scots as they went. As Robert and his men plunged towards the chaos, one such band came riding out of the flame-lit dusk.

At the sight of them, Robert rose in the stirrups, his sword swinging up in his hand. '*For Scotland!*' he roared, locking on an English knight, whose horse reared in alarm. Lowering his great head, Hunter barrelled into the animal, the momentum adding lethal force to his bulk. Robert felt the wind of one of the horse's hooves before it connected with the side of his helm. It was a glancing blow, but forceful enough to knock the helm clean from his head, just as the animal was lifted up and thrown back. Swinging his sword in a savage downward cut, Robert felt the concussive impact as the blade crashed into the falling knight's back, but he didn't see what damage was done as he was swept into the battle, flooded with that familiar vertiginous thrill, caught somewhere between terror and excitement.

It was a tight ground, hemmed in by trees and the spreading fire. Without the encasement of his helm, Robert had a wide view of the battle. He glimpsed a few dozen mounted Scots on the other side of a press of English knights. James Stewart was there, alongside James Douglas and Gilbert de la Hay. Before Robert could break his way through to them, a sword slashed at his face. He ducked and raised his shield, the crack of the blade biting into the wood harsh in his ears. Shoving the sword away, he punched his own weapon into his attacker's side. The tip tore the rings of the English knight's mail and drove the padding beneath into his flesh. Robert twisted the blade in the wound, before wrenching it free. The knight doubled over. As his horse pitched forward, he was tossed down among the pummelling hooves where scores of dead already clogged the ground.

Robert felt something thump into his back, but the impact was lessened as Hunter buckled, his hoof skidding in something slippery. The horse lurched upright in the press of men and animals. Robert went to strike at another knight, but found himself carried deeper into the fray by a sudden shift in the tide of the battle. Many of the Scottish peasants, bloodied and exhausted, were falling back, allowing the cavalry to surge forward. Some remained, most of them Highlanders with their long, lethal axes. One thick-necked man, close to Robert, roared as he chopped his blood-slicked weapon into the head of an English knight's horse. Wrenching it free as the animal collapsed, the Scot brought the axe swinging solidly into the knight's chest with a splintering of bones.

Robert heard John of Atholl shouting behind him, but he dared not turn, acutely aware of the blades carving all around him, horribly exposed without his helm. A man on foot came at him from the side, face contorted, soaked in blood. Robert blocked his blow. Their swords crossed in mid-air with a clash that shuddered through his arm. He battered away a second strike, before hacking at the man's neck. The man hoisted his shield to block. As Robert's sword smacked

into the wood he saw the symbol painted upon it: a white lion on a
blue background. Stunned, he left his defences open.

The man's eyes widened in anticipation and he lunged again.
Suddenly, there was a volley of ferocious barking and a blur of motion.
The man's sword went wide, missing Robert by inches, as Fionn leapt
at him. He went down screaming, the hound on top of him, ripping
bloody chunks from his face. Looking around him, Robert now saw
white lions everywhere, on shields and surcoats, dotted among the
arms of Pembroke and the myriad colours of his own men. The reason
for Galloway's brooding emptiness was suddenly clear. The Disinherited
had joined the English.

Robert's gaze locked on James Stewart, some distance away,
surrounded by English knights. Malcolm of Lennox was converging
on his position, along with Simon Fraser, both men fighting savagely,
but even as Robert watched, James's horse rose up, a spear embedded
in its neck. He yelled, seeing the animal go down, the steward disappearing beneath the seething tide of men. James Douglas was battling
to reach his uncle, but he had been unhorsed and was no match for
the knights amassing all around him. Robert glimpsed Gilbert de la
Hay grabbing hold of the young man's cloak, pulling him back while
fending off blows with great strokes of his broadsword. Malcolm of
Lennox had been cornered. Simon Fraser had disappeared.

Another Scot marked with the white lion of Galloway rushed in at
Robert. The man checked his blow at the last second, his face registering shock. He lunged instead for Hunter's reins. '*I have the king!*'

Hunter tossed his head, but the man held on, pulling the bit painfully through the warhorse's mouth. Robert stabbed out with his
blade, but couldn't reach him. Then, Christopher Seton was sweeping
in from the side. With a vicious arc of his sword, the knight cleaved
the man's head from his shoulders. The man's hands continued to
clutch Hunter's reins until the horse bucked away and the headless
corpse collapsed, spewing blood. But the Scot's shout had done its
damage. More men were turning on Robert, eyes alight at the promise of such valuable prey.

Away across the jostling crowd, through the clouds of smoke,
Robert caught sight of a powerfully built man astride an armoured
destrier, its trapper striped white and blue. The man's helm was
crested with a spray of feathers. He had snapped up his visor and his
gaze was on Robert.

Aymer de Valence's lips peeled back. '*Bruce!*' he bellowed, thrusting his sword in Robert's direction.

John of Atholl was at Robert's side, as were Edward Bruce and Neil Campbell, hacking desperately at the Galloway men pressing in on all sides. Hands reached out to grasp the man who had overthrown John Balliol, their former lord, and had murdered his nephew, John Comyn. There were too many of them.

'We must pull back!' Atholl cried hoarsely.

Smoke and sweat sour in his mouth, Robert wrenched Hunter towards the trees, into the shadows of which many Scots were fleeing. Yelling the retreat, he and his men spurred into the gloom, quickly overtaking foot soldiers and the wounded. The ridge echoed with fighting, many English having ridden deeper into the camp, aided by the men of Galloway. Men scattered through the trees in all directions like panicked ants pouring from the ruptured cone of a nest.

Robert passed a group running pell-mell through the undergrowth. He caught a glimpse of a youthful face and felt a shock of recognition, certain the young man was his nephew, Thomas Randolph. Then he was thundering on, no chance to slow or turn, the stampede carrying him out of the trees and down the steep hillside towards the river.

4

County Durham, England, 1306 AD

As the physician rubbed his hands in the basin, the odour of turpentine sharpened the air inside the tent. King Edward closed his eyes at the bitter smell, which had become a harbinger of pain these past weeks. Breathing through his mouth, he sat on the edge of the bed wincing at the spasm deep inside his bowels. The feather mattress provided scant comfort. Everything – the bed and cushioned stools, the smooth saddle of his horse, even the silks and linens he wore – felt rough and unyielding. It was as if his skin were thinning, exposing him little by little to every hard edge and coarse surface.

'My lord?'

Edward looked up to see the physician standing in front of him. His eyes narrowed as he saw the lancet and glass bowl in the man's hands. 'No leeches, Nicholas?'

'I'm afraid not, my lord. While the moon is in its current phase I must do all I can. Leeches are too slow for this work.' The physician's thin lips pursed. 'I say again, my lord, I would rather not do it at all, given your current weakness.'

Edward's face tightened at that last word. His grey eyes, one of which drooped at the lid lending him a permanent hooded scowl, fixed on the physician.

Nicholas Tingewick was a cool, self-possessed man, who had spent six years at Oxford studying medicine and canon law, but even he could not help but squirm under that gaze. Clearing his throat, he motioned to the stool he had set out. 'If you will, my lord.'

As he rose, Edward was gratified to see Nicholas take a step back.

Even with the stoop that curved his shoulders, the king stood at over six feet tall. Edward Longshanks, his subjects called him. His *weakness* may have stripped the muscle from his bones and hollowed out his cheeks until they were lanterns for the light to shine through, but it hadn't diminished the dread he still saw in the eyes of men when they were levelled with his displeasure. The elderly Dean of St Paul's had been so affected by it he had wilted and died right in front of him during a disagreement over Church taxes.

Crossing to the stool, Edward sat, hands on his knees, his body erect. A gust of wind rippled through the curtains that separated the bedchamber from the rest of the royal pavilion. Its cool breath whispered across Edward's sallow skin, which puckered in the bowl of his sunken stomach, his hip bones protruding over the waist of his braies. Coarse white hairs bristled on his chest, gleaming like spider threads in the candlelight. Scars riddled his arms and torso telling a long story of violence: faded tracks from his youth on the tournament grounds of Gascony, knotted ridges from his conquest of Wales, a depression in one shoulder where an arrow had pierced him at the siege of Stirling Castle and a whorl of scar tissue, close to his heart, from an Assassin's dagger in the Holy Land. But none of these scars was as livid as the wounds in his side – a series of neat red lesions, only just starting to scab.

Nicholas crouched beside the king, his eyes on the wounds. His face was intent as he set down the glass bowl with its slender stem of a neck. Placing two fingers to either side of one of the blood-crusted cuts, he opened up the skin with a decisive slash of the lancet. Edward grunted and gripped his knees, feeling the pressure as the physician pushed the cold lip of the bowl into his side, just below the cut. Nicholas muttered something, watching the line of blood trickling into the bowl.

'What is it?' Edward demanded, glancing down.

'The blood is dark and thick today, my lord. I will have to drain it well, until it comes red and thin.'

As the blood flowed, helped by Nicholas's fingers, which kept the wound prised apart, Edward focused on the folded book of parchment that hung from the physician's belt on a cord. The pages were covered in words, numbers, tables of astrological signs and phases of the moon. There were intricate diagrams of his body with its network of veins and descriptions of the look, taste and smell of his urine. The book charted the course of his disease, mapped out across its pages. On each of those stained sheets, Nicholas had painstakingly compiled detailed information on every facet of the enemy. But it was becoming clear that the sickness was hidden deep in the recesses of Edward's body and all the physician's strategies to draw it out and destroy it had so far yielded nothing but blood and pain.

Edward closed his eyes, feeling light-headed. Beads of sweat broke out on his forehead. After a time, Nicholas made a satisfied noise and the pressure of the bowl disappeared from Edward's side. It was replaced with a wad of linen soaked in laurel oil, which the king pressed to the wound, knowing the procedure well by now. The physician was conveying the glass bowl, half full of blood, to his table when the curtains opened.

Edward frowned as his son-in-law entered. Humphrey de Bohun's face, browned by the summer sun on the march north, was unusually animated. A new energy had sharpened the earl's green eyes, making him look younger than his thirty-one years. In him, Edward saw a fleeting memory of himself, so different to the shrunken ghost of a man he glimpsed now in mirrors and water. 'I said no interruptions, Humphrey.'

'I thought you would want to hear this, my lord. Word has come from Scotland – Sir Aymer's men.'

Edward felt the fog of pain dissolve. 'My robe.'

At the command, the physician brought the garment. The cut in Edward's side hadn't yet closed, but Nicholas knew better than to protest and stepped aside as the king pulled on the robe.

Edward strode through the pavilion, ignoring the expectant looks from his officials and servants. Humphrey de Bohun walked at his side, keeping pace with the king's long stride. The sunlight dazzled Edward as they headed out. Raising his hand to shield his eyes, he saw four men garbed in the blue and white striped surcoats of Pembroke. Horses, their flanks foamy with sweat, cropped the grass close by.

Seeing the king emerge, one of the men hastened over. Dropping to his knee, he bowed. 'My lord king.'

'What word from my cousin?'

The knight rose quickly at the king's impatience. 'Sir Aymer de Valence engaged Robert Bruce five nights ago, outside Perth. Men from Galloway under Captain Dungal MacDouall aided us. Their pledge of loyalty was proven, my lord. Together, our forces destroyed his army.'

'And Bruce?' demanded Edward, his heart thudding hard against the cage of his ribs.

'He evaded capture. But we came close, my lord.' Turning to his comrades, the knight gestured.

One of the others approached, carrying a bag. With a bow to the king, he reached inside and drew out a folded silk cloak. As Edward took it the material slipped open in his hands to reveal a red lion, rampant on gold.

'Many hundreds were killed in the assault,' continued the knight. 'Others we took prisoner, including a member of Bruce's own family. The rest were routed.'

Edward didn't answer, his gaze on the lion's narrowed eye. The red beast had been hoisted defiantly with the first declaration of war by John Balliol, the man he had chosen to be his puppet king, but who proved to be in thrall to the powerful Comyn family and by their will had stood against his attempts to dominate the kingdom. When he defeated Balliol and first conquered Scotland, Edward had thought the reign of the lion ended when his men ripped the royal arms from Balliol's tabard, stripping him of his kingship and sentencing him to a life in exile. But soon it had risen again, rearing over the heads of the rebels under William Wallace, who fought in the name of their banished king. He remembered the lion, huge and lurid on a wall in the ruins of Ayr, painted by the followers of Robert Bruce, who had turned on him.

There followed campaign after campaign, draining Edward's treasury and testing the loyalty of his barons. Two years ago, when the royal banner had been torn from the battlements of Stirling, the last castle to fall to his might, he believed it brought down for good. The magnates of Scotland had surrendered at St Andrews, the kingdom was relegated to a land and Wallace had been executed, his quartered body packed in barrels and sent to Newcastle, Berwick, Stirling and Perth to be strung up on their walls; bloody tokens of Edward's imperial might. But then Robert Bruce had risen up once more and with him that lion, proud as Satan.

He had taken the man into his household. Not once, but twice. He had fed him, trained him, sanctioned his marriage, given him land and authority. All the while, the serpent had been waiting to strike.

Humphrey's eyes, too, lingered on the cloak. 'It is a poor substitute for the man himself.'

Edward stirred. 'Did you find anything else? Any other possessions?'

'Only supplies and gear, my lord. We took a good number of horses, along with weapons and armour.'

'We will find him, my lord,' said Humphrey, turning to the king. 'And that which he took.'

Edward met his gaze, knowing his son-in-law had read his mind.

How many nights had he lain awake, pain gnawing at his bowels, his thoughts fixed on the box Bruce had stolen? His feverish mind had drifted often to the fate of the Gascon commander, Adam, missing since he was ordered to Ireland with a crossbow bolt meant for Bruce. Was Adam truly dead, as Bruce had told Humphrey, or had he been kept alive – proof of Edward's sin? And if Bruce knew enough to take the box from Westminster Abbey when he fled, did he also know the truth about King Alexander's death on the road to Kinghorn?

'Where is Bruce now?' Humphrey asked the Pembroke knight.

'He fled north into the mountains. We believe he will make for Aberdeen. Some of those we captured told us he sent his queen and the womenfolk there while he campaigned in Galloway.'

'Return to Sir Aymer,' Edward told the man. 'Tell him, if he cannot capture Bruce, he is to trap him in Aberdeen until I arrive. Tell him to use MacDouall and his followers to hunt down the rest of Bruce's supporters – any who weren't with him on the field. I want them picked off, like ticks.' He felt a sudden twist of pain in his gut. Edward doubled over, dropping the gold cloak. Humphrey was at his side in an instant, but the king pushed him away. Sweat trickled down his cheeks. 'Go!' he hissed at the knight, who bowed and hurried to his horse.

As the spasm subsided, Edward straightened, his face clenched. 'Summon my son, Humphrey. It is time for the new bloods to win their spurs. I will send them west to Bruce's lands.' He scanned the plain that stretched from the grassy slope on which his pavilion had been raised. The fields were covered with a sprawling mass of tents, wagons, men, horses and mules, all shrouded by a pall of smoke from countless campfires. His own body might be failing him, but this army arrayed before him was his iron fist and by its strength he would hammer Robert Bruce into the ground.

'We will leave no allies, no strongholds – no *rock* for the renegade to hide behind.'

At Edward's feet, the fallen cloak rippled in the breeze, the red lion distorted, its one eye staring up at the ashen-faced king.

5

Aberdeen, Scotland, 1306 AD

It was a ragged company that appeared before the gates of Aberdeen late that evening. The towering clouds that had shadowed them all afternoon had finally opened on their approach to the north-eastern port and rain poured from the heavens, drenching the column of men to the bone. It trickled down faces drawn with exhaustion, caused rust to bloom on broken rings of mail, soaked through bloodstained clothes and pooled in the depressions of empty saddles. Several of the animals were injured, some wounded in battle, others crippled during the desperate flight through the mountains. They limped along the road, barely able to carry their burdens these last unforgiving miles.

The guards who manned the town's south gate at first refused entry to the company, shouting down from the gatehouse that it was past curfew. It was only when they were commanded to open up in the name of their sheriff and the king himself that they obliged, allowing the line of men to trudge across the earthen bank that bridged the wide ditch.

Once inside, the procession wound slowly through the streets. Rain ran in rivers along the gutters, carrying the stink of night soil down to the Dee. As they made for the castle, which squatted on a hill above the town, faces appeared in doorways and windows, the people of Aberdeen summoned by the clatter of hooves and tramping feet. The gazes of the townsfolk lingered on the litters being carried in the midst of the company, bearing those too badly injured to walk or ride. Some nudged their neighbours and pointed out the king, riding beside the sheriff on a grey palfrey. Whispers became rumours, darting from house to house as the people of Aberdeen questioned what had happened and why the king had returned with less than half the army he had set out with in spring.

By the time the company reached the castle, word of their coming had spread before them and the guards were already hauling open the gates.

As the portcullis clanked up, Robert rode through the arched darkness of the gatehouse into the bailey beyond, where torches sputtered in the rain. His men funnelled in behind him. He caught a few voices lifted in relief as the weary and wounded saw the end of their journey, but to him these encircling walls that promised rest and shelter were cold comfort indeed. He slid down from the saddle, the sodden woollen cloak Nes had found to replace his royal mantle lost at Methven dragging at his shoulders.

The castle's steward hurried from the hall. 'Sir John!' He made his way over to the Earl of Atholl, who had dismounted beside Robert. 'My lord king.' His gaze darted across the crowd of men filing into the courtyard, some of whom were sinking to the steps of the great hall, helms and shields clattering down beside them.

In the steward's shocked and silent stare, Robert saw his defeat. It was burned into the remnants of his army like a brand, his failure laid bare in their depleted numbers and haggard faces. *The wheel turns. Always it turns.* The words, his grandfather's, echoed from some distant time. In his mind's eye, Robert saw himself bound to a great grinding wheel on its downward spiral towards earth. *It turns for all of us.*

'Clear the hall,' John ordered his steward. 'Bring wine, warm water, blankets. And wake my physician.'

As the steward moved to obey, more men hastened from the main buildings to help. A horse collapsed as its rider dismounted. Servants took litters from those who had carried wounded comrades.

Robert, turning to follow John, heard David murmur to his father.

'Did you see their faces? The townsfolk? Did you see the way they looked at us, Father? As if it was *us* who failed them?'

'Let it be, son.'

Nes emerged from the crowd, catching his attention. Robert noticed the knight was gripping the leather pack that contained the box. Looking at it, Robert felt a strange detachment. The thing he had risked his life to steal suddenly didn't seem so important.

Rain dripped steadily from Nes's nose. 'It's Hunter, sire. He's in mortal pain.'

Robert followed his gaze to where two grooms were leading his warhorse towards the stables. The destrier was limping between them, his head hanging low. Two nights ago, coming down out of the hills, Hunter had fallen. Nes had cared for him the best he could, but the horse was in agony, the bone of his fractured foreleg having punctured the skin. Robert knew he should have put the animal out of his misery, but he hadn't been able to bring himself to do it. Hunter's life felt bound up in his own fate, as if to destroy the horse that had carried him safely through so many battlegrounds would somehow seal this defeat.

'Do what you can for him.' Turning, Robert strode in through the doors of the great hall, where John and the others had sought shelter. A low hum of voices filled the chamber, punctuated by the screech of trestle legs on the stone floor as servants pushed the tables aside to make space. The wounded were set down by the fireplaces, which servants were hurriedly stacking with fresh logs.

Robert sat heavily on one of the benches that had been left in the centre of the hall. People milled around him, those from the castle quick with purpose, the newcomers slow and dazed. Feeling something brush against his leg, he saw Fionn. The hound was panting, his grey coat slick with mud and rain. Looking closer, Robert realised there were clots of blood around his muzzle, dried and crusted. Taking the hound by the collar, he began swiping them off.

'Sir.'

Robert glanced up to see a young lad holding out a glazed clay goblet, which was chipped at the base. Straightening to accept the drink, Robert's cloak parted, revealing the red lion on his surcoat.

The boy's mouth opened. 'My lord king!' He snatched the goblet away. 'Begging your pardon, sire, I'll fetch a more suitable cup.'

'This will do,' said Robert, taking the chipped goblet before the lad could protest. 'The wine comes out the same.' He drained the drink, some trickling through the stubble that shadowed his chin. The wine was rich and warming; a salve for his spirit. 'What's your name?'

'Col, sire.'

'Col?' Robert smiled at the name's simplicity.

'It was my father's name, sire.'

Robert passed back the empty cup, wondering if the lad had ever been outside Aberdeen's boundaries. He thought of the year he had spent as a page in Lord Donough's hall in Antrim, his world bordered by four walls, all his responsibilities decided upon by his foster-father. It had been the most simple time of his life. For a moment, he cursed the duty and the ambition that had driven him out of that hall all the way to this one, where it was not silver goblets and platters that lay in his hands, but the lives of all those around him.

'There're many here who need serving,' said John gruffly, appearing at Col's side.

Robert watched the lad hurry off. He knew his brother-in-law was staring at him, but didn't meet the older man's gaze.

The earl broke the silence. 'We won't be able to stay here long. Valence will be on our trail. Aberdeen is not Perth. Its defences aren't strong enough to keep out a determined assault and there aren't enough boats for us to escape by sea. We have to keep moving.'

As his brother-in-law spoke, Robert felt weariness pulling at his limbs. It was a deeper exhaustion than he'd felt after the battle or even during the flight through the mountains – helpless as horses fell lame and wounded men bled out in the darkness – a weariness that seemed soul deep. He stared across the gathering, picking out the faces of his brothers, the Setons, Gilbert de la Hay and Neil Campbell. There were so many holes in their number – so many missing. Malcolm of Lennox. Simon Fraser. James Stewart. Thomas Randolph. Their names had been repeating in his mind, each sounding a hollow note in his heart. He had wanted to wait longer in the hills, hoping more survivors would find their way to him, but after only a few score stragglers joined him there, he had forced his men on, knowing the English would not be slow to follow.

'Robert?'

He glanced up at the earl's insistent tone. 'I heard you, John.'

Edward Bruce headed over with Niall and the Setons. They were followed by Gilbert, Neil Campbell and David.

'We should post men on the gates at once,' said Edward determinedly, looking between Robert and the earl. 'Bolster the town's defences.'

'No,' John replied curtly. 'I believe we have a day or two's grace at most. We should spend that time getting what rest we can and gathering supplies. We leave as soon as we are able.' He told the others what he had told Robert.

David, standing at his father's side, looked at the floor and shook his head.

'So – we run?' questioned Edward roughly.

'We could make for Turnberry,' suggested Niall. 'Gather and arm as many of Carrick's tenants as we can?'

'Pit more farmers against English heavy cavalry?' said Alexander, his voice cold. Rain had tracked lines through the dirt and blood on his face. 'We might as well throw grains of sand before the incoming tide.'

'Cousin,' cautioned Christopher.

Alexander wouldn't be placated. 'We have lost. It is over.' His eyes, on Robert, were filled with condemnation.

Others countered, but Robert wasn't listening. He stood quickly, hearing female voices rising over the gruff tones of the men. A tall woman emerged from the crowd, eyes searching. Queen Elizabeth's cheeks were coloured by a flush, raised by her haste. Her black hair was piled up with jewelled pins, but her maid hadn't managed to gather all the strands and several drifted loose around her face. Her dove-grey mantle was darkened by rain, the sable trim glistening in the bloom of firelight. Seeing Robert, her face lightened with relief. For a moment, as she crossed to him, Robert thought she was going to throw herself into his arms and felt his own open in surprised expectation, but his wife stopped short before reaching him. Her expression changed and she appeared to compose herself, instead offering her husband and king a courteous dip of her head.

Other women were moving in among the men. Christian Bruce was already locked in an embrace with Christopher Seton. In her arms, crushed between them, her four-year-old son, Donald, protested loudly. John of Atholl's wife went to her husband, clasping the earl's grime-streaked face. The countess, a sister of Robert's first wife, kissed John fiercely before hugging David to her. David pulled back from his mother, the proud young man self-conscious at the display. The countess looked over at Robert. His sister-in-law's joy faded as she took in the beaten, worn-out faces of the men around him.

Robert's attention was drawn by a small figure who squeezed through the press of adults. With no bows, no formalities, his eleven-year-old daughter flung her arms around his waist, pressing her face into his sodden surcoat. Robert laughed, taken aback by the ferocity of Marjorie's grasp, then, with a surge of emotion, he crouched and drew her into his arms. Her hair was soft against his cheek and smelled of smoke and lavender. Holding his daughter at arm's length, he forced himself to smile at her grave expression.

'You are hurt,' murmured Marjorie, frowning at a spot over his eye.

Robert's hand drifted to the place. He felt a sting of pain as he touched it. A graze from a sword? A stray branch in the flight through the woods? He had no idea.

'Come away now,' said Elizabeth, grasping Marjorie's shoulders. 'Let your father be.'

Not so long ago his daughter would have shrugged angrily from Elizabeth's touch, but under the tutelage of a governess these past two years she had changed from a sullen, difficult child into a serious young girl. She let herself be guided to where her maid, Judith, was waiting.

Elizabeth turned back to Robert. 'What happened in Galloway? Why are you so few?'

'Valence.'

As Robert told his wife how they had been surprised outside Perth by Valence's forces, aided by the Disinherited, those around him quietened, the women straining to hear over the noise of the hall, the men silent, their faces mirroring the emotion of his words. Christian moved closer, whispering for her son to quiet. At her side was her younger sister, Mary, her blue eyes sharp as she listened to the grim tale.

By the time Robert had finished, Elizabeth's hand had strayed to her throat. He saw she was grasping the ivory cross she wore on the chain around her neck, a childhood gift from her father, the Earl of Ulster. Its edges had been worn smooth over the years by her worrying fingers. 'But how did they find you?'

'Valence's – or maybe MacDouall's men – must have been lying in wait. None of my scouts made it from the battle. My guess is they were killed just before the attack.'

Elizabeth shook her head, her gaze slipping from him to take in the men slumped on the hall's floor, too exhausted to strip off wet cloaks and bloodstained mail. 'I knew this fate, the day we were crowned.' Her eyes drifted back to him, full of unspoken meaning.

Robert remembered well her words, uttered that day on the Moot Hill; had thought of them while looking down on the walls of Perth and had felt the doom of them. As he put his hands on her shoulders, distress tightened Elizabeth's features, rendering her younger than her twenty-two years. He was reminded of the girl she had been in Ireland, trailing miserably behind him those endless miles through the wilderness, both of them trying to escape the prisons devised by her father – his a locked room, hers a marriage to a middle-aged lord. He had led her into danger then for the sake of his ambition. This was little different, only now the danger threatened to engulf everyone around him. 'It isn't over,' he told her, the force in his voice as much for himself as for her.

'If you could not stand against Valence and the men of Galloway, how can you hope to stand against the rest? King Edward and his knights? The Comyns?' Elizabeth searched the crowd, her gaze falling on the Countess of Buchan. 'Lady Isabel told us her husband was raising the men of Argyll against you.'

Robert followed his wife's gaze to where the countess stood. In her winter-white mantle, Isabel was a pale beauty, her arms folded tightly around her chest as if holding herself together. It was Isabel who had placed the crown upon his head at Scone, him bowing before her outstretched hands. The earls of Fife preserved the right to crown a new king and Edward had been shrewd enough to take into his custody the last kingmaker, a fourteen-year-old boy. Isabel, the young earl's aunt, was the nearest in blood. She was also the wife of the Earl of Buchan, head of the Black Comyns. Robert had sent John of Atholl to bring her to his coronation by force, but in the end she had come willingly, the faded bruises on her face telling him he was perhaps a better prospect than her husband.

Elizabeth's fingers crept back to the cross, her brow furrowing. 'Perhaps my father can help? If you surrender now, he may agree to petition King Edward on your behalf – persuade him to be lenient.'

Robert took his hands from her shoulders at the mention of the Earl of Ulster, Richard de Burgh. Elizabeth didn't know about the secret pact made between him and her father just before his submission to King Edward two years ago: that if Ulster endorsed him to the king, Robert would marry his daughter. By that pact, the ambitious Ulster had hoped to see his daughter become queen one day, but Robert knew the man hadn't envisioned this as the reality – his daughter now a rebel and a target of Edward's wrath.

Elizabeth took his silence as some indication of accord. 'He is one of the king's greatest allies. If any man can convince—'

'No, Elizabeth. I will not surrender. That isn't an option.'

Edward nodded adamantly. 'We've come too far to yield.' He scanned the circle. 'We, all of us, set my brother on the throne in defiance of John Balliol's right and took control of our kingdom against England's will. Does anyone here want to exchange this foothold, precarious though it may be, for one on the platform of a gallows?' He met Elizabeth's fearful gaze. 'Even the Earl of Ulster could not win the king's clemency now, my lady. I saw what he did to William Wallace. Mercy has become another victim of this war.'

Robert felt the fierceness of his brother's words spark a fire in him. He glimpsed Col in the crowd passing more goblets to grateful men and other servants crouched by the wounded helping them out of their armour. He saw his men, earls and lords of Scotland, all around him, defeated – yes – but still here with him. He had seized the throne, swearing to defend their rights and liberties, promising them a kingdom free of England's yoke. He would keep that promise, while he still had breath left in his body. Edward was right. They had come too far to yield. 'We head west,' he said, voicing the plan he had been considering these past days on the road.

'To Carrick?' questioned Niall.

'Not yet.' Robert addressed them all. 'Before my coronation I sent my brothers to Lord Donough, charging him to raise the men of Antrim. My foster-father will not have been slow to act and—'

'Your estates in Ireland will not offer safe haven,' warned John. 'You will be in easy reach of Ulster there. You cannot expect your past alliance to protect you. Sir Richard is Edward's man and will do what the king commands. No matter what,' he added, glancing at Elizabeth.

'Not Antrim, John. Islay. I told my brothers to take the same message to Angus MacDonald. His family has allied with mine in the past. I believe we may find sanctuary among his people. These last weeks Robert Wishart and William Lamberton have been raising their tenants from their dioceses and garnering supplies. We will send word for the bishops to join us on Islay, along with Lord Donough and the men of Antrim. And there are others,' he continued, his voice strengthening. 'The men of Carrick and Ayr. The MacRuaries—'

'The MacRuaries?' Neil Campbell cut in. 'You would trust the mercenaries to follow you, my lord? Those devils would stab you in the back the moment it was turned.'

Robert glanced at Neil, whose vehemence was easy to understand. The MacRuaries were kinsmen of the MacDougall lords, who had killed his father and taken Campbell lands around Loch Awe. 'Everything I know tells me the MacRuaries value plunder over kinship, Neil. Enough coins may buy their loyalty. As captains of the galloglass they have scores of fighting men and ships at their disposal. They could prove invaluable.'

'And from my uncle's lordships of Bute, Renfrew and Kyle Stewart you will find hundreds of tenants willing to fight, my lord.'

Robert saw James Douglas had entered the circle. The young man had been tight-lipped all through the flight from Methven Wood, his gaze often on the land behind them, hope draining from his face with every day his uncle failed to appear. Now, something else burned in his blue eyes, something fierce and vengeful.

'The steward fell,' John said quietly.

'None of us knows what happened to those left behind,' Robert answered him sharply.

James nodded in agreement. 'If my uncle escaped the field he would have returned to his lands. But either way, Sir John, his vassals will fight. William Wallace was of their stock. Many still harbour desire for revenge against his executioners.' He turned his gaze on Robert. 'I will follow you west, my lord.'

'As will I,' said Christopher Seton.

When Neil Campbell and Gilbert de la Hay added their support, Robert felt his confidence swell. He had underestimated his enemy and led his men blindly into Valence's trap. They had paid a terrible price for that mistake, but these men in this hall had followed him through years of blood. They had suffered other defeats and had fought their way on to victory. He had lost a battle. Not the war. 'We leave as soon as we are able. All of us,' he added, for the benefit of the watching women. 'We will rebuild our strength in the Isles. Then, when we return, Valence will pay in full for every life taken at Perth.'

As his men responded with grim accord, Robert saw his half-sister, Margaret, at the edge of the gathering. She was searching the circle, her face full of question as she looked for her son.

* * *

As the assembled men and women began to disperse, Christopher Seton watched Robert cross to his half-sister. Pity filled him as he saw the king's jaw tighten. No one should have to tell a mother her son was missing, possibly dead. It was against the law of nature. But, then, it seemed the law of man had been dominant these past ten years and nature had sat back to watch, more children being taken by the war than by her whim.

Feeling a hand on his arm, Christopher turned to see Christian, her eyes clouded with worry. Donald had quietened, resting his head in the curve of her neck, his blond hair brushing her chin. The boy's face was screwed up in a frown, sensing, but not understanding, the tension in his mother and the adults around him. Such a little mite, thought Christopher, to be head of one of Scotland's greatest earldoms. He cupped Christian's cheek. 'Don't look so frightened, my love.'

'How can I not?' Christian tilted her head from his touch, not wishing to be placated. 'My brother has lost half his army and our countrymen have joined our enemies, with the full strength of England still to come for us.'

'You heard Robert: Islay will offer refuge while he gathers more forces. You and Donald will be safe there, I promise.'

A cry made them both turn. As Margaret Randolph collapsed Robert reached to grasp her, but she sank to the floor, her cry stretching into a wail. The Countess of Atholl moved to hold her.

'My poor sister,' murmured Christian. She hugged Donald closer. 'Thomas was barely out of boyhood.' Her eyes switched back to Christopher. 'Do not make promises you don't know you can keep. They feel like lies.'

The strength of her tone took him aback. She was a quiet woman for the most part, gentle in manner and speech, but he was starting to learn that when roused there was a forcefulness in her that would come unexpected and sudden – thunder from a blue sky. His love for her had come quickly, bubbling up like laughter, but his deepening respect had turned it into something solid, immutable. 'Then I'll swear I would die protecting you both.'

Christian exhaled, her face softening. 'Don't say that either.' She hefted Donald higher on her hip so she could take Christopher's hand. 'Gartnait was a good man.' She looked down on the tousled head of the child that had come from that marriage. 'But I never truly loved him. Not as I know it now.' She squeezed his hand. 'You can say you'll always come back to me, no matter what. That, you can swear.'

Christopher wondered about the logic of making another promise that might be a lie, but judging by the look on her face she wanted him to make this one. 'You have my word.' At her smile he felt a question, playing at his lips these past few months, begin to emerge. 'Christian, I . . .' He faltered. 'What I mean to say is, I need your brother's permission, but if such an agreement was forthcoming, would you consider—' His attention was caught by Alexander, who pushed past him, heading for the doors. Christopher frowned, seeing the embittered look his cousin shot Robert before disappearing in the press of men. He turned back to Christian, whose face was alight with expectation. He could see it in her eyes, shining now, the worry gone: she knew what he had been going to ask. He could tell, too, what her answer would be. A grin threatened to spread across his face, but he forced back his joy. 'Give me leave for just a moment, my love.'

Tearing himself from her, Christopher pushed his way through the crowd, which was already stirring with new purpose, commanders relaying the king's plan to their companies, servants hastening to gather supplies. Christopher paused in the hall's doorway. The courtyard was crammed with men and horses, many hunched under the eaves of outbuildings, sheltering from the rain. Torches threw fractured shadows up the walls of the bailey. Christopher caught a glimpse of Alexander, headed in the direction of the stables. His cousin's hood was pulled up, a pack on his shoulder. Quickly, he descended the steps into the yard, churned to a thick soup of mud.

Alexander had been quiet for days now, but not in the same way as their companions. His had been an angry, restless silence. Christopher had been too preoccupied with his own thoughts after the battle to question his cousin's cold reserve. He knew Alexander harboured resentment towards Robert, for making decisions he hadn't agreed with and ignoring his counsel, but tonight his bitterness seemed different. He thought of his cousin's words earlier and the look on his face. *We have lost. It is over.*

Dodging kitchen boys hurrying to the great hall with armfuls of blankets and buckets of water, Christopher made his way to the stables. His boots slipped in the mire and rain trickled down inside the collar of his cloak. When he reached the stable block, he found himself in a chaos of grooms and horses, over which a stable-master was yelling to make himself heard. An agitated charger reared up, almost hauling the young boy gripping the reins off the ground. Christopher turned in a circle, scanning the courtyard, but saw no sign of Alexander.

6

Near Turnberry, Scotland, 1306 AD

Brigid paused halfway up the slope to catch her breath. Sitting back on her heels, she let her bag tumble from her shoulder and untied the skin from her belt. The watered wine tasted sour, but served to quench her thirst. It had been a hot climb in the late afternoon sun, the air alive with insects that swarmed in the gorse and heather. Her long hair was lank with sweat. She pushed it out of her eyes and surveyed the land that dropped away before her, pleased with how far she had travelled. The loch she had trudged alongside early that morning was now a distant shimmer.

She had worried she might become lost, having chosen the route that would bring her home by way of remote drovers' tracks through Carrick's southern uplands, but she had walked these hills as a child, hunting for coneys and adders, blackthorn and dog's mercury for her aunt's work. These lands hadn't changed. She doubted they had since the wild people raised their stone circles and chanted their prayers to the ancient gods. It was strange to be back in this timeless region after the last months spent in towns that were altering by the day. Man could change a landscape in just one season, by sword and by fire.

Feeling dangerously lulled by the sun's warmth, she forced herself on, legs throbbing as she tackled the last of the slope, the coarse grass scratching her feet through the holes that had opened in her shoes. The bag bumped against her back. Though still heavy with coins it was lighter than it had been, her supplies having dwindled to a hunk of rye bread and some salted herring. Her shabby dress hung loose on her body and her face, glimpsed that morning as she'd splashed in the loch, was gaunt. It didn't matter. She was almost home. Elena would be helping to prepare the evening meal, or fetching logs for the fire. The thought of her daughter drove her forward.

It was almost four months since King Robert's coronation at Scone, after which time Brigid had spent several weeks in Perth, selling the healing powders and charms Affraig had sent her with. Her aunt's craft had been suffering ever since the English raid on Turnberry five years ago, which devastated the community. With three mouths to feed and the last of their chickens having perished in the winter, the opportunity presented by the coronation had been too good to miss. Finally in May, when rumours reached Perth that the English had crossed the border and were headed their way, Brigid had set out for home.

The road felt different on the return journey. There was a sense of dissatisfaction in the settlements she passed through, stopping a few days to sell the last of Affraig's wares. People were angry, some saying King Robert had damned them by spilling blood on hallowed ground, or condemning him for overthrowing John Balliol, who, despite his exile in France, was still Scotland's rightful king. Others blamed the Comyns for their warmongering. Neighbours disagreed, men brawled quickly after too much ale and people wanted hexes not love spells. It felt as though the kingdom were fracturing, splitting across new battle lines. There were murmurs of a great muster against Robert taking place in Argyll. The further west she travelled the more armed companies Brigid began to see, until finally she made the decision to leave the road. She knew, all too well, the violence men were capable of.

Scrambling up on to the summit, Brigid was rewarded with a vast panorama. The view was dominated by the sea, a dazzling sheet of copper in the evening sun, ruptured in the foreground by the rocky dome of Ailsa Craig and in the distance by Arran's mountains. Shielding her eyes, Brigid scanned the land. The line of hills marched north for a few miles, before dropping away. In the distance, a solitary knoll reared over soft green woodland. Somewhere in the dusky shadows between the mound and the woods was Affraig's house. She need only head down and follow the skirts of the hills, and she would be home. As she took her first steps, Brigid caught sight of the hulking silhouette of Turnberry Castle on the coast beyond the woods. Her eyes told her something was wrong, halting her in her tracks even before her brain translated what she was seeing. Turnberry Castle was there, rising from its sea-bitten promontory of rock, but the village beside it was gone.

The bag slipped from her shoulder as her eyes fell on the blackened area where a small, but thriving settlement once stood. Though the distance made her vision blur, she thought she could see twisted stumps of buildings. It might have been the evening haze, but she fancied smoke still rose from the ruins. She looked south, seeing more scorched areas of earth, remains of farmsteads and crop-fields. Then, to the north, some miles beyond Turnberry, she saw the cause. On the bluffs that looked out over the curve of coastline towards Ayr was a great encampment. Campfires glittered among the expanse of tents.

Snatching up her bag, Brigid careened down the hillside, her trembling legs threatening to pitch her headlong down the slope. Her heart hammered in her chest, her breaths came in bursts and the hill never seemed to end. Once on the flat she went quicker, jumping burns and plunging through wider streams, gasping at the frigid waters that swirled around her thighs. The sun was slipping into the sea, throwing the land into blue gloom. Now and then she thought she smelled smoke tainting the breeze. All she could think of was Elena.

When the English razed Ayr, killing her husband and son, Brigid had saved her daughter from the fire that ravaged their home, but not without consequence. Eight-year-old Elena still bore the scars of her ordeal, outside and in. Her daughter would have smelled the village burning. She would have been terrified. Brigid cursed herself for leaving her so long with just a frail old woman for protection. Faint hope reminded her that Affraig's remote dwelling had always been safe from English raids, hidden by the woods, but as she neared it she saw that hope was in vain.

She cried out, running full tilt towards the blackened patch of earth, out of which thrust a few scorched timbers. Her feet crunched over charred remains of belongings, which turned to ash beneath her shoes. Even the mighty oak that loomed over the dwelling hadn't been spared. The branches that faced the house were blistered, the leaves shrivelled. She stood there, dragging in bitter lungfuls of smoky air. Here and there among the ruins cauldrons and pots were scattered about, the metal tarnished. She saw a leather-bound book, one of her aunt's prized possessions, half eaten by fire. Turning in a circle, she searched the woods, desperate for any sign of life. She wanted to scream her daughter's name, but had neither the breath, nor the heart.

Something moved. Brigid twisted round, focusing on a spot through the trees. In the shadows, she picked out a stooped figure. Her hope lifted, but as the figure limped towards her, she realised it wasn't her aunt, but a man leaning on a stick. Fear threaded cold fingers through her gut at the sight of the stranger. Searching the wasted ground at her feet, Brigid snatched up a half-charred piece of timber. He didn't look much of a threat, but the memory of the tents she had glimpsed in the north was still vivid. As the man came closer, she saw he was old, perhaps even older than Affraig. His face was skeletal, his skin like worn leather.

'Who are you?' she challenged, speaking Gaelic for the first time in months.

The old man stopped on the edge of the blackened circle, his eyes on the piece of timber she brandished. 'You'll find nothing of use,' he told her in the same tongue, his voice like grit rasping in his throat. 'I've looked.'

'What happened here?'

'Same as what happened in Turnberry and all about. The English.' The man ventured a little closer.

Brigid held her ground, her fingers clenched white around the makeshift weapon.

'Five nights ago they came. Young knights they were, under King Edward's son, and thirsty for blood one and all. Women and children weren't spared the sword.' His eyes clouded, the wrinkles in his brow deepening. 'No mercy. They took the castle and burned the rest.'

Brigid shuddered, thinking of her daughter.

'We fled into the woods, but the English followed us.'

Brigid realised how they must have found her aunt's house. Anger clenched its fist in her chest. The bastards had probably stumbled upon it and burned it for sport. *Don't let her have been in there.*

'They hunted us as if we were vermin,' said the man, 'sending their dogs after us.'

'How did you escape?' Brigid wanted to know, still not trusting him.

'I hid, like others. Up a tree for two full nights I was.'

'There are more of you?' Brigid felt a surge of anticipation.

'Not now. The others left three days ago. Went into the hills, towards Ayr.'

'Do you know the woman who lived here? Affraig?'

'The witch? I knew of her. Never met her.' The old man's mouth puckered and he made the sign of the cross. 'Never wanted to.'

'She is old,' Brigid said impatiently, 'very old. She would have had a child with her – a young girl with scars on her face.'

The old man's eyes lit up in recognition. 'Yes, I saw them, before I hid. But not since. Perhaps the English found them?' He lifted his shoulders in apology. 'Perhaps they went with the others?'

'Towards Ayr?' Brigid looked north. It was past midsummer but the nights were still long and this far west it would barely get dark. If she travelled through the night maybe she could catch up to them. Three days wasn't much of a head-start.

'Some folk talked of going into the mountains, where the English and their horses can't follow.'

Brigid's eyes were already roving over the ruins, searching for anything of use. Catching sight of a familiar forked stick lying beneath the oak she tossed aside the timber and picked it up, keeping a wary eye on the old man. The bottom half of the stick was charred, but the top, which tapered into two prongs, was solid. She stamped it on the ground, testing its strength. It would offer good support for walking and make a decent weapon. Affraig had used it to hang her spells in the oak. Brigid stared into the branches. There were a few cradles of twigs that were still whole, but most had been damaged by fire, the scraps of parchment, sprays of herbs and pouches of bone that hung in the centre of the woven webs burned to tatters. How many destinies had been destroyed? How many prayers would now go unanswered? Her eyes went to the place where Robert's web had hung. The crown of heather and broom wasn't there. She scanned the base of the tree, but couldn't see it. Had it fallen in her absence – its promise fulfilled? She remembered Robert's question, the day of his coronation. *My destiny. Did it ever fall?* And his dry, disbelieving laugh when she answered him.

'The English were going north too,' warned the old man, watching her.

Brigid hefted her bag and gripped the stick. She turned to go, then paused and looked back. 'Why didn't you leave with the others?'

The old man gave a croak of laughter. 'With my legs?' His laugh subsided. 'I'll stay and die in my own lands. God willing, the English will choke on the stench of my corpse.'

With another rough laugh he turned back towards the woods, leaving her alone in the gathering shadows.

Perth, Scotland, 1306 AD

'Ask around. Find out who holds the authority here.'

The two knights nodded and kicked their horses into a trot. Alexander watched them part at the market cross, each taking a different street.

'Sir?'

He looked round to see his squire standing there expectantly. 'Water the horses, Tom.'

As Tom led the weary animals over to a trough in the market gardens, Alexander crossed to the stalls. Traders' wares were shadowed from the sun by cloth sheets, beneath which were rows of oatcakes and golden loaves fresh from the bakehouse, the smell causing his stomach to groan. A heavy chop-chop came from a flesher hacking meat off the carcass of a lamb, while women stood waiting, baskets on their arms. Past a girl selling curds and milk, two fishwives were busy gutting salmon. One paused to toss the slop of guts from her bucket on the ground behind her, making several mangy dogs lunge out of nowhere and begin lapping up the waste.

At first glance it was a normal day in the royal burgh, but beneath the hustle and bustle Alexander sensed how subdued the place was. The market didn't echo with the usual brisk shouts of traders, women gossiping, men haggling over prices. The crowds seemed nervous, glancing at the stone houses of the burgesses that ringed the square, outside which groups of armed men loitered, sunlight sparking off the pommels of their swords. The gardens were scarred with the ruts of wagon wheels, the ground littered with the detritus of a mass of men. But the most obvious sign of Perth's occupation were the nooses still dangling over a row of empty stalls, twisting slowly in the air. The men hanged there had since been taken down. Only a posy of flowers remained, lying in the dust beneath one of the knotted ropes, wilting in the heat. The townsfolk gave them a wide berth.

Alexander paused at the baker's stall. While he was fishing in his purse for a coin, a pimple-faced youth pushed past him and asked the baker for two loaves. Grabbing the youth by the scruff of his tunic, Alexander pulled him back. 'Wait your turn.'

The youth looked Alexander up and down, his expression changing from startled to indignant. 'Get your hand off me!'

In the pimpled youth's contemptuous gaze, Alexander saw himself: face streaked with dirt and a beard grown full around his jaw, hair greasy with sweat, his cloak frayed and his boots scuffed bare. He looked, he knew, little better than a beggar. Feeling a surge of anger, he pulled aside his cloak, revealing his broadsword to the sneering youth.

The lad backed away, eyes on the blade, his bread forgotten. Alexander watched him turn and flee before he let his cloak fall back in place. Once, he had been lord of a rich estate, his hall filled with servants, his stables crowded with horses, meat and wine to grace his table and minstrels to entertain him. Now, violence was his only authority – his retinue reduced to the paltry sum of two knights and a squire, the only men who had left Aberdeen with him. Everything else had been taken from him by his decision to follow Robert Bruce.

After the baker had served him in silence, Alexander took the loaf and leaned against an empty stall. Passers-by shot him suspicious glances and went out of their way to avoid the unsavoury stranger. Tearing off a few pieces of bread, Alexander chewed without pleasure, his appetite gone. While he was standing there, he noticed a man ride up to one of the stone halls. He watched him dismount and disappear inside. Moments later, several others emerged and crossed to the market gardens, from which they began to haul a wagon, drawing it up outside the hall. Alexander handed the bread to Tom when the lad joined him with the horses. He kept his eyes on the wagon as armed men moved around it, issuing orders to grooms, who harnessed four horses to the front.

'Ewen's back, sir.'

At Tom's voice, Alexander drew his gaze from the wagon to see one of his knights riding into the square.

'It is as you thought,' Ewen said as he reached them. He swung down from the saddle. 'Valence is going after King Robert. He's already headed for Aberdeen.'

Alexander had expected as much, but he had hoped Valence would have left a commander in Perth in his stead – someone with the authority he needed. None of the guards he had seen at the gates or over by the stone halls wore the colours of Pembroke. 'Did you discover who has been left in charge of the town?'

'Those I spoke to weren't very forthcoming. Too scared for the most part. But I was told prisoners taken from Methven Wood are being held there.' Ewen nodded to the hall.

Alexander wondered if the wagon was being readied to cart prisoners. He sucked the remnants of bread from his teeth. Were friends and allies locked up in that building? James Stewart perhaps, or Malcolm of Lennox? The shadow of guilt that had trailed him from Aberdeen darkened, but he forced it away. 'We'll wait and see what Will finds out.'

Alexander lapsed into silence. His manor at Seton was scarcely more than a day's ride – frustratingly close. His lands in East Lothian had been forfeited to the English crown for his role in the rebellion, but King Edward was a shrewd man and Alexander was certain the king would look beyond his crimes to see what a blow his desertion would strike at Robert. He couldn't let guilt overrule reason. All ten years of loyalty had brought him was bad fortune. The attack outside these walls at the hands of Valence and their own countrymen – which he had warned Robert about and yet again been ignored – had been the last nail in the coffin of his faith. While he trusted Robert would deliver them from Edward's tyranny he had fought with every sinew for the man and his cause. But he hadn't believed in a long time. Now, the English had raised the dragon and Alexander refused to relinquish the last things he had left – his life and his freedom – to fight for a doomed king whose own subjects were turning against him.

He thought of Christopher, standing in the rain in the courtyard of Aberdeen Castle. Alexander had watched his cousin from the shadows of the stables, knowing the young man was searching for him. Compassion had urged him to call out, but sense had kept him silent. Christopher was as a brother to him, but although he was English, born and bred, Robert was his true master and he would follow his king down into hell if ordered. There would have been no persuading him otherwise. Alexander could only hope, by submitting to Edward, that he would be able to secure his cousin's safety. In time, God willing, he would be reinstated as Lord of Seton, Christopher would be free of Robert's influence and they would no longer be outlaws on the run, living hand to mouth. Life as a nobleman under an English king had to be better than no life at all.

'Sir.'

Alexander was roused from his thoughts by Ewen, whose eyes were on the main street. A company of men was advancing on the market square, some riding, others marching alongside. Alexander's eyes narrowed on the white lions emblazoned on blue shields and surcoats. He cursed. Valence had left someone in charge, just not someone he wanted to parley with.

At the head of the company rode Dungal MacDouall, former captain of the army of Galloway, now leader of the Disinherited: men whose lands had been divided among the barons of England when John Balliol was exiled in France. MacDouall held the reins of his horse one-handed, sitting back against the cantle. The Galloway men were laughing and calling to one another, a few banging on their shields with their swords. It was the entry of men who had just won a victory.

'Wait here,' Alexander told Ewen and Tom.

He slipped into the market crowds, keeping MacDouall in his sights. The captain was headed for the stone hall with the wagon outside. Grooms were still moving around it, adjusting straps on the harnessed horses. As MacDouall reached the hall, a man emerged. Squeezing past two portly women haggling with the butcher, Alexander saw this man was wearing a blue and white striped surcoat, adorned with red birds. Pembroke's colours. His anticipation sharpened. Would this man have the authority to deliver his surrender to King Edward?

Moving closer, Alexander pulled up his hood, the better to conceal himself. He had known Dungal MacDouall for years and had fought on the same side as him for most of them, but the captain had been John Comyn's right-hand man. Alexander had been at Dumfries and it was his cousin's sword that had spilled blood that night, changing for ever the fortunes of MacDouall and his men, who had found a new master in Comyn. The Seton name was black among this company.

'Captain,' greeted the Englishman, as MacDouall swung down from the saddle. 'I've prepared the prisoner's transport, as your man requested.'

'Good.' MacDouall's voice came harsh over the low hum of voices in the market place. 'He'll have a friend to keep him company on the journey.'

Following the captain's gaze, Alexander saw a figure in the midst of the Galloway men, hands bound with ropes to the pommel of his horse, which was being led by one of MacDouall's knights. The recognition was a shock. The man was William Lamberton, the Bishop of St Andrews. The bishop sat erect, head held high, despite the ignoble position he was in.

'We caught his grace outside his diocese,' said MacDouall. 'He was stockpiling meat and grain for Bruce. We took what we could and burned the rest.'

'King Edward will be most pleased with this bounty,' assured the Englishman, appraising the bishop as though he were a prize stag.

Lamberton's cloak was dust-stained and his tonsured head had been burned by the sun. There was a bruise darkening to purple on the side of his face. But his eyes, one blue the other pearl white, remained unwavering as he met the gaze of his captors.

Watching from the cover of the market crowds as the bishop was hauled from the saddle, Alexander felt a rush of shame. This proud, formidable man, humbled and bound, was a friend of his. He had shared bread and conversation with Lamberton around many campfires, enjoying his passionate, plain-spoken company. His resolve faltered. Did he want to surrender himself to men who would treat one of the highest-ranking clergymen in the realm like a common outlaw?

'I will be most pleased to serve this bounty to the king,' replied MacDouall, 'but first I have another errand. While pursuing our enemy near St Andrews I received word that Sir John has returned from Argyll. I must meet him at his wife's manor.'

Alexander listened intently. The last they knew, the Black Comyn had been in the west raising the lords of Argyll against Robert in retaliation for the murder of their kinsman.

The Englishman's interest also seemed piqued. 'Do you have word of how many men the MacDougalls have raised for our cause?'

'The message just said to join him, with all speed, at Leuchars. If I leave now, I'll be there by nightfall.'

'And the prisoners?'

'As instructed, I'll take them south to King Edward at Durham. Do not fear. Lord Edward will have his pound of flesh.'

'*That's him!*'

Alexander jerked round at the shout. The crowd behind him had parted and he saw three men standing there. One was the pimple-faced youth he had threatened at the baker's stall. The other two looked enough like him, with their sallow complexions and pock-marked faces, to be related, only older, and brawnier. One had a stained apron and was wielding a cleaver.

Alexander held up his hands as they advanced. 'I meant no harm,' he said, acutely aware of MacDouall, not more than twenty yards away.

The man with the cleaver glanced over Alexander's shoulder, checking the attention of the guards outside the hall. His eyes flicked back, narrowing with enmity. 'You threatened my boy?'

Before he could answer, Alexander caught a rush of motion behind the man. He went to shout, but Will, who had appeared from nowhere, barrelled into the man, sending him crashing to the ground. A young girl standing nearby screamed, the shrill sound piercing the subdued market. Will was on top of the brawny man, trying to wrest the cleaver from his hand. Ewen and Tom were shoving their way through the press as the other man rushed to the aid of his struggling compan-ion. Alexander stormed into the skirmish, shouting at his men to get the hell out. His warning came too late. Within moments, the place was swarming with armed men from the hall.

Alexander was knocked violently as people scattered in all direc-tions. Someone crashed into a potter's stall, sending pots smashing to the ground. Alexander felt a fist grab the back of his cloak. He reacted quickly, bringing his elbow crashing back. As it connected with something soft, he heard a grunt of pain and the hold on his cloak disappeared. Ahead, between the fleeing market-goers, he glimpsed Will being hauled off his victim by two men with the white lion of Galloway on their surcoats. The pimple-faced youth had vanished. Ewen had drawn his sword and was backing away from two guards, Tom at his side.

A blow landed heavily on the back of Alexander's head. He stum-bled to his knees with the impact, pain blurring his vision. He tried to push himself up, but while he was still dazed someone grasped his arm. He went for his sword, but another man grabbed at his wrist, bending it back until he yelled. Hauled to his feet, he was marched to the hall, his head still ringing. Will, Ewen and the two companions of the youth were similarly manhandled and brought before Dungal MacDouall and the English knight.

Alexander hung his head as he approached MacDouall, whose one hand was curled around the hilt of his sword. His hood had stayed up in the skirmish and helped to hide his face.

'What is the meaning of this?' demanded Valence's man, looking between the brawlers.

'A misunderstanding, sir,' said Will quickly. 'Nothing more.'

The Englishman frowned. 'I'll not put up with disturbers of the king's peace. You should know this by now. Throw them in the cellar with the others,' he told his guards brusquely. 'I'll decide how to punish them later.'

Alexander kept his head lowered as the men holding him began to usher him towards the building into which Lamberton had been taken.

'Wait!' MacDouall's voice rang out.

Out of the corner of his eye, Alexander watched him cross to Will.

MacDouall stared at the knight, eyes sharp with question. 'Who are you? Why do I know your face?' When Will didn't answer, MacDouall grabbed a fistful of his hair and pulled back his head, inspecting him intently. After a moment, recognition dawned on his face. He let go of Will and turned.

Alexander felt MacDouall's gaze fall on him as a blow. He tried to twist away, but MacDouall strode over and ripped back his hood.

'Seton!'

There was a scatter of exclamations from the Galloway men in earshot.

MacDouall's triumph faded fast. He scanned the now deserted market square, then gestured to the Englishman. 'Alert your guards. There could be more.' He turned his attention back to Alexander. 'Did Bruce send you? Are you here to rescue his men?'

'No,' murmured Alexander. 'I came alone.'

'One of Bruce's commanders — come alone into the lion's den? Tell me the truth, Seton, or I'll rip it from you.'

'It is the truth. I am no longer Bruce's man.' Alexander looked over at the English knight. 'I came to surrender to King Edward.'

The knight took a step forward at this, but MacDouall turned on him. 'This man is one of John Comyn's murderers. I request the right to question him on behalf of the Comyn family.'

'Sir Aymer will want to interrogate the murderer of his brother-in-law.'

'Sir Aymer is occupied hunting down Bruce. Seton may have vital information on our enemy's plans – information that should be extracted as soon as possible. Let me take him with the other prisoners. My master will be grateful for the opportunity to question him, personally.'

7

St Fillan's Shrine, Scotland, 1306 AD

Robert watched the river foam past, its rush loud in his ears. Rains from the summer storms that had drenched his company on their slow progress west from Aberdeen had made their own way to this point, tumbling down out of the mountains of Drumalban by tracks and tributaries to meet in the white rapids of the Fillan. A short distance upriver they converged in the icy depths of St Fillan's Pool, the waters of which were said to cure sickness of the mind and the soul.

'It is a wild beauty, is it not, my lord?'

Robert turned. Abbot Maurice was approaching, his black habit brushing the tall grasses. He shielded his eyes from the afternoon sun as he came, smiling in question. Behind him, the roof of St Fillan's Chapel rose from a copse of birch trees. Above the foaming water, Robert caught music and laughter coming from beyond the trees. As the abbot came to stand beside him, he looked back across the river where waterlogged meadows, iridescent in the sunlight, ascended into hills carpeted with heather. Beyond, higher peaks climbed to the sky, their bare flanks darkened by the shadows of scudding clouds. The shrine of St Fillan's, which lay in a remote valley, was imprisoned by mountains on virtually all sides.

'Do you know the legends of our blessed saint?'

Robert glanced at the abbot. The old man was still smiling, but Robert sensed something else in his tone now. 'My family is more familiar with the history of St Malachy of Armagh.'

Abbot Maurice nodded sagely. 'Ah, yes. The curse.'

Robert thought of his grandfather's obsession with atoning for the sins of their ancestor, cursed down the generations by the wrathful Irish saint. He wondered if Thomas and Alexander had now returned the Staff of Malachy, taken in his flight from Westminster Abbey, to its rightful keepers – the monks of Bangor Abbey.

'When St Fillan first came to this valley it was haunted by savage creatures. Before he could build his place of worship he had to confront these beasts. First, he drove off a vicious boar. Next, he tamed a wolf, rendering the ferocious animal so obedient he was able to lash it to a cart to carry stones for his chapel. For hundreds of years his sanctuary has provided solace for pilgrims and his pool has cured the sick. It is a shame only a ruin now stands to mark such a legacy.'

Robert's eyes narrowed at the none-too-subtle intimation, but he owed the abbot no less than a donation. Descending through the rain-swept mountains his company of five hundred men, weighed down by baggage and slowed by the women and children, had found welcome shelter in the Abbey of Inchaffray. Abbot Maurice, on learning of Robert's intention to head west, had offered to escort him by the old pilgrim road to St Fillan's, beyond which he could easily follow routes to the sea. 'You have my word, when my reign is secured St Fillan will have a shrine worthy of his deeds.'

Abbot Maurice inclined his head. 'Blessings upon you, my lord.' He paused, his gaze lingering on Robert. 'This valley has long been a place of healing. Not just of the body, but of the soul. Absolution can be found here, by those who seek it.'

Robert smiled coolly. 'I thank you, Abbot, for officiating over the marriage of my sister. I should join in the celebrations while they last.' He made his way back towards the copse of trees, his smile vanishing.

The sounds of merriment grew louder as he approached the camp, spread out across a meadow by St Fillan's shrine. The small, ramshackle chapel, besieged by ivy and creeping moss, had been festooned with wildflowers for the wedding of his sister and Christopher Seton. Despite the bright sprays of colour, gathered by the children who had been set the task to keep them occupied while the army set up camp, the chapel's musty interior remained full of gloom. Staring into its cobwebbed darkness, Robert felt a chill. He had barely set foot inside a church since Greyfriars. The abbot wasn't the only one to have offered him absolution. Four months ago, his brother Alexander had urged him to give his confession. In response, Robert had sent him to

Antrim. He had been defiant that the attack on John Comyn had not been an act of murder, but of self-defence. Though this wasn't an outright lie, the truth was more complicated.

It was James Stewart who first advised him to seek the endorsement of John Comyn in his bid to claim the throne. Despite his misgivings, he had followed the steward's counsel, but unbeknown to them, Comyn had his own eyes fixed on the crown and in Robert's offer of an alliance against the English had seen his chance to take it. Orchestrating the capture of William Wallace, Comyn had documents planted on the rebel leader that exposed Robert's plan to take the throne in defiance of his pledge of loyalty to Edward. The king, discovering the conspiracy after Wallace's execution, ordered his arrest and so Robert had fled, taking the Staff of Malachy and the precious box that contained the king's dark secret with him.

That night in the church of the Greyfriars, Comyn looked as shocked as if he'd seen a ghost when Robert stepped out of the shadows. The son of a bitch had expected him to be dead, or at least rotting in the Tower. They fought and, yes, he defended himself, but although he might fool those around him, Robert could not fool himself. He had gone to that church with murder in mind, the tortured screams of William Wallace, sacrificed on the altar of Comyn's ambition, still ringing in his ears. He could say it was justice for the rebel leader, or that it was fate; that his and Comyn's path had been set years before, furrowed by the hatred of their fathers and grandfathers, and half a century of bad blood had, that night, been fulfilled in them. But if he was to be truly absolved he would first have to confess that not only had he wanted to kill Comyn, but that he had taken pleasure in it.

Robert wondered if events since – his humiliating defeat at the hands of Valence, the men of Galloway joining forces with the English, the loss of so many friends and followers – were not caused by errors of judgement, but rather by his own sin. He imagined it as a cloud, following him wherever he went, God's displeasure hanging over him like a thunderhead.

Thou shalt not kill.

Distracted by a burst of laughter, Robert forced his gaze from the derelict shrine. Beyond the graveyard, the men and women of his company were relaxing in the sunlight, children playing among them. Two minstrels were entertaining the crowd, the rhythm of drum and pipes lending speed to the children's races.

Matilda and Mary, at nineteen and twenty the youngest of Robert's siblings, were clapping in time to the music. The women, both slim and dark-haired, were almost identical in appearance, but opposites in manner. Mary took after Edward, sharp-tongued and stubborn, while Matilda, cut from the same cloth as Alexander, was studious and quiet. Marjorie raced past them in pursuit of Niall. Her skirts were bunched in one hand, thin legs pounding the grass. Christian's son, Donald, toddled determinedly in her wake. Marjorie screamed delightedly as her uncle turned and whirled her into his arms, causing Fionn to leap from his patch of sun, barking. John of Atholl reclined with a goblet of wine, threading the fingers of his free hand idly through his wife's hair, while her head rested on his chest. Their daughter Isabel, a pretty girl of sixteen, was speaking to the daughter of one of her father's knights, while David sat close by with James Douglas, talking intently.

Robert's gaze drifted to Elizabeth, who was sitting a little way from the crowd, observing the festivities. The breeze blew a strand of his wife's hair across her face and she reached up to tug it behind her ear. Beside her sat Isabel Comyn. Robert was struck again by how similar his wife and the countess were – not just in appearance. The two women had the same brittle quality that rendered them cautious and guarded, even in times of joy.

Scanning the rest of the company, he caught glimpses of the true gravity of their situation in the grief-worn face of Margaret Randolph and in the bloodstained clothing of those wounded at Methven Wood, but for all that they appeared more like revellers at a summer fair rather than a war-band on the run. It was as if the sanctuary of St Fillan was isolated by more than just its location; a place of peace that existed outside the world. It helped that his scouts were out in the hills around them, bringing back regular reports. So far, his men had seen no one in the wilderness, allowing the company a welcome moment of respite after the hardships of the last weeks.

At the centre of the sunlit meadow, Christian rested in the arms of her husband, her hair crowned with flowers. She smiled as Christopher murmured something in her ear. Robert remembered witnessing the moment of affection they had stolen beneath the shadow of the Moot Hill the day of his coronation. He had vowed then to return to them the days of peace before the death of King Alexander, a desire that still shimmered in his vision, only now it was more of a mirage, leaving him uncertain as to how he would reach it.

Catching Robert's gaze, Christopher kissed his bride and hastened over, a wide smile splitting his face. Dropping to one knee he clasped the king's hand in both of his, his expression at once solemn. 'My lord, I swore after you saved my life at Carlisle that I was in your debt. Now, that debt is doubled.'

Robert drew the knight to his feet. 'To see my sister happy is all the payment I need.' He embraced the beaming Yorkshireman, laughing at his infectious joy. 'Congratulations, brother.'

When Christopher pulled back he was still smiling, but it was as if a cloud had passed across his face, weakening the brightness. 'I only wish Alexander was here.' He paused. 'I should have said something to him sooner.' He lifted his shoulders helplessly. 'Done something.'

Robert felt his joy fade at the mention of Alexander Seton, who had disappeared with three of his men shortly after their arrival in Aberdeen. 'He is his own man, Christopher. You aren't responsible for him.'

'I want you to know, Robert, that I am with you.' Christopher's tone was intent. 'Alexander may be my kin, but he's a fool to have left your company.'

Robert didn't answer. He might resent Alexander for his desertion, but he could not call the man a fool. His had been the voice of warning at Methven Wood and the one he hadn't heeded. His desire to prove himself worthy as Scotland's king – to wash clean his tarnished reputation with the blood of the English and show his detractors his mettle – had blinded him to the danger posed by Valence. If he hadn't been so reckless: if he had waited to confront the English when he was at full strength, with the support of the men of Antrim and others who may have joined his army, he might not now be reduced to five hundred men, fleeing through the wilderness.

His mind filled with an image of the Wheel of Fortune spinning him towards the ground, threatening to crush him in its unrelenting course. He hadn't been able to get that image out of his mind since Aberdeen. From his coronation at Scone Abbey to this, in just four months.

'Husband!'

Christopher turned to see Christian beckoning to him. She did a twirl in time to the minstrels' spirited tune. Grinning again, the knight took his leave and ran to his bride. Catching her, he spun her into the air, causing her to shriek and spill her wine.

'It reminds me of Turnberry,' said Edward, appearing at Robert's side. He handed him one of the two goblets he was holding. The wine had been a gift from Abbot Maurice. Taking a sip, Edward smiled slightly at their sister's laughter. 'Do you remember the feasts? Our father was never happier than when he and our mother were dancing.'

'He was only happy then,' corrected Robert.

Edward turned his full attention on Robert. 'How long do you plan to stay here?'

Robert noted the impatience in his tone. Often on the journey through the mountains, he caught his brother looking behind them, back the way they had come. At first he thought Edward was checking for signs of pursuit, until he realised it wasn't fear, but hunger in his eyes: hunger for the victory they had been denied.

'A few more days at least. They should rest while they are able.' Robert's gaze moved over the scores of women and children he'd led, exhausted and scared, through the heights of Drumalban. 'The way ahead will be harder still.'

Edward nodded in grim agreement. 'The route will take us deep into the territory of the lords of Argyll. I agree it is better than attempting the pass, but it is still not without risk.'

'No route is without risk for us,' Robert told him, not wanting to be drawn into another debate about their chosen path, the subject of most of his conversations these past days. The obvious choice was to make for the Pass of Brander, but Dunstaffnage Castle, the chief seat of the lords of Argyll, stood sentry over the coast beyond and the pass itself, a narrow ridge overshadowed by the slopes of Ben Cruachan, was a dangerous place to be caught. Robert had opted for the proposal put forward by Neil Campbell: to keep east of Loch Awe and make their way through the hills until they reached the sea. There, they would have to commandeer a boat to Islay. Robert would go first with a small force of men and as many of the women and children as possible. If Angus MacDonald agreed to aid him, galleys could then be sent to ferry across the remainder. 'I trust Neil to lead us. He knows these lands better than anyone here.'

'At your coronation, Lady Isabel told us the Black Comyn was raising his kinsmen against you. We have no idea of the force John MacDougall and his father may have gathered in that time.'

'Whatever force the MacDougalls have gathered will most likely be based at Dunstaffnage, within easy reach of the sea and the pass. As Neil said, our route will take us many miles east of the castle. The hills around Loch Awe are densely wooded, affording us good cover, and our scouts will keep watch ahead and behind.' Robert held his brother's gaze. 'No one knows which way we're headed. By the time they do we'll be safe on Islay.'

'God willing.' Edward took another drink, his eyes on the company spread out across the meadow. 'We have a lot of mouths to feed. I just hope MacDonald agrees to shelter us all.'

'I'm his king. I'll give him no damn choice.' Robert drew a breath, pushing down his frustration at his brother's questions. 'Angus was at Turnberry with his father and brother when Grandfather called on their support against John Balliol. The MacDonalds pledged themselves willingly to our cause that night. I have no reason to think Angus will not continue his family's allegiance, especially if I can make it worth his while. The MacDonalds have warred with the MacDougalls for years over territory. I can exploit their animosity to my advantage.' Robert drained his wine. 'The enemy of my enemy . . .'

'And the MacRuaries? You've heard the same stories I have and not just from Neil.'

'One mountain at a time, brother.'

'Father!' Marjorie ran over, her cheeks flushed. 'Come, dance with me.'

Robert handed his empty goblet to Edward. 'With the most beautiful girl at the wedding? It would be my honour.'

As he allowed his daughter to lead him into the crowd, out of the shadow of the ruined chapel and away from his brother's doubts, Robert thought of Abbot Maurice speaking of St Fillan and the beasts of the valley.

Just how many wolves would he have to tame if he was to rebuild his kingdom?

8

County Durham, England, 1306 AD

The flaps of the royal pavilion were splayed apart, affording Edward a wide view across the fields to where the road curved north towards the line of hills that barricaded the horizon. His gaze didn't stray from the vista as the last of the sun's radiance faded across the western sky. When he finally turned his attention back to the meal in front of him his eyes remained branded with the silhouettes of those hills.

Servants moved around the king in their usual unobserved dance, feet hushed on the silk rug that covered the ground inside the pavilion. Edward drank from his goblet after it had been refilled. The wine was laced with herbs and honey as directed by his physician. It didn't taste as it ought to. Neither did the dry bread or thin strips of salted meat, but he could keep nothing else inside him. He remembered banquets at the palace in Westminster, sugared almonds piled high in silver bowls like pale gems; feasts in Bordeaux, his wife's lips stained with wine, dark juices bleeding from slabs of venison; sticky dates and the perfume of a thousand spices in the markets of Acre. He wished he had savoured them more.

As he picked up a crust of bread, Edward caught movement on the road – a dozen or more riders heading south, followed by a wagon. Tearing a morsel from the crust, he watched the company draw closer. The sides of the pavilion snapped in a gust of wind that made him shudder, even through his ermine-trimmed mantle. It was mid-July, but the evenings seemed colder of late. Across the encampment fires were winking into life, his men settling in for another night on Durham's plain. Edward wanted to have moved on by now, leading his army north in the wake of his son and Aymer de Valence, but his physician had told him plainly that the march could kill him. His bowel movements were watery and bloody and he spent most of his days crouched over a pot while whatever was left in him spattered out.

Frustration burned, fever-hot, inside him. Through endless, pain-riddled nights and the dull fog of his waking hours he thought of nothing else except the events taking place beyond those hills. So far, reports were good – Bruce was on the run with Aymer de Valence in pursuit and his son was ravaging the traitor's lands in Carrick – but it was all happening without him. He had been the commander of countless campaigns in Scotland, Wales and Gascony, and was accus-tomed to the control his presence on the field gave him. Now, he felt like a puppet master whose creations had upped and learned to dance without him.

He knew this war would be his last act on earth. Only victory here would complete his legacy. By the power of prophecy he had drawn men to his cause and with the swords of the faithful he had conquered Britain. To the men of his Round Table he was Arthur, the Dragon King. He had executed the bloody conquest of Wales and had survived the struggle against his cousin in France, securing the duchy of Gascony for his son and heir. But it was Scotland that had eluded him, time and time again; Scotland he had spent the last ten years fighting and failing to control.

In this pursuit he had bled his lands dry of taxes, grain and men. England had suffered, poverty and lawlessness growing, while all his attention remained fixed on the north. The nobility had protested over the protracted conflict in Gascony and if victory was not soon won here he might risk again the diminishing of their support. He could not endure another civil war; the memory of his father humbled and humiliated before Simon de Montfort at Lewes forty-two years ago as clear now as if it were yesterday. But neither could he rest until Scotland was conquered and all those who had defied him were crushed. Only then would he let them lay his wasted bones in a tomb.

As a servant appeared to pour more of the bitter wine, Edward realised the company of riders had veered off the road and were head-ing towards the encampment, the wagon trundling behind them. He set down the bread, hungrier to know who these new arrivals might be. He squinted into the dusk, but they were too far for him to discern any coats of arms. Royal guards rode out to meet them as they neared the fringes of the encampment. There was a brief exchange. Edward wiped his mouth with a cloth as a lone rider cantered through the midst of the army. Passing the campfires of the infantry and the domed tents of the barons, the rider urged his horse up the shallow hill towards the royal pavilion. It was Henry Percy.

Bringing his horse to a halt outside the tent, the Lord of Alnwick dismounted heavily. Henry had grown fat over the last few years and his horses had likewise become larger to compensate. His fair hair appeared almost white against the red of his face, mottled with wine and sun. 'Captain Dungal MacDouall has come, my lord. He requests to speak to you in person. He says he has a gift from Scotland.'

Edward leaned forward. 'Gift?' His mind sharpened with anticipation. His first thought was whether it could be Bruce himself, but he couldn't imagine Aymer trusting a Scot to deliver such a prize.

'He wouldn't say what it was, my lord, just that it would please you to receive it. I can compel him to tell me, if you wish.'

Edward waved his hand impatiently. 'Bring him to me.'

Henry heaved himself into the saddle and retreated with the order.

Edward set down his wine, suddenly aware of the meagre meal in front of him. It was why he now ate alone – the extent of his weakness revealed in the paltry offerings. There were beggars in his realm who would eat better. 'Clear this,' he ordered his servants, pushing the plate roughly away from him.

Humphrey de Bohun, Earl of Hereford and Essex, and Constable of England, lay drunk in his tent. He had vowed that morning at prayer that he would not end another day like this, but as the afternoon stretched on and the empty hours opened up the dark places in his mind where his dead wife, Bess, still lingered, he had ordered his servant to pour one goblet. The wine was potent, softening the jagged edges of his thoughts as he watched the sun slip beyond the hills. One goblet became five, before he retreated to the warm womb of his tent, nursing the sixth.

The dome of the tent seemed to spiral above him in the ethereal glow of a lantern Humphrey couldn't recall his servant lighting. Meadowsweet, spread on the ground, clogged the air with its sickly perfume. His thoughts were jumbled, floating in a soup of mixed emotions. On the one hand he felt comfortably drowsy, lying here waiting for sleep to claim him. On the other he wanted to rise up and do something; as if by his own action he could galvanise the king's army and move it forward from this godforsaken plain.

Voices filtered into his consciousness. Hearing the word *prisoners*, Humphrey turned his head to the sound. Through the flaps he could see a figure. The bright yellow of the man's surcoat told him it was Sir Ralph de Monthermer. Humphrey sat up, his head spinning. Feeling like an old man, he struggled on to his hands and knees.

As he stumbled out of the tent, Ralph looked round, as did the other speaker. It was Robert Clifford. The two men paused in their conversation.

'Prisoners?' Humphrey asked thickly. He frowned when neither man answered. 'Well? Am I to guess?'

'Dungal MacDouall has come,' Ralph told him. 'He has two of Bruce's men.'

Humphrey made for the royal pavilion.

Ralph caught his arm. 'Perhaps you should wait, my friend. Speak to the king in the morning?'

Humphrey focused on Ralph's face. He hated the look he saw there – part consternation, part pity. They had come up together at the royal court, both of them Knights of the Dragon, along with Robert Clifford, Henry Percy, Aymer de Valence and other young noblemen: England's elite, who had sworn to uphold their king's cause. Ralph had recently become Humphrey's brother-in-law by his marriage to the king's daughter, Joan, a marriage that had landed him the earldom of Gloucester. Still, Humphrey would be damned if he'd let the man tell him what to do.

Pushing past Ralph, he made his way towards the pavilion, staggering as he negotiated the guy ropes of tents, ignoring the greetings from his knights, who were sharing a meal around a campfire. The smell of food made Humphrey's stomach knot with hunger. He couldn't remember when he'd last eaten. He pushed a hand through his hair, aware of the state he was in, his face rough with stubble and his shirt stained with wine, but he had to see who these men of Bruce's were. It was an urge driven by a powerful need for answers. The memory of Robert holding him while his grief for Bess poured out of him as though his soul had turned to water haunted him still. The man had been betraying him even as he comforted him. Judas with a kiss for Jesus. If he looked Robert in the eye now would he see an enemy staring back at him, or would he see his old friend? He had to know.

As Humphrey approached the pavilion, he saw Dungal MacDouall at the head of a company. Scanning the devices on shields and surcoats, he realised there were knights of the Black Comyn with the captain, as well as men from Galloway. Royal guards stood to attention around the edges of the pavilion, their eyes on the Scots. Henry Percy was with them, standing by the king's table, his stomach straining against his belt. The lord looked preposterously fat; a big blond egg set beside the king, whose gauntness could not now be concealed, even by the sumptuous folds of his mantle. Humphrey concentrated his shifting vision on two figures in the centre of the ring of men. They were kneeling on the grass, their tonsured heads shiny with sweat in the light from the lanterns. The prisoners were William Lamberton and Robert Wishart.

Even through his stupor, Humphrey was well aware of the value of this prize. The bishops had been at the heart of the rebellion since the earliest days, especially Wishart, the aged, but bellicose Bishop of Glasgow, who had been one of the guardians of Scotland in the interregnum that followed the death of King Alexander. An advocate and friend of William Wallace, he had since thrown his considerable influence behind Robert's uprising. Wishart was sagging against Lamberton, hands bound tightly behind his stooped back.

Edward, seated at his table, looking down on the two men, appeared pleased with his bounty, although Humphrey found his pain-clenched face hard to read these days.

'. . . and we caught his grace at Cupar, my lord king,' Dungal MacDouall was saying. 'He was using the gift of timber you sent for repairs to his cathedral to build siege engines. They were to be employed in Bruce's war against you.'

Edward fixed Wishart with his barbed stare. 'What say you?' When the bishop didn't answer the king rose, planting his hands on the table. 'Answer me, damn you! Why did my charity warrant such flagrant abuse?'

Wishart raised his head. 'What good, Lord Edward, is a new roof to a congregation who are prisoners in their own land? The people of my diocese want freedom, not shelter.'

The bishop was nudged roughly in the back by the knee of one of MacDouall's men. He pitched forward, but managed to avoid falling on his face by steadying himself against Lamberton.

'Peace, old friend,' Lamberton murmured, as Wishart struggled upright.

'Have you questioned them on Bruce's whereabouts?'

'They would not say, but I do not believe they know. They seemed most unsettled,' MacDouall added, with a ghost of a smile, 'when we told them of Bruce's plight. Besides, my lord, we do not need their cooperation. I can tell you myself where he is.'

Edward's eyes flashed with expectation at this, but he wasn't yet finished with the bishops. He looked down on them, his thin hair drifting around his haggard face like cobwebs. 'I see not the robes of your orders, only the rebels inside. I cannot send men of the cloth to the scaffold, however deep their treachery. But be assured you will spend the rest of your lives in irons. Look to the north, both of you. Mark it well.' Edward pointed to the distant hills. 'This will be the closest you will ever come to your land again.' He gestured to his guards. 'Take them.'

As the condemned bishops were marched away, Humphrey made his way over to the king. Edward acknowledged him with a brief glance. Feeling a wave of dizziness, Humphrey gripped the edge of the table. Henry Percy frowned at him, disapproval plain in his cold blue eyes.

He, along with Humphrey, had been the greatest beneficiary of Robert's treachery. The king had granted Percy Turnberry and Carrick, while Humphrey had been given Robert's lands in Annandale and his estates in England. The prize, although great, had not been enough to soothe the deep wound gouged in Humphrey by Robert's betrayal, a wound since poisoned by his own anger, humiliation and creeping self-doubts. His mind tormented him, telling him he had been closest to Robert; he was the one who should have seen the enemy masquerading as his friend. He didn't want land – he wanted answers. Answers as to how he had been made such a fool and what, in turn, that said about him.

Humphrey met Percy's disdainful gaze, determined to assert himself here. If anyone was going to be given the task of hunting Bruce down, he wanted it to be him.

The king had turned his attention back to Dungal MacDouall. 'Tell me, Captain. Where is Bruce?'

'We know he left Aberdeen ten days ago with what was left of his army, my lord. He is heading for Islay. There, he plans to rebuild his forces with the strength of the men of the Isles and his tenants in Antrim.'

'Islay?' Edward's face was pensive in the coppery lantern light. 'So, he hopes to sway the loyalty of the MacDonalds? Is my cousin in pursuit?'

'This I do not know, my lord. Sir Aymer had left for Aberdeen by the time we discovered Bruce's plans. I have sent word to him.'

'And how, exactly, did you discover this?'

'I captured one of Bruce's followers in Perth. Alexander Seton claimed to have deserted and wished to surrender, but he wasn't willing to divulge Bruce's plans, at least not at first. I took him to Sir John of Buchan. My master wrested the information from him. Sir John has gone with all speed to warn the MacDougalls that Bruce is headed their way. Bruce, we were told, has women and children with him. His progress will be slow. God willing, my master and the lords of Argyll will be able to bar his route to Islay and capture him.'

Edward was silent, thinking. Finally, he nodded. 'Thank you, Captain. My men will show you where your company can rest for the night. We will speak again at first light.'

The king watched as the Scots were ushered down the hillside, before turning his attention to Humphrey. His grey eyes were alert, the pain that clouded them replaced by fierce intent. 'Prepare your men, Humphrey. You will ride to Carrick and there join forces with my son. Take MacDouall with you, he can escort you to the Black Comyn. Use the Comyn's strength by all means, but I want you to confront Bruce and his men.'

'I will not fail you, my lord.'

'All his possessions must be brought to me intact. You understand?'

Humphrey knew what Edward spoke of. 'I swear, my lord, by Michaelmas you will have Bruce in custody and the Staff of Malachy will be back in Westminster Abbey. I will not let him undermine all we have sacrificed in the struggle to protect our kingdom.'

Edward drummed his thin fingers on the table top. 'Do not forget the prophecy, Humphrey. I want that box returned to me at all cost.'

'Of course, my lord.'

The king held his gaze, looking as if he might say something more, but then he turned to Henry Percy. 'Go to Aberdeen. Tell Aymer to stay in the city in case Bruce evades the trap and attempts to head back east. I want the son of a bitch surrounded.' Edward made a fist of his hand. 'With a noose tightening around his neck.'

Dismissed, Humphrey made his way back to his tent, surer and more sober with every step. Feeling new energy pulsing through him, he thought of the day he was initiated as a Knight of the Dragon, tasked by the king with a quest on which the future of their kingdom depended.

He had first learned of the *Last Prophecy* from his father, who told him of its discovery at Nefyn in Wales, following the fall of the Welsh prince, Llywelyn ap Gruffudd. Translated by a Welshman loyal to King Edward, the prophecy revealed that the four relics of Brutus, the founder of Britain, must be gathered together again, united under one ruler. According to the ancient text, consigned to a locked box to prevent it crumbling into dust, the division of the kingdom between the sons of Brutus, who had each taken one relic as a symbol of his reign, had caused Britain's descent into centuries of chaos, war and poverty. The island's final ruin was now approaching, as foreseen in a vision of Merlin, and only the unification of the treasures – and thus the kingdom itself – would prevent it.

The king had charged his knights to seize the relics alluded to in the prophecy from the four corners of Britain. Curtana, the Sword of Mercy, symbol of English royal power, had been the first to be presented at the shrine of the Confessor in Westminster Abbey. Next, the Crown of Arthur, taken from the rebels during the conquest of Wales, and the Stone of Destiny, removed from Scotland. Last was the Staff of Malachy, Ireland's holiest relic, brought to the king by Robert Bruce on his surrender; a peace offering.

Telling his knights to finish their meal and be ready to receive orders, Humphrey asked his servants to fetch food, a basin of water and a razor. Ducking inside the tent, his eyes went to his armour and broadsword. Rust had bloomed on the mail. He would have his squire clean it and whet his sword. Bending to pull a fresh shirt from his pack, his gaze alighted on the half-finished wine by his bed. Picking it up, he stared into the red depths.

He remembered raising his goblet to Robert the night of the young man's inception into the Knights of the Dragon at Conwy Castle, drinking to their sacred brotherhood. Robert had taken the same oaths he had. The man had seemed so sincere in his utterance of them, but how could he have been when, by taking the staff and the prophecy from Westminster, he had set Britain back on the path to destruction? His betrayal had made a mockery of everything Humphrey had worked for; everything he trusted. It made a mockery of him too. He had stood up for the man when no one else would, defended him. How could he have been so foolish? Had Robert ever believed, or was it all just lies?

Writtle, England

1302 AD (4 years earlier)

*H*umphrey felt Bess's arm brush his as she leaned forward to push the ivory pawn across the chessboard. He glanced at her and smiled, distracted for a moment from his study of Robert, who sat opposite with his young wife.

A servant left the great hall carrying an armful of silver plates, soiled with the remains of the feast. As the man opened the door a blast of air blew into the chamber, causing the banners on the walls to flutter against their nails and a large cobweb that laced the oak beams to billow and break. The fire in the hearth gusted, sending sparks roaring up the chimney. Writtle Manor was a draughty old place, thought Humphrey, in need of some urgent repairs, but Robert's father seemed more interested in spending his money on a steady supply of Gascon wine. The old lord had retired drunk to his bed some hours ago, leaving the four of them alone to finish the game.

Bess drew her crimson mantle, brocaded with flowers, tighter and leaned into him for warmth. Slipping an arm around her waist, Humphrey returned his attention to Robert, whose eyes were on the chessboard, his goblet gripped in his hand. He appeared preoccupied, but not, it seemed, by the contest. His stare was distant and unfocused as if he were looking through the board to something only he could see. Firelight bruised his face, highlighting the frown that creased his brow. Not for the first time, Humphrey wished he could see into that closed mind.

It was seven months since Robert had surrendered to the king at Westminster and in all that time, despite searching for it, Humphrey had seen nothing to indicate that his submission was anything other than genuine. But, still, he could not bring himself to trust the man. After his desertion to join the insurrection led by William Wallace, Robert had spent five years fighting against them. Humphrey's gaze drifted to the fragment of iron that hung on a leather thong around Robert's neck, visible in the cleft of his shirt. He remembered the king's order, issued on the day of Robert's surrender: that he was to rebuild their old friendship and, in doing so, find out what had happened in Ireland. Robert had been wounded by that crossbow bolt and Edward wanted to know who his attacker was and whether or not they were still alive. He had been very explicit about this.

Robert's eyes flicked up suddenly, meeting his gaze. Humphrey covered himself by taking a sip of wine. Robert's wife, Elizabeth, moved her knight across the board taking one of their pawns, her young face taut with concentration. Bess smiled and countered.

As Robert's eyes returned to the board, Humphrey recalled the evening six months ago in this hall when he had asked the king's question. Robert had said he hadn't known the man who attacked him, who was killed by Ulster's knights before he could find out. Humphrey thought he had glimpsed a lie in Robert's face, but drink and resentment had been hot in both of them that night and thoughts of the truth had been swept aside in the fight that followed. In reporting back to Edward, Humphrey had suggested the king ask Sir Richard de Burgh for his version of events, but the king surprised him, saying the Earl of Ulster had already corroborated Robert's story. Clearly, even the word of one of his staunchest vassals hadn't satisfied him.

Humphrey sensed something secret and unspoken, spun like a web between Robert and Edward, that he now found himself caught in. The notion the king was asking after a killer sent by his own instruction had entered his mind, but he had forced that thought aside. The secret slaying of a man of Robert's rank, without trial or judgement, was unthinkable. Nobles died heroic in battle, like his father, or else were captured for ransom. They weren't even executed, let alone murdered in cold blood.

'It is your move, my lord.'

Elizabeth was looking expectantly at Robert.

'You take it.'

Elizabeth glanced at Bess and Humphrey, then lowered her eyes. Pressing her lips together, she picked up another piece. The flared sleeve of her dress toppled a bishop, which rolled off the board. Humphrey snatched out his hand. Elizabeth reached for it at the same time and grabbed his hand instead. She withdrew sharply as if burned by the contact, her cheeks flushing. There was a clatter as the bishop struck the floor. Humphrey bent and picked it up, setting it back on the board. He smiled at Elizabeth, who smiled self-consciously back. She was seventeen, but seemed much younger.

Bess yawned deeply. 'I believe that heralds the ending of our game.'

'Indeed,' said Humphrey, feeling her pinch his side softly. 'We should retire. I'll need to leave early tomorrow. I have matters to attend to on my estate.'

Elizabeth's face fell, but she covered her disappointment with a forced smile. 'Of course.' She looked meaningfully at her husband, who seemed to come back to life.

'I'll have Edwin show you to the guest quarters,' Robert said, rising.

A short time later, after the steward had escorted them to their room and the servant who banked up the fire had left, closing the door behind him, Humphrey sat on the bed and let out a sigh, feeling the tension of the evening ebbing slowly. Across the room, Bess had shrugged off her cloak and was fiddling with the laces on the sides of her gown. Like all the king's children, she was tall and long-limbed. Her dark hair was trussed up under a pearl-studded net, which matched her crimson dress. Firelight flushed the skin of her neck as she twisted to pick at the knots. Humphrey crossed to her. 'Allow me.'

She smiled as he pulled gently at the bindings. When he bent forward to kiss her neck, she closed her eyes and sighed. 'Poor Elizabeth. She seems so unhappy.' Her eyes opened and she looked over her shoulder at him. 'I'm not even sure they share the same bed. I'm not sure they ever have.'

Humphrey withdrew, discomforted. 'A man's marriage is his own business, Bess. I'll not get involved. Neither should you.'

Bess took his hand and drew it back to her waist to continue undoing her gown. She pressed her shoulders into his chest. 'I'm just glad for what I have.'

'Not as glad as I,' Humphrey murmured in response, but even as the gown slipped down to her waist and Bess turned to kiss him, his thoughts remained fixed on Robert.

9

Dunstaffnage Castle, Scotland, 1306 AD

The hooves clattered off the drawbridge as a dozen riders funnelled in through the stone bulk of the gatehouse. The guards stood aside, allowing them to pass under the iron fangs of the portcullis and into the courtyard beyond, enclosed by high, quadrangular walls, from which projected great towers at the north and west corners. Built along one wall was a grand, two-storey hall, its whitewashed walls glazed by torchlight.

John MacDougall, Lord of Argyll, strode out through the hall's doors as the riders dismounted by the well, his steward following in his wake. John pushed a hand through his red hair, dishevelled from sleep. Even though the hour was late the courtyard was cast in pale twilight. It would barely get darker than this tonight, although it was now several weeks past midsummer and John discerned a faint change in the light. Over the next few months the nights would slowly deepen to pitch, darkness stretching into the days; a creeping tide of shadows that would eventually fill all hours, the castle besieged by howling winds and winter's bone-marrow chill. But, for now, all was calm and the breeze mild.

'Sir, the earl has some fifty men with him, waiting in the grounds.'

'Make space for them and their horses,' John told his steward. 'Clear out the boathouse if you have to.'

As John headed over to the riders he glanced up, checking the parapet walk. Half a dozen guards were stationed there, the half-light making them look more like statues built out of the fabric of the castle. Below, in the bailey, other guards stood sentry: two outside the north tower, the bottom chamber of which was piled high with sacks of oats and grain, and another four beside a long row of spears propped against the wall, ready to furnish an army. Gratified, John approached his kinsman.

John Comyn, Earl of Buchan and head of the Black Comyns, dismounted his palfrey with a metal shiver of mail and spurs. He handed the reins to one of his knights, all of whom were dressed, as he was, in black surcoats adorned with three white sheaves of wheat. The Black Comyn was an imposing man, broad in the shoulders and built like a barrel, but with most of his bulk still muscle rather than fat, surprising in a man of his advanced years. Ten years John MacDougall's senior, the earl was approaching sixty, his face creased with age and webbed with battle scars.

Holding back his impatience to discover why his kinsman had returned so unexpectedly, John embraced him. 'Welcome, brother.' As his steward spoke to one of the earl's knights, John saw the man gesture to a large sack draped over the back of one of the horses.

The Black Comyn scanned the courtyard imperiously. As his dark eyes alighted on the row of spears, he nodded slightly.

John bore the inspection without comment. He and his father might rule Argyll – their dominion radiating out from Dunstaffnage across the water to Mull, northern Jura, Coll and Tiree, and far inland through the wilds of Lorn – but the Black Comyn controlled a vast swathe of the north-east of the kingdom and was the former Constable of Scotland. Although he had lost some of his standing in the coup staged by Robert Bruce, he was still one of the most formidable men in the realm and commanded the utmost respect.

'How is Sir Alexander?' asked the earl, his deep voice gruff.

'My father is recovering well from the last bout of fever. His strength returns day by day.' John pressed in, impatience getting the better of him. 'I know he would have wanted to greet you himself, had he known you were coming.'

The Black Comyn grunted. 'I'm afraid haste took precedence over etiquette.'

'Haste? Are the English set for war?' John felt a surge of anticipation. When the Black Comyn left his company a month ago, he hadn't expected to see him again until he received word to head east and join forces with him and King Edward. 'Are we to move on Bruce?'

'The plan has changed.'

John listened as the earl told him of Bruce's defeat at the hands of Aymer de Valence, aided by Dungal MacDouall and the men of Galloway. He scowled at this, his initial eagerness dampened by his lack of involvement in the victory.

The Black Comyn read his mind. 'Do not fear, John, you will have your chance to make good on your blood oath. Indeed, sooner than we thought. By the time I returned to my wife's estate at Leuchars, Valence had marched on Aberdeen, but I learned there that Bruce had already left the port and was making for Islay.'

'The whoreson seeks the aid of Angus MacDonald,' John murmured. His eyes narrowed as he plotted the various routes in his mind. Aberdeen to Islay would take Bruce directly through his lands. 'Do we know when he left?'

'A fortnight, give or take.'

John shook his head. 'Then he should have passed through already.'

'There are women and children in his company. I suspect they came down through Drumalban, using the mountains as shelter. He may make for the pass.'

'A dangerous road. If he takes Brander he'll have to come by Dunstaffnage.'

'He has five hundred men or more. He may hope to fight his way through.'

'With women and children? He would have to be desperate to risk being trapped in the pass. No. There are other routes he could take.' John's frown deepened as he thought of Bruce's allies. 'Campbell,' he muttered, thinking of the young man whose father he had slaughtered ten years ago. 'He knows these lands.'

'If we can block his path to Islay, will you and your men be ready to face him?'

John smiled grimly. 'Come.' He led the earl to a set of stone steps that climbed the wall to the parapet. 'You cannot see it from the road in.'

They emerged on to the walkway above, the Black Comyn breathing hard, weighed down by mail. The guards nodded respectfully, making room for the two men to pass along the wall.

Up here, the wind buffeted them, carrying on its currents the sour tang of the sea and the pungent stink from the outflow of the latrine chutes that opened on to the rocks sixty feet below. Banners, decorated with the black galleys of the MacDougall arms, snapped and billowed. The view was spectacular: dominated by rugged hills and immense stretches of water, all washed in twilight. Built on a wide slab of rock, Dunstaffnage glowered from its promontory over the Firth of Lorn towards the dark ramparts of Mull's mountains. In the foreground was the lower lying hump of Lismore, over which the MacDougalls had fought bitterly with the MacDonalds for years. The two families, along with the MacRuaries, were all descended from the same man, Somerled, the King of the Isles, but that hadn't stopped each branch warring for supremacy over the western sea kingdom.

In one corner of the castle grounds stood an ornate chapel, bordered by a graveyard which together with gardens and an orchard made a patchwork of green. Ignoring the scattered collection of outbuildings, stables and boathouses, John pointed to the northern end of the promontory. 'There.'

The Black Comyn's gaze focused on the scores of tents just visible through a shroud of trees. Many shadowy figures were highlighted by the glow of campfires. The camp stretched down to the water's edge where, in a shallow bay that opened into the wide mouth of Loch Etive, a score of galleys undulated. At this distance, with their sails furled, the vessels looked like leaves floating on the current.

'Almost a thousand at last count,' John said, looking at the earl to see his reaction. 'With more still coming in.'

'Ready fighters?'

'Ready and able,' replied John, thinking of the rough Highlanders who had come down out of the hills and the leather-skinned men of the Isles who came from the sea, summoned by the beacons. These mercenaries and pirates, all keen for plunder, were augmented by disciplined knights of Argyll. Many had served his father for years, but it was he – John MacDougall – who would now lead them into battle against Bruce; he who would avenge the murder of his cousin, John Comyn. Blood demanded blood.

'I have nigh on seventy with me here,' said the earl, turning to him. 'And I've sent word for my tenants, now gathering in Buchan with men from Sir John's lands in Badenoch, to make their way west. Together, we'll outnumber the bastard three to one.'

'What about the English? Will they join us here?' John's anticipation was further whetted by the thought. His family had been enemies of the English king since the early days of John Balliol's rebellion, only submitting with reluctance to Edward's authority two years ago, along with the rest of Scotland's magnates. But now Bruce had rebelled, taking the throne in defiance of John Balliol's right and murdering his nephew, things had changed. If he helped defeat their common enemy, what would King Edward grant him in return? Perhaps the MacDougalls might finally hold sway over the Western Isles as their ancestor, Somerled, had.

'I sent Captain MacDouall to the king at Durham to tell him Bruce's plan, but it will take time for Edward to muster his forces. Indeed, I'm counting on it. The kinsmen of John Comyn deserve this victory. Not the English.'

John smiled grimly. 'I agree.' Turning from the encampment, he led the way back down to the courtyard. A thought occurred to him. 'Brother, how did you discover Bruce was headed for Islay?'

The Black Comyn motioned to one of his knights. Grooms had led away most of the horses, except for the one with the sack draped over its back. As the earl ordered the knight to untie the burden, John realised it wasn't a sack at all, but a man.

As the ropes were unbound, he slid from the horse's rump and collapsed in the dust of the courtyard. John thought him dead, until the earl's knights hauled him to his feet. The glow of the torches highlighted the injuries on his face, a bloody mess of bruises and cuts. The skin around one of his eyes was swollen and purple, the eye itself red with blood. His lips were torn and more blood coated his neck and stained his shirt. He was a well-built man, about the same age as himself, John guessed, with black hair and a beard filthy with dust. 'Who is he?'

'Alexander Seton,' answered the Black Comyn with satisfaction. 'One of Bruce's commanders. He gave up the information. Eventually.'

The broken man licked his lips and murmured something. John thought he caught the word *bastard* in the rasp of his voice.

The earl nodded to one of the knights, who punched a mailed fist into Alexander's stomach. Alexander doubled over in the clutches of his captors, retching and gasping.

'I'll send out scouts tonight,' said John, looking back at his kinsman. 'We'll waste no time. If five hundred men are hiding in these hills, believe me they will find them. My galleys will patrol the coast, blocking the sea routes to Islay. By the blood of my cousin, Bruce will not make it to the haven of the MacDonalds.'

'One last thing, John,' said the Black Comyn, gripping his

shoulder. 'I am told my wife is still in Bruce's company.' His voice was low, but emotion now simmered beneath the surface, his dark eyes glittering. 'I want Lady Isabel taken alive – her and the man who took her to Scone, John of Atholl. They are mine, you understand?'

'Of course, brother,' said John, his own mind on the prize he wanted: the head of the false king, Robert Bruce.

Near Ayr, Scotland, 1306 AD

'You were a lion on the field today.' Prince Edward watched Piers Gaveston recline on the rug beside him. It was damp where the evening dew had seeped through the weave.

The Gascon knight rested his elbow on the ground and propped his head against his hand. In the other, he cradled a silver goblet, over the lip of which he met the prince's gaze. 'Proud, you mean to say?' His eyes were black in the gold haze of the candles and his olive skin glistened with the sweat of a day spent fighting on the sun-baked bluffs.

Edward smiled. 'Fierce.' He took a sip from his own goblet. The wine was warm and slightly tart. Setting it on one of the chests that lined the tent he lay back, resting his head on the rumpled blankets that formed his bed. Young men's shouts and laughter echoed outside. The night air was redolent with wood-smoke, horse dung and roasting meat. 'I'm surprised anyone else dared face you after you knocked poor Henry de Bohun so soundly from his horse.' Edward's smile faded. 'I thought you had killed him.'

'He was fine,' retorted Piers. 'The lad has spirit.' He exhaled sharply when Edward's expression didn't change. Placing his own goblet on the rug, he reached across and touched his friend's hand, where it was splayed on his stomach. 'What is wrong, my prince? You've been quiet all afternoon.'

Edward closed his eyes, feeling the heat of Piers's palm as it closed over his hand and the calloused ridge of skin where the lance had rubbed, even through the protection of his gloves. 'My father wouldn't approve.' Opening his eyes, he glanced at Piers. Seeing the knight was unsure of his meaning, he added, 'Of these tournaments. Of our' – he waved a hand to indicate the outside world – 'frivolity.'

'The king is hundreds of miles away.'

'That does not mean he will not find out,' said Edward darkly.

Every error he made, his father always somehow unearthed it and brought it up to chastise or humiliate him. 'What if Henry had died today? He's the constable's nephew!'

'Your father has long been a lover of the tourney. My own father told me it was his greatest passion when he was in Gascony, a youth of your years now. His knights called him King Arthur, did they not?'

'I know my father's history,' said Edward shortly. How could he not? It was part of the long shadow the man cast over him.

'Then you are doing no more than he himself has done. You've often spoken of the jousts he organised in Wales for the men of his Round Table. He was famous for them. And, lest we forget, those celebrations in Perth a few years ago – a whole week of tournaments.' Piers's mouth curled in a self-satisfied smile. 'At which I was crowned the victor.'

Edward recalled Piers's swagger at the victory feast and his drunken antics, the Gascon laughing as he leaned in and kissed him on the mouth in full public view, then slid a hand up the inside of his thigh under the table. He remembered too the looks and mutterings among the older barons and the stone-cold disapproval in his father's eyes as he presented the cocksure knight with his prize. He frowned, not wanting to be distracted from the point of the conversation. 'Those were celebrations of victory – when he had conquered his enemies.'

'And what have you done here?' pressed Piers. 'You've taken Bruce's castle, burned his lands and soaked the ground with the blood of his people. He will find no shelter in Carrick. We've destroyed his home.' Piers threaded his fingers through Edward's. 'You are the conqueror now, my prince.'

Edward turned his head to look at the knight, whose angular face was half cast in shadow, half flushed with candlelight. There was a blade of grass caught in his black hair. Piers, accepted into the royal household after the death of his father who had served the king in Gascony, had a blind spot when it came to the king. Despite the fact he had grown to manhood at court, assigned to the prince's household six years ago when the two of them turned sixteen, he still didn't realise how unforgiving – how *dangerous* – the king could be. Edward stared up at the dome of the tent. 'A conqueror, am I? Yet still my father treats me like a dim-witted child.' He gritted his teeth at the words, humiliated by the truth of them. 'I'm sick of his damned disapproval!'

'I've told you, Edward, you must stand up to him. You are Prince of Wales, Duke of Gascony and commander of the king's army. He has given you the authority. Now, you must command his respect.' Piers gripped the prince's hand, forcing him to listen. 'Your father is old and ailing. I do not believe it will be long before you take his place. The barons must learn to honour and fear you now, if you are to keep them in check once he is gone. I will be at your side, always, but you alone will control them. Make a stand. Tell the king what you want. *Demand* it!'

Edward felt the familiar weight pressing in on his mind. More and more since the sickness had begun stripping his father's strength he had dwelled on his future, which stood waiting in Westminster Abbey – a coronation chair made at his father's behest, beneath which Scotland's Stone of Destiny was encased. The prince's brow knotted. He was named after his father and with his fair hair and tall, strapping frame everyone told him he was a mirror of the king in youth. But that was where any similarity ended. His father had wanted to create from him a mould of himself, but since the death of Edward's mother, Eleanor, only Scotland had been granted the attention of the king. Over the past ten years it was as if the kingdom had become an errant child that needed to be beaten and cowed into obedience, while Edward, who tried to be the good son, waited in the shadows for his father to notice him.

God, how he hated this place.

Feeling Piers's hand tighten around his, Edward met the knight's eyes. Things would change when he was king. He sat up, determination rising in him. The rug shifted, toppling Piers's goblet. Edward grabbed for it, cursing as wine spilled over his hand. He went to shake it off, but Piers grasped his wrist. The knight smiled slyly, then slid his tongue lightly up the side of Edward's hand, droplets trickling into his mouth. Edward felt a spasm of pleasure. Grabbing Piers by the back of the neck, he pulled the knight towards him, opening his mouth over his. They kissed deeply, tongues entwined. Edward tasted the salt of Piers's sweat, felt the man's stubble scraping his skin. Beneath his hand, pressed into the wine-soaked rug, he sensed a shudder, like thunder rumbling through the earth. He drew back abruptly, looking to the tent flaps, in the gap between which the evening sky was a thin strip of blue.

'What is it?'

'Do you feel that? Hoof-beats?' Edward strained to listen, but all he could hear were the raucous voices of his knights, enjoying the wine and food they had taken from the stores of Turnberry Castle.

'It is just our men out there.'

Edward kept his gaze on the tent opening, until Piers pressed his palm to his cheek and turned him to face him. The knight's lips glistened in the candlelight, his black eyes smouldering like coals. Feeling desire bite deep, the prince pressed in. He dug his fingers into Piers's shoulder. Beneath the knight's shirt, muscles tightened. The outside world disappeared. Edward no longer heard the faint drum of hoof-beats approaching.

They had been careful for a long time, ever since Edward Bruce had glimpsed them together during the hunt in the woods of Burstwick Manor, the prince fearing the truth of his friendship with Piers would be discovered. His father had become suspicious, he knew, and had spoken with new determination and frequency of Edward's forthcoming marriage to Isabella, daughter of the King of France. His father wasn't the only one. Edward's cousin, Thomas, the Earl of Lancaster, with whom he had once been close, had become increasingly cold and aloof, often making cutting remarks about Piers. For months on end, Edward had suffered for the touch he craved, dreaming of Piers and waking fitful, drenched in sweat. But out here on campaign with the men of his own household, far from the king and his barons, he had let down his guard. The two of them had come together in the dark cocoon of the tent these past few nights like men starved.

'My lord prince!'

Edward jerked from Piers at the call from outside.

'A company has come, my lord.' The voice was Henry de Bohun's.

The young squire, Edward was relieved to see, was standing to the side of the gap in the tent's opening. His heart slowed from gallop to trot. He wouldn't have seen anything. 'Whose company?' he demanded, wondering who on earth would have travelled all the way out to his remote camp on this wild strip of coast.

'It's my uncle, sir.'

Edward felt a jolt go through him at the unpleasant surprise. He glanced at Piers, who stared calmly back. 'Tell him to wait,' he called, after a pause. As Henry's footsteps receded, Edward sat back on his heels and pushed his hands through his hair. 'God damn it!' He looked over at Piers, anger and shame prickling inside him. 'I said my father has eyes everywhere!' Leaning over, he snatched his goblet from the chest and drained the sour wine in one swift draught. 'Now he has sent his right-hand man to spy on me and no doubt report back on my inadequacies. I told you we must be careful!'

As Edward set down the goblet, Piers took hold of his wrist. 'And I told you, my prince, to seize the authority your father has bestowed upon you. It isn't God waiting outside, nor is it the king. It is Humphrey de Bohun. The constable is a powerful man, yes, but you are more powerful still. Go, speak to him, find out why he has come, but do it with your head raised, for you will be his king and however high he thinks himself he will soon be on bended knee before you.'

Piers's eyes were intent, his gaze unwavering. Edward gave a small nod. Pushing himself to his feet, he smoothed down his tunic and ducked out into the warm evening, followed by Piers. Making his way past the campfires of his comrades, who were all flushed with wine and laughter and suddenly seemed far too relaxed, he fixed his attention on the company of horsemen who had gathered a short distance from his tent, the horses stamping, excited by their ride.

Humphrey de Bohun was at their head, the six gold lions on his mantle glittering in the flame-light. The earl had dismounted and was speaking to his nephew. Edward thought of his fears that Henry could have been killed in the tournament and what trouble that would have caused him. It was a horrible coincidence that the squire's uncle should now turn up in his camp. He wondered uneasily whether the bruises and cuts the young man sported after coming off his horse in the joust would look like war wounds.

'My lord prince,' greeted Humphrey, with a brief bow.

Edward thought the earl seemed even more direct than usual, his tone curt. He noticed Humphrey's gaze flick to Piers and seeing the flash of disapproval in the constable's green eyes found himself moving to block his view. 'Sir Humphrey, it is a surprise to see you here, so far from my father's camp. Do you have word from him?' Edward went on before Humphrey could answer. 'Has Master Henry been telling you of my success? I have taken Turnberry Castle and burned Bruce's lands. His tenants have been scattered to the—'

'I beg your pardon, my lord prince,' interrupted Humphrey, 'but time is of the essence. I have come with all speed from Durham with orders from the king. Robert Bruce is fleeing west. We are to intercept him.'

Near Tyndrum, Scotland, 1306 AD

From the sprawling thicket of birch and alders, Alexander Seton stared at the distant wooded fringes of the River Fillan, where a broad meadow curved out of sight, folding into a valley. His eyes strained, searching for movement beyond the great plain of grass that rippled like a green sea. Around him, crowds of men were adjusting helms and armour, hefting weapons. Some spoke in low voices to comrades, or to quieten horses. Most were silent. The muggy air was clogged with their combined stink – stale sweat, leather and tarnished steel.

Alexander's attention was diverted as his arm was knocked by one of his two guards who viciously swatted a fly from his face. There were scores of them buzzing about the nostrils of the horses and the piles of dung around the cavalry lines; more still around the six corpses. Alexander glanced at the bodies. He didn't know any of them by name, but he recognised two as Robert's scouts. The dead men's eyes and mouths were already busy with flies, laying eggs in the openings. Come nightfall, worms would make a feast.

'Eyes forward.'

Alexander realised the guard was staring at him. The man's fist was raised as if to strike. He looked back at the plain, not wishing to give Comyn's thugs any more excuses to beat him. They needed little encouragement – the myriad bruises that throbbed and ached across his body a painful testament to that.

'That's right. You don't want to miss the approach of your king.'

Alexander felt a surge of hatred, bitter as bile, as the guard chuckled, but he couldn't say anything, even if he dared, for a filthy gag, which tasted of his own blood, was tied over his mouth.

Dear God, let him see them. Let him see them before it's too late.

As he clasped his bound hands together behind his back to cement the prayer, Alexander felt again how loose his bindings had become after endless hours of struggle, his skin chafed raw by the ropes, but the possibility of freedom offered little hope. Where the hell would he run to? He was surrounded by fifteen hundred men.

The Black Comyn and John MacDougall had two hundred horsemen on palfreys and hobbies. The rest, on foot, made a grim band, armed with spears and the wicked, long-handled axes of Highlanders. Alexander thought of the women and children in the king's company and closed his eyes. However angry he was with Robert, however much he had wanted out of the man's company and his own life back, he hadn't wanted this. He should have let the Black Comyn and that one-handed thug MacDouall kill him – but his wasn't the only life they had bargained with.

After MacDouall took him from Perth to Leuchars, Alexander had been beaten for hours, the earl demanding to know everything about Robert's plans. At first he resisted the punches, the kicks and the threats against his life. Finally, when he was barely conscious, the earl had Will dragged in. Alexander had watched through eyes misted with blood as the knight was forced to his knees in front of him. Will's face was ashen, but he held his head high, looking him in the eye, even as Alexander refused to answer their questions, even when the dagger was pressed to Will's bared neck. Even when they slit his throat. They did the same to Ewen and, still, Alexander did not speak.

It was Tom who had broken him. Young Tom, his squire, begged as they put the blade to the corner of his eye, threatening to put it out. When the tip punctured his skin the lad, sobbing, had pissed himself. Alexander had surrendered then, one of the earl's men having to lean right down into the pool of blood and spit he had made to hear his words.

'Islay. He's going to Islay.'

His submission did not matter. The sons of whores had killed Tom anyway.

Alexander had wished then that they would end him, but the Black Comyn had ordered him kept alive, in case he might still prove of use.

'If nothing else,' he had heard the earl say, 'his delivery into English custody will help strengthen the king's trust. Bring him with us. I'll hand him over myself. I imagine Lord Edward will relish dealing with one of Bruce's commanders.'

A shudder of expectation rippled through the army hidden in the woods as away across the plain a host of men came slowly into view. Alexander stiffened, seeing the column wind its way up from the valley into the sea of grass like a thick black snake. The column lengthened as more men appeared, some on horses, others on foot. Around him, the murmurs were accompanied by the scrape of weapons and stamping hooves. Within moments, after sharp commands from the captains, the waiting army quietened. Men tensed, sweat trickling down their faces.

Alexander's heart beat a rapid tattoo in his chest as he fixed his eyes on the host emerging on to the sunlit plain. He strained against the ropes around his wrists, the knots biting into his skin as he fought to pull his hands apart. His guards didn't notice, all their attention fixed on the approaching army. The company was a long way away, but however hopeless, he had to act. There was one thing he could do – though it would most likely be his last act on this earth. At last, wrenching his hands free from the bindings, Alexander pulled down the gag, threw back his head and roared Robert's name.

Robert glanced round as John of Atholl urged his horse up alongside him at the vanguard of the column of men.

'No sign of them?' murmured John.

The visor of Robert's helm was raised. Beneath its iron rim, his eyes were narrowed, scanning the plain before them. A wedge of cloud was looming over the peaks of Lorn, all the blacker in contrast to the gold of the afternoon sun that bathed the broad meadows beyond the River Fillan. It had rained a short time ago and the plain was a vast shimmering cloak, spread out beneath the mountains. Finches and plovers darted from the flower-dappled grasses.

'You told them to scout out the road,' reasoned John. He nodded north towards Tyndrum, where the mountains became densely wooded hills. 'It's a fair way.'

David manoeuvred his horse up alongside his father. 'The scouts?'

John shook his head.

'They should have returned by now,' said Robert, looking over his shoulder down the first dozen rows of mounted men. Sunlight caught on the metal bosses and rivets of shields and winked on the domes of helms. His gaze moved on, past the lines of foot soldiers who trudged alongside the knights, to where the women and children rode in a tight group. He had put them in the middle with the servants, grooms and pack-horses, partly to keep the company moving at the same pace, partly to surround them with a shield of men.

Elizabeth rode at the head of the women on a sleek white palfrey. His wife wore the grey mantle he'd had lined with sable to surprise her years ago in Essex. The garment was frayed and sun-bleached. Beside the queen was Marjorie on a sturdy-legged pony. His daughter looked tired. His sisters and the wives and children of his men rode behind in silence. Gone was the gaiety of the wedding day. That had faded days ago while they prepared for the next leg of the journey, James Douglas and Gilbert de la Hay leading hunting parties to supplement their dwindling supplies. As they had loaded the pack-horses that morning, Robert noticed Elizabeth was pale and anxious. Overhearing her talking to Isabel Comyn, he realised she was worried about the sea voyage to Islay. His wife had almost drowned as a child and had been terrified of water ever since.

'Maybe they met with company and had to lie low?' offered John. 'The road leads to the Pass of Brander before it splits. It's unlikely to be free of travellers.'

Fixing his eyes forward again, Robert cursed. 'We're travelling blind.'

'We could wait.' John shifted in his saddle, one hand sliding to rest on the pommel of his sword. It was an instinctive movement, but one that betrayed his own unease. 'Give the scouts more time to return?'

'No,' said Robert, after a pause. 'The longer we stay out here, the longer we're in danger of being seen. We move on. With luck we'll make the head of Loch Awe before nightfall and we can disappear in the hills. Tomorrow evening, by Campbell's reckoning, we'll reach the coast.'

He flicked his spurs across Ghost's sides, urging the palfrey into the waving sea of grass at a brisk walk that was quickly matched by the men of the vanguard. Ghost moved easily across the marshy ground, even with the weight of Robert's mail, augmented by a coat-of-plates over which he wore his surcoat and a woollen cloak. Hunter would have been too heavy for such terrain. The thought brought a painful memory of the night in Aberdeen when he'd been forced to confront

the reality of the animal's injury. The warhorse had lain down in the
stables at his command, snorting as he stroked his nose. When Nes
crouched beside him in silence, holding an iron spike and a hammer,
Robert had taken the tools himself. He had talked softly, setting the
tip of the spike against the animal's head. One strong swing of the
hammer, as the stable-master had instructed.

Robert was brought back to the present by a noise somewhere off
in the distance. It sounded like an animal's howl. A flock of crows
burst from the tangled canopy of a wood, half a mile or so to the
south, their calls rising ragged on the breeze.

'What is it?' asked John, seeing his intent expression.

Robert strained to listen over the jingle of mail and bridles, the
grunts of horses and thud of hooves, but all he caught was the wind
singing in the grass. 'I'm not sure.'

Neil Campbell, riding to their left, looked round, his eyes alert.

'You heard it?' Robert asked him.

Neil nodded. 'Could have been a wolf,' he ventured, although his
hand was curled around the grip of his sword.

'What's wrong?' Edward kicked his horse up alongside his brother.
He was quickly joined by Christopher Seton and Niall.

Robert held up his hand, gesturing for the men of the vanguard to
halt. They did so, one by one, their horses fanning out. The black
wedge of cloud was drifting over the mountains, trailing curtains of
rain down into the foothills. Robert stared into the woods, out of the
depths of which the birds had scattered. He felt the first drops of rain
misting the air. The clouds were advancing on the sun, bringing a
wave of shadow towards him. Before the sun winked out, Robert
caught several flashes along the tree line. Sunlight on metal. His
instincts flared. He went for his broadsword, shouting the alarm, just
as a tide of men came pouring out of the woods.

Their distant roar was drowned by the thunder of hooves as two
hundred riders broke from the front lines, urging their horses into a
gallop. Behind, men came running, the stormy light sparking off spear-
heads and axe-blades. Banners billowed above the riders, decorated
with the black galleys of Argyll and the arms of the Black Comyn.

All around Robert, men began shouting and drawing their weapons. Horses reared in fear as alarm swept through the company. A few
pack-horses broke free from the grasp of startled servants and bolted.
Some of the women began to scream, setting the dogs barking and

threatening to send more horses into flight. Christian had snatched Donald from the arms of his wet nurse and was grasping the wailing boy tight to her chest. Mary clutched at the reins of Matilda's horse, her sister's animal panicked and stamping. Isabel Comyn was staring numbly at the incoming charge of horsemen, transfixed by the sight of her husband's banner.

Robert, the blood pumping through his veins, looked from the cluster of terrified women and children to the approaching riders. The horsemen were still some distance away, but the gap was closing rapidly, more and more of the plain disappearing under the pummelling hooves. Behind them, men continued to emerge from the trees. There were hundreds – maybe thousands.

'There're too many!' shouted John. 'We'll be overrun!'

Robert made a decision; no time to think whether it was right or wrong. 'Niall! Edward!' He pointed his sword towards the women. 'Get them out of here! Take the foot soldiers and archers. Go back to the valley – make for the woods beyond the Fillan. We'll hold them off as long as we can.'

'Like hell——' Edward began.

'*Do it!*' roared Robert, so fiercely his brother flinched.

Edward's jaw pulsed, but he wheeled his horse around and, with Niall's help, drove the foot soldiers into a protective wedge around the women, children and servants, forcing them back the way they had come.

Robert had one last glimpse of Marjorie – looking over her shoulder at him, stricken with terror – before he snapped down his visor. Kicking viciously with his heels, he spurred Ghost towards the advancing mass of horsemen. '*On them!*' he roared, his voice echoing around the encasement of his helm.

His men rode with him, their horses ripping through the grass, kicking up black clots of mud. The rain was falling harder, gauzing the air. Ahead, the enemy were coming swiftly to meet them. Finally it was upon him: the reckoning Robert had known was coming for the murder of John Comyn. These men rushing towards him, swords and axes raised, were his judges and executioners, come to avenge the blood of their kinsman. But he would not falter, nor give them ground. The lives of all those he loved were at stake. With the image of his daughter's face imprinted on his mind, Robert compelled Ghost, with brutal rakes of his spurs, into the front lines of the enemy.

The two forces came together in a vicious clash that resounded across the plain. Men and horses smashed into one another, spears splintering on shields, bones breaking under impact. Some men were hurled from saddles and sent tumbling to the marshy ground, where the mud was as slick as pitch. More managed to right themselves, shaking off the initial concussion, and set about those they found themselves among, hacking and battering. The rain pelted them all, blinding in its intensity, as if the heavens wanted to join in the battle.

Robert swept into the heart of the enemy line, thrusting his blade into the throat of a man who slashed out at him, eyes wide and white through the slit of his helm. The man convulsed and blood spewed over Robert's blade as he wrenched it free. He felt a concussive crack on the side of his helm, which made his head ring. He roared as he struck at the men and horses crushed in front of him, ignoring the brutal pain in his shoulder as his shield was knocked and battered. His world narrowed into the shifting wall of flesh in front of him, which needed to be struck in every vulnerable place to bring it down.

The two cavalry forces were almost evenly matched, but all that would end when the foot soldiers, charging across the plain, reached them. Robert's only hope in these few desperate minutes was that he and his men could kill or wound as many cavalry as possible so as to slow pursuit. That should give the women long enough to escape into the forest beyond St Fillan's. His breath bursting hot inside his helm, he slammed his shield into the face of a man whose surcoat was adorned with the arms of Argyll. As the knight recoiled, Robert drove his sword into his ribs.

John of Atholl was fighting fiercely alongside his son. James Douglas was close by, his pale cheeks splattered with blood. He fought like a fury, teeth bared, his blade moving in whip-quick arcs. Christopher Seton had been carried deep into the mêlée, along with a dozen of Atholl's knights. They were clashing with men wearing the arms of the Black Comyn. Gilbert de la Hay went at one unfortunate Argyllsman, whose helm had fallen off. As Gilbert swung a mighty blow towards his neck the man ducked, but not low enough. The blade bit into his forehead and went on through, taking the man's scalp clean off, padded coif and all. Looking obscenely like an egg with the top sliced off, he sank from his saddle, a stunned look on his face. His horse bucked, its back hoof catching the face of one of the fallen man's comrades. He reeled, retching blood and teeth. Other horses were going down, struck by swords and axes, squealing as they collapsed, pulling men down with them.

As another Argyll knight fell, gored by his blade, Robert twisted in his saddle. The women had disappeared from the plain, herded into the valley by his brothers and the infantry. The enemy foot soldiers were almost upon them, their fell voices ragged on the air. Robert went to yell the retreat, but his cry was cut off abruptly as he was jerked to one side. An Argyllsman had grabbed hold of his cloak and now wrenched him towards the point of his sword. Robert pulled back. The brooch that pinned his cloak snapped apart and the garment came away in his enemy's fist. The man snarled and clutched for Robert's reins instead. Crushed in between two horses, Robert couldn't free himself. James Douglas, seeing the danger, lunged in at the Argyllsman's blindside, hacking his sword deep into the man's thigh before jerking it free, with an arc of blood.

As the man tumbled from the saddle, Robert hauled Ghost around. '*Back! Back!*'

Alexander gasped, struggling to draw breath back into his lungs. He was doubled up on the damp ground, curled around the knot in his stomach, where Comyn's man had slammed a fist, cutting off his warning shout. It was from this perspective that he had seen the cavalry ride out from the trees, the plunging hooves shaking the earth beneath him. He had choked in the first few merciful breaths as the foot soldiers charged in their wake. The world, which he hadn't expected to see again, came back into focus as his lungs were filled. The army had gone, out over the fields, the only ones left his two captors. One was at the tree line watching the battle unfold, the other was looming over him, the fallen rope in the man's hands, ready to tie him up again.

Taking one last lungful of blessed air, Alexander grabbed hold of the rope and pulled his captor sharply towards him, at the same time thrusting his head up. His forehead connected with the bridge of his captor's nose. The man reared upright in pain, clutching his face. There was a distant, resounding clash as the two forces met on the field. Faint screams rose above the roars of the foot soldiers, still surging across the grass. Tearing the rope from his captor's hand, Alexander pushed himself to his feet, his bruised and beaten body screaming. Over the sounds of fighting, the other guard didn't hear the snap of undergrowth as Alexander threw himself on his comrade, twisting the rope apart in his hands and bringing it down over his head to yank it tight against his neck. The man's gurgled shout was cut short as his windpipe was crushed, but now the other guard was alerted. Seeing his comrade bucking and choking as Alexander strained on the rope, he drew his sword and ran towards them.

Alexander charged. Using the guard as a shield, he propelled him on to the outstretched point of the other man's sword, forcing the guard down the length of the blade. The second guard toppled back with the momentum. The two men went down together, one on top of the other like lovers. Alexander lunged for the skewered guard's sword, hauling it from his scabbard. He swooped on the man who had gone down first, ready to punch it into his vitals. He had no need. The guard had fallen back on to a tree root, splintered into a sharp shard by a charging horse. The root had gone clean through his skull and burst up through one of his eyes.

Breathing hard, Alexander staggered to where the guards' horses were tethered. Keeping the sword in his fist, he freed one with a trembling hand. His captors had left him with only his undershirt and hose, torn and bloodstained. Digging his bare foot into the saddle, he mounted. Wrenching the beast around, he kicked at its sides with his heels. Once out of the woods, the rain soaked him to the skin, but its chill revived him and his mind sharpened as he urged the horse into a furious gallop. Across the great meadow, churned by hooves and pounding feet, the two forces of cavalry had merged, the different colours of coats of arms bleeding into one another. Racing past the first lines of foot soldiers, Alexander caught a glimpse of yellow, bright among the black of Comyn's men. He recognised John of Atholl's arms. Robert wouldn't be far from his brother-in-law. The two were inseparable in battle. Alexander jerked on the reins, steering his horse towards those colours.

With a desperate burst of speed, he overtook the rest of the foot soldiers, the front lines of which had almost reached the skirmish. His horse crashed into several running men on the way past, knocking them flying. He entered the battle just behind Atholl's men, barrelling through Comyn's knights, hacking at their backs with his stolen sword. They didn't expect attack to come from behind and those he struck toppled easily. Alexander felt a crushing pain in his leg as his horse was forced up against another. A stray sword grazed his arm, opening flesh to the bone, but the madness of battle was raging through him, taking him dancing along the brink of life itself, and he barely felt it.

The wet air stank of mud and opened bowels. Alexander was close enough to see the faces of some of Atholl's knights. He felt a jolt go through him, catching sight of a young man among them, snarling over the rim of his shield. Strands of fair hair had come free from his mail coif and were stuck to his face.

'*Christopher!*'

Alexander's hoarse shout was swallowed instantly by the din of the mêlée, the crack of blades on shields harsh over the clamour of the foot soldiers, who had now entered the battle, axes and spears raised for a first strike at the enemy. They were too late. Robert and his men were breaking away, galloping back the way they had come, leaving scores of dead and dying behind them. Not all the king's men followed, some caught too deep in the battle to leave it so easily. Christopher was among them with a small band of Atholl's knights, hewing desperately at Comyn's men who were pressing in, threatening to overwhelm them. Alexander roared in desperation, jabbing his blood-slick sword into every inch of flesh he could see, trying to reach his cousin. For a moment, the tide of fighting swept them close together. Over the shield, Christopher's eyes widened in recognition. Alexander went to shout to him, then the metal rim of a shield cracked into the side of his head. The world vanished.

Alexander came to, coughing mud from his mouth and nose. He pushed himself up on to his hands and knees, vomiting up a vile stream of brown liquid. His eyes stung. Wiping them with the soaked sleeve of his shirt, he blinked his vision back to clarity. The world around him had changed. For a moment, he thought he had died and woken in another place. Hell, surely, for all the moans and whimpering. The rain had ceased and the plain was cast once more in sunlight. It shone garishly on the red mess of severed limbs and opened corpses that clogged the marshy ground. Wounded horses twisted among the dead and the dying. The air reeked. The marsh birds had vanished and crows had taken their place, winging their way from the foothills, drawn by the stench of carrion. Alexander sank back on his heels, staring at the plain. Where had the battle gone? The men? The thought brought his cousin's face to mind.

Swaying with pain and exhaustion, Alexander managed to rise from the mud. His whole body was shaking uncontrollably. He stared around him, trying to keep his balance, until his gaze fixed on a patch of yellow and black stripes, vivid between the broken blades of grass. He staggered over and crouched beside the knight, one of Atholl's.

'Christopher Seton.' Alexander's voice came out as a croak. 'He was fighting with you. Did he escape?'

The man's eyes were open. He stared at Alexander with dazed incomprehension. Looking down the length of him, Alexander saw the knight had a wide gash in his side. The rings of his mail coat had been torn apart and the straw that padded his gambeson had burst up out of the gash. Like a scarecrow, thought Alexander numbly. The raw pink and yellow of intestines glistened beneath. The man continued to stare at him, licking his lips. Hearing the long note of a horn, Alexander jerked round. His eyes focused slowly on the great mass of men riding towards him. For a moment, he thought Comyn and MacDougall had returned, but these men weren't dressed in black. He fixed on a banner, raised at the vanguard. The device was unmistakable – three golden lions on scarlet.

Pushing himself to his feet, Alexander forced one foot in front of the other, finally managing to break into a run. He heard distant shouts and the horn's call ring out again. He was still running as hoofbeats came pounding up behind him.

PART 2

1306 AD

It is your country which you fight for, and for which you should, when required, voluntarily suffer death: for that itself is victory, and the cure of the soul.

The History of the Kings of Britain, *Geoffrey of Monmouth*

Finlaggan Castle (Islay), Scotland, 1306 AD

The procession made its way across the causeway that spanned the reed-fringed waters of Finlaggan's northern shore; the stone umbilical cord linking the two islands of Eilean Mor and Eilean na Comhairle. Ahead, at the end of the causeway, the council hall dominated the smaller man-made isle. Torches burned at the entranceway, their reflections jewelling the water. Cattle lowed in the velvet dark of the surrounding hills. Beyond, in the distance, the scarred flanks of the Paps of Jura were stark against the pearlescent evening sky.

As the line of men filed in through the hall's arched doorway, Thomas Bruce looked over his shoulder, past the cluster of buildings on Eilean Mor, where smoke plumed from the chimney of the great hall. For a moment, he thought he saw the shadow of a boat, lying low in the water, where another causeway joined the larger island to the shore beyond, but the reflections of the hills made it impossible to be certain.

Cormac had to bring himself up short to avoid knocking into him. 'They're not coming, brother.'

Thomas met his gaze. 'Perhaps.'

His foster-brother looked steadily back, his red hair seeming to flame in the torchlight. Like the ten Irishmen who had accompanied him from Antrim, Cormac wore it in the traditional cúlán, the front matted thick and hanging in his eyes, the back shorn short. 'For what it's worth, I think that a good thing.'

'Come, Thomas,' called Alexander Bruce from the hall's entrance, where his hooded brown robe made him one with the shadows. 'Let us not keep our host waiting.'

Turning, Thomas hefted his bag higher on his shoulder, feeling the weight of the chest straining the leather. He would have thought the promise inside would have drawn the lords of Garmoran like wolves to blood.

As he entered, closely followed by Cormac, Thomas scanned the chamber. He had been on Islay for almost a month, having sailed from Ireland where Lord Donough had been raising the men of Antrim for Robert's war, but this was the first time he had set foot in the council hall on Eilean na Comhairle – the heart of the MacDonald lordship. Torches spread fans of light up the whitewashed walls. Above, beams criss-crossed into shadow where bats skimmed the air, disturbed by the murmuring voices as the men shuffled into rows of benches, all facing a dais at the far wall on which stood a solitary chair.

The man who had led them here climbed the steps of the dais and seated himself. Angus Og MacDonald, the Lord of Islay, was a broad-chested man in his early forties with nut-brown skin and a strong face framed by sandy hair, streaked grey at his temples. He scanned the chamber as the men settled into the benches, his sharp blue eyes watchful. They had come at his summons from across his lands in Kintyre and Islay, southern Jura, Oronsay and Colonsay. Seasoned chiefs who had fought the Norsemen at their last battle on western shores forty-three years ago were joined by strapping sons and eager grandsons, many of whom now aspired to knighthood rather than the wild, sea-governed existence of their plundering forefathers.

Directed by Angus's usher, Thomas sat at the front, placing the leather bag on the floor between his feet. He hadn't trusted anyone else with the burden since Robert passed it to him at Dumbarton Rock along with the Staff of Malachy, now returned to the monks at Bangor Abbey. Alexander moved in beside him, hands folded in his lap, the silver cross he wore around his neck glinting in the torchlight. Cormac and the men from Antrim, who had been ordered to escort the brothers to Islay by Lord Donough, were shown into the benches behind. Looking up at Angus seated on the dais, a banner on the wall behind displaying the MacDonald arms – a black galley with sails furled – Thomas thought the man looked more like a king than a lord. As the great-great-grandson of Somerled, he supposed in some way he was.

The ancient sea kingdom, made up of more than five hundred islands that curved along the western coast of Scotland at the mercy of the moods of the Northern Ocean, had been carved up on Somerled's death among his sons. The influence of the Norse kings, who plundered and settled along the chain of islands, had divided the allegiances of Somerled's descendants, plunging them into a feud that had echoed down the generations. Forty years ago, once the Norsemen had conceded control, the Western Isles had been drawn under the authority of Scotland's kings, but the lords of the three families who governed the fractured territory were fierce, proud men with long memories and they still commanded a king-like respect from the communities they governed. Thomas had seen that clearly these past few weeks on Islay.

'Welcome,' said Angus, his Gaelic rich and deep. His eyes swept the company, seeming to connect with every man in turn. 'I have summoned you here at the behest of my esteemed guests, Sir Thomas Bruce and Alexander, Dean of Glasgow. They have come under the authority of their brother, King Robert, who requests my aid in his war against King Edward.'

The hall filled with a rumble of surprise.

Thomas glanced behind him, taking in the frowns and shaking of heads. He had expected as much. The MacDonalds, like his father and other Scottish magnates, had been supporters of King Edward since the start of the war. The statement presented a dramatic volte face.

'My lord,' spoke up an old man, whose hands were planted on a stick as gnarled and bent as he was, 'while the war with England has ravaged the mainland we have remained untouched. Why risk King Edward's wrath after all these years?'

'We have a new king now, Gillepatrick,' answered Angus.

'A king who took the throne by force, my lord, against the will of many.'

There were murmurs of agreement at this.

Thomas wanted to speak, but held his tongue. Angus might have shown him great hospitality, but he had no authority here.

'Gillepatrick is right,' said a younger man. 'By his actions Bruce has made many powerful foes, not just in England. It is only three years since Richard de Burgh was ordered to attack the stronghold of Sir James Stewart on Bute. All our lands lie in easy reach of Ireland. Who is to say the galleys of Ulster will not be seen on our shores if we ally ourselves with King Edward's enemy?'

'Right now, the Earl of Ulster has his own troubles to attend to,'

Cormac said, rising. 'My Irish countrymen continue to press in on the borders of English settlements in the south and west. My father, Lord Donough of Glenarm, is preparing a fleet of ships that will bring the warriors of Antrim to King Robert's aid. So preoccupied is Ulster by the advance of my people, he doesn't even have the resources to stop my father. He will not come for you.' Cormac caught Thomas's warning look. 'With respect,' he added, nodding to Angus.

Angus raised his hand for silence. 'My father pledged himself to the Bruce cause before John Balliol was crowned – before the war began. I was at Turnberry when the oath was sworn to the Lord of Annandale. His grandson has now called upon me to uphold that oath. It would be an insult to my father's honour to refuse.'

'Honour? Is that what you call it?'

At the harsh voice that came from the back of the hall most of the men turned, craning their heads to see who had addressed the lord so insolently. Thomas saw a figure step from the gloom into a pool of torchlight. He was a tall man, wiry of build, with dark hair that fell to his shoulders. He wore a sky-blue cloak, pinned at the shoulder with a silver brooch. A few days of stubble darkened his angular jaw, partially concealing a defect, or perhaps a scar, that twisted the corner of his upper lip. The man's gaze remained fixed on Angus.

'I call it ambition.'

Angus sat forward, hands curled around the arms of the chair. 'Lachlan. I was expecting you days ago.'

At the name, Thomas knew this was Lachlan MacRuarie, West Highland captain of the galloglass, bastard son of the Lord of Garmoran and another of Somerled's descendants. He nudged the leather bag at his feet with his boot, his anticipation sparked.

'You would support Bruce not because of your father's pledge, but because you believe it may bring you what you desire most. Do not pretend otherwise, cousin.' Lachlan's twisted lip curled. 'You must know the MacDougalls have been raising an army against Bruce, planning to strike at him for the killing of John Comyn. You know, too, if you aid Bruce and he is triumphant, he may finally grant you their island.'

Angus rose. 'Lismore is ours by my brother's marriage to that MacDougall bitch. The lords of Argyll's refusal to honour her dowry doesn't make it their island. It makes it stolen territory: territory my brother lost his life for, as well you know, *cousin*, since you aided the whoresons.' Angus gestured to two of his men, standing near the back. 'Seize him.'

As they made towards him, Lachlan shouted a command. Through the doors of the hall burst a band of men. Most were clad in patterned woollen tunics, their bare arms sun-browned and corded with muscle. All had swords or daggers in their hands. Two of them held a man between them, a blade pushed up against his throat.

Thomas recognised the captive as Angus's steward. Reaching down, he grasped the leather bag as the hall erupted with shouts of indignation and the scrape of swords. Behind him, Cormac and the men of Antrim were on their feet, weapons drawn.

'Hold!' Angus shouted at his men. He held up his hands to Lachlan; a gesture of peace. 'Do not do this.'

Lachlan's mocking smile had vanished. His green eyes were glacial. 'Did you think I would be fool enough to come alone into the hall of the man who imprisoned me and my brother on a godforsaken rock for five damn years?'

'Five years? As Christ is my witness you didn't serve one — the MacDougalls saw to that.'

'Ruarie wasn't so fortunate though, was he? Your guards made him pay for my escape.'

A man emerged from the group to stand beside Lachlan. He was shorter and broader of body, his bald head laced with ugly scars. One of his eyes was missing. There was a dark, empty hole in its place.

'I negotiated your brother's release,' said Angus, hand on the hilt of the dirk that hung from his belt. 'Even though King Edward wanted him detained for life for the burning and looting of one of his royal galleys.'

Ruarie stared back, his one eye unblinking. He looked like a mastiff, poised to attack. There was an axe gripped in his fists.

'How honourable of you,' said Lachlan coldly.

'You would charge *my* lord with dishonour?' growled one of Angus's men. 'When the MacDougalls laid waste to our islands and slaughtered our people you followed, picking through the spoils. Like crows after carrion you and your kind are, MacRuarie. There's no honour among you — you and your clan of bastards!'

The men with Lachlan bristled. The steward cried out as the dagger bit into his neck. Angus strode down the steps of the dais, wrenching his dirk free.

It was Alexander who stopped them.

Thomas started as his brother swept out into the aisle, putting himself between Angus and Lachlan.

'Peace!' Alexander raised his hands, palms upturned to each of them, like Moses parting the Red Sea.

Angus halted at the command. Lachlan's eyes narrowed, but he made no further move.

Alexander looked from one man to the other. 'Whatever disputes lie between you they are neither my nor my brother's concern. We are here for one purpose only – to deliver a summons from your king, calling you to arms against a common enemy of Scotland.'

Thomas stared at his brother in dumb surprise at this strident declaration. Since leaving Scotland, shortly before the coronation, Alexander had been deeply troubled by their brother's part in the death of John Comyn. In Antrim, while Thomas and Lord Donough gathered the men for war, he had done little except to return the staff to the monks at Bangor and pray for Robert's soul.

'Your support,' finished Alexander, his eyes on Lachlan, 'will be rewarded.' He nodded curtly to Thomas. 'Brother.'

Suppressing his astonishment, Thomas gathered himself. The leather bag held tight in his fist, he headed down the aisle, past Alexander. Lachlan's men were still poised for a fight, as were Angus's, but all eyes were now on Thomas. He stopped a few paces from Lachlan, taking in the blades pointing towards him. He remembered someone, Neil Campbell most likely, saying the MacRuaries were as unpredictable and capricious as the seas they ruled. Crouching, he set the bag on the rush-strewn floor and pushed the material down in folds to reveal a wooden chest. Unsnapping the catch and opening the lid, he picked it up and held it out.

Lachlan continued to hold Thomas's gaze for a moment, before his eyes flicked down to the open coffer. Inside, hundreds of silver coins glinted in the burnished light of the torches.

Ruarie leaned forward, his one eye squinting into the coffer. 'I've seen more silver in the fists of one of my bairns.' His voice was husky.

'This is but a token,' Thomas assured them, 'to show our good faith. The king will give you more, much more, if you agree to enlist your fighting men and ships to his cause. Isn't this why you came to this hall? Because you were told of the reward?'

For a while, Lachlan said nothing. Then, reaching forward, he closed the lid. 'I am not sure King Robert will be in any position to make good on such a promise. A force of English knights aided by men from Galloway defeated your brother near Perth, over a month ago.'

'Dear God.'

Ignoring Alexander's murmur, Thomas took a step forward. 'You lie.' As he said this, he searched Lachlan's green eyes, but could see no trace of falsehood. He turned to look at Angus MacDonald for any sign he knew about this, but the lord appeared genuinely surprised. He and Alexander had been far from their brother's camp for months now, in Antrim and Islay, with no access to word from the mainland. Such a thing was conceivable. 'How do you know this?' he demanded, turning back to Lachlan. 'Was he captured?'

'The last I heard, he was on the run. But with the MacDougalls, the Comyns and the English after him, I doubt he will be free for long.'

Images of Robert, Niall and Edward, his sisters and his friends crowded in Thomas's mind. He pushed them away, knowing he must not falter here, not if there was still a chance. 'Then you do not know my brother. For I tell you now, whatever defeat he has suffered he will come back from it. He is cut from the same cloth as our grandfather, who fought the infidel in Palestine and was named heir to the kingdom when he was barely out of boyhood.' His voice strengthened. 'You can walk away now without these coins and be seen for ever by your king as cowards and freebooters. Or,' he finished, turning to include Angus MacDonald's men in his address, 'you can throw your strength behind him and help him take back our kingdom.'

I2

Loch Lomond, Scotland, 1306 AD

'There's no way across.'

Robert looked round, hearing the exhaustion in Gilbert's voice. The tower of a man was slumped on the bank, unable to hold himself upright any longer. His usually hale face was drawn and his blond hair was clotted with blood. Around him, other men were collapsing on the sandy ground, or leaning on comrades for support, breaths ragged, faces oily with sweat. The damp dawn air was clouded with flies that swarmed about bloodstained clothes and oozing wounds.

All eyes were fixed on the loch that stretched away before them. The tree-bristling backs of islands broke the glass-smooth surface in places, but for all the tantalising glimpses of land the vast expanse of water remained indomitable. The far shore was veiled in mist curling down from the sides of the mountains. To the north, where the loch narrowed over the course of many miles, the peaks were giants. Distant waterfalls, white as milk, gushed silently through rifts in their stone faces.

'It's got to be three miles across here,' said Neil Campbell, thrusting a hand through his sweat-slick hair.

'Nearer four,' answered Robert. He wanted to shout his frustration to the sky.

From the deep valleys of the surrounding mountains they had struck blindly for the banks of Loch Lomond, hoping to tackle it from the south where it tapered into the mouth of the River Leven. They had emerged at least ten miles too far north. Robert wanted to sink down with the rest of them, close his eyes and let weariness overwhelm him, but to falter now was to risk ruin. The enemy, who had trailed them relentlessly from the battleground, would not be far behind. Now they had left the sanctuary of the mountains, stumbling on foot through the dense woods that fringed the loch, they were easy prey for their mounted pursuers, who had spread far into the region until every wooded hollow and crag-shadowed valley was filled with possible death.

Watching some of his men cupping water from the shallows to revive themselves, Robert recalled a hunt with his grandfather years ago in Lochmaben. He remembered riding into a clearing and coming unexpectedly across the wolf they had been trailing. The wretched animal had been hunched over a puddle, lapping desperately at the stagnant water. It had been so exhausted it hadn't heard them approach.

'We have to keep going.' Robert raised his voice so the men clustered on the shore would hear him. 'We'll head south from here. Make our way along the—'

'My lord!' James Douglas had waded into the shallows, past the men splashing water on their wounds. He was staring intently up the banks. 'There's a boat!'

Pushing past Gilbert de la Hay and Neil Campbell, Robert strode into the water. It gushed through the holes worn in the leather of his boots, stinging the blisters that had bubbled up on his feet. Following James's finger, he looked north along the tree-fringed banks. Sure enough, he glimpsed the outline of a small vessel. Some sort of fishing craft, it appeared half submerged in mud. 'It will take hours to ferry everyone,' said Robert, calculating quickly and not liking the conclusion. 'A day at least. MacDougall's men could be on us before that. Those left on shore would be trapped.'

'Not if the stronger swimmers among us go across with the boat, using it to aid them when they tire,' ventured James.

'He's right,' said Edward, joining them in the shallows. His jaw was bearded with several weeks' growth and his lean face was dark with sun. Blood had dried in a brown crust along a deep gash on his neck. His surcoat had soaked up most of the flow from the wound. The smell coming off the stained garment was sour. 'If it takes a day we'll still be quicker than if we skirt the loch and attempt the river.'

'Take David and his men with you,' Robert told James, after a pause. 'Be quick.'

James hastened back up the bank, motioning to David of Atholl, who was with a band of knights from his father's earldom. The young man nodded at the instruction, but Robert saw him throw a glance in his direction. David's dirt-streaked face was tight. He had barely said two words to him since the battle. Robert knew he resented the fact he had been ordered from his father's side, but he had no time to appease recalcitrant youths. They had all had to make sacrifices.

'Here,' said Edward, passing Robert his skin.

Pressing it to his lips, Robert upended the container. The water, taken from a mountain spring, had a coppery taste. When he'd finished, Edward took the skin, but held his gaze. Robert tensed, thinking his brother was going to challenge him again over his decision to split their forces, but Edward simply put a hand on his shoulder. After a moment, Robert broke from his brother's grasp and made his way back to the bank. Emotion could overwhelm him if he let it.

Ahead, someone was shouting. A man fought his way through the crowd to reach the king. Seeing it was one of the men he'd set on lookout, Robert felt apprehension fire life through his leaden limbs. 'What is it, Alan?'

'Horsemen,' panted Alan. 'In the next valley.'

'Show me.'

As the word went round, the men began drawing weapons, faces tight with unease. Alan led Robert through the trees, Edward, Gilbert, Neil and Nes following closely.

'How many?' asked Robert, as he climbed the steep, bracken-covered bank they had descended earlier, using tree roots and branches to haul himself up. Robert, along with the rest of his men, had removed his mail the quicker to move by, but it was a tough ascent nonetheless and after three days on the run his legs and lungs screamed with the effort. Sweat broke out on his forehead and dripped from his nose.

'Fifty at my reckoning,' panted Alan.

At the top of the ridge another scout was waiting, eyes fixed on the land before him, which fell into pleated valleys bristling with birch, ash and towering pines, dark against the pallid dawn. As the man pointed north, Robert picked out a slow-moving line of mounted men, maybe a mile or two distant. They were coming their way.

'MacDougall's men?' questioned Neil Campbell, moving up beside them, breathing hard.

'Too far to tell, sir,' said Alan.

Robert cursed bitterly. All he needed was a few goddamned hours more.

'We could hide?' said Gilbert, tossing his blood-streaked hair out of his eyes. 'Wait for them to pass?'

'The moment we take that boat out we'll break our cover. They would be on us before we could get even half our men across.' Robert scanned the vale south of the horsemen. 'There.' He fixed on a place where the folds of the hills narrowed the valley into a bottleneck. 'If we're quick we could lie in wait for them.'

Edward's eyes narrowed keenly. 'Agreed.'

Sending the order for one hundred of his men to join him, leaving the others to begin ferrying the first men across once James and David had transported the boat, Robert led the company into the cleft of the valley.

Occasionally pausing to check their bearings, they moved swiftly, lightly, like hunters on a trail. The lack of mail and other armour rendered their progress virtually silent, only the snap of twigs and swish of surcoats against the undergrowth betraying their passing, but what was now an advantage would make them vulnerable in the fight. Robert knew they would have to attack fast and hard, overwhelming the enemy with surprise and superior numbers. He kept a tight grip on the hilt of his broadsword, the gold pommel glinting dully in the dreary light seeping through the trees. Still sheathed in its jewelled scabbard, the magnificent blade seemed incongruous strapped against his blood- and sweat-soiled surcoat, which was ripped in places and hung loose over his gambeson and hose. He looked like an outlaw who had stolen the sword of a king.

As they reached the place seen from the ridge, Robert heard the unmistakable ring of bridles. The horsemen were drawing near. Sending Alan shinning up through the splayed branches of an oak to check on their approach, Robert gestured for his men to settle. They hunkered down on the slope above the narrow valley, hiding in the tangle of undergrowth. The rustling of branches faded, broken only by soft whispers of breath that were soon drowned by birdsong.

Robert, crouched by the silvery trunk of a birch, glanced around him at his men, concealed among the green fronds of bracken. Only weeks ago there were almost a thousand in his company. The attack at Methven Wood and the ambush orchestrated by the Lord of Argyll and the Black Comyn had reduced them to less than four hundred, and a quarter of those were now gone from his side. Robert's brow furrowed, the fracturing of their company all too fresh in his mind.

Leading his men from the plain, leaving behind scores of dead and wounded, Robert had caught up with the women in the woods beyond St Fillan's shrine. Here, with the horns of the enemy sounding a strident pursuit, he had made the excruciating decision to split the company. Ordering his brother, Niall, and John of Atholl to lead a large group of men, he bade them take the horses and bear the women north into the mountains to the stronghold of Kildrummy, the great fortress of the earls of Mar, held in trust for his nephew, Donald. The farewells had been brief and bitter.

Christian was beside herself, screaming for Christopher, missing in the chaos of the battle. The Countess of Atholl had grasped David's face, kissing his cheeks until John pulled her away, his eyes on his son, no words to say. Marjorie clung to Robert, begging him to stay with her. Of all of them, it was Elizabeth who surprised him most. Though visibly shaken, his wife remained calm, promising him she would take care of the women. Lady Isabel, who had seen her husband's banner on the field, also managed to keep control of her emotions, taking the wailing Donald from his mother's grief-tight grip and leaving Christian in the care of her sisters, Mary and Matilda. Thrusting his weeping daughter into Elizabeth's arms, Robert had led his men at a run through the woods, heading south towards the rising hills. They had dumped helms, greaves, shields and mail coifs as they went, leaving a trail of detritus for the enemy to follow.

Robert looked up as Alan whistled from the heights of the oak. In the valley, the ring of bridles was now accompanied by thudding hooves. Robert gripped his sword. His heart began to pound, sending blood racing through his veins. His eyes fixed on the breaks in the trees through which he saw the first riders appear. He waited until the company was stretched into a long line by the narrow valley, then propelled himself to his feet. Roaring, Robert plunged down the slope, followed by his men. They hurtled through the undergrowth to burst out on the fifty horsemen.

Robert went straight for the man at the head of the company, the momentum of his charge allowing him to throw himself bodily at his enemy. He yelled as he leapt, bringing his sword crashing down towards the startled man's side. The man managed to bring his own sword round in time to deflect the blow, but he was rocked back with the impact. Panicked horses squealed and reared. Some of the animals attempted to bolt, but Edward and Gilbert were blocking the bottle-neck with a cluster of men, whose ranks bristled with swords, hammers and axes. The vale echoed with the clash of steel, as the enemy wrenched their own weapons free to engage.

Robert ducked as the man he had targeted thrust his sword at his face. Swinging upright, gripping his broadsword two-handed, he slammed the blade towards the man's exposed thigh in a blow that could have taken his leg off had it struck. His opponent reacted quickly, bringing his shield in to block. As the blade crashed into the wood, Robert saw flashes of red – a saltire and four red roses were painted on its scarred white surface. As the man shoved his sword away with the shield, Robert caught sight of a handsome face and a pair of blazing blue eyes. He pulled his sword wide, recognition flooding him like ice water, shocking him out of the heat of the battle.

'*Halt!*' he roared, backing away and yelling the order down his line of men. '*Halt, damn you! Sheath your weapons!*'

It took a few moments for the order to cascade through the ranks and the clash of weapons continued briefly, but most men were drop-ping back, many now seeing what Robert himself had realised. These were not enemies.

Robert turned back to the man he had attacked, who was staring at him in astonishment.

After a moment, Malcolm of Lennox swung down from his saddle. Throwing his shield and sword to the ground, he dropped to one knee. 'My lord king.'

Robert grasped Malcolm's outstretched hands, feeling relief flood him. God hadn't abandoned him: He had sent him a friend in the wilderness.

'Blood and thunder, Robert,' breathed Malcolm. 'You almost killed me!'

'Forgive me.' Robert raised the earl to his feet.

As the knights calmed their horses and dismounted, men began embracing comrades they had never expected to see again, laughing in amazement, eyes bright with emotion.

Edward had made his way to the head of the company, along with Gilbert, Neil and David. All were grinning broadly.

'You're the last person I thought we'd meet out here, Sir Malcolm,' said Edward, gripping the earl's hand.

'When these are my lands?' remarked Malcolm, gesturing to the valley, still astonished.

In his exhaustion, Robert realised he hadn't even thought of Lennox – the earl of this region. 'We're being pursued. We thought you were part of their company.'

Malcolm's levity faded. 'I had reports of bands of men moving through my lands. My men and I have been hunting for them. Who are they?'

'Men of John MacDougall of Argyll and the Earl of Buchan.' Robert told him briefly of the battle near St Fillan's shrine, but despite Malcolm's deepening frown, he wanted his own questions answered first. 'How did you make it alive from Methven Wood?'

Malcolm let out a heavy breath. 'I fought my way out with the aid of my men. I lost . . .' He shook his head. 'I lost many.' He met Robert's eyes. 'It was chaos, my lord. I didn't know which direction you had gone. The only thing I could do was make for my lands. I've been here ever since.' He nodded in the direction of the loch. 'My castle on Inchmurrin offers good protection. I've been sending out scouts, trying to get word of what happened to everyone. I heard you made for Aberdeen.'

'We weren't safe there.' Robert's mind filled with an image of James Stewart going down, surrounded by a seething press of men. Steeling himself, he asked the question. 'The steward? Do you know if he lives?'

'I saw him ride from the field – that I can say.'

'Truly?' Joy swept through Robert at these tidings. He felt an acute need to see the high steward, all his animosity towards the man now gone. 'What about the others?'

Malcolm's face remained grave. 'I heard your nephew, Thomas Randolph, was captured, as was Simon Fraser. I cannot speak as to Thomas's fate, but I know Fraser was hanged.'

A few of the men exclaimed at this, but Robert nodded grimly. Simon Fraser, along with William Wallace, had been a thorn in the English side for a long time and was one of the few nobles who had consistently refused to surrender to Edward. His life had been claimed forfeit for years. The news about his nephew, although unwelcome, was also not unexpected. Robert remembered passing Thomas fleeing on foot through the woods – the fear in his face.

'I'm afraid there is more,' Malcolm warned. 'Robert Wishart and William Lamberton have been taken.'

Robert closed his eyes, the last joy at meeting his friend and ally dissipating. How many men's lives now hung in the balance for his star-crossed cause?

'Where is Sir John?' asked Malcolm, taking in the men around Robert.

Robert shook off the weight of Lennox's black news. He couldn't dwell on the fates of those beyond his influence. Not now. He had to worry about those still with him. 'We parted company three days ago. Elizabeth and my daughter, all the women, were with us. We were attempting to reach Islay, hoping to find shelter with the MacDonalds. John has taken the women to Kildrummy. They should be safe there for the time being. We went south to draw MacDougalls' men from them.'

Malcolm shook his head as the gravity of Robert's words sank in. 'What do you plan to do?'

'I still intend to reach Islay. I'm surrounded here. I need to evade the nets my enemies are throwing up around me.'

'How can I help?'

'Do you have galleys?'

'One of twelve oars two miles up-water and another moored at Inchmurrin. They are yours.'

Edward and Gilbert exchanged gratified looks at the good fortune.

Robert gripped Malcolm's shoulder. 'Thank you.' He gestured to the woods. 'We should go. I do not know how far behind MacDougalls' men may be.'

As he turned to go, Malcolm caught his arm. 'There is one last thing, Robert.' He paused, seeming hesitant to speak.

'Tell me.'

'Word has come from France. Pope Clement has excommunicated you for the murder of John Comyn.'

13

Kildrummy Castle, Scotland, 1306 AD

Niall Bruce sat up, throwing back the blankets. It was early September, but the night was unseasonably warm. He was exhausted yet sleep had eluded him again, his mind refusing to lie still like his body. Leaning back against the curtains that draped the head of the bed, he stared at the sheets, yellowed with his sweat after a month of restless nights.

He felt like an intruder in this grand chamber, which once housed his sister, Christian, and her first husband, Gartnait, the former Earl of Mar. It reminded him of when he was young, roused by dark dreams that sent him creeping into his parents' bedchamber. His mother would awaken quickly, parting the covers to let him slip into the warmth beside her, but he would never stay long, afraid to be caught there by his father, who would not be so forgiving of his fears. On arriving at Kildrummy, Niall assumed Christian would take up residence here, but his sister, in torment over Christopher's disappearance, had taken refuge with her sisters. They had all left with John of Atholl, over a fortnight ago, leaving him alone; master of the great north-eastern castle.

Niall rubbed at his face, grinding his palms into his bloodshot eyes in an effort to revive himself. If he was awake, he might as well do the rounds. Forcing himself to his feet, he crossed the room, avoiding the hole where a rope dangled into darkness, floor after floor, to a well from which water could be drawn up to each level. As he took his gambeson from a clothes perch and shrugged it on over his shirt a fine white dust misted the air. The stuff was everywhere – caught in hair and clothing, layering furniture and gritting up food.

After pushing his feet into his boots, Niall took up the leather bag and slung it over his shoulder. Robert, on thrusting it at him in the woods, had made him vow not to let it leave his sight. Niall understood little of the broken box inside, except that his brother had risked his life to seize it and hoped to use it somehow against King Edward. It seemed a trifling thing to base any hope on at all. But, still, he had kept his word. Snapping up the latch, he opened the door and moved into a narrow passage, where arrow slits let in shafts of coppery light. As he made his way up a steep spiral of steps, the smoke-tinged night air blew down at him, cooling the sweat on his face.

When he emerged on the battlements in the shadow of the Snow Tower, those on watch greeted him with nods. In the torchlight their beards were grey with more of the dust, created by the smashing of the engines' stones against the smooth ashlar of the curtain walls. A short distance along the battlements part of the wall was gone and rubble littered the walkway. A wooden screen had been hastily erected in its place, but the enemy kept battering it down into the courtyard with shot from their engines, cheering when they succeeded as if it were a game. Two days ago it had taken one of the archers with it, sending him screaming to the flagstones.

'All quiet?'

'Yes, sir,' answered Roland, one of Kildrummy's garrison. He ducked from his spot, allowing Niall to take his place.

A breeze whisked up the mortar dust, stinging Niall's eyes. Earlier that day, the castle's constable had likened the brutal pounding of the walls to grain being milled to powder. The magnificent castle, which backed on to a ravine and was shaped like a shield with four corner towers and a twin-towered gatehouse, was redoubtable, but no fortress was impregnable. The fractures that now scarred its flanks were testament to that.

Through the thin aperture of the arrow slit, Niall stared out over the encampment that ringed the castle in a crescent of tents, dug-out latrines, horses, mules and wagons. The flames of campfires highlighted the garish colours of the banners that thrust up out of the crowded site, the largest of which was a scarlet standard, emblazoned with three golden lions. At three points, trebuchets had been erected on platforms over the castle's ditch, each protected by screens. The dread machines loomed against the fire-bruised sky; skeletal beasts with ropes for sinews to bind their limbs. Their massive heads were bowed and still, but tomorrow, some time after matins, they would begin to rise, throw back their long necks and, from the jaws of those great baskets, spit their loads at Kildrummy's walls.

Niall pressed his cheek to the stone, squinting to the front of the castle where the greatest concentration of men was camped. Four days ago, they had bridged the ditch with a sow. The long platform, mounted on wheels and covered with a timber roof to protect them from archers, led right up to the gatehouse. Yesterday morning he and the rest of the garrison had watched in silence as a felled pine was hauled by oxen from the surrounding woods. Hacked of branches and looped with chains it had since become a ram. He imagined it thumping like a giant fist into the doors of the gatehouse. Kildrummy's constable had ordered oil brought from the stores, ready to be boiled up and tossed, molten, over the heads of the enemy, but unless they could set fire to the roof of the sow, Niall didn't see how they could halt an all-out attack on the gates. There were almost one hundred men in the castle with him, but he had never felt more alone.

Through much of the war with England, Niall had been in fosterage in Antrim, training for knighthood, as Robert and Edward before him. Even when he became swept up in the conflict, as the youngest brother he had always felt protected from the burdens of responsibility and pressures of strategy. Now, with an English army encircling Kildrummy, the war had landed on his doorstep and it was his task to keep it here, for the longer the enemy were occupied in this place the more chance it gave his family to get to safety. For the first time, Niall understood something of the enormity of the weight Robert must feel every day.

Focusing on the red standard at the head of the camp, planted next to a blue and white striped banner, he reminded himself that despite his own predicament Prince Edward's arrival last week was a good sign. That the prince had joined forces with Aymer de Valence and Henry Percy left the west clearer for Robert. Furthermore, since they were concentrating all their efforts here, the English must surely believe the king's family were still inside, which is exactly what he and John of Atholl had intended.

None of them knew how Valence had got word of their arrival at Kildrummy, but it was apparent their enemies were everywhere. It was as if the kingdom itself were turning against them; hills and valleys that once sheltered and fed them now full of danger and watching eyes. When the news reached them from some of Atholl's people fleeing north from Valence's advance, Niall and John made their decision. God willing, John would have seen the women safely to the north coast by now and they would be on a boat to Norway, where Isabel Bruce was queen. Niall just hoped he had done right by his brother; that Robert would not be angered by the fact he had sent his wife and daughter abroad.

Allowing Roland to return to his place at the arrow slit, Niall started off on his nightly route along the walls, stepping over piles of rubble, broken arrows and buckets of sand. He had climbed to the top of the second tower and was talking to the guards there, when he noticed firelight shimmering in the windows of the great hall. Niall turned from the men and crossed to the edge of the battlements, staring towards the building, which projected into the courtyard. The timber-beamed hall had been used as a grain store since the start of the siege, but even when in use there were no fireplaces. Besides, the pulsing glow was too bright for any hearth fire.

'Christ!' hissed one of the guards. 'That's all our food in there!' He made towards the bell positioned on the tower top.

Niall caught his arm. 'No! I don't want to alert the English. Keep to your post.'

Hastening to the archway in the battlements, he charged down the spiralled steps, the bag that contained the precious box bouncing against his back. His ankle turned on an uneven stair, pitching him forward. He threw himself sideways, slamming into the wall, only just managing to halt his fall. Righting himself he plunged on, pushing out on to the walkway, back the way he'd come. The fire seemed brighter, dancing in the windows. White smoke was curling from under the hall's doors. Other men around the compound had seen it now, their shouts rising. Guards rushed from the gatehouse carrying buckets of sand and water. Somewhere a bell began to clang, the sound terribly loud in the stillness. Niall cursed. If the English attacked while they were all occupied with a fire? The thought stopped him in his tracks.

He scanned the courtyard, his gaze moving over the men dashing towards the hall, briefly catching on the constable, who had emerged from the Warden's Tower and was directing others to bring more buckets. Niall fixed on a lone figure, moving towards the gatehouse, keeping close to the line of the wall. When the figure paused and looked towards the hall, Niall recognised him as the castle's black-smith, a bad-tempered bull of a man called Osbourne. The blacksmith continued, quickly now. Niall felt cold doubt turn to sickening certainty. As he cupped his hands around his mouth and yelled the man's name, Osbourne whipped round, his face tilting towards the battlements. He was too far for Niall to see his expression, but his intent was clear as he turned and ran for the gatehouse.

Niall began to sprint, yelling at the guards in the courtyard as he went, gesturing wildly towards the running man, but his cries were lost in the commotion of the fire and the mad clanging of the bells. The hall's doors had been flung open and smoke billowed thickly around the men, all tossing in sand and water in an attempt to quell the blaze. Leaping the pile of rubble by the broken section of wall, Niall fixed on the sentries by the Snow Tower.

'Roland!' he roared. '*Archers!*'

The guard was at the battlements, his attention caught by something else. Through an arrow slit, Niall glimpsed a host of men massing at the English siege lines, all cast in the copper light of the campfires. There were horsemen at the head, funnelling across the makeshift bridge of the sow. Racing on, he reached the sentries and grabbed one of them, an archer, by the scruff of his cloak.

'Shoot that man!' Niall forced the archer round to face the gate-house, where Osbourne was charging into the mouth of the passage between the twin towers. 'Shoot him now, or we all die!'

The archer swung his bow from his shoulder and snatched an arrow from the basket on his belt. Fixing it in place with one rapid move-ment, he drew back the string, aimed, and shot. The arrow flew straight and true into the darkness where Osbourne had disappeared. Niall held his breath, listening for a scream. Instead, he heard the drum of hooves and the unmistakable rattle and clank of Kildrummy's portcullis.

St Duthac's Shrine, Scotland, 1306 AD

Elizabeth sat in the window, staring out over the firth, beyond which mountains rose black against the blanched dawn. The wide water was dew-pond calm, filled with vertiginous reflections of the surround-ing crags. To the others, coming down out of the hills, the sight of the channel leading into the open sea beyond Tain had been a blessed relief. To her it whispered only death. She closed her eyes, fingering the ivory cross around her neck, her mind caught in the rushing dark of a different body of water, long since left, but not forgotten.

Mother Mary, give me strength.

Hearing a rustle of blankets and the slap of bare feet on stone, she looked round to see Christian disappearing behind the wicker screen that shielded a latrine from the chamber. A moment later came sounds of vomiting. Elizabeth's gaze drifted over the sleeping forms of the other women, curled up under blankets. They covered the floor of the draughty lodgings the priest had offered them, huddled together for warmth. Fionn was lying beside Marjorie, his shaggy head resting between his paws, eyes half open, glinting and watchful. The other dogs and all the horses were in the stables or out in the pastures, but the hound had refused to leave the girl's side since they had left St Fillan's. Close by, Donald shifted beside his wet nurse, whimpered, then silenced. His mother emerged from behind the screen, wiping her mouth with a trembling hand. Christian started, seeing Elizabeth sitting there in the gloom. She came to the window seat, stepping carefully over the bodies of Marjorie and Lady Isabel Comyn.

'The priest told me one of his chaplains is a skilled healer,' Elizabeth said quietly, shifting her legs to allow Christian to sit beside her on the stone seat. The frayed hem of her dress caught on a cobweb, snapping the strands. 'I think you should allow him to examine you if you keep getting sick.'

'I'm not sick, my lady.' Christian's eyes filled with pale dawn light as she looked out across the firth beyond the grounds of St Duthac's Chapel. 'I'm with child.'

Elizabeth felt her breath catch in her throat. Instinctively, before her customary reserve could stop her, she reached out and took Christian's hand. Her sister-in-law looked at her, surprised by the contact, then smiled sadly and squeezed her hand in return.

'You are certain?'

'I haven't bled since St Fillan's and it feels the same as it did with Donald.' Christian pressed her arm against her breasts, nodding to confirm it. She let her hand fall into her lap. 'Christopher would be so happy.'

'He *will* be,' Elizabeth assured her. 'And when we return he will be able to tell you so himself.'

Christian stared out of the window, her brow furrowing. 'John has been gone three days now.'

Elizabeth followed her gaze to where a stone cross loomed above a spit of sand on the shore of the estuary. It was one of four that marked the boundaries of the Girth of Tain, which cradled St Duthac's Chapel. The shrine was a holy sanctuary that could not be breached, but nonetheless their tension had risen since John of Atholl left with most of the men to seek out a worthy vessel and captain. The earl planned to rejoin Robert's company, but the women were to be sent to Norway. The others, though distraught at leaving their husbands, had mostly resigned themselves to their fate with its promise of safety for them and their children. But to Elizabeth it still seemed an intolerably drastic measure, even beyond her own implacable fear of the journey through endless miles of deep water.

She found it unreal that less than six months ago she had been crowned queen and now she was fleeing her kingdom with a rag-tag band of noblewomen, bound for a country she knew nothing of, besides stories of dragon-prowed ships and men who had once preyed on the coasts of Scotland and Ireland. She fought another urge to touch the cross at her throat as she thought of her father and the hope that refused to be crushed that he would surely shelter them. Earl John, however, had been adamant: Norway was the only safe place for them, until Robert secured his kingdom.

'Sir John said we could make Orkney in just a few days with a good wind. From there it is not much further to Norway and my sister's court.'

At Christian's soft tone Elizabeth knew her sister-in-law was trying to comfort her about the sea voyage, but another feeling had started to push its way up through her fear. 'I cannot help . . .' She paused, wanting to speak her mind, but cautious of offending Christian. Her relationships with these Scots women were still forming. Some, especially Mary Bruce, had quick tempers that caught her off guard. Elizabeth had siblings of her own, but they had been much older and she'd never been close to any of them. Her first friendship had been with Humphrey's wife, Bess, but the English princess was two years buried. Now, she was alone, responsible for these new sisters and a daughter who wasn't her blood. Seeing Christian looking at her expectantly, she let her anger well to the surface. 'I cannot help but blame Robert for all this' – she motioned to the women spread out on the floor – 'all our misfortune.

If he hadn't spilled John Comyn's blood and revolted against the king, we wouldn't be here, fleeing for our lives.'

'No, my lady. We would be living under King Edward's rule in a land that was no longer our own, watching our people break their backs to fill his coffers with silver. I've heard tell of what life is like for the Irish and the Welsh. We would be little more than slaves.'

Elizabeth could not respond to this. Born in an English settlement in Connacht to the Earl of Ulster she only knew the Irish as barbarians, with coarse customs and savage natures. In that, she was still her father's child. 'The end cannot be justified if the means of getting there is by murder. Our husbands were both involved in committing a deadly sin. That sin now haunts us all.'

'Men kill one another all the time.' Christian's voice had hardened.

'You know it is different in war,' said Elizabeth quietly. 'The Church does not call it murder.'

Christian pressed her lips together, seeming to consider her next words. 'My brother has his faults, certainly, and he has done wrong. I do not deny it.' She fixed Elizabeth with her blue eyes. 'Robert has been led most of his life by his ambition – our *family's* ambition – for him to be king. All of us have paid a price, for some the highest price, for him to fulfil that desire, but we have done so because we see in him something that lifts him above most other men; something that makes us hope. He has the iron will of our grandfather and, yes, the hot blood of our father, though he'll not hear the latter said, but he also has the heart of our mother. It is a true heart. A *good* heart. You must keep faith, my lady.' She took Elizabeth's hand. The ruby on the queen's gold ring was almost black in the half-light, gleaming alongside the bright silver of Christian's own wedding band. 'He is your husband and king. He needs you by his side.'

As her voice broke on these last words, Elizabeth drew Christian into her arms, pity overwhelming her. Was this what family felt like? Anger and love and grief all bound up together?

There was a low growl.

The two women pulled back from one another to see Fionn had risen and was standing stock-still, staring at the door. The hound's hackles were up, his ears pressed flat against his head.

'Sir John?' murmured Christian.

Elizabeth felt a chill prickle its way along her arms. She shook her head, eyes on the hound. 'Fionn knows him.'

There were sounds of shouting outside. Fionn launched into a torrent of snarling barks, causing Elizabeth and Christian to jump up. All the other women woke, scrabbling to their feet in startled confusion.

Marjorie threw off her blanket and grabbed the hound's spiked collar. 'Fionn!' The animal took no notice of the girl, still barking ferociously at the door.

'My lady?' Isabel Comyn crossed to Elizabeth, her long dark hair curling loose around her shoulders. 'What is it? Who is out there?'

Elizabeth realised Christian was still grasping her hand. She could feel the sweat slick on both their palms. She came to her senses. 'Mary! Bolt the door!'

Mary, the closest, hastened to do as bid. Before she reached it, the door flew open with a bang. Lora, Elizabeth's maid, screamed shrilly. Marjorie just managed to stop Fionn lunging at the chaplain, who rushed in and slammed the door shut behind him. Donald began to wail, shushed vainly by his wet nurse. Judith, Lora and the other maids and governesses were clustered together, some holding their charges tight to their breasts, others grasping one another.

The chaplain looked over his shoulder at the terrified women as he snapped the bolt in place. 'Men have breached the girth!' he gasped. 'They wear Earl William's colours. They have Sir John.'

The Countess of Atholl put her hands to her mouth. Her daughter, Isabel, went to her side, clutching her mother's arm.

'They come for you, my lady.'

Elizabeth flinched as the chaplain's gaze fell on her. He twisted round. There was a bright red stain on the front of his white robe, blooming like a rose unfurling.

Marjorie cried out. She ran to Elizabeth, who put an arm around her shoulders, shielding the child from the sight of the chaplain sliding down the door.

'Earl William of Ross was a loyal follower of John Balliol,' said Christian to Elizabeth, her face white.

Mary Bruce turned to them. 'They cannot take us,' she said fiercely. 'This is a sanctuary!'

'I am not sure they care, sister,' murmured Margaret Randolph, stepping backwards to the window along with the other women now clustering around Elizabeth.

They all started as several loud crashes echoed outside. More shouts rose, this time closer. They were followed by guttural screams. The other chaplains? Or the few men Sir John had left them with? The sound galvanised Elizabeth. 'The window,' she urged, turning Marjorie towards it. 'Go!'

The girl clambered up on to the window seat and ducked into the narrowing aperture, which opened on to the field outside. 'It's too small!' she said, her voice quavering.

'Try!' Elizabeth ordered.

Marjorie put her hands to either side of the thin, arched opening. She was pushing herself forward when she suddenly screamed and staggered back. Her scream was echoed by others as a man's face appeared in the window. His eyes lit with triumph, seeing Marjorie being pulled back by Elizabeth.

'In here!' he yelled, turning his head to someone they couldn't see, before leering at the women, huddled together in the centre of the room. His expression changed as Fionn lunged at the window.

Marjorie cried a command, but the hound was gone, leaping through the opening. There were now sounds of shrieking and snarling outside.

A fierce bang shook the door. Some of the women began to cry as it rattled violently in its frame. Donald was howling. Elizabeth drew Marjorie close, feeling the girl quivering against her. Her eyes darted around the room, searching for escape or some means of defence. There was nothing. Screams burst from the group as the bolt snapped and the door crashed open.

Men appeared, their red surcoats and tunics decorated with three white lions. All had swords drawn. Some were wet with blood. One, a thickset man with a crooked nose, pushed his way to the front. He scanned the group of women and children. Elizabeth found his cold stare far more unsettling than the unpleasant grins of the men with him.

'Which of you is the wife of Robert Bruce?'

Elizabeth released herself from Marjorie and stepped out of the group. 'I am.' It came out as a whisper. Swallowing back the terrible dryness in her throat, she tried again, this time more forcefully. 'And as your queen I command you to leave this place.'

'You're not my queen. You're the bitch wife of a murdering bastard.'

There were gasps of shock among the women.

Elizabeth paled. Then, her anger rising, she stepped closer. 'How dare you come into this place of refuge. You have violated a holy sanctuary with your foul presence.' She pointed a rigid finger at them 'May the wrath of St Duthac descend upon you!' She may not have lived among the Irish, but she knew how they cursed. 'Go now, or may God Almighty strike you down! You and all your sons!' As she spoke, she realised Christian and Mary Bruce, Isabel Comyn and the Countess of Atholl had moved to join her, facing the men blocking the doorway.

A couple of Ross's men's grins disappeared. They looked nervously at their master, who didn't quail, but met Elizabeth's outburst with dispassionate eyes. 'Seize them.'

As the men poured in, the women began to scream and protest. Mary Bruce fought like a cat, scratching and biting as one of the men tried to grab her and Matilda. The man reeled back, surprised, then backhanded her across the face with his mailed fist. Matilda swooped over her fallen sister with a strangled cry, but was dragged away. Margaret Randolph and some of the others submitted, calling to their sisters to do the same and avoid being hurt. Lady Isabel Comyn had crumpled against the wall, holding her hands out in front of her face, eyes wild with fear, trapped in some old, familiar place of horror. One of Ross's men cruelly snatched a handful of her hair and hauled her to her feet. Christian had grabbed Donald and was clutching her son. Elizabeth tried to keep hold of Marjorie as long as she could, but the men were strong and it was easy for them to rip Robert's daughter from her arms.

14

Lanercost Priory, England, 1306 AD

They were drawn in carts, exposed to the midday sun and evening's chill, their wrists and ankles bound with rope. The year had begun its languid fall towards winter and over the many miles they travelled they watched the last glory of summer burn in the leaves of trees and the bright blaze of heather on the mountainsides. Its death was both beautiful and heartbreaking.

In the front cart the women sat in two lines facing one another, their spines knocking painfully against the timber sides with every rut in the road. Dust kicked up by the harnessed horses had turned their dresses grey. During the first few days of the journey south they had whispered to one another, passing words of consolation or reassurance back and forth. Now, as they wound down out of the hills to see the great edifice of Lanercost Priory dominating the landscape beyond the broken line of Hadrian's Wall, they were silent.

Elizabeth looked at Christian, sitting opposite. Her sister-in-law's eyes were fixed on the second cart which followed in the procession of mounted men, where her son Donald was swaddled against his wet nurse. The maids had their ankles bound, but their hands had been kept free to allow them to suckle and care for their charges. Christian's blonde hair hung bedraggled, blanched by the sun, and her face was freckled after months spent living in the wild. Her dress was torn and had slipped off one brown shoulder. She looked, thought Elizabeth, more like a shepherdess than a countess. They all did.

When Earl William of Ross had delivered them into the custody of Aymer de Valence and Prince Edward, Elizabeth had told the English that her sister-in-law was with child. They granted Christian the concession of a cushion to sit on, but showed no sympathy for her sickness, instructing her to vomit over the side of the cart or else sit in her own mess. On seeing Humphrey de Bohun, Elizabeth had thought the earl, whom she had once counted a friend, might be persuaded to offer more lenient treatment, but her hope had been dashed when Humphrey parted their company almost immediately, no doubt riding on to tell the king of their coming.

The cart jolted over a stone, causing the women to lurch into one another. Christian glanced at the Countess of Atholl, who bumped shoulders with her. The older woman communicated an apology with her eyes, before returning her gaze to the front, squinting into the early evening sun. Her daughter, Isabel, hunched beside her, joined her mother's vigil, watching the back of her father. John of Atholl was some distance ahead, his black and yellow surcoat glimpsed occasionally between the swaying backs and switching tails of the knights' horses. Stripped of mail and weapons, the earl was seated on a horse, hands tied to the pommel. Behind him, Niall Bruce was similarly trussed. The brief joy of the Bruce sisters on seeing their younger brother in the prince's company had quickly faded with the realisation Kildrummy had fallen. Elizabeth, catching snatches of conversation among the knights, heard talk of the castle's garrison being executed, only those of high rank kept alive, reserved for the pleasure of the king.

As they trundled across tree-fringed fields, approaching the priory's precinct, Elizabeth caught clear voices rising over the din of the hooves and the creaking cartwheels. A group of children were running along the flower-speckled verge. They called to the knights, who ignored them, before stopping in a curious huddle to watch the carts roll past. The eldest, a skinny boy with lank hair, pointed at the women and said something to his companions that made them cackle. Elizabeth felt heat rise in her cheeks. The children's faces were mocking. The little group jogged alongside the carts for a while, still laughing, until they got bored and ran off into the fields, chasing one another. Their screams faded slowly. Feeling the sun vanish and a cold gloom move across her, Elizabeth realised they had passed through the gateway of the priory wall.

Now they were level with the buildings, the height of the church at the centre was even more imposing. It towered before them, its stone façade ruddy in the sunlight. Clustered in its shadow was a colourful multitude of tents, the larger ones displaying heraldic banners beside them. The largest of all was a scarlet pavilion made up of several sections, hemmed with fluttering gold flags. Elizabeth's heart began to hammer in her chest at the sight of it. Behind the pavilion, a timber building was under construction, men working on scaffolds. Many other figures moved about the camp and the priory's lawns, which were crowded with wagons, horses and mules. The royal court had come to Lanercost.

As the vanguard came to a stop, Elizabeth saw Humphrey de Bohun heading across to greet the prince and his men. Aymer de Valence and Henry Percy dismounted and joined them. Her attention was distracted as the cart lurched to a halt. Men came to the back with knives in their hands. Matilda Bruce flinched as one leaned towards her, but he merely grabbed the rope that bound her ankles and began sawing through it. One by one, the women were helped from the carts. Elizabeth saw Margaret Randolph jump down unaided and crane her head to the camp. Of all of them she had something to hope for here – knowledge of her son, Thomas, missing since the battle at Methven Wood.

Elizabeth looked over her shoulder as she was led towards the pavilion, seeking Marjorie in the crowd of men and horses. Despite her protestations, Robert's daughter had been separated from her in the third cart, which had travelled some distance behind the others. She was gratified to see the girl had now been freed and was following, the hand of one of Valence's men on her shoulder. Ahead, Humphrey de Bohun was making his way back towards the pavilion, accompanied by the prince and the barons who had led the raid into Scotland. Another of Valence's knights drew Fionn after his new master. The hound, scarred from several brutal whippings, whined unhappily, twisting his head towards Marjorie, but was pulled forward by a jerk of the leash.

As the women were escorted, struggling, with hands still bound, to hitch their skirts over the fresh piles of horse dung littering the priory's lawns, they were brought alongside the men who had been taken prisoner at Kildrummy and Tain. Seeing the countess lock eyes with her husband, Elizabeth found it unsettling that a face could communicate so much relief and despair at once. John of Atholl gave his wife and daughter a fortifying smile, which didn't reach his brown eyes. Niall Bruce was leaning heavily against his captors, his surcoat ripped and covered in blood, but he managed a brief nod to his sisters.

'*My God.*'

Hearing the breathless exclamation, Elizabeth saw Lady Isabel Comyn staring at the royal pavilion. Outside was a host of men, watching their approach. Near the front was an imposing, well-built man, dressed all in black. Seeing the arms decorating his surcoat, Elizabeth realised he must be the Black Comyn. Isabel had frozen at the sight of her husband, the knights escorting her having to compel her forward.

Elizabeth found her own eyes transfixed by a figure seated on a throne in the pavilion, the sides of which were stretched out to either side of him like red wings. She had last seen King Edward two years ago at Dunfermline Abbey. The man before her was scarcely recognisable. Edward's face was haggard and wan, as if all the blood had been leached out of it. He sat hunched in a flowing, scarlet mantle, which failed to conceal the shocking gauntness of his once powerful physique. A gold crown perched on his head, where patches of scalp were clearly visible through the thin white hair. Elizabeth was reminded of pictures of Death she had seen on murals and in religious books – an emaciated, claw-fingered figure, leering from behind tombstones. A shudder ran through her as the skeleton in the throne fixed his bloodshot eyes on her.

Prince Edward bowed before his father, then swept a hand to the prisoners being lined up before the king. 'My lord, I present to you Bruce's family and followers,' he announced grandly.

The king's gaze shifted to his son, but remained glacial. 'But not the man himself.'

The prince glanced at Humphrey de Bohun, standing at the king's right. 'My lord, I believe Sir Humphrey has informed you that Bruce fled into the wilderness before we could confront him.'

Piers Gaveston stepped in. 'We have had reports that place Bruce in Kintyre. The Scots are in pursuit.'

Prince Edward shot the Gascon knight a warning look, before turning back to his father. 'My men and I are ready to join the hunt whenever you command it.'

The king didn't respond. Instead, he addressed one of his knights. 'Bring the prisoner. I am ready to pass judgement.'

Despite her fear, Elizabeth stepped forward. As queen it was her duty to stand up for her countrywomen and, as the daughter of Richard de Burgh, she was perhaps the only one who could. 'My lord king, I beg you, have pity. These women and their children have endured great hardship and I implore you to—'

Her entreaty was cut off by a sharp cry from Christian Bruce. Following her sister-in-law's gaze, Elizabeth saw a man being dragged through the crowd. It was Christopher Seton. The knight from Yorkshire had been badly beaten, but his bloodied face lit up like a candle at the sight of his wife. The men holding Christian had to tighten their grip as she tried to run to him.

'My lord,' Elizabeth began again, but fell silent as the king rose, his face stained by the red hues of the evening sun.

'There are no innocents here. No blameless victims.' Despite his frailty, Edward's tone was all iron authority. 'Time after time I have extended the hand of forgiveness and I have suffered the bite of betrayal for it. I will be merciful no longer. All who have aided or supported the renegade, Robert Bruce, who helped cloak his treachery in false folds of friendship and loyalty, will be judged enemies of the crown.'

Elizabeth saw many of the king's men nodding. Among their number were those whom Robert had once called friends: Ralph de Monthermer, Robert Clifford, Thomas of Lancaster. She caught the eye of Humphrey de Bohun, who looked steadily back at her, before returning his attention to the king.

'Lady Elizabeth.'

She snapped back at her name.

'You will henceforth be taken to the royal manor at Burstwick, where you will be confined indefinitely.' The king's eyes moved to Christian. 'Your son, the Earl of Mar, is hereby removed from the wardship of your brother. He will be placed in my court, under my authority.' Ignoring her cry of protest, Edward continued. 'You and your sisters will be held in Sixhills nunnery, where you will live out the rest of your days in silent prayer.'

Matilda hung her head, but Mary faced the king, eyes glinting with loathing.

'Lady Isabel Comyn.' The king stared at the pale countess, his eyes narrowing with fresh enmity. 'For the act of placing the crown upon the rebel's head, you will be kept in a cage, fashioned appropriately for your crime, at Berwick Castle.'

Elizabeth stared at the king in astonishment. Looking to the Black Comyn to see his reaction, she saw the man was smiling and guessed the brute had not only known of, but welcomed this cruel sentence. Close by, Aymer de Valence wore a similarly exalted expression. Elizabeth felt sickened. But Edward wasn't finished.

'I have a second cage being built. This one will be placed in the Tower of London and will hold Bruce's daughter.'

Elizabeth's shout was drowned by the rest of Robert's family, who erupted around her. Niall lunged at the king, but was roughly forced to his knees by his guards. Christian and Margaret tried in vain to get closer to Marjorie, who had blanched in terror at the judgement. It was Mary Bruce who broke free. Twisting round, she bit the hand of one of her captors. Hands still bound, she flew across the grass before anyone could stop her and spat full in Edward's face. Two of Valence's knights were on her in moments, wrestling her to the ground. But the deed had been done. Shock rippled through the gathering around the pavilion as the king wiped the spittle from his cheek with a trembling hand.

'Another cage for this animal!' he hissed, as Mary was hauled to her feet. Edward stooped suddenly, clutching his side as if in pain. After a moment, he righted himself, his gaze swivelling to John and Niall. 'And you – you who have sheltered the traitor, who fought and bled for him and his cause.' He looked at Christopher. 'You who murdered John Comyn in cold blood. John of Atholl. Niall Bruce. Christopher Seton. I sentence you to death.'

At this, even some of the watching English looked surprised. As John's wife let out a strangled cry and Christian Bruce collapsed in the arms of Valence's men, Elizabeth turned helplessly to Humphrey, with her eyes beseeching him to intervene. The earl's jaw clenched as he looked away, now unwilling to meet her gaze.

Berwick Castle, Scotland, 1306 AD

Alexander Seton felt the damp stone bruising his back, but he didn't move. The discomfort served to remind him that he was still alive. His wounds had healed, his skin sealing imperfectly over cuts and bruises to create new marks on his arms and chest. He had no idea what his face looked like. Only his fingers could create a picture of the crooked breaks in his nose and the knots of scar tissue around his eyes and lips.

Sounds of scraping fingernails, the wet pad of feet on the slimy floor and agitated murmurs rose around him in the dank gloom as other men shifted their positions. The newer prisoners still stalked about the cramped cell like caged animals, walking endless circles. Those who had been in the dungeon longest huddled against the sides or lay curled, facing the mildewed walls. One, a scrawny, toothless man who had been in here longer than he himself knew, crawled around on hands and knees, chattering to himself. Old Bones, the others called him.

Alexander closed his eyes, hearing the knocking start up again as men went to work on the town walls. He had seen hundreds of them up on scaffolds and down in the deep trench of the fosse when his captors carted him in. Berwick, once a thriving Scottish port, had been the first casualty of the war and a bloody one at that. Livid tales of the two-day slaughter that saw the deaths of over seven thousand townsfolk and made the River Tweed run red reached everyone in Scotland. Thereafter, Berwick had become an English town and seat of King Edward's administration in Scotland. The distant hammering entered Alexander's head, maddening in its monotony. He had been able to handle the squalid, confined space, the foetid stench of his fellow prisoners, even the repulsive rations the guards slopped in, but not that endless knocking. It felt as though the workers had their picks and hammers inside his skull, slowly chipping away at his sanity.

He sank into himself, squeezing his hands into fists and trying to block it out. Dark thoughts began creeping in and he allowed them – anything to stop that banging. His mind wandered, walking the same endless circles as the new prisoners. Guilt came first, an old enemy, picking at his soul. It tormented him, telling him what his actions had caused; reminding him of comrades bleeding out on that marshy plain, their bodies hacked into red ribbons. Guilt twisted down into a sick self-loathing. Finally, another voice spoke, first quiet then more compelling, telling him that none of these things would have happened if not for Robert Bruce. Normally, such thoughts could loop for hours, but today the cycle was interrupted.

Hearing footsteps echoing down the passage, Alexander opened his eyes. Other prisoners were looking round. There was a jangle of keys, which made some of the more withdrawn ones sit up. Old Bones took no notice, still crawling about.

'Get back,' ordered one of the guards, coming into view through the bars of the cell.

The prisoners did as they were told, shuffling against the far wall. Two more guards appeared, hauling a man between them. His head was drooping and his blond hair hung like a curtain in front of his face. The first guard unlocked the door, allowing his comrades to throw the limp man into the cell. As the man collapsed, his hair fell away from his face.

Alexander let out an exclamation that made some of the other prisoners flinch. As the cell door clanked shut, he threw himself down beside the man. His face was horribly bruised, but wonderfully familiar. Alexander cradled his cousin's head in his hands. 'Christopher.' His voice sounded strange after so long without use.

After a moment, Christopher mumbled something and one of his eyes cracked open. It was sore and weeping, crusted with blood. Alexander pushed away Old Bones who had appeared at his side and was chattering curiously over Christopher. 'Gil,' he said, glancing at one of the prisoners. 'Bring me some water.' When Gil looked hesitantly at the bucket in the corner that contained their rations, Alexander glared at him. 'By God, Gil, if I have to ask you twice . . .'

Gil relented, bringing him the bucket. Alexander tore a strip off his ragged shirt and dipped it in the bucket. As he squeezed it over Christopher's cracked lips, his cousin coughed, then swallowed. Life sparked in his eyes. He clutched Alexander's wrist, opening his mouth for more.

'Not too much,' Alexander warned. 'It will make you sick.'

Christopher focused slowly on him. 'Alex?'

Alexander felt emotion tighten in his chest. Christopher hadn't called him that since they were boys. Christopher licked his lips and struggled to sit.

Alexander helped him until he was propped against the wall. 'What happened?'

'We were attacked,' Christopher said, teeth gritted with the effort of holding himself upright. 'By John MacDougall and the Black Comyn. I escaped with some of Atholl's men and rode to Robert's castle at Loch Doon.' He shook his head. 'The English took it.' His brow creased. 'I dreamed I saw you in the battle. But you couldn't have been there, could you.' His eyes cleared, flashing with anger. 'You deserted us.'

'I was there. At the battle. I tried to save you.'

As Christopher stared at him, uncomprehending, Alexander told his cousin of his capture in Perth by Dungal MacDouall and torture at the hands of the Black Comyn. He told him how he had tried to warn them at St Fillan's and broke his bonds to ride to aid them. 'But I fell,' he finished. 'The English, under Prince Edward, arrived soon after the battle. I was taken from the field and brought here.'

Christopher met his gaze for a long moment, then threw out his hand to push him away. 'How could you?' His voice rose. 'How could you *betray* us!'

'Cousin—'

'No! Don't you call me that!'

Alexander sat back on his heels. He had never seen such raw fury in his cousin's face. The other prisoners were staring at them. Old Bones was rocking excitedly.

'After all Robert has done for you – for us! We owe him our lives! God damn you, Alex, you should have let them kill you rather than betray your king!'

Alexander's shock turned to surprise, before anger rushed in on a hot tide. 'What Robert has done for us? I'll tell you what. He led us straight into Valence's hands at Methven Wood, ignoring the counsel of his own men, not just mine, the steward's too. He had you help him murder a man on holy ground – a deadly sin, Christopher. And, lest we forget, all this after he submitted to King Edward, without one word to us, his faithful followers – leaving us to fend for ourselves for two goddamned years!'

'All to free his kingdom.'

'No!' Alexander spat back. 'All for the sake of his ambition.'

'Ambition?' said Christopher, breathing hard, sweat causing old blood to run down his cheeks. 'If that is his crime, then I will charge you with the same. Do you remember how you deceived him back in Ayr all those years ago? How you wanted him to be rid of Katherine because you thought her a distraction, so you paid that lad to lie with her and made damn sure Robert caught them?'

Alexander laughed harshly. 'You're still bent over that? A maid!' His laughter vanished. 'She was the first of many mistakes. The gravest of which was mine for following him for so long!'

At their rising voices, there was a shout from one of the guards that echoed down the passage, telling them to be quiet.

Alexander swallowed thickly, trying to quell his rage. 'I regret, more than I can say, that my yielding to Comyn's torture led to the bloodshed on that plain, but despite my own failings, I believe Robert, through his actions, is the one to blame. I've given up everything, Christopher. I will not now die for him.'

'I will.'

Alexander saw something new in his cousin's eyes – a flicker of fear in the defiance.

Christopher held his gaze for a long moment, then looked away. 'I've been sentenced to hang.'

Alexander shook his head, disbelieving. 'There must be some mistake. Who gave this order?'

'King Edward himself.'

Alexander remained silent, stunned, as Christopher told him of the sentences passed at Lanercost.

'Aymer de Valence and Humphrey de Bohun will oversee the executions of me and Niall here in Berwick,' he finished. 'John of Atholl has been taken to London with the other prisoners.' Christopher looked sideways at him. 'Now do you see what your actions have caused?'

Alexander closed his eyes.

Christopher wiped his cheek with the back of his hand. He stared at the streak of red that stained his knuckles. 'Valence told me Christian is with child.' He laughed, but there was no humour in the sound. 'The bastard thought he was tormenting me. But I can die now, Alex.' He looked at him. 'I can die with the knowledge there's something of me in her – that she'll have a piece of me still.'

Alexander felt something twist in him as he watched a bloody tear leak from the corner of his cousin's eye. After a moment, he rose and banged on the bars with his fists.

'What are you doing?'

'Guard!'

'Shut your hole,' shouted the guard. 'Or I'll put my fist in it!'

'Christ,' muttered Gil.

Old Bones let out an excited squeak.

'*Guard!*'

There was a curse and the sound of stamping feet. One of the guards appeared, glaring through the bars. 'I said shut your mouth!'

'Sir Aymer,' Alexander said quickly, 'tell him I have something to say to him. An offer.'

'Alex!' Christopher struggled to sit, grimacing with pain.

'Offer?' The guard's eyes narrowed mistrustfully.

'Tell him I can bring him Robert Bruce – if he'll spare my cousin the gallows.'

'Don't listen to him!' Christopher hissed at the guard. 'I give my life willingly!'

'Silence!' The guard stared at Alexander. 'If you're lying, I'll make sure you're strung up on the scaffold beside the wretch.'

'So be it.'

15

Dunaverty Castle, Scotland, 1306 AD

The men worked in lines, hefting sacks of grain and rolling barrels of ale down to the boats, where others were waiting to load them. Now and then, they would glance up at the castle, rearing above them on a grassy outcrop, where the jagged rocks that tumbled into the foaming waves formed the last broken pieces of land before the realm of the sea began. The men's faces were taut, eyes watching the battlements for any sign of warning from their comrades.

It was early morning, mid-October. Tattered clouds chased across the sky, driven by the wind, which tore at the men's clothes and sent sand dancing like smoke across the beach. Every so often the sun would appear, turning the white-tipped waves from deep indigo to emerald green, scattering shards of sunlight across the churning surface. Gulls competed for fish, screaming at one another. Just off shore, the dog-like face of a seal appeared, then vanished.

Gilbert de la Hay hoisted another barrel of salted meat into one of the boats. Straightening with a wince, the tall man looked uneasily out to sea.

'It isn't far,' said Robert, giving the lord a brief smile as he tossed the pack he was carrying into the boat.

'It's far enough,' murmured Gilbert. Sniffing in a breath of salty air, he hitched up his braies, which no longer fitted his once broad girth.

Robert looked at the men piling supplies into the four boats, among them Malcolm Lennox and his company, with him since Loch Lomond. All were leaner, forced to live hand to mouth these past weeks, scavenging nuts and berries in the woods, occasionally making a meal of a bird or a coney. Beards had grown thicker, hair was longer and clothing was ripped and filthy. There was barely a scrap of armour between them, just weapons, which would only fall when they did. Even in the depths of the Forest, in the midst of William Wallace's peasant army, Robert hadn't seen a more ragged band.

'This should do for a few months,' observed Edward, jumping down from one of the boats.

Robert nodded, surveying the supplies being stowed at the prows under sheets of waxed canvas. Along with the provisions were ropes and blankets, buckets, axes and hunting spears. He thanked God for his foresight with the restocking of Dunaverty Castle, which had been commandeered by his forces late in February, one of several that had fallen to him during the uprising. Dunaverty stood sentry over the sea route to the Isles – the nail on the fingertip that was Kintyre, ever pointing towards Ireland.

'Sire!'

Robert looked round as Nes called to him. The knight was gesturing to the battlements. Following his gaze, he saw the lookouts waving their arms. It was time to leave.

'Let's take them out,' Robert called sharply.

The last few packs were hurled into the boats as the men climbed in, some taking the oars. Robert vaulted over the side as those on the beach pushed them into the shallows, faces straining with the effort. Robert felt the vessel lighten and lift, borne aloft by the waves. The men at the oars dug them into the water to get them through the first rollers. A wave smashed into the prow, drenching those at the front and misting the rest of them with spray. Gilbert, on a bench in the centre, closed his eyes and mouthed a prayer, clinging on for dear life. The rush and drag of stones being ground beneath them sounded like a lion's roar.

While the men heaved on the oars, taking them through the rough green shallows out into the deep blue, others wrenched on the ropes to unfurl the sail, which came down with a great snap, filling at once with wind. Shouts and creaking timbers rose on the air as the crew in the other three boats did the same. A few of the men left on the beach raised their hands in farewell. Robert saw others salute back, before their comrades turned and headed up the cliff path that led to the castle. It was a small garrison he had left there, but he hoped it would be enough to fool those who were coming for them.

Their enemies, led by John MacDougall, had pursued them from the shore of Loch Lomond to the head of Loch Fyne and down through the woods of Argyll. Sleeping in thickets and caves as the autumn air grew chill and the first storms swept in from the west, they had been hunted like beasts until they were stumbling through the miles, as dazed as sleep walkers. Desperate to make Islay, on reaching the coast they found their path barred by scores of galleys patrolling the sea, sails adorned with the MacDougall arms. Unable to stop, or else risk being overrun, Robert led them south past rings of stones and barrows where the ancient dead slept under the green skin of the land. As they followed the serrated shoreline, Islay and Jura rose ever from the waters to their right, tauntingly close.

In this desperate flight, Robert lost several men through wounds that had become infected. He lost more when a band of the enemy caught up with them. With the fresh strength of Malcolm of Lennox and his men, who hadn't been harried as long, they won the skirmish. When it was over and the corpses were looted for boots and weapons, Robert saw familiar arms on the surcoats of several. The men were John of Menteith's, who had drawn William Wallace into John Comyn's trap and had been made keeper of Dumbarton Castle by King Edward for that service.

In this time, Robert dwelled often on his excommunication, proclaimed by the pope, condemning him for the blood of John Comyn that had stained his hands and his soul. Outlawed from Christendom. Outcast by God. It was a terrible sentence, carrying the promise of eternal damnation unless he repented. He thought, too, of the Stone of Destiny encased within Edward's coronation chair in Westminster Abbey: Scotland's sovereignty entombed in the heart of England. Did these roads all lead back to the desperate moment he helped the Knights of the Dragon take it? The stone, on which Scotland's kings had ever been made, tied the king to the land and through it to the people. Had Scotland rejected him because he hadn't been crowned upon it?

As the boats edged out into the churning deep of the stretch of water known as the race, Robert watched the green edge of the land diminish. Dunaverty's walls shone gold in a flash of sunlight. He had hoped to rest there longer, but an army was sighted that morning approaching in the distance and he knew then that they had run him out of his kingdom. He needed a safe haven where his men could rest, where wounds could heal and strength could be regained; somewhere his enemies could not find him, close to friends and allies.

Robert thought of his daughter and his wife, his sisters and his brother, Niall, John of Atholl and Christopher Seton: all those he held dear now scattered to the winds. He thought, too, of his trusted supporters, bishops William Lamberton and Robert Wishart, languishing in one of King Edward's dungeons, his nephew, Thomas Randolph, and James Stewart, still missing. Sending up a prayer for all of them, he turned his face to the prow. In the distance, the black cliffs of Ireland's northern coastline loomed. Nearer, just a few miles off that dark forbidding shore, was a tiny speck of an island.

Berwick, Scotland, 1306 AD

As autumn wrapped its withering gold mantle around Britain, the king's judgements were carried out across the land.

One raw, bright morning in London, when the streets were mottled with the first frost, John of Atholl was taken from the Tower with a host of Scottish prisoners captured at Methven Wood. Passing London Bridge, where the rotting head of Simon Fraser and the skull of William Wallace leered down the Thames from their pikes, the Scots were drawn through the jeering crowds to Smithfield. After the sentences had been passed at Lanercost, John had appealed to Edward, reminding him of the high-born status of those he condemned to death. Here, on Smithfield's plain, was cruel evidence of the king's acceptance of this: a gallows thirty feet higher than the others for the earl.

Closing his eyes as he stood on the gallows, in the place where William Wallace had been butchered the year before, John cradled the images of his wife, his son and his daughter in his mind. Asking God to deliver them from harm and to lend all His strength to Robert and his cause, he felt the noose snatch him up, high above London's roaring mob.

Many miles north, at the royal manor in Burstwick, Elizabeth Bruce stared at the cramped, gloomy chamber she had been ushered into. There was a bed, a table, a small fireplace and a stool. The dour woman at her back told her brusquely that a meal would be brought twice a day, before the door was shut behind her. Elizabeth listened to the key twist in the lock, her thoughts on Marjorie – eleven years old and on her way to a cage in the Tower. After a moment, the queen crossed to the narrow bed and sat on its hard edge, staring numbly at the cracks of light bleeding through the shuttered window.

Not far away, in Lincolnshire, Christian Bruce wept as her fair hair was cut away by one of the Gilbertine sisters of the Sixhills nunnery. To either side of her, Matilda and Margaret knelt on the cold stone floor, sharing the same fate. Locks of hair, blonde, brown and grey, fell around the knees of the three sisters, the only sounds the scrape of the knives and Christian's muffled sobs. Margaret Randolph, who had been told at Lanercost that her son, Thomas, was alive and in English custody, leaned across and took her sister's hand, telling her she must take heart – Donald would be well cared for in the royal court, his young life guaranteed by the king. She could do nothing for Christopher, but she could keep her strength and spirits up so as to nourish his child, now growing inside her.

In a turret of Roxburgh Castle, Mary Bruce sat hunched against the bars of her newly made cage, knees drawn up to her chest. She had screamed herself hoarse for the first few days in the prison, feeling the bars and the walls closing in around her. Now, in shocked silence, all her defiance and protest gone, Mary wrapped her arms around her head and wept, not knowing that some thirty miles to the east, in the tallest tower of Berwick Castle, in an iron cage, eight foot by eight and fashioned in the shape of a crown to remind her of her crime, Isabel Comyn was doing the same.

The countess's face, arms and thighs were livid with bruises, a parting gift from her husband, the Black Comyn, who had come to visit her that first night. Despite her pleas, he had shown no mercy in demonstrating the consequences of her betrayal, first by exercising his right as a husband, forcing her down on the wooden boards of the cage floor, then by beating her with his fists until even her screams were silenced.

Isabel's bloodshot, swollen eyes flickered open as a ragged cheer came from somewhere beyond the castle walls. She closed them again and curled even tighter around her pain. The sound could only mean another hanging.

Humphrey de Bohun, seated on his palfrey in Berwick's market square, watched as Niall Bruce and Christopher Seton were drawn, stumbling, through the seething mob. The young men already had nooses looped around their necks, the ends of which were tied to the horses of the royal knights who had escorted them from the castle. Their hands were bound behind their backs. A light rain misted the air, which stank of mud and brine from the River Tweed.

A cheer went up as Niall collapsed in the street and was dragged a few yards on his stomach, before he managed to get to his knees and then to his feet. As he did so, Humphrey saw one man, wearing the white apron of a stonemason, make a fist at the side of his neck and pull on an invisible noose, his face contorting grotesquely. His companions laughed and raised their tankards as the man swaggered back into their midst. The crowds had swelled with these labourers, granted a few hours off their back-breaking work on Berwick's defences to watch the executions. Many were from towns in Northumberland, which had been sacked and raided by the Scots over the past ten years of the war. All were keen to witness these men swing for their crimes and more appreciation filled the air as other Scots, taken at Kildrummy and Tain, were led into the square behind Niall and Christopher, each man sentenced to be hanged and beheaded.

'A great day for England.'

Humphrey glanced round at Aymer de Valence's harsh voice.

The Earl of Pembroke was seated beside him on his horse. He didn't take his eyes off Niall and Christopher, who were being led towards the gallows erected in the market. 'A great day indeed.'

Humphrey nodded but said nothing, thinking of the similar displays taking place across Scotland and England. Edward, ensconced in new, comfortable lodgings at Lanercost, wouldn't witness any of his judgements, but Humphrey had no doubt he would agree.

When ordered by the king to escort the prisoners to Berwick and from there head west to join Prince Edward on his way to Dunaverty Castle, where Bruce was reported to be trapped, Humphrey had thought Edward seemed in rare good spirits. He was still weak, but his skin was flushed with new life and his appetite increased. Humphrey had listened to his instructions, while watching the royal physician place the leeches on the king's arms. Seeing the colour in Edward's cheeks, he had been struck by the thought that while the worms fed on him, the king himself seemed to be feeding on the blood of the Scots.

After the sentences had been passed at Lanercost, Humphrey,

Ralph de Monthermer and several other barons had privately petitioned the king to temper the harshness of his judgements. John of
Atholl's execution, especially, had left them all uneasy. No one could
remember the last time an earl had been executed. Edward, however,
was in no mood to be lenient and even when Queen Marguerite
implored him to reconsider his treatment of little Marjorie Bruce, he
bluntly refused.

Humphrey watched Christopher flinch as someone pelted him
with mud. 'Sir Ralph told me you released Alexander Seton? That he
pledged to apprehend Robert if you spared his cousin's life?'

Aymer's dark eyes flicked to Humphrey at the questioning tone.
'He seemed adamant he could bring me Bruce. I judged the promise
of the prize to be worth the risk of losing a prisoner who would have
otherwise rotted in a cell.'

'But if he learns you reneged on your word?' asked Humphrey,
gesturing to Christopher. 'If he hears of his cousin's execution before
he brings you Bruce?'

'Then he can tell the son of a bitch all about it.' Aymer's handsome
face hardened. 'I want Bruce to know exactly what has been done to
his family. I want him crushed – body and spirit.' His gaze moved back
to the condemned men.

The soldiers had untied Niall and Christopher from the cruppers
of the horses and now compelled them on by the tips of their swords,
up the steps of the platform, past the block and axe where they would
be beheaded after they were cut down, still alive. When Niall hung
back, his white face tilted to the beam above, he had to be marched
forcibly up the steps, much to the jeers of the watching crowd.

'The king's brother has pissed himself!' someone shouted. There
was a scattering of loud jibes.

Humphrey swallowed back the knot that had collected at the back of
his throat. This wasn't the way noblemen should die, whatever their
crimes. He remembered Robert speaking fondly of his carefree younger
brother. What measure of grief would assail him when he learned of
Niall's death? Would he feel the way he himself had after Bess? He
forced away the pity, angry at himself for feeling it. This was Robert's
doing – this, here, was the price of his betrayal. He deserved this. The
thought, however forceful, didn't quite reach Humphrey's heart.

'The whelp told me his brother would avenge him,' said Aymer, his
lip curling as he watched Niall being forced up the steps. 'I told him

he could charge Bruce with that when he sees him in hell. Whether by Seton's hand or by your men at Dunaverty, the whoreson will soon be brought down and this goddamned war will be over.'

People at the back of the jostling crowds craned their necks the better to see as the ropes of the nooses around Niall and Christopher's necks were thrown over the beam of the gallows. There were scattered calls of approval from some of the watching men; supporters of John Comyn, glad to see one of his killers receive this justice. Among them was Dungal MacDouall. A cold smile graced the captain's face.

'We still have to retrieve the Staff of Malachy and the box containing the *Last Prophecy* and return them to Westminster,' Humphrey reminded Aymer. 'Then, perhaps, this will be over.'

'The box?' Aymer's brow knotted. 'I found that on the brother.' He gestured to Niall, who had raised his head to the leaden sky. 'He went down fighting at Kildrummy with it on him.' His frown deepened with Humphrey's surprise. 'Did the king not tell you?' When Humphrey shook his head, Aymer looked puzzled. 'Lord Edward forbade me from speaking of it, but I assumed he would have told you at least.'

The crowd surged forward, eager to see the hanging. A few people fell in the crush. Others were shoved back by soldiers.

'Tell me what?' When Aymer didn't answer, Humphrey pressed him. 'Robert betrayed us both, Aymer. I deserve to know.'

'The box was broken,' confessed Aymer. 'There was nothing inside it. My guess is we will find the prophecy when we find Bruce. Either that or he has destroyed it.'

Humphrey didn't answer. His eyes narrowed as he watched Niall and Christopher being hauled into the air above the roaring crowds. Why on earth had Robert charged his brother to guard an empty box?

PART 3

1306–1307 AD

Then shall there be a slaughter of foreigners; then shall the rivers run with blood. Then shall break forth the fountains of Armorica, and they shall be crowned with the diadem of Brutus.

The History of the Kings of Britain, *Geoffrey of Monmouth*

16

Rathlin, Ireland, 1306 AD

In the heart of the fire a log burst with a crackle of sparks that gusted into the night sky. Around the courtyard weathered walls ascended to the broken teeth of battlements. Inside the castle's chambers, veiled with dust and cobwebs, most of the chimneys had been blocked by the matted nests of seabirds and so the men had set their fire outside. The tang of wood-smoke mingled with the smell of roasted meat from the geese, bartered from an old woman in the village. Their lips and beards glossed with the grease of their meal, they nursed the last of the wine and listened to one another's stories, rendered in a mixture of French, Scots and Gaelic.

As Neil Campbell finished a stirring account of William Wallace's bravery against the English at Stirling, Cormac rose. 'My lord king, may I tell the tale of the salmon?' The young Irishman looked over at Robert, who was seated beside his brother, Edward, faces bronzed by the flames.

Robert said nothing, but gave a half-smile, permitting his foster-brother to continue.

'On this night,' began Cormac, eyes glinting with humour beneath the thick fringe of his cúlán, 'my father invited two neighbouring chieftains to our hall in Glenarm. His cooks had baked a salmon for the occasion, caught by my father himself.'

Edward Bruce chuckled at the memory. He leaned in to Gilbert de la Hay and James Douglas, quietly translating Cormac's words. Others of the king's company who didn't speak Gaelic crowded closer to listen.

'The day before, my father had been telling young Lord Robert and Sir Edward about the ancient heroes of Ireland and Robert's blood had been stirred by the tales of Fionn Mac Cumhaill and his band of warriors, the Fianna. One story had been about the time Fionn, as a boy, had cooked the Salmon of Knowledge for the Druid, Finegas, and on accidentally brushing the flesh with his thumb had sucked it and gained the gift of wisdom. Robert, then my father's page, was waiting in the hall for the guests to arrive, with the feast laid out and that salmon on a platter in the centre.' Cormac spread his hands wide to show the watching men the size of the fish. A few grinned. 'As my father and his men entered, with God as my witness, there was young Robert leaning over the table with his thumb stuck in the creature.'

Laughter echoed around the walls. Even David of Atholl cracked a rare smile.

Robert found himself surprised by how many of these stories he had forgotten. They all seemed part of someone else's life. Someone without the weight of the world on his shoulders.

'Have you heard the one about the maid and the miller?' ventured Gilbert de la Hay.

More laughter burst up as the barrel-chested Lord of Erroll began the joke. Robert saw his brother, Thomas, pour out more of the rationed wine for himself and the Irishmen seated with Cormac. He let it go. It was the eve of the Christ Mass.

His gaze wandered over the tight circle of men. Less than a year ago, most had stood on the Moot Hill, witness to his coronation. They had been dressed then in silks and velvets. Now, they were swaddled in tattered cloaks, with holes in their boots and hair and beards long and unkempt. Looking at them, he recalled another tale of Fionn Mac Cumhaill. In this one, the Fianna had been invited to sup in the hall of a rival and, on entering, had been awed by the splendour of their enemy's court, where tapestries of every hue adorned the walls, fires burned merrily and wine flowed from a fountain. Slowly, this vision had changed and Fionn and his men found they had been lured not to a magnificent hall, but to the House of Death, their table the damp floor of a cave with rough walls shrouded in rags and their cracked cups filled with blood.

As Gilbert started another lewd tale, Robert realised Alexander was staring at him. His brother's eyes narrowed expectantly.

When a few calls and whistles joined Gilbert's story, Alexander rose, his face taut. 'Lest we forget, brothers, we have come together this evening to honour the birth of our Lord Jesus Christ. I believe, my lord,' he added meaningfully to Robert, 'a story from the Gospels would be more appropriate.'

Robert bridled at the chastisement, but after a pause he motioned for his brother to speak. Some of the men exchanged looks, but most settled down to listen as the former dean retold the story of Christ's birth from the Gospel of St Luke.

Alexander and Thomas had arrived on Rathlin after receiving Robert's message, delivered to Islay in the hands of a fisherman. In his report, Thomas had told Robert of Alexander's intervention at the council of Angus MacDonald, which might otherwise have ended in bloodshed. It was his impassioned speech, Thomas said, that led to the Lord of Islay and his men pledging their support for the war and to Lachlan MacRuarie agreeing – for a price – to build a fleet of ships and fill them with his galloglass. Robert, surprised by Alexander's actions, had expressed his gratitude, which his brother accepted, seemingly with some pleasure. But, on learning of Robert's excommunication for the murder of John Comyn, he once again distanced himself, spending most of his days alone in prayer. Robert had meant to speak to him, but the business of planning his return to the mainland had taken up all his time, and he had let it.

In the next few days, when the full moon calmed the seas, Thomas and Alexander would return to Ireland with Cormac, bearing orders for Lord Donough and the men of Antrim to launch an assault on Galloway. While his foster-father was attacking the lands of his enemies in the south-west, Robert, bolstered by the combined strength of Angus MacDonald and Lachlan MacRuarie, would strike for Carrick by way of Arran. He had no doubt King Edward's men would have occupied his earldom, but he intended to retake it, gathering more men and the much-needed revenues from his vassals with which to pay his debt to the MacRuaries. The Irish, meanwhile, would make their way north from Galloway, scouring the west of enemy forces before joining him in Turnberry, the prelude to a larger campaign, which he would lead east against his English and Scottish foes.

Alexander finished his solemn retelling of the birth of Christ to a muttering of amens.

In the quiet that followed, James Douglas lifted his cup. 'Blessings

upon those beyond our circle.' The young man met Robert's gaze, his
eyes glittering in the firelight. 'To the missing and the fallen.'

As Robert raised his goblet his men followed suit, among them
Edward and Thomas, Cormac, Gilbert, Malcolm of Lennox, Neil
Campbell and David of Atholl. When they were done drinking they
lapsed into silence, staring into the flames, each man thinking of those
they had lost and those they had left behind.

The spell of silence was broken when Nes got up to gather more
firewood. As low-murmured conversations started up again, Robert
rose. Leaving Edward to preside over the gathering, he climbed the
crumbling steps to the battlements, his mind crowding with thoughts
of his daughter and the rest of his family. He couldn't regret his decision to divide the company back at St Fillan's, for the women and
children would have suffered on this rock, dogged by cold and hunger,
but neither had he been able to dispel the gnawing concern for their
safety. Where were his wife and daughter this Christ Mass? Holed up
in Kildrummy, or elsewhere? He tried to conjure an image of Marjorie
sitting by a fire, eating gingerbread and drinking spiced wine, but the
vision faded quickly in the face of his fears.

Away from the fire the night air was glacial. Robert's breath
steamed as he made his way around the walkway to where the walls
fell sheer to the shore. Far below, waves dashed themselves against the
rocks, booming as they rumbled on into caves in the cliffs. Here, in
the ruins of this sea-girt fortress, his men had made a home, finding
shelter within its walls and encouragement in the promises of support
from Islay and Antrim. To him, however, it remained a place of exile.
Across the race, the waters of which glimmered like quicksilver in the
moonlight, the cliffs of Kintyre rose from the sea, blacker than the
star-studded sky. Only twelve miles away, his kingdom had never
seemed so far.

Robert leaned on the battlements, watching the waves rush
towards the cliffs, trailing skirts of foam. This place reminded him so
much of Turnberry. As a boy he would stand on those battlements and
lean out, arms stretched, until it felt as though he were in the sky,
wheeling above the salt spume with the gulls and cormorants.

Turnberry. The place where he was born, thirty-three years ago,
pulled into the world by Affraig's hands on a night when Mars smouldered like a coal in the heavens. It was there that he learned of the
death of King Alexander and watched his grandfather make his claim

to the throne; where he witnessed the births of his brothers and sisters, delighted in his mother's laughter and dwindled in his father's bitter silence. Turnberry: where he learned to fight and to ride, and waited one endless summer for the men to return from their war against John Balliol in Galloway. His leaving of its walls had heralded the ending of his childhood and his march towards manhood, which began in the hall of his grandfather at Lochmaben and took him to the daunting majesty of King Edward's court.

In the Knights of the Dragon he had been seduced by prophecy and power, finding new purpose among England's elite. On the road to war in Wales he was promised fortune and glory, only to discover that the promise was soaked in the blood of nations. Years later, it was to Turnberry that he came home a man, disillusioned by Edward's desire to unite Britain under one crown, sickened by his father creeping on his belly to beg the king for a throne, and riddled with guilt for his part in the theft of the Stone of Destiny. In defiance of the king and his father, making good on the oath sworn to his grandfather in Lochmaben, he had sought out Affraig and there, in her house in the woods, had watched her weave him a crown out of heather, wormwood and broom.

And what is your destiny?

To be King of Scotland.

He had felt the ghosts of his ancestors gathering around him in the shadows, their will working within him, the voice of his grandfather reminding him that the blood of kings flowed in his veins. That same night he had tossed the scarlet shield with its golden dragon from Turnberry's battlements and watched it disappear beneath the waves, before telling his family and followers that he would be their king.

Everything had seemed so clear – the road wide open before him. He hadn't foreseen the twists and turns that had followed: the rough politics of William Wallace's Forest court where he was plotted against by those who still supported John Balliol, the relentless campaigns of the English, the horror of Falkirk and, always, his rivalry with John Comyn, heating like a slow, inevitable fire. Sailing to Ireland to keep the Staff of Malachy from Edward's hands and deny his ambition to fulfil Merlin's prophecy, he found himself hunted by an assassin who turned out to be the last man to have seen King Alexander alive. Robert had survived the crossbow bolt only to be struck a greater blow in the rumour of Balliol's return to the throne.

It had been the bitterest of pills to swallow; his submission to Edward in Westminster Abbey, with the staff in his hands and his darkening suspicion that the king may have been involved in King Alexander's death. For two years he bided his time in Edward's court, hated and mistrusted, forced to lie to those he loved and spill the blood of his countrymen to prove his loyalty. His final move towards the throne, the result of months of careful plotting, had been ruined by John Comyn's betrayal, after which the tumbling of stones had become an avalanche: Wallace's execution, the flight from England, Edward's declaration of war, the murder at Dumfries and his swift coronation.

Now, here he stood, with a gulf much greater than twelve miles of water between him and his kingdom. Exiled by his people and excommunicated by the pope, what was he but king of a windswept rock with rags on his body and two hundred outlaws for an army? Robert clenched his fists on the battlements as he thought of the men in the glens of Antrim and out in the Isles gathering under his name. They would be a bridge to his country and the route back to his throne.

It was then that he saw the boat.

The vessel was gliding slowly towards the shore, carving a broad wake through the moon-washed waters. Like all West Highland galleys, the birlinn had a long, curved prow; an echo of the dragon-stemmed ships of the Norsemen. Robert tracked the boat's trajectory to the beach where the vessels that had borne them from Dunaverty were moored. Quickly, he made his way back down the crumbling steps to the courtyard.

As he entered the pool of firelight, his men, seeing his expression, faltered in their conversation. The festive atmosphere vanished as he told them about the boat. Men set down wine and drew weapons. The fire was doused. Ordering some men to man the battlements and watch for other ships, Robert led the rest out of the castle.

They moved as ghosts in the moonlight, making their way down the rocky path to the shore. The birlinn had almost reached the shallows, nearing the pools where seals played. The splash of oars could be heard. On the beach, Robert motioned for his men to spread out. They did so, crouching behind rocks or pressing themselves against seaweed-draped boulders. After a time came voices and the sound of the galley grinding ashore. Robert risked a glance to see twenty figures leaping on to the beach. He nodded to Malcolm of Lennox and Gilbert de la Hay, hunkered down beside him, then emerged from his hiding place, sword drawn.

'State your business!'

The figures at the boat started round at Robert's harsh call. Seeing the host of armed men appearing, a few reached for their weapons.

One, taller than the others with a shaggy cloak that looked like a bearskin, raised a hand to stay them. 'My lord king?' His Gaelic was broad and deep, his tone wary, but self-assured.

Robert didn't recognise it, but Thomas did. He grinned, teeth flashing in the moonlight. 'It's Lord Angus, brother.'

'Is that Sir Thomas?' Angus MacDonald strode up the beach, pebbles clattering under his feet. He was followed by his men.

As the Lord of Islay came closer, his features became clearer. Robert was struck by a memory of a young man with startlingly blue eyes passing him a spoon at his father's table in Turnberry. He had been a boy then and Angus a squire in his father's company, but there was something familiar in the lord's strong-boned face. Robert held out his hand. 'Well met, Sir Angus,' he said, unable to conceal his surprise.

'My lord.' Angus took his hand, his grip tight. He bowed, then raised his eyes to Robert. 'Forgive my abruptness, but I must come straight to the matter that brings me here.'

Robert felt his surprise turn to apprehension. 'Please do so.'

'Lachlan MacRuarie left my company two months ago to begin building a fleet of ships in honour of your request. I have now received word that he wants his payment doubled.'

Robert said nothing. Behind him, he heard Neil Campbell curse.

'He wants it now, my lord,' Angus continued gravely, 'before he gives you the boats and the men. May God strike him down, but the son of a bitch says he'll sell his galleys to the English if you refuse.'

Lochmaben, Scotland, 1307 AD

Humphrey de Bohun woke to the screaming of gulls. The pillow was damp against his face and his skin felt clammy, prickling under the coarseness of the sheet. The fever seemed to have burned its way out of his skin during the night, but his head still pounded like a tight drum when he pushed himself upright. He sat on the edge of the bed, letting the intensity of the pain subside.

The debilitating sickness had swept through the army during the last weeks of the siege against Dunaverty Castle, when autumn winds and driving rain had given way to leaden December skies that augured snow, already lacing the hills of Arran, visible across the Firth of Clyde. When the first fall came to Kintyre it fell as a mantle, covering the world in white. Each frozen dawn, the men had to scrape snow and ice from the frames of the siege engines. Almost three months battering the castle, with the weather battering them in return, and what did they have to show for it?

Humphrey crossed the sparse chamber to the table by the window, the bare boards hard under his feet. He had noticed a few of the timbers were blackened, perhaps salvaged from the fire five years ago when the Scots, led by John Comyn, had attacked and most of King Edward's new fortress at Lochmaben had gone up in smoke. He remembered that night now with a different kind of loss. This was yet another place tinged with the memory of Bess. She had kissed him on the battlements and spoke of her desire for the war to be ended, just before the arrows had come flaming out of the darkness. If only her body could be as a fortress, resurrected from ashes and dust.

Rebuilt, using more material from the nearby motte and bailey castle that once belonged to Robert's grandfather, the fort had fallen to Bruce early last year, following the uprising at Dumfries. Now, it was back in English hands, along with most of the kingdom, the Scots turning from the rebel king in their hundreds to lay swords and pledges of loyalty at Edward's feet. Yet, still, the man himself evaded them.

When the garrison at Dunaverty capitulated to the English and Scots forces under Prince Edward and John of Menteith, Robert Bruce was nowhere to be found. Humphrey had ordered the castle searched from top to bottom, three times, without success. Neither was there any sign of the Staff of Malachy or the *Last Prophecy*, apparently missing from its vessel. Infuriated by the rapidly souring victory, he had his men interrogate the garrison in an attempt to discover where Bruce had gone, but either none of them knew, or else they were all playing the same game, for each had offered up a different location. Some said he had never been there, others that he'd sailed to Ireland or Orkney, or some remote Outer Isle. One man even thoughtfully suggested Norway, with a mocking glimmer in his eyes that had angered Humphrey beyond belief. Whatever the truth, the rebel was in the wind.

Instructing John of Menteith to remain and guard the castle, Humphrey and Prince Edward crossed the firth to Carrick, bearing the prisoners and the bad tidings. After a brief stay in Turnberry, in the command of Henry Percy, where Humphrey sent word to John MacDougall to maintain his patrols along the west coast, the company had wound their way south through the snow-covered wilds of Galloway, heading for the border.

Humphrey planted his hands on the table, either side of a silver platter. On the plate was a remedy his squire, Hugh, had procured from the prince's physician. He stared at the thing – a ball, about the size of a sheep's eye, covered in a paste that bound its ingredients together and, according to the physician, made it easier to swallow. Humphrey felt his inflamed throat tighten in protest just looking at it. Sweeping aside the curtain, he winced at the flare of sunlight, a surprise after all these weeks of grey. The sky was the colour of lapis lazuli, as blue as the Virgin's robes. A flock of gulls wheeled over the loch, come inland from the frozen marshes of the Solway Firth to find food. The window looked out over the courtyard, which was crowded with carts and horses. Grooms and porters were making preparations for their departure. Humphrey hoped to reach Lanercost by tonight. The sooner he told the king of Bruce's disappearance and the next course of action was decided the better.

Peering into the jug beside the platter, he saw the wine was as dark as blood. His servant had forgotten to water it down. Humphrey turned to the door, meaning to call for the man, then stopped and looked back at it. His head throbbed and his throat burned.

Dear God, would this struggle never end? He wanted Bruce in his custody – not some ghost in the heather that slipped through his fingers. It had been so many months since anyone had seen him Humphrey had started to wonder if Robert might even be dead. Maybe he would never get his chance to look the man in the eye. Maybe he would never get his answers – answers to questions that had since begun to breed in dark corners of his mind, spawned by Aymer's revelation that the empty prophecy box had been found on Niall, a vital fact King Edward had kept from him, for what reason or purpose he could not fathom.

Humphrey reached for the jug of wine, then drew back at a knock on the door.

It opened and Thomas, Earl of Lancaster and nephew to the king, entered. The young man looked furious. 'My cousin has gone.'

'Gone?'

'Hunting, so my grooms tell me. He left just after matins with twenty of his men.'

Humphrey's frustration swelled. Now, they wouldn't make Lanercost until tomorrow – yet another day for Robert to be free.

Thomas closed the door behind him. 'How long, Humphrey, will we let this continue?'

'I will speak to the prince when he returns. Impress upon him the carelessness of his actions.' Humphrey kept his voice calm, stifling his own ire. Thomas had become increasingly vocal in his waning opinion of the prince. It wasn't a good time, with Edward ill, to have his son and nephew at odds with one another. He needed to play the advocate. 'He is still young, Thomas. We must forgive him some mistakes.'

'Young? At twenty-two years? At sixteen I was fighting in Wales. At seventeen my uncle was commanding an army against Llywelyn ap Gruffudd! Hunting, God damn it, when the king lies sick in England waiting for our return? When our enemy remains at large and our vision for a kingdom united hangs in the balance?' Thomas stalked about the chamber, his whole body rigid with pent-up feeling. As he passed through a slant of sunlight his eyes, pale grey like the king's, flashed. 'Neither his youth nor his carelessness are the issue here. It isn't my cousin's actions that trouble me, so much as the company he keeps. You've seen as well as me the influence that knave exerts over him.'

Humphrey knew Thomas meant Piers Gaveston. The young earl had never liked the Gascon and had made his antipathy plainer of late. Thomas wasn't the only one. Many barons abhorred the way Piers lorded it over the rest of the court, acting, some said, as if it were he who was heir to the throne. Humphrey had little love for the arrogant knight, but he sensed that the resentment of some was fuelled more by jealousy, for not only did Piers have the ear of the future king, he was also one of the most accomplished fighters in their circle. For those reasons, if nothing else, the Gascon had garnered many enemies.

Thomas scowled as he read Humphrey's face. 'This isn't mere rivalry, or gossip-mongering, Humphrey. Their friendship is – unnatural.' His expression changed, his anger shifting to uncertainty. He stared at the floorboards, appearing to be struggling with some dilemma. Finally, he raised his head. 'Two years ago, at Burstwick Manor, the prince led a hunt while the king convalesced. Do you remember?'

Humphrey's jaw pulsed. How in God's name could he forget? Bess had died at that manor. Thomas went on, not seeming to notice his stiffness.

'I had tracked the boar to a glade where it was hiding. My cousin and Piers had got there first, but they hadn't seen the quarry, or me.' Thomas's brow furrowed. 'I saw them kiss. Not the kiss of brothers. They kissed as man and woman.'

Humphrey didn't speak for a moment, as he took this in. 'Did you confront them?'

'In truth, I was too shocked. I said nothing, hoping it was a moment's madness – the thrill of the hunt causing their passions to run wild. But I have seen signs since that tell me otherwise.' Thomas paused. 'Edward will take the throne of our kingdom, soon if my uncle's health continues to deteriorate. Something must be done, before his authority becomes absolute. I believe I should speak to the king on our return to Lanercost – tell him what I saw.'

'No,' said Humphrey quickly. 'As you say, the king is frail. Such a revelation will only weaken him further.' He paused, trying to think through the throbbing in his head, increased by Thomas's disclosure. 'I will speak to the prince and counsel him to take responsibility for his conduct. He has heeded me in the past. On our return, I will advise the king to bring forward the prince's impending marriage to Isabella of France. Edward wanted to wait until Scotland was fully under his control, but I can suggest the wedding would be better served sooner rather than later, especially as the king is ailing.'

Thomas pressed his lips together. 'Just remember, Humphrey, we both have a duty to defend the realm against all dangers, without and within.'

18

The Inner Hebrides, Scotland, 1307 AD

The galley ploughed through the waves, creaking with every upward surge and downward plunge. A fist of purple cloud, looming over the distant peaks of Argyll, was spreading dark fingers westwards.

'Start heading in,' Angus called to his men.

The crew of the birlinn moved into action at their lord's command, tacking into the wind. Ropes sawed through iron rings on the galley's sides as they heaved in the slack. The mainsail flapped wildly until the ropes were drawn taut again, then it ballooned once more. The man at the stern shifted the rudder, the vessel pitching to the opposite side. Away to starboard, the monstrous finned back of a whale arched out of the water and disappeared.

Robert stared at the Isle of Muck, now directly ahead. All around, other islands rose from the rolling expanse of water, some near, some far; dark towers of rock that thrust from the sea, or long strips of land barely breaking the surface. Out here in the Western Isles, water ruled all. During the voyage from Rathlin, Robert had come to understand how Somerled and the Norsemen had held sway over this sea kingdom for so long. The ocean was power: lifeblood and life taker, a road for armies, a route of escape and an endless larder. He who controlled it could control the west coast of Scotland. The understanding made him even more determined to get what he had come here for.

A gust of wind snatched his cloak from around his shoulders. It couldn't be much past nones, but already the day had gone, extinguished like a candle on the chill breath of dusk. The faint warmth he'd felt in the sun had vanished. As he drew his cloak tighter, his eyes caught on the red lion on his surcoat. There was a tear in the cloth that went straight through the beast's head. It provoked a thought of John Balliol at Montrose, the royal arms ripped from his tabard by Edward's knights. Toom tabard, they had called him. King nobody.

Robert felt his brother shift beside him, turning to Angus MacDonald who was seated behind them on one of the benches, his shaggy black cloak augmenting his broad form.

'How long till we make land?'

The Lord of Islay squinted at the island. 'An hour if this wind keeps up, Sir Edward.' He looked to the mainland, where the dark clouds over Argyll were stretching towards them. 'But the same wind will bring that weather our way.'

Robert followed the lord's gaze to the storm-bruised eastern sky. So far on their journey, skirting the Inner Isles, they had been blessed with clement days. The men who had accompanied him from Rathlin – Edward, Nes, David and Malcolm, along with an escort of knights – had been relieved, well aware of the Northern Ocean's reputation for violence, but Angus and the crew had been less grateful. Robert, noting their watchfulness as they passed Islay and sailed north through the narrowing channel between Mull, Coll and Tiree, realised the fair weather, while making for a gentle voyage, also made them more visible to John MacDougall's patrols.

Fortunately, Angus's crew knew these waters better than they knew their own wives – the hidden coves and sheltering rocks, the shifts of the tides – and although they spotted numerous vessels flying the colours of Argyll near Jura, their enemy had not spied them. Now, sailing out of the channel into open water, they were leaving the bounds of the MacDougalls and entering the vast, remote territory of the lords of Garmoran.

'We'll be safe on Muck, Sir Angus?' Malcolm of Lennox had to raise his voice above the sail, which was snapping in the rising wind.

The vessel lurched as a wave rolled them from the side. The crew, even those standing, moved easily with the motion, but one of Lennox's knights was only saved from being pitched overboard by grabbing hold of the mast. Nes gripped the bench he was sitting on, eyes wide.

'The isle is owned by the monks of Iona,' Angus told the earl. 'We'll find sanctuary there for tonight at least. If the wind allows we'll strike for Barra at first light. The weather is on the turn and with the changing tide . . . Well, if we don't attempt the crossing we could be stranded here for weeks.' Angus glanced at Robert to check his agreement.

Robert nodded. The sooner they reached Barra the better.

Before leaving Rathlin, he had sent Thomas, Alexander and Cormac to Antrim as planned, to order the assault on Galloway. Neil Campbell, Gilbert de la Hay and James Douglas had meanwhile sailed to Arran with the rest of his men to establish a staging ground for the invasion of Carrick, James vowing to send a message to the high steward's lands in the hope his uncle would receive it and raise his vassals for the return of their king. But all Robert's plans, laid these past months on Rathlin, now hung in the balance with the word of just one man. If Lachlan MacRuarie switched sides and the galleys and men Robert so desperately needed for his attack on the mainland were given over to his enemies, all would be lost. So here he was, out on these treacherous seas, making his way to the Outer Isles to persuade the duplicitous bastard to make good on his pledge.

The thought that a mercenary could decide his fate, after all he and his men had suffered these past six months, had lit a righteous fire inside him. He might be exiled, a hunted man, but he was still king and Lachlan MacRuarie and his freebooting brood would obey his command, or suffer the consequences. Robert was determined, whatever happened, that he would be leaving Barra at the head of a fleet, or else with the head of the man who had dared to defy him. He was going home to wrest his kingdom from the hands of his enemies and God help anyone who stood in his way.

The galley groaned as it crested the white-capped swell. Now they were out of the shelter of the channel the waves rose to meet them like hills, lifting them up and casting them down. Darkness raced to overtake them on a black chariot of cloud. Great curtains of rain had obscured the mainland and lightning whipped the sky over the mountains. A wave broke hard over the prow, lashing Robert with spray.

'Take my place, my lord,' called Angus, moving to allow him to sit on his bench.

Robert and Edward staggered from the prow. The wind was moaning.

'Just like riding a horse,' Edward shouted as they sat heavily on the bench, but his grin turned into a grimace as they smashed into another wave.

The crew worked in silence, white-knuckled as they fought to keep the boat on course, concentration tightening their faces, just visible in the deepening gloom. Robert's men had crowded together on the benches, holding on to their packs. Nes was praying. One of Malcolm of Lennox's knights twisted away to vomit over the side. Rain engulfed them, hammering on the deck and needling the water. The galley climbed steadily up the flank of a wave, then rushed down the other side, slamming into the water as if it were a wall. Robert grabbed hold of the side, feeling his body threaten to leave the bench. Salt water dashed him, splinteringly cold. He wiped his eyes and focused on the island, the outline of which was disappearing in sheets of rain.

'How much longer?' he shouted to Angus, who was clutching the stem of the prow.

The lord turned to answer, but halted, his brow furrowing. As Angus pushed his way past them to grip the mast, Robert followed his intent gaze. For a moment he saw nothing but the rolling darkness. Then, as they crested another wave, he caught sight of a huge shape, some distance behind. It was suspended briefly on the side of a wave, before disappearing behind another. Shock jolted through him with the thought that it was some enormous creature, then, as the shape reappeared, he realised it was three galleys lashed together in a row to form one great vessel. With black sails billowing, the three-headed ship was coming straight at them.

'*MacDougalls!*' yelled Angus.

'Christ!' hissed Edward.

As Angus barked orders, the crew struggled against the pelting rain to let out more of the mainsail.

'What can we do?' Robert shouted.

'We'll try and outrun them!' Angus bellowed back. 'They have more power with three sails, but they're heavier in the water.' He lurched down the deck to the prow again, checking their position.

Robert blinked rain from his eyes, his gaze on the pursuing vessels. 'Why bind them together?'

'Makes a good fighting platform, my lord,' one of the crew responded.

There were faint voices on the wind. Robert caught the word *halt*, repeated several times. The triple-vessel reared up behind them. It was gaining. Their own mainsail was bulging with wind, straining against its ropes. There were several ominous creaks and groans.

'Sir!' cried one of the crew. 'The wind is too strong! We'll lose the mast!'

Angus cursed. 'Pull her in, Patrick!' he hollered. 'Just a little!'

As Patrick was fighting his way to the ropes he suddenly pitched overboard. Robert pushed himself from the bench, slamming into the side as they careened down another wave. A second later, David of Atholl was there with him. Steadying themselves, they leaned over and fished for the man. After a few attempts, Robert snatched a fistful of cloak. Angus was roaring at the other crewmen to pull in the sail. With David's help and the aid of a timely wave that lifted the man almost level with the side, Robert heaved Patrick back into the boat. As the man slid on to the deck with a wash of icy water and lay unmoving, Robert saw an arrow protruding from his back.

'*Down! Get down!*'

Even as the shout left his mouth and he was shoving David of Atholl to the deck, more barbs shot out of the darkness. Most stabbed into the waves, but one struck the shoulder of one of Malcolm's men, who collapsed with a cry. The others, realising the danger, were throwing themselves down. Robert, hunkered on the deck, risked a glance over the side to see the enemy vessels were nearly on them. Angus lunged for the ropes as a fierce gust of wind stretched the sail. They were listing dangerously, the vessel threatening to capsize with the strength of the squall. It was taking two men just to hold the rudder.

Robert, seeing Angus alone, fighting to pull in the sail, struggled to his feet. He swayed sickeningly, skidding on the slippery deck as he tried to reach him. There was a mighty crack as the mast broke in two. The top half came crashing towards Robert in a tangle of ropes and cloth. He raised his arms to protect his head. As he did so, the galley lurched violently and he was lifted free from the rolling deck. For a moment, he was flying, weightless. Then, he struck the water.

The shock slammed him like a fist. His head went under the rushing darkness, the cold carving through him like knives. For a moment, he wasn't sure which way was up and which was down and he began to panic, twisting and flailing. A wave turned him, then spat him to the surface. He came up choking salt water. He glimpsed the galley

— a mess of ropes and sail — his brother and Nes shouting, arms outstretched towards him, before they all disappeared down the side of a wave.

Robert felt himself carried under, caught up in his cloak. He tore desperately at the brooch, ripping the garment away. He was still too heavy, his body wanting to sink beneath the rain-peppered surface. His sword. He still had his broadsword attached to his belt. Thrusting his head above the water, gulping air, he took hold of the hilt. Something stopped him pulling it free. As he kicked and thrashed, the weight of the forty-two-inch blade around his waist, all he could think of was James Stewart handing him the weapon on the night of his enthronement. It was the last goddamned thing he had of his kingship.

He went under again, the cold freezing his brain. When he broke the surface, he heard more shouts. Fear stabbed in through the numbness as he realised he had been carried some distance from the boat. He glimpsed it again on the ridge of a wave. The MacDougalls' vessels were almost upon it. It looked as though they were going to ram it. Robert yelled in the darkness, overcome by helpless rage. It couldn't end here, like this, the pitiless ocean stripping away the last of his authority, his possessions, his life. The weight of the sword was dragging him down. He had to let go. His legs and arms weren't working any more. It was as if his body were turning to ice, solidifying.

Just let go.

Buoyed up for one last moment on the crest of a wave, he saw six dark shapes with glowing yellow eyes bearing down on him. At his cry, water flooded his mouth and poured down his throat. As the sea closed over his head, he had the faint thought that they weren't monsters, but galleys with lanterns on their sides, then the thought slipped away and he was sinking into the black.

19

Lanercost Priory, England, 1307 AD

Prince Edward stared out of the window, across the priory's snow-clad grounds towards his father's lodgings. The timber house, construction of which had begun last autumn, was complete and a separate two-storey building was now being erected behind it for the queen, who had joined her husband on the northern frontier. As Edward's gaze lingered on the structure, which squatted by Lanercost's magnificent church like an ugly child beside a tall, graceful parent, he felt its windows stare back at him, filled with darkness. He thought of the man inside, pent up all these months with his leeches and his fury.

A boy's shout caught his attention. Looking past the porters, still busy unloading gear from the wagons, the snows churned black by the arrival of his company that afternoon, the prince saw his half-brothers, Thomas and Edmund, racing one another towards the drifts banked up along the priory's wall. Following the snaking lines of their footprints, Edward saw two women walking in their wake. One was his stepmother, Queen Marguerite, her scarlet robe trailing like a sweep of blood through the snow. Sister of King Philippe and known as the Pearl of France by her people, Marguerite had been seventeen when she was married to his father in Canterbury. She had since blessed the sixty-seven-year-old king with three children. The third, born last year, was a girl named Eleanor. The prince had wondered what Marguerite thought of her child being named after the king's first wife, his mother, whose beloved ghost she could never live up to.

Edward's gaze lingered on the queen. Despite the fact Marguerite was the same age as himself he had always found her motherly and protective. Gentle in manner, she had often acted as a balm to the king's temper. He pondered speaking to her first to gauge his father's mood, perhaps even asking her to petition the king on his behalf? The moment he thought it he felt like a coward and berated himself bitterly.

The door opened, making him start. Piers entered. The knight had already changed out of his travelling clothes and had somehow found time to sit with his barber, for his handsome face was clean-shaven, his black hair swept back with scented oil. Edward caught a waft of the sweet fragrance as Piers closed the door. At once he felt terribly shabby, his cloak soiled with horse sweat, boots mud-caked and his chin coarse with stubble.

Piers threw a disparaging glance around the chamber, which was located in part of the monks' quarters. Chests and bags brought up by the porters were stacked against the walls. There was a narrow bed in one corner. 'These are your lodgings? My prince, you should have asked your father for his pavilion, since he is not using it.' When Edward didn't answer, Piers's dark eyes narrowed. 'You haven't seen him yet, have you?'

Edward turned back to the window. He felt Piers move up behind him.

'You're having second thoughts?'

'No,' Edward said sharply. 'I'm . . .' He trailed off, not wanting to tell Piers the real reason for his reluctance. 'Sir Humphrey has been to see him already.'

'All the more reason you should go to him now. You must give him your version of events.' Piers put a hand on Edward's shoulder, turning the prince to face him. 'Don't let Humphrey and the others take the credit for the fall of Dunaverty, then blame you for Bruce's disappearance. You know that is their way.'

Edward said nothing, but inwardly he disagreed. Whatever else he might say about Humphrey, the constable had always been a fair and honest man. Indeed, it was his honesty that was the issue for he was worried the earl would have told his father about his behaviour on campaign. Humphrey had spoken to him, gravely and at length, after the hunt at Lochmaben, which delayed their arrival at Lanercost. The earl told him it was time to stop acting like an errant youth and start behaving as the king he was destined to become.

Frivolous pursuits, Humphrey advised, must wait until he had reported to his father on the state of the war. The earl had no idea he had organised the hunt to avoid doing just that. Not only did Edward want to delay the admission to his father that he had failed to capture Robert Bruce, he also wanted to avoid, as long as possible, the promise he had made to Piers.

That evening, their last in Lochmaben, smarting from Humphrey's chastisement, Edward had drunk too much wine and neglected to rein in Piers, who told the silent barons only those who had joined the hunt could eat the flesh of the boar he had caught. Thomas of Lancaster had risen, tossing aside his plate and telling the men present he would rather eat air than linger any longer in the company of degenerates. The following morning the barons and the prince's household rode down to the border in separate companies, the atmosphere between them as frigid as the weather.

'In Lochmaben you promised you would petition your father.' Piers held Edward with his gaze. 'You gave me your word.'

Edward shrugged from his touch, his gaze fixing on the timber building across the priory's grounds. His mind filled with a memory of the grand feast after his knighting at Westminster, at which his father made him and all the young bloods present swear an oath over two golden swans, never to sleep in the same place twice, like Perceval on his Grail quest, until Robert Bruce and the Scots were defeated. 'God damn it, why do you all want so much of me! Will you never be satisfied?'

Piers's hand dropped away. There was silence. Edward steeled himself to it, refusing to relent. After a moment he heard a creak of boots.

'Forgive me.'

Hearing the voice come from the floor, Edward realised Piers had dropped to his knees. He turned.

Piers's head was bowed, strands of his black hair falling in front of his face. 'All I want is to serve you, my lord. If, by my actions, I have given any other impression it was done in ignorance and I beg your pardon for it.' He glanced up at the prince. 'I thought, with more authority – more influence in court – I could better support you.' Piers continued, his voice sharpening. 'I have seen how Thomas of Lancaster, your own cousin, belittles you and how Humphrey and others in your father's circle treat you as if you were a wayward child in need of disciplining rather than the king you will soon become. The reason I hoped you would petition your father on my behalf is so that I may stand as a loyal ally in the face of those who do not have your best interests at heart. Now I am a knight of your household, with little power except that which you have generously bestowed upon me. You have let me be your champion on the tournament ground. Let me be the same at court.'

Edward softened. Reaching down, he took Piers's hands and pulled the knight to his feet. 'I want that too.' His brow furrowed. 'But I fear my father's response.'

'As I have told you, the king will respect you if you stand before him as a man and tell him what you want. You've said yourself how much he abhors weakness.'

'I will go to him,' Edward said quietly.

Piers smiled. He put a gloved finger under Edward's chin and lifted it. 'Look him in the eye when you ask him.'

'Again, my lord king, I beg your forgiveness for not speaking out sooner.'

King Edward watched Thomas of Lancaster rise from bended knee and leave the chamber. When the doorward closed the door behind his nephew, the king sat back in his chair, the strength of his feelings flooding his weakened body with new life. He gripped the chair's carved arms, feeling an intense need to crush something. Thomas's words buzzed in his mind like angry bees, stinging him with poisonous images. The worst of it was that although he felt fury, revulsion and betrayal, he did not feel surprise. He had known this. Deep down, he had known it for years.

The war in Scotland, this war without end, had distracted him from all else. It wasn't just England that had suffered in his absence, bridges and roads falling into disrepair, towns taken over by thieves and racketeers, his people starving. His son, too, had fallen to ruin. He had thought, by sending him on campaign as a leader of men, that the damage could be reversed; that his son would be moulded by battle and bloodshed into the man who would continue his legacy when he was gone.

Edward closed his eyes, thinking of the children he had fathered – nineteen in total – and all those he had buried. He thought of serious little John, who had reached five years, and sweet smiling Henry who made it to six. Then there was Alfonso, dark like his beautiful Castilian mother, tall like him, a fine and fearless rider with a clear head on his young shoulders. Certain the boy would be his heir, he had poured all his ambition and expectation into him. Edward had been at Caernarfon, celebrating his conquest of Wales, when messengers had come from Westminster to tell him Alfonso was dead. His hopes had therefore turned to his one surviving son, his namesake, then a squalling infant in his nurse's arms.

The king opened his eyes and stared into the flames leaping in the brazier beside him. Was it that his seed had been weakened, diluted over the years? Animals, after all, produced runts at the end of a litter. But his son had never been a weakling, indeed he was the very image of him: long-limbed, athletic and handsome. What had caused such a hideous defect in his character? Piers. He had to be the cause – the root of the infection. Edward gripped the chair. God strike him down, he had invited the young man into his household, had raised him as his own.

There was a rap on the door. As the doorward pulled it open, the king saw his son filling the frame. The prince entered. Edward felt his heart begin to thump, images invoked by Thomas's revelation rising in his mind to torment him. His son, who looked as though he had just got off his horse, came forward, tracking mud across the rug.

'My lord king,' he murmured, bowing his head.

Edward realised his hands, white-knuckled on the chair's arms, were shaking, such was the intensity of his emotion. His son seemed not to notice.

'Dunaverty Castle fell to me, my lord, but I'm afraid I must tell you Robert Bruce was not to be found among the garrison.' The prince spoke in a rapid monotone, which the king recognised as one he slipped into when afraid. 'I sent word to John MacDougall to continue the search for him along the coast and—'

'Sir Humphrey gave me his report.'

The prince pressed his lips together. For a moment, he looked as though he might turn and walk from the room, then he blurted, 'My lord, I ask that you grant me permission to give the County of Ponthieu to Piers.'

For a long moment, the king did not speak. A log burst in the brazier, making the prince flinch.

Then, Edward was pushing himself from the chair and rushing at his son. Before the young man could move the king had seized him by the hair. Wrenching the prince's head down with both hands, Edward felt one of his nails break against his son's scalp. '*You bastard son of a bitch!*'

'*Father!*'

'You would give your lands away? You who never gained any? You would give them to *him*! God damn you! I'll die before I see you give away a single acre!'

'*Father! Please!*'

'Shut your mouth, you disgusting little worm. Crawl on your belly, you bastard!' Spittle flew from the king's mouth as he dragged his son down by his hair, forcing him to double over. 'Crawl like the worm you are!'

The prince grasped his father's wrists, trying to pull him off, but it only made Edward tighten his grip.

'*I should have drowned you at birth, you shit!*' As the king roared this, the full force of his fury came bursting up out of him, raw and relentless, causing him to pull at his son's hair in a frenzy, ripping hanks of it from his head.

At the prince's screams, the door flew open. Neither man saw the doorward framed there, stock-still with shock, before he turned and raced down the stairs.

'I know what you did!' Edward raged. 'Your cousin saw you in the woods with that whoreson! All these years with the devil in you! *By God, I'll beat him out!*' With that, the king brought his knee smashing up into his son's down-turned face.

There was a crack as the prince's nose broke. Blood flowed, splattering the rug and the king's robes. His son was yelling incoherently, but Edward refused to relinquish his hold, digging his fingers deeper into his scalp, breaking skin.

Pounding footsteps sounded on the stairs. The doorward reappeared with Humphrey de Bohun.

'My lord!'

The king didn't heed the earl's shout. He kicked his son above the knee, causing him to collapse. Now Edward let go, strands of blond hair falling from between his fingers as he swung his fist into his son's face. His jewelled ring ripped through the prince's lip as it struck. Pain lanced through the king's arm with the impact, but it only served to fuel his rage. He hadn't felt so alive, so *strong*, in an age. All these months lying impotent, racked with pain, close enough to Scotland to see its hills, yet unable even to rise from his bed. He punched out again, his fist slamming into his son's jaw. All these months praying that his men would return with Robert Bruce in irons and his conquest would at last be complete. Once again, they had failed him. Another vicious punch sent his son reeling to the floor. The young man wrapped his hands around his head to protect his face.

The king drew back his foot for a kick. His eyes caught the silver brooch on his son's travel-stained cloak, flashing in the firelight. Eleanor had given their son that brooch, years ago. He remembered her smile as she pinned it on him and the flush of love in the young boy's face. Looking down on the prince, bleeding, curled like an infant, Edward staggered back.

Humphrey de Bohun caught him. 'My lord.' He guided the king back to his chair.

Edward slumped in it. 'Get word to my cousin in France,' he breathed. 'My son is ready to wed Isabella.' The king wiped the sweat from his brow with a shaking hand. 'And I want Piers Gaveston banished from my kingdom.'

The Outer Hebrides, Scotland, 1307 AD

Lightning danced in the east as the storms continued to batter the distant isles of Muck, Canna and Rhum, but out here the air was still and the ocean rolled, huge and slow, under a lifeless sky. Ahead, a chain of islands threaded like a broken string of jewels.

Robert sat at the prow, the hood of the woollen cloak grazing his cheek. He smelled the sea trapped in the weave and something sweet: heather, or grass. He couldn't recall how he came to be wearing it. As he watched the Outer Isles grow larger with every sweep of the oars, he recalled the belief of some that these islands stood at the bounds of the world. As a youth he'd heard a different tale in his grandfather's hall – men speaking of the Norsemen who had found distant lands far beyond these isles. There were other stories, too, of the black empire of Gog and Magog that encircled the known borders of the earth; Satan's army, walled up behind gates of iron, ready to be loosed upon the world. The thought took him, as many had these past hours, straight to his daughter, who, years ago in Writtle, had been told by his drunken father that Gog and Magog would be coming for her as she hadn't eaten her meat. That night the terrified child had refused to sleep anywhere but in Robert and Elizabeth's bed.

The memory brought a fresh wave of torment twisting up through Robert's gut. It clogged his throat, a knotted lump of fury, horror and helplessness. He turned suddenly, wanting to order these men to steer the galley around and bear it south towards England. He would sail it himself if he had to, up the Thames, all the way to the Tower, where he would scale the white walls and free his daughter from the cage that vile bastard had locked her in.

Dear God, was it true? What the woman had told him?

Robert searched the deck, his eyes passing over the oarsmen on the benches and his comrades who sat apart from them in silence, as still as statues amid the activity of the crew. The woman stood tall among the men, easily marked by her hair, the colour of autumn leaves and winter hearths. She wore it bound up with plaited threads of golden silk, but the wind and rain had dragged much of it free. The shorter strands curled at her temples, stiff with salt. Her brown dress, girdled with a belt of gold rings, was thin and seeing her cheeks chapped pink with cold Robert wondered numbly why she wasn't wearing a cloak. Feeling the weight of the garment around his shoulders, he now remembered her placing it there.

The woman looked round, locking eyes with him briefly, before turning back to her crew. Those eyes were the first thing he'd seen when her men had hauled him from the sea, frozen to the marrow and retching salt water. Pale green, almost liquid in the lantern light, they had widened when the woman caught sight of the red lion on his surcoat.

'It is the king,' he had heard her say, her Gaelic broad and pure. 'It is my brother.'

After that everything was just scattered images and sounds. He remembered other men being pulled from the sea, their broken birlinn adrift on a wave lit by the flare of lightning, the MacDougalls' triple galley retreating, outnumbered, the faint cries of those lost in the rushing dark and the shouts of the crew of the six vessels who had come to their aid, caught in the howling maw of the storm. Soon, the chill in his body had seeped into his mind, taking him down into an icy well of blackness, from which he had only emerged many hours later.

Part of him wished he had stayed in that place of nothingness. No thoughts. No dreaming. No knowledge. If he had known what he would wake to find he never would have surfaced.

It was his brother he had seen first when he opened his eyes. Edward had been sitting beside him on the damp deck, cast in a pallid dawn. As he stirred, his brother turned to him. Robert had never seen such an expression on his face. It was a look of utter despair. Struggling to sit, disorientated, he had seen Angus MacDonald talking to a tall woman with auburn hair and the memory of their wrecked ship had returned.

Seeing him awake, the woman had crossed the crowded deck, moving gracefully with the motion. Bowing her head briefly, she had crouched beside him and introduced herself as Christiana MacRuarie, Lady of Garmoran. The name had been a surprise. Although he'd not met her before, Robert knew the woman was his sister-in-law by his first marriage to Isobel, daughter of the Earl of Mar. Christiana, the only legitimate child of the Lord of Garmoran, had been wed to one of Mar's sons, but more than this he did not know, the woman being only a name to him; a name synonymous with the brutal reputation of her half-brothers, Lachlan and Ruarie.

'Are you hurt, my lord?' Her voice had been all brisk authority.

Her tone had taken him aback before the question itself and the knowledge of who she was had sparked an anger that burned away the last of his confusion. 'Hurt?' He had gestured at Angus MacDonald and Malcolm of Lennox, both of whom had men missing. 'Will you ask the same of those who drowned, my lady?'

She had narrowed her green eyes, unsure of his meaning.

'If not for your brother my men and I would not have been out here.' Robert had raised his voice, not caring that the crew, MacRuarie's men no doubt, were looking over. 'Demanding I double his fee or he'll sell his fleet to the English? By his insolence and greed I lost good men last night. We would have all been lost if not for . . .' If not for her, he had meant, but did not say.

Christiana had studied him in silence for a pause. 'I've been on the mainland, my lord, at my castle, Tioram. Until Lord Angus told me, I knew nothing of my brother's demands. I will speak to him of this. You can be sure.'

Robert had wanted to know how a mere woman, even a lady of standing, could possibly alter the ambitions of a predator like Lachlan, but he had fallen silent, seeing a look pass between Christiana and Edward. It was a look full of unspoken meaning. 'What is it? What aren't you telling me?' He had stared at his brother, searching his bleak expression, fear snaking a cold tendril around his heart. 'Edward?'

Christiana had begun to speak then, her Gaelic soft and low. She told him that she had been running supplies from her lands on the north-west coast out to the Isles. She had also been ferrying people, a steady stream of whom had been coming north over the past months, looking to escape the occupations of Carrick and Ayr, and the men of Argyll and Lorn who had sided with the English. Some of these people, she told him, had brought with them tidings. King Edward, they said, was once again in control of Scotland. Robert was gone, presumed dead by many. The rebellion was over and all those involved were being hunted down. Already, many had been captured by Aymer de Valence and others of the king's men. At the look that passed again between Christiana and Edward the tendril of fear around Robert's heart had become a gripping hand.

'My family?' he had managed to say.

John of Atholl, Christopher Seton, Isabel of Buchan, Margaret Randolph, Niall, Mary, Matilda, Elizabeth, Marjorie — these names and the horrors attached to them had come in a quiet stream from the woman, who had spoken unflinchingly, still meeting his eyes.

For some moments, Robert had not been able to take any of it in. He had looked over at his men, hoping to prove the insanity of her words, but in their desolate faces and David of Atholl's red-rimmed eyes he saw only truth. Yet, still, he had not been able to understand it. The news from Malcolm of Lennox on the banks of Loch Lomond — the arrest of Robert Wishart and William Lamberton, the imprisonment of his nephew, Thomas Randolph, the hanging of Simon Fraser — had been dire indeed, but it hadn't surprised him. But this? This made no sense. John and Christopher executed? Niall strung up for a mob in Berwick? Mary in a cage? His wife locked away?

My daughter . . . ?

At the thought of Marjorie, his child, caged like an animal in the Tower, a quake had begun deep in Robert's body, shuddering up through his chest. Then he knew it — the price of his ambition, his desire to be king. Then he knew it. The wheel had made its last turn, crushing him beneath its grinding weight. Unfastening her cloak, Christiana had shrugged it from her shoulders and placed it around his. Leaving him alone, she had instructed her crew and those of the five accompanying galleys to head for Barra, then just a dark line on the horizon.

Now, the island's rocky shores rose before them and the air was filled with the cries of gannets that plunged the waves like great white arrows. With Christiana's galley taking the lead, the oarsmen pulled the six birlinns through a narrow channel between Barra and a smaller adjacent island, where the beaches were as pale as sugar and the waters milky blue in the February dusk. Inching round to the west coast of the island, timbers creaking as the boats were lifted once more on the ocean's swell, they headed for a curve of sand, above which stood a chapel.

The light was fading fast by the time they made land, the crew leaping into the shallows to haul the vessels ashore, alongside several others. Robert smelled fish and the briny odour of rotting seaweed. Calls echoed as men appeared, heading down through the grasses of the machair to greet them. Some held torches, the flames pluming brightly against the darkening sky. Beyond, the swell of a great hill disappeared in shadow.

Taking the proffered hands of two crewmen, Christiana jumped lightly to the sand. Robert followed her, his muscles stiff with cold and inertia. Nes came next, clutching Robert's broadsword, saved from the sea. He stayed close to his lord, eyes fixed warily on the approaching men. Edward, Angus and Malcolm followed with David, who stood apart with his four surviving knights. The young man hadn't spoken a word since he learned of the execution of his father. His eyes were haunted.

Leaving her men to unload barrels of meat, sacks of grain and the few exhausted-looking refugees from the other galleys, Christiana strode up the seaweed- and debris-strewn shore to meet the men.

One at the head bowed. 'Welcome, my lady.'

'Thank you, Kerald.' Christiana glanced over the man's shoulder to the path he had come down by. 'Did the storm do much damage?'

'Nothing that cannot be mended.' Kerald nodded to Robert and the others. 'More come seeking sanctuary?'

Christiana's gaze fell on Robert. 'No, Kerald, he is our king.'

As the eyes of the company of men turned on him, Robert saw surprise, suspicion and hostility, but certainly nothing akin to respect or awe. He realised he looked scarcely like a king; standing there without weapon or armour, in soiled clothes and with Christiana's cloak still draped about his shoulders. Pride flashed through his grief and he came forward to meet them, shrugging off the cloak to reveal the red lion on his torn surcoat. His men came with him, Edward gripping his sword, Angus bristling at the frosty reception. After a pause, Kerald gave a slight nod.

Christiana broke the taut silence. 'Come, my lords,' she said, lead-ing the way up the beach towards the dunes. 'My village isn't far.'

Robert fell into step beside her, his men close behind him, followed by Kerald and the others, their torches spilling light across a sandy track that wound through the machair. A monolithic shadow loomed up. Robert thought it was a giant figure, until the flames revealed a weathered standing stone.

'A Viking's grave,' Christiana said at his side.

Glancing at her he saw for the first time how tall she was; almost face to face with him. He realised, too, that he was still holding her cloak and her hands, hitching up her skirts, were tinged blue with cold. 'My lady,' he said, passing her the garment.

She smiled and swung it round her shoulders, sighing gratefully as the warmth of the wool enveloped her.

Ahead a few stunted trees appeared, tracking the course of a burn that trickled down from a narrow glen in the shelter of the great hill. There was wood-smoke on the wind. Following the line of the burn, they came to a settlement, dominated by low stone houses inter-spersed with smaller dwellings, most of which were of timber with turf roofs. Several fire pits cast the buildings in a ruddy light.

There were scores of people here, sitting around the fires eating, or busy with errands: young women hauling buckets of water from the burn, children feeding goats in a paddock, men laying the last few sheaves of broom, weighted down with stone-strung nets, over gaps in roofs damaged by the storm. Many of them called a welcome to Christiana as she entered the settlement. Others appeared in doorways, peering curiously at the king and his companions. Surprised by the crowd, Robert thought of the refugees Christiana had been ferrying here from the mainland. He wondered at her generosity in feeding and sheltering so many strangers, given this rocky island in the middle of the Northern Ocean was clearly anything but a land of riches.

'Christiana.'

At the harsh voice, Robert saw a tall, wiry man emerge from one of the larger stone buildings. He wore a sky-blue cloak and was pale-skinned with long black hair. As he advanced, scanning the company, Robert realised the man had the same green eyes as Christiana, only his were darker and less welcoming. His expression was hard, his unsmiling mouth twisted by a scar. He was followed by several strapping men, a few of whom clutched goblets and bowls, evidently caught in the middle of a meal. One was short and stocky, his bald head criss-crossed with scars and an empty socket where one of his eyes should have been.

'Brothers,' greeted Christiana, her tone sharp.

The tall man's gaze fell on Robert, fixing on his surcoat. There was a flicker of surprise, then a glint of triumph, but before Robert could speak, Angus MacDonald pushed his way past, drawing his sword.

'Lachlan! I should strike you down where you stand!'

The men with Lachlan MacRuarie moved protectively in front of their captain. One tossed aside his goblet and drew a dirk from his belt. A couple of the watching women shooed children into the safety of their houses. The realisation that the man before him was the one he'd come here seeking made little impact on Robert. The war he had been so determined to resume now felt like a distant dream, surreal and intangible. He knew Lord Donough's galleys would be on their way to Galloway and that Neil Campbell and Gilbert de la Hay would have reached Arran, but he couldn't imagine having the strength to lead men into battle. All his power had been leached from him by Christiana's words.

Angus kept his sword trained on Lachlan, his blue eyes alight with fury. 'I lost three men last night! Their blood is on your hands.'

Lachlan pushed through the protective circle of his men to face the Lord of Islay. 'You know as well as me the perils of the sea. I do not rule her appetite.'

'It wasn't the storm, God damn you, it was the MacDougalls!'

Lachlan took this in with little reaction. 'Then you understand full well why I have raised my fee. My scouts tell me the western shores, from Galloway to Argyll, are crawling with ships. All looking for you, my lord.' His eyes flicked to Robert. 'To aid you has become a hazardous business. One for which a man must be properly compensated.'

Edward Bruce joined Angus, hand around the hilt of his sword.

'My lords,' said Christiana, moving in front of them, 'the hour grows late and you and your men need food and sleep.'

Angus, finding he now had his blade levelled at a woman, lowered it reluctantly.

'Our council can wait until tomorrow,' Christiana continued, 'along with any reparations.' She gave her half-brother a look that caused him to yield his ground, though not without a flash of anger in his eyes. 'Please sit,' she invited, gesturing Angus and the rest of Robert's company towards one of the fires. 'I'll have food brought. Kerald, have lodgings readied.' Her eyes came to rest on Robert. 'It won't be much fit for a king, my lord, but it is all I can offer. My lord?'

Robert didn't answer. Out of the growing crowd, come from their homes at the rumour the king had landed on their shores, stepped a woman, holding the hand of a girl. The woman had a gaunt face and dark hair that drifted in the breeze. He moved towards her, disbelieving, half expecting her to vanish, but she remained a solid presence, lit by the flames of a fire, the girl frowning up at her, revealing that one side of her face was ravaged by burns.

'Brigid?'

The woman inclined her head. 'My lord king.'

'Why are you here? How?'

'A story for another time, my lord.' A smile caught somewhere between gratitude and sadness played about Brigid's lips. 'I prayed you might come, before the end.'

She held out her free hand. Ignoring Christiana's questioning call and the astonished stares of his men, Robert took it. Feeling the strength in her grip a memory was awoken of the day when, as a boy, he had trailed her through the heather into the woods beyond Turnberry to that house in the shadow of the oak. As Brigid led him towards one of the timber huts, he knew who he would find inside.

Stranraer, Scotland, 1307 AD

In the darkness, the eighteen galleys glided through the mouth of the loch like a phalanx of black swans. The vessels were packed with men, come from the glens of Antrim at the summons of their lord. Almost seven hundred in total, their faces were cast in the spectral glow of thousands of stars, the light of which glimmered on the silvery mesh of mail coifs and the domes of basinets.

The hiss and drag of waves on the shingle became more persistent, the waters agitated as the galleys neared the sweep of beach. As the largest, a vessel of twenty-six oars, ground ashore, Cormac gripped the mast to steady himself. He winced at the grating sound as the other boats entered the shallows. Looking towards the loch's southern shore he could just make out the buildings of Stranraer.

'The wind is in our favour, son. They'll not hear us.'

Cormac looked round at the gruff voice to see his father standing beside him. The lord's face was in darkness, but Cormac caught the shimmer of his eyes.

Turning, Lord Donough signalled to his men. There were muffled thuds as the oars were stowed, followed by the splashing of feet as the men began jumping over the sides, gripping spears, swords and axes as they made their way up the beach. Cormac went to follow, but his father caught his arm.

'I think the dean might need waking.' Lord Donough nodded to the stern.

Cormac realised Alexander Bruce hadn't moved from his position despite the action going on around him. The dean's head was lowered, the bald dome of his tonsure catching the starlight. Cormac made his way down the length of the vessel, negotiating the sacks and barrels stowed between the benches. 'We're here,' he murmured, placing a hand on Alexander's shoulder. When the man didn't move, Cormac went to try again, then stopped, hearing the whispered words. Alexander, he realised, was praying. 'Have no fear, brother,' he reassured the man quietly. 'Stranraer is little more than a village. There is no need to pray for our souls. Not tonight at least.'

Alexander raised his head. 'I am praying for theirs.'

Cormac stared at him, piqued. 'The men of Stranraer are among those who sailed from these shores to raid the north of Ireland. Over the years my people have suffered greatly at their hands. None here is innocent. Save your prayers for those who deserve them.'

'The women and children here, who will suffer for the crimes committed by husbands and fathers, are they not worthy of mercy?' Alexander stood, pulling up the hood of his brown robes. 'Our capacity for it is what raises us above the beasts, Cormac.'

Cormac's jaw tightened. He had closed his mind to any such compunction on the crossing and refused to have it opened again. Stranraer was the key to Galloway. Taking it would unlock the door to their invasion, as well as keeping open their escape route to Ireland. Drawing his dirk from his belt, he thrust it at Alexander. 'Mercy can wait until we've won back your brother's kingdom.'

'Alex?'

At the voice, Cormac saw Thomas Bruce had appeared at the galley's side, wading through the shallows.

Thomas's face was taut beneath the rim of his helmet as he looked from his brother to Cormac. 'Let's go,' he urged.

Alexander stared at the blade in Cormac's outstretched hand. After a moment, he took it.

Grasping his axe, Cormac jumped over the side and strode through the water up the beach to where his father was waiting at the head of the gathering army. A few men who had hastened to relieve themselves on landing rejoined them quickly. Cormac felt a twinge in his bladder, but ignored it, knowing it wasn't need, but apprehension. He reached up to adjust his helm, feeling the tug on his scalp as his matted hair shifted inside the iron shell. Some said the cúlán could repel a sword-blow, but he wasn't going to take the chance.

Leaving two dozen men to secure the galleys, Lord Donough led the company along the shore towards the sleeping settlement. To the east, the land flattened into darkness. The raw wind carried the pungent stink of marshes. Ahead, beyond the cluster of buildings, hills rose black against the sky. It was almost dawn, but daylight would be a long time coming. Moving quickly, feet muffled by the sand, they neared the buildings on the outskirts of the settlement, most of which were barns and storehouses. There were fishing boats outside several, nets trailing over the sides. Wicker baskets for snaring crabs and lobsters were scattered about the place. The air was tainted with the acrid odour of decaying fish.

A wide street led into a cluster of houses beyond the barns, the spaces between which were filled with more boats, bakehouses and frozen midden heaps. The men stared about them as they made their way down the street, eyes darting across darkened doorways, alley mouths and shuttered windows. No firelight glowed in any of the houses. The only sounds came from the men themselves: the unavoidable tramping of footsteps, clinks of weapons against armour and the muted hiss of breath.

Directed by gestures from Donough, Thomas Bruce and the other leaders, the company spread out. They knew what to do, having been given their instructions on the crossing from Antrim. Nodding to his father, Cormac peeled away with three of his men. Reaching the door of a dwelling, he pressed himself up against the wood, keeping his eyes on his father, who remained by a well in the centre of the street, one hand raised. Alexander Bruce was at his side, the dirk held loosely in his grip. Donough let his hand fall. At the signal, the company began breaking their way into the houses, kicking down doors and hacking through shutters. The harsh sounds shocked away the night's silence, swelling to engulf the town as those who had ventured down alleys and into gardens were spurred to action by the war cries of their comrades.

Cormac shouldered his way through the door, bursting into the chamber beyond. He raised his axe, ready to strike at whoever might come rushing out of the shadows. His men fanned out around him. There was a scrape and a curse as one of them crashed into a table. Eyes adjusting to the gloom, Cormac saw cups and bowls on the table, along with a platter of salted herring and half a loaf of rye bread. The smell of fish was strong. In a hearth, a frail glow came from the ashes of a dying fire. Cormac strode to the wicker screen that divided the chamber. He pulled it roughly aside to reveal a low bed with a cradle beside it. Both were empty. There was a small window beyond, the shutters open into darkness, through which came the stench of the marshes.

Cormac turned away, aggravated, his energy for the fight dampened by the absence of an enemy. Pushing past his comrades to the door, he realised he wasn't the only one. Sounds of crashing and banging continued as more houses were broken into, but many men were emerging into the streets, weapons clean of blood and faces filled with confusion. Cormac saw Thomas Bruce turning in a circle, eyes sweeping the streets, his broadsword hefted expectantly. Cormac began to make his way to his father, standing by the well, a frown knotting his brow. 'They must have seen us coming.'

Suddenly, one of the men with Donough collapsed with a cry, clutching at his arm. Cormac halted, seeing the arrow stuck fast in the man's shoulder. As other barbs stabbed out of the darkness, thumping into doors or clattering off walls, he threw himself down, yelling a warning. Screams sounded as more men were hit. Lord Donough pulled Alexander down behind the stone rim of the well. An arrow lanced past, missing them by inches. Beneath his palms, Cormac felt a tremble in the earth. Hoof-beats. As an arrow skidded along the ground beside him he picked himself up and lunged for the house he'd just left. One of his men emerged from the doorway, alerted by the cries. He took an arrow in the face and twisted back. Cormac threw himself over the body of his comrade into the shelter of the interior.

The hoof-beats were unmistakable now, a mad thudding that beat on the air. Harsh shouts were joined by the clash of weapons. Risking a glance around the door, Cormac saw scores of riders surging through the streets. Some of the horsemen carried torches, the flames of which turned night to amber day. The white lion of Galloway was daubed on blue shields. He saw their swords carving red slashes through the heads and backs of his scattering countrymen. Others held their ground and tried to fight, but separated from their comrades they stood little chance against the horsemen. The arrows ceased to fly, but foot soldiers, all marked with the white lion, came charging in the wake of the riders. Seeing his father trapped against the well, cut off from his men, Cormac gripped his axe haft in his sweat-soaked palm. With a roar, he pitched himself into the tide of men.

Barra, Scotland, 1307 AD

Robert leaned his head against the wall, the timber damp beneath his skull. Under the door a crack of light was turning the threads of straw that covered the ground to gold. It was dawn, he realised. His eyes ached from lack of sleep and his throat was raw from talking. He looked over at Affraig, who stared back at him in silence.

It was hours since Brigid had left him standing in the doorway, his eyes adjusting to the gloom, nose filling with the earthy smell of herbs and sour odours of sweat and urine. It had taken a moment to distinguish the old woman from the pile of blankets she was swaddled in. Even in the dark, after ten years, he had recognised her. Affraig's hair, once a grey knotted curtain, was virtually gone, bald patches showing scalp between the wisps of white. Her face, which he remembered as strong-boned, even handsome, had folded in on itself, the skin sagging around her mouth and drooping under her chin.

Seeing him in the doorway, she had struggled to sit, eyes gleaming in the red glow of a brazier. Her lips had parted and her breath held the whisper of his name. He had knelt beside her and there in the darkness, out of sight of the hostile eyes of the Islesmen, away from the anguish in Edward's face and the blame in David of Atholl's, the frozen numbness inside him had cracked and out of the fissure his grief came pouring.

Words had followed, at first a faltering trickle, then a flood. He told her of his struggles these past ten years: the months in Ireland searching for the Staff of Malachy, his escape from Ulster's prison and the moment, in that abandoned town, when a stranger strode out of the shadows and aimed a crossbow at his heart. He recalled how James Stewart had stood with him over his attacker's body in Dunluce Castle and recognised him as Adam, one of King Alexander's squires, the last man to see the king alive that storm-tossed night on the road to Kinghorn. He spoke of his dawning suspicion that King Edward may have ordered Alexander's murder to gain control of Scotland, and how, after surrendering to the king, he had tried to find evidence of this, his doubts kept alive by an ancient prophecy that rightly predicted Alexander's death. He spoke of his triumph, seeing that black box split open on the floor of Westminster Abbey to reveal the lie – the proof contained in that empty vessel.

He told the old woman, who had brought him into this world, everything. Things even his brother, Edward, didn't know. Secrets he had kept from everyone. It was a relief, this unravelling of the years, unburdening himself of the weights he had carried, as well as a blessing to be talking about anything but the fates of his family. Affraig didn't speak. Only her whistling breaths acknowledged the admission of his part in the theft of the Stone of Destiny and that he had gone to Dumfries to meet John Comyn with murder in his mind.

Now, with the dawn light bleeding through the door, Robert searched her age-ravaged face for some reaction to his long confession.

Affraig continued to meet his gaze. At last, she spoke, her voice a rasp. 'When Brigid found me after the English razed Turnberry, she said she spoke to you at your coronation – that you said you sought my help. I have wondered what for.'

Robert toyed with the fragment of crossbow bolt around his neck. 'The box,' he said finally. 'It was the only proof that there was no ancient prophecy, only the king's translation, which I believe was invented to manipulate the things he wanted and to predict events he knew would happen. I hoped I could somehow show the king's men they had been loyal, all these years, to nothing more than an elaborate lie. I thought it might weaken their support for his war. Without them he could not fight it.'

'They would say you destroyed the prophecy,' Affraig told him. 'An empty box proves nothing.'

Robert hesitated. It had been a nebulous idea, but one that had fuelled his wish to keep that box safe. Now it seemed ridiculous; a fool's hope. He raised a helpless hand. 'You deal in men's destinies, Affraig. I thought you could write me a prophecy of my own. I thought

I could use Edward's lie against him – say this new prophecy was what I had found in the box.'

'Your enemies would say you had written it.'

'Perhaps. But Sir James Stewart once told me a lie is easier to swallow if embedded in truth. Edward would not be able to prove my prophecy false, any more than I could prove his. Maybe some in his circle would begin to doubt?' Robert met her cynical gaze. 'It does not matter now. I gave the box to Niall. They would have found it when they . . .' He closed his eyes. 'Do you believe in the Wheel of Fortune?'

'Yes.'

'The course I have steered.' Robert shook his head. 'My taking of the Stone. That night in Greyfriars Church. Methven Wood. Abandoning my family.' He stared down at his hands. 'Now, I am crushed beneath it.'

Affraig shifted, leaning forward to force his eyes back to hers. Her skin was as creased and translucent as old parchment. 'What does the wheel do? It turns. It will raise you up again.'

'I have lost too much.'

Moving her arm from beneath the blankets, she crooked a finger towards the corner of the hut. 'There.'

Robert saw a leather bag sagged against the wall. Seeing she meant for him to get it, he rose. He was weak with exhaustion, his body protesting with every movement. His right side felt bruised where Christiana's men had hauled him into the boat. Bending, he picked up the bag. The contents shifted and knocked against one another. A memory was stirred of the first time he met Affraig, emerging out of the woods with her black dogs, a gnarled stick in one hand and a sack gripped in the other, inside which things slithered and writhed. He handed the bag to her.

Opening it, Affraig reached in. Carefully, she withdrew a lattice of twigs, woven together to form a cage. In the centre, held by a thread, was a circle of heather, broom and wormwood. It was his destiny, fashioned by her hands the night he pledged to be king.

'When I saw the smoke from Turnberry, I took Elena and fled. This is what I saved – what I carried with me all the months and miles since.'

Robert took it when she offered it to him. He felt the suppleness of the web of twigs, worn as smooth as bones by wind and rain. 'It never fell?' He watched her shake her head. 'You told me they fell when the person's destiny was fulfilled.'

'Yes.'

'Then why did it not when I became king?'

'Are you king?'

His anger at the question dissipated when he glanced down at himself; ragged as a beggar. He gave a wry laugh, which faded quickly. 'Did I curse my reign by taking the Stone for Edward? By not being crowned upon it?'

'The man makes the king. Not the Stone.'

He frowned, remembering his grandfather saying something similar.

'Yours was the only destiny I saved from the oak,' Affraig continued, 'the only one worth saving. The others, they all came for themselves, hearts set on wealth, love or revenge.'

'I came for myself,' he reminded her, 'came because I wanted to be king.'

'Why?'

The creases in his brow deepened. 'Duty, I think – duty to make good on the oath I swore to my grandfather. That and my right.' He met her eyes. 'I was told, from the moment King Alexander died, that my family were the rightful heirs to the throne. In my mind, I think it was always mine. After I joined Wallace's rebellion and saw the damage Edward and his men were doing to our kingdom I wanted to stop them, to take it from them.'

'And now?'

'I'm no longer sure I want it,' he said quietly. 'This crown has cost me everything.'

Affraig nodded, her eyes hard and bright. 'Now you can begin,' she murmured. 'Now you can be the king your grandfather and I saw in you, years ago.'

'I don't understand.'

'Through these years of war your people have lost homes and livelihoods, sons and daughters. Do you know how they feel, my lord?'

He didn't speak, but she knew his answer.

'Then you can stand with them – for them. Be their voice.'

Robert felt something flicker to life inside him at her words. It was a fragile flame, but the moment it was ignited he knew what it was. Hope. He looked at the web of twigs in his hand; the crown at its centre.

'Can you recover what we have lost?' she asked him, her voice low, but compelling. 'Can you reclaim what is ours? Take back our kingdom?'

Before he could answer, there was a knock on the door. As it opened, flooding the hut with sunlight, Robert shielded his eyes.

Christiana MacRuarie stood there, her hair flaming in the golden dawn. 'My lord, will you walk with me? I have something to show you.'

Stranraer, Scotland, 1307 AD

Cormac pressed himself up against the barn, breathing through his teeth at the pain in his side. His mail and the straw-filled gambeson beneath had saved his life when the sword struck, but he guessed the blow had broken several ribs. He was still bleeding from a gash in his neck, but most of the other cuts had clotted, the freezing mud of the marshes helping to seal the wounds. His helm had come off in the ferocity of the battle and his hair was plastered with slime. Rank odours of mud, animal dung and human faeces clogged his nose.

The voices were louder. Cormac chanced a look around the edge of the barn. From here he had a good view of Stranraer's main street with the well in the centre. The blood-spattered ground was littered with fallen helms, broken arrows and the dead. Several score men with the white lion of Galloway on their tunics were working in lines, dragging bodies down to the shore. In the gap between two houses, Cormac saw corpses piled up on the beach, limbs sticking out at angles from the heap. There were more bodies at the loch's edge, drifting back and forth in the waters. He guessed many of his countrymen had attempted to flee to the boats. Counting the galleys, he realised two were gone. The rest were still moored in the shallows, being picked over for spoils by the men of Galloway.

The battle was over, gone in a shuddering rush of motion, pain and panic. Cormac had tried and failed to reach his father. Almost cut in half by a sword, he'd been knocked aside by a charging horse, losing his axe, before being tackled by a mad-eyed man, who pounced on him with a dagger. He had twisted from the attack, feeling a hot sting as his neck was grazed by the blade, then wrenching free his food knife had stuck it as hard as he could into the man's groin. Screaming shrilly, his attacker had peeled away, swept up in the flood of men and horses. Seeing his countrymen being overwhelmed, instinct had sent Cormac scrabbling, injured and weaponless, into the house he'd emerged from. He had struggled out through the window, dropped into a midden heap, and crawled away into the marshes, the sounds of slaughter tearing the air behind him.

Cormac had no idea how long he had lain in the mud, eventually passing out from the agony in his ribs, but the stars were now gone and the sky was washed with sullen dawn. His eyes focused on the group gathered in the street beyond the piles of dead. One man stood slightly apart from the others. Dressed in a blue surcoat adorned with a white lion, he was facing a row of men, all of whom were on their knees, hands bound behind their backs. As he walked the blood-soaked ground before them, Cormac realised the man's left hand was missing. He held a broadsword in his right. Among the kneeling men were Lord Donough, Thomas and Alexander Bruce. Thomas was badly wounded, struggling to remain upright, his face blanched, his fair hair streaked with blood. Seeing his father humbled and defeated, shame coursed hot through Cormac. He should be at his side. Instead, he had fled the battle and was now watching from a distance like a coward.

'Where is your brother?' the pacing man demanded. 'Where is Robert Bruce?'

'If we knew,' answered Thomas, his voice strained, 'you would not hear it from the lips of any man here. Do with us as you will, MacDouall.'

At the name, Cormac realised this was Dungal MacDouall, former captain of the army of Galloway, loyal supporter of John Balliol and John Comyn, and leader of the Disinherited.

MacDouall turned on Thomas. 'Oh, I shall, you son of a whore. I've waited years to take my revenge on those who murdered my father.'

'Our father is dead,' said Alexander, his eyes on the captain. 'You will not now attain vengeance for the attack on Buittle Castle.'

'Not from the man himself,' said MacDouall coldly. 'But I can take it out of his sons.'

As MacDouall raised his sword, Alexander flinched and Thomas gave a hoarse shout, but it was one of the captain's own men who stayed his hand.

'Sir! These men will be more valuable to us alive. Such a prize might persuade King Edward to give us what we want. Our lands returned to us?'

As MacDouall began to lower his sword, Cormac let out a breath.

'You're right. The brothers of the king may prove useful. But not the Irish scum.' Before anyone could stop him, Dungal MacDouall brought his sword swinging round towards Lord Donough's neck.

Barra, Scotland, 1307 AD

Huge white clouds scudded across the dawn sky, blown by the glacial February wind. The air was so sharp it was hard to breathe and Robert's eyes smarted as he walked beside Christiana down the track towards the beach. Nes followed at a discreet distance, having handed Robert his broadsword. On leaving Affraig's hut, seeing the knight sitting by a fire outside, Robert realised he had been keeping guard through the night. The rest of his comrades and Angus MacDonald were asleep in the lodgings they had been given, with the exception of David of Atholl, sitting hunched by the fire. The young man hadn't even acknowledged him.

Christiana glanced at Robert as they neared the shore. 'When she first arrived here Affraig told me she knew you. She helped deliver you at Turnberry, yes?'

Robert was discomforted by the intimacy of the question. He shifted the subject. 'I'm surprised by your charity, my lady, welcoming those dispossessed by the war to your lands. It must be a task to feed and house them all?'

Her green eyes sharpened at his tone, but she smiled cordially. 'We offer them safe passage to a new life. They offer us skills and labour in return.'

Robert drew the heavy black mantle, trimmed with rabbit fur, closer around his shoulders. Christiana had handed it to him outside the hut, saying it belonged to her late husband. Robert had accepted the garment awkwardly, unaware that the Earl of Mar's son had passed, leaving her a widow. She was wearing her blue patterned cloak and her flame-coloured hair was as dishevelled as it had been the day before. She looked tired, he thought, as if she too had been up all night.

Ahead, the sea appeared, a dazzling sheet, brocaded with sunlight.

Waves broke hard against the sand, spray gauzing the air. Robert saw two more boats had arrived in the night. There was a group of men around them, hauling out deer carcasses.

'From Rhum,' Christiana told him, raising a hand to the men. 'My family have long used the island as a hunting park. It is not so hard to feed many mouths out here. Our crops may be poor, but meat and fish we have fit for a king's table.'

Feeling someone rushing up behind him, Robert reached automatically for his sword. He stayed his hand as a young girl raced past them.

She sprinted down to the beach, bare feet kicking up sand. 'Father!'

Robert saw one of the men, hands bloody from the carcasses, turn. Bending with a grin, the man swept her into his arms. Robert felt a wrench in his chest. He thought of the moment he first held his daughter; placed in his arms by the midwife, while his wife lay unmoving in a soup of bloody sheets, and smoke billowed above Carlisle. Marjorie. Born into a war she had now become a victim of. He thought of Affraig's words, but the faint hope that had been kindled already felt as if it were fading, too frail to push back the shadows in his heart.

Christiana was looking at his hand, curled around the sword hilt. 'You are safe here, my lord. You have my word.'

'Even from your brothers?'

'These are my lands. They have been for ten years, since the passing of my father. Lachlan and Ruarie will do as I say.'

Hearing his name called, Robert turned to see Edward approaching. He was tugging a woollen cloak over his surcoat, the arms of Annandale partially hidden by filth.

Edward looked between him and Christiana. 'I didn't realise you were awake, brother.'

'I wanted to show Lord Robert something,' Christiana told him. 'You are welcome to join us.'

Robert nodded his agreement and Edward fell into step beside them as Christiana led the way across the dunes, to where another track wound through the machair above the shoreline. Moving inland, past a reed-fringed loch in the shadow of the hill, whose green flanks were scattered with boulders, they passed a couple of fishermen, nets slung over their shoulders. The men greeted Christiana courteously, but cocked their heads suspiciously at Robert and Edward.

Robert frowned at their backs. His cloak was open at the front, displaying the red lion. 'They do not know the arms of their king?'

'They do.' Christiana laughed. 'I doubt, by now, there is a man, woman or child on this island who doesn't know that you are here, my lord. Word moves faster than the tides on Barra.'

He didn't share her mirth. 'I am their king, my lady.'

Her smile faded. 'You must understand, for many years the kings of Scotland have seemed' – she struggled for the words – 'foreign to us. A distant power that tried to impose its will by force, without respecting our rights and customs. We were Norse-led for a long time before we were ruled by Edinburgh. My uncle was chosen as King of the Isles by Hakon of Norway. On his death, my father succeeded him. It is difficult to go from king to king's man.'

Robert nodded after a pause. Although the Western Isles were part of his kingdom, he hadn't fully understood how intricate their politics and history were. Shifting on the sands of Norse and Scottish rule for centuries, Somerled had been the cement that bound them together for a time, until the islands were broken up among his sons, then sold to Scotland on the parchment of a Norse treaty.

The track began to rise, sloping over the headland. Redwings and golden plovers cast from the carpet of rock-strewn grass, wings flickering. The sun disappeared behind a cloud, throwing them into chilly shade. Hearing the shrill cries of gulls, Robert looked towards the sea, realising that they had climbed a fair way up a steep promontory. The sun appeared again, gilding the waters.

'My God.'

At Edward's murmur, Robert looked back round to see they had crested the rise. He stopped in his tracks. Spread out before him was a bay, sheltered by two encircling arms of headland that created a huge, natural harbour. In the wide mouth between the rocky bluffs, he could see the surge of the green ocean, but in the harbour the waters were as calm as a mill pond. In the centre was a small island, from which rose a stout castle. But it was what lay between the island and the shore that had caught his attention. There, where the waters turned jewel blue as they neared the sands, were scores of galleys. Forty, he guessed, at first count. A few were fishing craft and there were a couple of round, merchant cogs, but most were slender birlinns – the war galleys of the Isles. His heart quickened.

Christiana turned to him. 'I spoke at length to Lachlan last night, my lord. My brother will keep his pledge. You will have twenty ships at your command, equipped with fighting men, all for the promised price.'

Robert, noting again the shadows around her eyes, wondered what this had cost her. 'I do not have the revenue to pay him yet,' he warned. 'I won't until I've collected the rents from my lands in Carrick.'

'He will wait. I persuaded him of the benefits we might one day enjoy for loyal service to our king, especially if our galleys help turn the tide of the war.'

Christiana's smile was light, but Robert caught a shrewd glint in her eyes. He thought of the refugees she had so generously conveyed here and wondered how many of the men and boys might be destined for service as mercenaries aboard MacRuarie war galleys. His sense of her shifted to the guarded respect he might feel towards a worthy rival. This was, he thought, not a woman to take lightly.

'With the fifteen galleys Lord Angus promised from Islay, we'll have a fleet of thirty-five,' said Edward, surveying the distant rows of galleys. 'We can take the bastards,' he said, grasping Robert's shoulder. 'We can avenge Niall's death.' His tone was fierce, but his voice cracked with emotion on their brother's name.

Robert thought of Affraig's questions, back in the gloom of her hut. *Can you reclaim what is ours? Take back our kingdom?*

He felt his answer begin to rise.

22

The West Coast, Scotland, 1307 AD

They sailed on the spring tide, the twenty birlinns making short work of the fast-flowing channel between the Outer and Inner Isles. The long ships were slung low to the water, which surged around their prows as the oars carved white circles through the blue. Rising and falling in perfect time, all along the sides of the vessels, they looked like wings, propelling these beasts through the deep.

The ships were crowded with men, clad in an assortment of mail hauberks, quilted gambesons and leather aketons, boiled and steeped in oil to stiffen them. Some were barelegged, others clad in hose, but all had iron basinets and double-headed axes, the hafts of which were six feet long. They were the galloglass, West Highland mercenaries, shipped and sold by the MacRuaries to Irish chieftains for the war against Ulster and the settlers. Recruited for their stature and moulded, through ruthless training, from lean farmhands and fishermen's sons into lofty, muscular men, they formed a fearsome company. Almost five hundred in number, they had all been bred to fight the English.

On the second morning, heading south to Islay under sail, the fleet was escorted briefly by a school of dolphins, the young bulls leaping before them. Even the hard-bitten veterans among the crew smiled at the spectacle, declaring it to be a blessing. Robert watched them from the largest galley, a vessel of thirty-four oars with a crimson sail, captained by Lachlan himself. He was accompanied by Angus, Edward and Malcolm, along with Nes and the other knights who had survived the MacDougalls' attack. There was one notable absence, in the form of David of Atholl. Two days before they were due to leave Barra, the young man and his band of knights had disappeared. Questioning Kerald, Robert discovered that David had bartered his way on board one of the supply ships returning to the mainland. The man hadn't been able to look at him since learning of the execution of his father and Robert guessed grief had turned to blame. He took the news with little emotion. Let deserters fall by the wayside, he wanted only the ready and willing on this campaign.

Robert and his men wore new armour and clothing: coats of polished mail, helms and woollen cloaks for the lords, gambesons for their men. Robert's surcoat had been cleaned and mended by Brigid, watched closely by her daughter, Elena. Scotland's red lion now had a scar running the length of its snarling face. When Christiana handed out the garments and weapons, Robert had wondered how much of the gear had been stolen by her brothers, recalling tales of Lachlan and Ruarie plundering their way across Lewis and Skye. If, before, such stories had given him pause, they now gave him heart. He would need that brute audacity in the coming days. He just prayed the MacRuaries would not switch in the wind at the first sign of trouble. Proof they would not came the day after they reached Islay.

The sight of the MacRuarie fleet entering the harbour at Dunyvaig, in the shadow of Angus MacDonald's cliff-top castle, must have appeared as an invasion to the people of Islay, for beacons had been lit on the castle walls and a host of men were there to meet them on the beach, ranks bristling with spears. Seeing their lord jumping down from Lachlan's galley, safely returned to them after two months at sea, their alarm had turned to joy and there, in the harbour, Robert found the remainder of his promised galleys and three hundred men, come from across MacDonald's lands at the call to war. This past year, after death, capture and desertion had whittled his army down to scarcely more than two hundred, he now had almost the same size force he had commanded at Methven Wood.

After re-supplying, the thirty-five galleys set out, negotiating the wild waters around the Mull of Kintyre before heading up towards the southern tip of Arran in sight of the Carrick coast. Here, the dome of Ailsa Craig filled Robert's vision like a marker, counting down the miles to home. It was off Carrick that they encountered their first enemy patrol – four English galleys. At the sight of the great fleet bearing down on them, they had come sharply about, but the heavy, cumbersome vessels were no match for the sleek birlinns. One managed to escape, making for the coast of Galloway, but the other three were grappled and boarded. Lachlan's mercenaries proved not only their loyalty, but their reputation for savagery. After making a bloody slaughter of the crew they had slung the dead and dying into the waves, a feast for fish and gulls, before stripping the vessels of anything valuable and sinking them. That afternoon, as the setting sun gilded the tip of Holy Island, the fleet arrived on the shores of Arran. Here they were met by a patrol headed by Gilbert de la Hay, who greeted Robert with a fierce embrace, and led him to where the rest of his men were camped.

The reunion with Neil Campbell, James Douglas and the others, raised Robert's spirits in a way he hadn't thought possible. The company, hidden in their remote coastal camp, hadn't heard any word of events on the mainland and it was with heavy hearts that they listened to Robert's account of the fates of his family and friends. James Douglas, his voice resolute, informed the king he had sent a message to Bute and avowed, if his uncle was alive, he would answer the call to arms. Neil privately told Robert that James, who'd led several night patrols along the coast and had discovered Henry Percy was in command of Turnberry Castle, had proven himself a keen and capable leader.

In honour of this, Robert placed the young man in command of the first company to cross from Arran. If the garrison at Turnberry was judged ripe for attack, James was to light a beacon as a signal for the rest of fleet to follow. He had left the next night, leaving Robert and his men to settle down to wait, watching the Carrick coastline for a point of fire.

Near Turnberry Castle, Scotland, 1307 AD

His eyes on the castle, James cursed beneath his breath. He heard Alan creep up alongside him in the tangled darkness of the woods.

'What is it?' asked Alan, breathing hard after the climb from the beach.

'See for yourself.' Moving aside, James pointed through the branches of wych-elm and ash towards the next headland, which jutted into the sea across a small bay.

Alan, one of Gilbert de la Hay's squires who had come across with him from Arran, stared at the castle that rose from the promontory. Torches on Turnberry's battlements blazed against the midnight sky, an orange halo of fire. There were more lights down in the courtyard, the glow of them wavering up the walls. Alan shook his head in question, unsure of the reason for James's frustration.

'The banners,' James explained. 'The gold one with the blue lion – those are Henry Percy's arms.' He moved his finger along the battlements to where another standard snapped in the breeze. It hadn't been there on his last scout along the coast. The banner was striped blue and white. James couldn't see the red birds at this distance, but he knew they were there. 'Pembroke,' he murmured to Alan. 'Aymer de Valence is in residence.'

There was a crackle of twigs behind them. James turned to see the other two men who had climbed up the cliffs with him emerging from the undergrowth. Relaxing, he let Alan convey the bad news as he scanned the bluffs beyond the castle gates. The village of Turnberry had stood there until Prince Edward burned it to ash. Now, there was a large encampment in its place, scattered with campfires, which highlighted scores of tents and wagons. James had glimpsed the camp from the sea, but it appeared much bigger now. No doubt augmented, he thought grimly, by Valence's men.

James's gaze flicked back to the battlements, lingering on the banners. How he wanted to see another beside them, one whose colours were burned into his mind: a blue and gold chequered ground cut in half by a wide red band, the arms of Robert Clifford, the man who had been granted the lands of his father.

Lord William Douglas, governor of Berwick and the first nobleman to join Wallace's insurrection, had been a tower of a man, whom James had loved and revered. Captured at the fall of Berwick, he had died in chains in the Tower of London. James, sent by his mother to live with an uncle in Paris, had returned to Scotland three years ago in the company of William Lamberton, who took him in as his ward with a pledge to help him regain his lands. Toughened by his uncle's training in France, determined to avenge his father's death, James had joined the rebellion with a fire in his heart. But now the Bishop of St Andrews was languishing in one of King Edward's dungeons and, with his uncle still missing, he felt as though all the hopes of his family had settled, heavy, on his shoulders.

Forcing his gaze from the battlements, James nodded to his companions. 'Come. We must tell the others.'

'Do we light the beacon?' asked Brice, one of Neil Campbell's men from Argyll.

'No. We need to know how large the garrison is. Percy's company we could have overcome, but Valence is the king's lieutenant. He commands a formidable force.'

'The king has almost one thousand, Master James,' Brice reminded him.

'Valence had more than that under his banner at Methven, many of them horsed, and that force was increased by the men of Galloway. Who knows how many he has here.' James felt a tug of impatience as he spoke. Caution was not a familiar counsellor and he was as keen as the others to move to action, but he wanted to get this right. Victory here was crucial to the campaign. Added to that, Robert had given him the opportunity to prove himself. If he helped the king win the war, his lands would be returned to him. Maybe then the restless ghost of his father – carried within him these past years – could finally find peace. 'We'll return at daybreak. Try to get a closer look.'

James led the way back through the undergrowth, blackthorn and briars scratching at his hands and snagging his clothes in the darkness. Emerging on the cliff edge, he and his men picked their route down carefully. It was a clear night and the new moon washed the crags with its insipid light, revealing the animal tracks that criss-crossed down to the shore, heart-clenchingly narrow in places. The rocks were freezing beneath the men's hands, mottled with lichen and rosettes of saxifrage, already brittle with frost.

The tide was out, the beach strewn with black ropes of kelp. Once on the gleaming expanse of sand, the four moved quickly. At the far end, behind a tumble of rocks where James and his men had hidden their boat that morning, was a cave. As they approached, a voice called sharply from the shadows.

'Who's there?'

'It's us, Fergus.'

At James's voice a man appeared from behind the rocks, the blade of his sword glinting in the moonlight. 'You'd better come. We could have trouble.'

Instantly alert, James climbed over the stones. 'What is it?'

'See for yourself,' answered Fergus, leading the way up the shingle towards the narrow entrance of the cave.

James entered, his nose filling with the stink of seaweed and dankness. Fergus and his three companions had lit a small fire, the glow of which pulsed on the slimy walls. A band of serpentine in the granite glistened like snakeskin. As James followed Fergus in, the men parted to reveal a figure on his knees before the fire. The man's hands were bound. James picked out the glimmer of mail and the bulk of a gambeson beneath his filthy tunic. His face was horribly bruised and there was a jagged cut, crusted shut with dried blood, along his neck. His hair, thick and matted at the front, was so caked with mud James could barely tell the colour, although he caught a glint of red in the firelight.

'We caught him spying on us when we went to gather wood for the beacon,' Fergus said. 'He tried to run.'

When the man saw James, his injured face lit up. He began speaking in a rapid stream. James caught enough of the words to know it was Gaelic, although he didn't understand much. He stared at the man, thinking he looked incredibly familiar. Squinting past the mud and the bruises, he knew him. 'Cormac!' He turned on Fergus. 'Christ, man, it's the king's brother you've been beating!'

Fergus's eyes widened at the man's identity, but he raised a hand to proclaim his innocence. 'We didn't touch him, Master James! I swear he was like this when we found him.'

James crossed to the Irishman and untied his hands. Cormac rubbed at his wrists, his eyes on Fergus. Picking up one of the water skins, James handed it to him. The spark of life in Cormac's face at seeing James had already vanished, replaced by exhaustion, but he took the skin gratefully and gulped at it.

'Brice,' said James, turning to his comrade. 'Ask him what he's doing here.'

The Argyllsman stepped forward and repeated the question in Gaelic. Cormac listened, looking between James and Brice. After a moment he began speaking.

'He has come from Galloway,' said Brice. 'He was with his father, Lord Donough of Glenarm, and King Robert's brothers.'

A ripple of excitement spread through the others at the mention of the company that was due to join them from Galloway, but James said nothing. The Irishman's injuries, his wretched appearance: all told a story of anguish. Cormac's voice broke on his father's name.

'Some food, Fergus,' James said quickly. 'And a blanket.'

Fergus ducked out of the cave, heading to the boat where their supplies were stowed.

'What happened in Galloway?' James asked, not taking his gaze off Cormac as Brice asked the question.

Cormac lowered the skin, then spoke quietly. Brice's face fell.

'Brice?' pressed James, when the man didn't speak.

'He says they were ambushed on the shores of Loch Ryan by men of Galloway, allies of the Comyn family. Many were killed. Lord Donough was executed by Dungal MacDouall.' Brice looked at James. 'Thomas and Alexander Bruce were taken prisoner.'

'The Irish?' asked Alan, his voice hoarse with shock.

Brice shook his head.

The sound of footsteps dashing on shingle interrupted them. Fergus entered the cave, food and blanket forgotten. 'Come! Quickly!'

Drawing his sword, James followed him outside.

Fergus led him at a run past the boat to where the cliffs tumbled down on to the rock-strewn sand. Waves murmured across the beach, the tide creeping in. 'There!' Fergus clutched James's shoulder and pointed north, in the opposite direction to Turnberry. A mile or two distant, up on the bluffs, a fire was burning. 'An English patrol?'

James didn't answer, his eyes on the flames leaping high in the night. 'The beacon! Dear God, they'll think it's the beacon!'

23

Turnberry Castle, Scotland, 1307 AD

The black cliffs loomed before them, great towers of rock veiled by mist. Seabirds cried in the heights, their ghostly forms occasionally visible, wheeling in the murk. During the crossing from Arran the sky had gradually lightened from pitch to inky-grey, but even though it was now past dawn the world was still shrouded in gloom.

Ahead, the rush of waves was louder. Robert gripped the mast, feeling the swell thrust the galley towards the beach. He smelled seaweed above the metal tang of mail and the warmer odours of sweat and breath. Men crowded around him, their eyes on the approaching shore. The galloglass gripped the long hafts of their double-headed axes, breaths pluming in the damp air. Pearls of mist clung to matted hair and beards. Each had a foot up on the vessel's side, ready to vault into the shallows at their captain's command. Through the shifting vapours, Robert caught glimpses of the six other birlinns that accompanied them and saw row upon row of galloglass, similarly poised.

Since leaving Barra his fears over their loyalty had vanished. When ordered, these men moved as one, without question or compunction. He had only witnessed a similar level of discipline in William Wallace's camp in the Forest, when the rebel leader was training his schiltroms of spearmen. In his experience, common soldiery were hard to organise and knights and squires followed the lead of their own lords. There was something single-minded about the galloglass. It made him think of a hive.

Glancing round, he sought out Lachlan, who was staring ahead, eyes narrowed in concentration. Catching his gaze, the captain cocked his head in question. Robert nodded an affirmation that they were still on course. This broken line of land was as familiar to him as his own skin. Even though he couldn't see it, he knew Turnberry Castle rose sheer from the rocky foundations of its promontory, just to the right of their position. He offered up another thanks to God for the freezing fog that had curled around them as they neared the coast, shielding them from enemy eyes, although the same mists had caused their guiding beacon to wink out of sight several hours earlier. He prayed it was as impenetrable on the other side of the bay where the greater part of his fleet, commanded by Angus MacDonald and Ruarie MacRuarie, was due to land. Certainly, there had been no sound of alarm from the castle as yet.

All at once, the veil parted and the walls of Turnberry Castle appeared high above them, crowned by an amber haze of torchlight. Robert's heart sang at the sight. After all these desperate months on the run, his back to his enemies, he was coming home to face them head-on. He thought of the dragon shield he had tossed from those battlements, lying somewhere beneath the surf, its red paint long since peeled away, wood rotted, iron rusted. He slid his gloved hand from the gold tear-drop pommel of his sword down to the hilt, tightening his fingers around the worn, leather-bound grip. As he did so, he caught the eye of his brother, pressed in close at his side. He saw the fierceness in Edward's face, the passion in his eyes as the breaking waves propelled the galley on to the shingle.

Robert went over with the first few men, the water rushing up to his thighs. The current was strong, threatening to pull him back, the weight of his mail dragging him down. He fought against it, propelling himself into the shallows. With Edward and Nes close behind him, followed by Malcolm of Lennox and the rest of his men, Robert led the galloglass to where a well-worn path wound up to the bluffs beyond the castle walls.

He knew from reports that Turnberry had been razed, but it was still a shock as he came up over the edge of the cliffs to see a mass of tents disappearing in the gloom, where once the small, but bustling settlement had stood. The sight added fuel to the fire inside him. He let the fury take him over, singing its song of violence inside him as he charged towards the English camp, broadsword drawn, a cry tearing from his throat.

It was still early, but a fair few men in the camp were awake, cooks preparing morning meals, grooms tending to horses and clearing piles of dung, servants stoking fires. A few knights and squires had risen to use the latrines and dress for the day, shrugging gambesons over sleep-crumpled shirts and hose, cupping palms and blowing warmth into hands stiff with cold. The first thing these men heard was the muffled pounding of many feet on the springy turf. Some started round, others froze, as a roar shattered the hush and out of the mist came a horde of men.

Leaping the guy ropes of a tent, Robert hacked his sword into the neck of a stocky, half-dressed Englishman, who was bellowing a warning. His shout cut off abruptly, blood spewing from his mouth. Wrenching his sword free, Robert shoved the man aside, sending him lurching into a tent, which buckled inward. Another figure loomed up. Robert glimpsed an iron pot clutched in a white-knuckled hand and a mouth stretched in fear. The cook reacted at the last moment, swinging the pot at him. Robert ducked the blow and ran him through. He felt the resistance of skin and tightened muscles, before the blade slid on through the tenderness of organs and bowels. The cook sagged over him, convulsing. Twisting his sword free, Robert charged towards the next target.

The blind fury of battle possessed him, compelling him to strike at anyone who stood before him. He would cleanse this ground of his enemy; wash it clean with their blood. At his side was Edward, storm-eyed, the blade of his sword already slick with gore. His brother looked more alive than he had in months, slashing and carving his way through the scattering men. The roses on Malcolm of Lennox's surcoat were like splashes of blood in the blaze of the campfire, the war cry of his family on his lips. With them was Lachlan MacRuarie, leading his galloglass into the heart of the camp. The captain fought like a fiend, swinging his mighty, double-bladed axe into backs, scalps and chests as if he were chopping firewood.

Cries of panic tore through the camp. Knights, shocked from sleep, scrambled from tents, snatching up swords. Others grabbed shovels and stakes; anything that could be used as a weapon. Grooms and servants quailed in the face of the galloglass. These weren't Scottish knights or peasants, who dressed and looked much like their own kind. These barelegged, barefooted giants brandishing axes as big as themselves seemed another race entirely. Many of the younger men were turning and fleeing at the sight of them, but the veterans switched quickly from shock to defence, roaring at infantry to seize arms.

Within moments the tide of Scots was slowed, a growing wall of English knights and squires rushing in to halt their advance. Many wore surcoats, emblazoned with the blue lion of Henry Percy. Most hadn't had time to put on mail, but their gambesons offered some protection. Robert glimpsed one galloglass take an iron-embossed buckler in the face. As the man rocked back, choking on his own teeth, the English knight who delivered the jaw-shattering blow crouched and thrust his sword up under the man's tunic, between his bare legs. Another mercenary, struggling to free his axe from a young man's scalp, had his head pulled back by an English squire and his throat slit. A tent collapsed into a campfire as two grappling men staggered into it. The material smouldered, then flickered into bright life. Smoke rose into the mist.

Robert, caught up in the press, realised there were many more English here than anticipated. He had expected, based on his scouts' estimates of enemy numbers, to overrun the camp and destroy it before the castle garrison could come to their aid. He felt a wave of unease. Where were Angus MacDonald and the rest of his company? Scores of galloglass had stormed deep into the camp, urged on by Lachlan's battle cry. His forces were spread out, hemmed in by tents and wagons, latrines and campfires – vulnerable. As a sword smacked against his helm, Robert's attention was snatched forward.

The fight quickly became tight and vicious, men wrestling one another to the ground, stabbing dirks into eyes and throats. Robert, his sword cuffed wide by one of Percy's knights, slammed his head into the man's snarling face. The front of his helm connected solidly with the man's nose. As the knight pitched back, Robert caught sight of two huge figures striding out of the fog, hacking a bloody path through the back of the line of men in front of him. One was Angus MacDonald, the other, Gilbert de la Hay. He realised he could hear horns blowing. The rest of his army had arrived. Feeling a surge of life through his limbs, he pressed forward, Percy's knights trapped in a killing ground between the two forces of Scots, come together in the centre of the English camp.

'My lord!' Gilbert fought through the seething crowd to get to Robert. 'My lord king!'

Behind the Lord of Erroll, Robert saw James Douglas, Neil Campbell and others struggling towards him. They all looked agitated. He realised there was another figure with James, a young man with a mud-caked thatch of hair, clutching an axe and holding his side as if injured, his face a mask of pain. So unexpected was the sight of him that it took Robert a moment to recognise his foster-brother, Cormac. Dimly, through the chaos, he heard Gilbert shouting.

'Valence is here! Our men didn't set that beacon!'

At that moment, the gates of Turnberry Castle groaned open. Out of the courtyard scores of knights came riding, the sound of their destriers' hooves filling the air. The mists were lifting and the first pale shades of morning shed light across the camp. Robert now saw, among the colours of Henry Percy, the blue and white stripes of Pembroke on dozens of surcoats, trappers and shields. One knight at the head, mounted on a muscular black warhorse, wore a great helm, crested with a spray of goose feathers dyed blue. At the sight of Aymer de Valence, a maelstrom of emotions swept through Robert, shock followed by hatred and livid anger. His eyes on his enemy, he didn't see one of Percy's knights, left for dead at his feet, curl his fingers around his fallen sword and heave himself upright.

Nes lunged, swiping aside the knight's blow with his own blade before thrusting it into the man's throat.

Robert staggered back as the knight jerked on the length of steel. He met Nes's gaze, but there was no time for gratitude. Valence and his knights were coming for them.

In their wake, more men were pouring from the castle's gates, pulling on helms and grabbing spears. Some mounted horses, hastily saddled by squires. Archers were lining up on the walls. For all the fearlessness of the galloglass, Robert knew at once that they would be no match for Valence's cavalry. Caught up in the maze of tents, unable to form protective lines, those who had ventured far into the camp were the first to go down, knocked flying by the armoured horses or ripped apart by the blades of the knights. A few English horses went down, caught by axe swings, but more rode on over them. The voice of James Stewart sounded in Robert's mind, warning him that one armoured knight was worth ten foot soldiers. He thought of the trap Valence had set for him at Methven Wood and the ambush in the wilds of Lorn by John MacDougall and the Black Comyn. He couldn't risk another catastrophic defeat. These men were all he had left.

'*Back to the boats!*'

At Robert's command, Gilbert de la Hay and Angus MacDonald, forewarned by James Douglas, spared no haste in withdrawing, moving back the way they had come with the men of Islay and Ruarie MacRuarie's galloglass, fending off attacks from the English, who had rallied at the appearance of Valence and Percy.

Edward grasped Robert's arm. 'What are you doing? This is our chance! Let's end the bastard!'

Robert wrenched himself free. 'We've no choice, damn it!'

Shouting to the rest of his company, he headed for the cliffs, retracing his steps through the bloody trail of destruction he and his men had left. Malcolm of Lennox went with him, taking up the cry, as did Nes. More and more of his men followed suit, pouring through the labyrinth of tents. Robert snatched a buckler from the debris-strewn ground, holding it aloft against the arrows stabbing down from the archers on Turnberry's walls. A galloglass running just ahead of him took one in the face. Vaulting the fallen man, Robert saw Lachlan away to his left, grappling with one of Percy's men. The haft of his axe had clashed in mid-air to form a cross with the Englishman's sword. As the man spat in his face, Lachlan didn't flinch, but with his free hand tugged his dirk from its sheath and rammed it into his eye, twisting the blade savagely. The captain's back was to Valence's cavalry, riding straight for him.

Robert hollered at him, but Lachlan, caught up in the chaos, didn't hear. Letting the blinded man fall, he turned on another, who rushed at him. Robert pitched himself towards Lachlan, who despatched his attacker with a swing of his axe that caved in the Englishman's head. As Robert grasped Lachlan's shoulder the man turned on him, raising his dirk. Recognition flooded his wild green eyes and he just managed to check the blow.

'To the boats!' Robert shouted, thrusting the captain towards the cliffs. '*Go!*'

Lachlan, seeing the cavalry storming towards them, came to his senses. With a curse, he began to run, calling his men to follow.

'*Bruce!*'

The roar of his name ripped through the air behind him. Robert glanced over his shoulder to see Aymer de Valence bearing down on him. His visor was raised and Robert saw the earl's hard face light up in triumph as he turned. At the sight of him – the arrogance in that grin, the cruelty in those black eyes – a dam broke in Robert. Rage swept through him, washing away sense and fear. This man, who destroyed his army at Methven Wood and forced him into exile, had captured Niall, his beloved brother, and John of Atholl, who had been as a father to him. He had seized his wife, his sisters and his daughter, and delivered them all into King Edward's merciless hands.

At once, Robert was charging forward. There was a bellowing in his ears that he dimly realised was coming from his own mouth. Aymer's destrier crashed between two pavilions, ripping one free from its stakes and dragging half of it behind it. As Robert ran headlong towards him, he saw a flash of fear in Valence's eyes. The earl jerked on the reins, but the horse, agitated by the tangle of ropes and canvas around its hooves, didn't respond. Dropping the buckler, Robert grasped the hilt of his sword in both hands and brought it swinging round over his head. Dropping into a crouch, he let the momentum of the strike carry on through to connect with the animal's front leg as it plunged down in front of him. The blade carved flesh and bone, severing the beast's limb.

The great destrier gave a piercing scream. It plummeted in a rush of mail and a billow of blue and white silk. Aymer was hurled from the saddle. He rolled with the impact, his armour absorbing some, though by no means all, of the fall. His helm was knocked off, leaving just a coif of mail over his arming cap. He staggered to his feet, shaking his head dazedly and spitting blood. Turning, he managed to draw his sword, just as Robert launched himself at him. Their blades met with a clash, slivers of metal sparking from them. Life returned to Aymer's eyes at the vicious strike. He snarled in Robert's face, lips pulling back to reveal the gleam of silver, smeared with blood.

Robert seeing that wire, remembering his fist shattering Valence's teeth in Llanfaes, felt new strength flood him, swelling his desire to finish now what he had started all those years ago. He pushed against the man's blade, forcing it down, hissing through his teeth with the effort. When Valence, unable to resist, was pulled to one side, Robert released a hand from his sword hilt and elbowed him in the face. The earl's head snapped back. Reeling away, he wrenched his sword out from under Robert's, metal screeching against metal. Though blood was gushing from his nose and his eyes were full of water, he came straight in again. Robert lurched from the strike, then retaliated. He was aware, from the clang of swords and din of hooves, that fighting

was continuing around him, but the realisation was faint, all his attention fixed on Valence.

Their swords smashed together, sprang apart, arced and met again,
each man blocking the death strike the other aimed at him. Robert
had forgotten what a ferocious fighter Valence was. Every blow jarred
through his arms until his muscles were burning and sweat was pouring down his face. The thick cloak Christiana had given him was dragging at his shoulders, slowing him down. He'd not slept during the
crossing from Arran, nor had he eaten a proper meal since leaving
Barra. He'd lost weight during the months on the run and his strength
was depleted. Aymer, on the other hand, was fresh and fit. Robert had
rage on his side, but he knew this would burn out quickly. Battering
away another strike, he spun out of Aymer's reach, circling around a
campfire to catch his breath. Tearing off the brooch on his cloak, he
let the heavy garment fall. At once, his limbs felt lighter.

Aymer swiped blood from his face, pacing round to face him. 'Your
little brother pissed himself when they led him to the gallows. I
watched the whelp dance on the rope for an age, but he was still alive
when they put his neck on the block for the axe.'

Robert gripped his sword, feeling his hands begin to shake. 'As you
will be when I scalp you.'

Aymer grinned. 'It ends today, Bruce – your pathetic reign, your
pitiful life. Your family will die in their prisons. Your last supporters
will be strung up alongside the rotting corpses of their friends and
your lands will be divided among us. In a few years no one will even
remember you existed.'

'Arrogance has made a fool of you,' murmured Robert, moving to
keep the campfire between them. 'You couldn't vanquish me in
Llanfaes. You couldn't catch me in Westminster. Even at Methven
Wood you failed to take me.'

'Will you fight us all?' asked Valence, his eyes flicking over Robert's
shoulder.

Robert risked a glance behind him. He saw several squires had
come to Valence's aid, clad in the Pembroke colours. They carried
spears and falchions and were advancing on him.

'He's mine!' Valence called to them.

Robert realised, with a sick rising fear, that he was now alone.
Lachlan had gone, as had the rest of his men, swept away in the tumultuous retreat. He glimpsed a few galloglass among the tents and

wagons, still fighting hard with the English, but most had retreated, pursued by Henry Percy's knights.

Aymer's smile widened. Suddenly, the earl lunged. Robert kicked at the campfire. As glowing embers burst up around him, Valence threw up an arm to shield his face, allowing Robert to barrel past, knocking him roughly aside as he went. Aymer hit the ground hard, his sword slipping from his grip.

Robert wove through the tents, Valence's shouts lifting behind him. His whole back twitching with the expectation of a sword strike, he raced past two men locked together, hands around one another's throats. Skidding in a pool of blood, he pushed on, hurdling over sacks of grain that had spilled from a wagon. Hooves were drumming up behind him. Any moment, they would catch him.

'Robert!'

At his name, he twisted round, lifting his sword to defend himself. A rider was bearing down on him. He saw a thatch of dirty red hair and wide eyes in a bruised face.

As he brought the horse to a stamping halt, Cormac thrust out his hand. Seeing Valence's squires running towards him, Robert grasped it. He dug his foot in the stirrup and hauled himself up. One of the squires threw himself forward, slashing at the animal's hind leg. The horse squealed, but Cormac jabbed it hard with his heels, compelling it on. Robert gripped the pommel, only half in the saddle, as the horse careened through the camp and out across the mist-wreathed fields.

Aymer cursed bitterly as he saw his enemy being borne away. He ordered his men to follow, then shouted at his squire to bring him a fresh horse, his mighty destrier now bleeding out in a tangle of ropes and canvas.

Wiping sweat from his eyes, Aymer caught sight of Robert's cloak lying crumpled on the ground by the scattered remains of the campfire. He crossed to it and snatched up the garment. 'And bring me the hound!' he roared at his retreating squire.

Aymer looked across the fields, his eyes on the horse, galloping towards the woods. His fingers curled around the cloak. 'We'll have ourselves some sport.'

They fled through the woods, splashing through mud and wading across narrow burns. They had left the horse some miles back, the animal's injured leg finally buckling under their weight. A tree root snagged Cormac's foot, sending him flying. He lay there panting, sprawled on the mossy ground.

Robert raced back and grabbed his foster-brother's arm. 'Come on!' Cormac raised his head. '*No!*' he gasped. 'I can't!'

In the gloom, Robert saw Cormac's face was white beneath the faded bruises and fresh blood, his eyes sunken deep in their sockets. He looked as though he hadn't eaten or slept in weeks. Again, the question of what his foster-brother was doing here spiked in through his own exhaustion, but as he heard the distant barking of a hound all such thoughts left him. 'We have to keep moving!'

The Irishman managed to struggle to his knees, but agony flashed across his face as he tried to stand. He clutched Robert's wrist. 'You need to listen. You need to know what happened in Galloway.'

'It can wait!' Robert tried to heave him up.

Cormac's eyes were desperate. 'The bastard killed my father, Robert. Took his head.'

Robert stopped pulling at him.

Cormac stared up at the king, anguish etched in his face. 'Dungal MacDouall was waiting for us at Loch Ryan. They must have seen our fleet crossing from Antrim. My lord, he captured your brothers. Thomas and Alexander have been taken.'

'The men of Antrim? The ships?'

'Gone, brother. All gone.'

Robert staggered back, his hands lifting as if to block the words. Thoughts rose, whirled and collided. The barking was louder. The forest was echoing with hoof-beats, rough shouts and ringing horns. Their pursuers were almost upon them. With a desperate effort of will, Robert reached down and grasped Cormac by the waist. Grunting, sweat dripping from his nose, he hefted the man up over his shoulder. Ignoring his foster-brother's groans of pain and protest, he stumbled forward, feet sinking in the boggy ground.

Three deer crashed across their path, fleeing the approaching party. Robert, hunched under Cormac's weight, skidded down a muddy slope into a wooded hollow, overgrown with blackthorn and brambles. Forcing his way through the thicket, he made his way towards the far side of the dell. There, in the sandy bank, he saw a dark opening. It was partially draped by the snaking roots of a tree that had fallen some time ago, leaving a bowl in the earth. The woods behind them filling with the deep call of the horns, Robert dropped Cormac at the entrance to the hole. Crawling inside, he pulled his foster-brother in after him. Over Cormac's body, through the trailing curtain of roots, Robert saw a large, grey shape appear on the bank. The hound paused on the edge, then darted forward in a flurry of leaves.

Robert, wedged in behind Cormac, earth trickling down his neck, tried to draw his sword, but the space was too tight. 'Your knife!' he hissed at Cormac, as the animal tore through the undergrowth towards them.

It was too late. The hound emerged from the thicket and thrust its muzzle through the roots of the hole, jaws slathered with saliva. Cormac kicked out at it, but the dog whined and tried even harder to scrabble its way in.

'Fionn!'

At Robert's exclamation the hound went into a loud volley of barks. Leaning over his brother, Robert pulled aside the roots, allowing the panting, mud-soaked dog to squeeze into the hollow with them. Cormac winced in pain as Fionn pawed at his chest, trying to crawl over him, desperate to reach his long-lost master. Robert snapped a command in Gaelic. Immediately, Fionn dropped down, just as several riders came into view, hauling their horses to a halt at the edge of the dell. One was Aymer de Valence. Feeling Cormac tense beside him, Robert laid a warning hand on Fionn's head. The animal had been taught to obey commands of silence during hunts, but it was almost a year since he had sent the hound to Kildrummy with Niall and the women, and he had no idea what the animal might have been through in that time.

Aymer turned in his saddle, shouting to someone off through the trees. A few moments later a man appeared on foot. He had a whip in one hand and a cloak slung over his shoulder. Seeing the garment Christiana had given him, Robert realised how they had got Fionn to track him. In the gloom of the hollow he saw whip marks on the hound's back, glistening pink beneath his fur. There were older scars alongside the wounds. The man, a squire or a huntsman, gave a sharp whistle. Fionn's ears twitched under Robert's hand, but the dog made no sound, even when the man continued to whistle more frantically.

Valence turned on him. 'Quiet, God damn you! Let me listen.'

Robert's heart thudded as he watched Aymer walk his horse around the lip of the dell, his head turning this way and that, searching.

'Bruce!' he yelled, his shout echoing off through the trees. 'I know you're here!'

Robert felt Cormac's chest rising and falling beneath his arm. His nose was filled with the smell of mouldering earth. Something skittered across his face.

'Bruce, you whoreson! If you don't give yourself up to me I swear, by Christ, the first thing I'll do when I cross the border is pay a visit to your wife at Burstwick!' A few of the riders with Aymer chuckled unpleasantly. The earl urged his horse on around the clearing. 'After that I'll take a look in at your daughter!'

Robert fought back the fury that began to boil beneath his skin. Fionn whined softly. Cormac's breaths came fast and shallow.

'She screamed for you when they put her in her cage! Cried until her voice was gone, they tell me.' Aymer wrenched on the reins as his palfrey tossed its head. 'Show yourself, or I'll make that little bitch scream so hard you'll hear it for yourself!'

Robert's rage boiled over. He jerked forward, but Cormac clutched hold of him.

'No, brother,' he breathed. 'Not now. Not today.'

Robert clenched his teeth and closed his eyes, trying to block out Valence's words.

After a few more moments, the earl wheeled his horse around and spurred it on, commanding his men to follow. 'Spread out! Keep looking!'

24

Lanercost Priory, England, 1307 AD

At the anguished cry, Humphrey turned to see Thomas Bruce being hauled down from the wagon. The man's blond hair was stuck to his scalp with sweat and his broad face had a sallow hue. His leg, carved across the thigh by a sword strike during the fight with MacDouall's men, had been crudely splinted and bandaged, but the wrappings were soaked with blood.

'Careful,' Humphrey called.

As his knights glanced over he saw the question in their eyes, but they did as ordered, letting Thomas lean on them for support. Alexander Bruce was helped from the cart, his hands and feet bound. The dean's robes were bloodstained and one of his eyes was bruised shut, but his injuries were minor in comparison to his brother's.

Alexander met Humphrey's gaze. 'My brother needs help.' His tone was calm, but there was a pleading look in his eyes.

'I'll have a physician sent.' Humphrey turned to his squire. 'Hugh, ask the steward where they are to be kept. See they're made comfortable.'

Passing the reins of his horse to one of the grooms, Humphrey made his way across the priory's grounds, his breath fogging the air. He guessed his men would wonder at his compassion for the brothers of his enemy. In truth, he wondered at it himself. All he knew was that he took no pleasure in their suffering. The brutal executions of Niall Bruce and Christopher Seton had left an unpleasant taste in his mouth that lingered still.

It was almost March, but winter still held the north in its frozen grip. The wagons had struggled on the road down from the border, two horses falling on the ice. Here in Lanercost, which had housed the two hundred members of the royal court since autumn, the constant comings and goings had turned the snow to a dirty slush. Humphrey's boots crunched through the frozen muck as he headed for the two-storey building, which stood in the shadow of the priory's church.

The doorward greeted him outside the king's bedchamber. 'Sir Humphrey.'

'How is he today, Simon?'

The man pursed his lips and shook his head.

As Simon pushed open the door for him, Humphrey took a deep breath of the corridor's musty air, knowing it would be blessedly sweet in comparison to the chamber beyond. He realised he had come to loathe this place; the smell of sickness that saturated it and the volatility of the man trapped within it.

Despite the fact it was still daylight thick drapes were pulled over the windows. The chamber was lit by a fire and several candles, slumped in pools of their own wax. The chair by the hearth was empty. Humphrey's gaze went to the large bed that dominated the room. The curtains were partially drawn and he could see a shape under the covers. 'My lord?'

Drawing the curtains aside, Humphrey looked down on his father-in-law. He was shocked by the change in the king. He had seen him only two days ago, but the man seemed to have aged another year in that time. In the candles' jaundiced glow, his skin was ashen, his face sunken in on itself. His head, webbed with white strands of hair, looked too small for the pillow it lay on. The shadow of death itself seemed cast upon him. Indeed, if not for the whistling breaths emitting from the king's puckered mouth, Humphrey would have said it had already claimed him. One of Edward's hands was outside the covers, which were stained with sweat and other fluids. Humphrey noted the dark marks across his knuckles. It was over a week since the confrontation with his son, who had been sent to London, but the bruises had been slow to fade.

Thinking the king's rapid decline was most likely due to the fight and the revelation that preceded it, Humphrey felt a stirring of anger towards Thomas of Lancaster, who had ignored his counsel at Lochmaben. As he had feared, rifts had now opened in the royal court;

bitter lines drawn between father and son, cousin and cousin. It was
the last thing they needed.

The king's eyes flickered open. Seeing Humphrey standing over
him he at once looked alert, all the life left in him concentrated in
those steel-bright eyes. He licked his desiccated lips and tried to sit.
'Do you have them? Bruce's brothers?'

Humphrey leaned in to help, banking the pillows up behind
the king. 'Dungal MacDouall was as good as his word, my lord.
He delivered Thomas and Alexander into my custody at
Lochmaben.'

'What were his demands?' asked Edward, grunting as he sat back.

'As you thought, he wants his lands in Galloway returned to him
and to those of his men who were disinherited after John Balliol's
exile. He was reluctant to hand over the prisoners without formal
agreement of this, but I assured him you would give it serious
consideration.'

'I am preparing to send a company to join MacDouall's force in
Galloway, in case Bruce tries to retaliate. I'll have my men take the
message that when the rebel king is captured, MacDouall and the
Disinherited will be granted their estates, subject to me.'

Humphrey was surprised by the king's curt response. Edward
seemed less gratified by the arrest of Bruce's brothers than he'd
expected.

The king coughed dryly and motioned to the table, on which stood
a jug and goblet. As Humphrey crossed the room, the king continued.
'While you were gone word came from the captain of one of the ships
I sent out from Skinburness to hunt for Bruce.'

Humphrey listened as he poured out the spiced wine. He watched
it swirl into the goblet, ignoring the desire to have some himself. As
he returned to the king's side he caught sight of a large wooden chest
that stood at the end of the bed. He had seen it before and knew it
stored Edward's personal belongings. Looking at it now, he recalled
Aymer de Valence speaking of the recovered prophecy box. He
wondered if it might be inside.

'The captain encountered a large fleet off Kintyre. He managed to
sail to safety, but the three vessels with his were captured. The ships
were Highland galleys, flying the colours of the MacDonalds and the
MacRuaries.'

Humphrey paused, the wine forgotten in his hand. 'Robert?'

Edward beckoned impatiently. As Humphrey passed him the goblet, the king seized it with shaking hands. He slurped at the lip, wine dribbling from the corners of his mouth. When he was done, he closed his eyes and rested his head back against the pillows. The effort of drinking seemed to have leached even more life from him. 'It would seem the bastard has emerged from whatever hole he's been hiding in.'

'So the landing at Galloway by Bruce's Irish kin was perhaps part of a larger invasion? Or a distraction?' Humphrey pushed a hand through his hair. 'Did the captain have any idea where the fleet was headed?'

'North.' Edward handed back the goblet. 'I've sent messengers to Henry at Turnberry and Aymer in Ayr.' Pain animated his face. He gritted his teeth and continued. 'I expected the MacDonalds to aid Bruce. They have always blown in the same direction as his family, but the MacRuaries are a force I had not reckoned on. I haven't the power, Humphrey, to challenge such a fleet. Not out on the water. Not even with the support of John MacDougall of Argyll.'

'What about Richard de Burgh, my lord?'

Edward nodded. 'A summons has already been drafted. It is time to test Ulster's loyalty, with his daughter in my custody.'

Humphrey thought of Elizabeth, locked up in Burstwick Manor. Now and then, he would catch Bess's voice in his mind, asking why he hadn't petitioned the king for a more lenient sentence for the young woman, who had been her good friend. He eased that nub of guilt with the knowledge that Elizabeth, of all Bruce's women, was the one suffering the least. 'What do you need me to do?'

'I want you to go to Carrick. Meet with Aymer at Ayr and find out what is happening. I need to know, Humphrey.'

'Of course. I will leave whenever you command it.' Humphrey paused. 'My lord, Thomas Bruce is gravely wounded. His brother, the dean, requested aid. We may benefit from granting the request. I have questioned them on the whereabouts of the Staff of Malachy. Thomas refused to answer, but I got the impression Alexander may be willing to speak if we help his brother.'

'I'll not have any here waste time on a condemned man. They are both to be hanged in Carlisle.'

Humphrey fought to conceal his shock. Alexander – a man of the cloth? 'But, my lord, if they know where the staff is we can—'

'God damn it, Humphrey, the staff is not important!'

Humphrey stared at him, astonished.

Edward drew in a long breath. 'What I mean to say is that it isn't important at this moment, not while the Scots are massing in the west. I'll not have you, or any of my men, following more false leads and lies from that family. The retrieval of the relic can wait until Bruce is destroyed.'

Humphrey fought back the clamour in his mind as all the questions seething in him these past months now rushed to the surface at the king's outburst. He tried to keep his focus. 'Forgive me, my lord, but do we not run the risk of making martyrs? If Bruce has managed to elicit the support of the lords of the Isles, he may win more sympathy as word of these sentences spreads. Even some of our own men have been . . . discomforted by the treatment of his family.'

'Then those men should remember that not only did Bruce betray them and break faith with me, but that he is a murderer and an excommunicate. With the killing of John Comyn he set himself beyond the bounds of all laws, temporal and spiritual. He and all who support him are subject to punishments as befit that heinous crime.'

Humphrey felt a prickle of anger. He knew full well that John Comyn's murder was the lesser of the reasons the king wanted Bruce to pay. The burning issue was that not only had the man personally betrayed Edward, but – by claiming the throne of Scotland – he had effectively disinherited him. Humphrey understood, well enough, the king's wrath. He just wished Edward wouldn't try to make him swallow the same propaganda he had his clerics promoting far and wide.

The king held Humphrey in his gaze. 'You need not fear the will of those Scots who have pledged their loyalty to me, Humphrey. The Comyns, the MacDougalls and many other barons want swift, harsh justice for the slayers of their kinsman. They will not mourn the deaths of two more bad seeds from Bruce's clan. By God, even a member of his own family has expressed deep disgust for that act.' The king's mouth twitched. 'And a willingness to enter my service against him.'

Humphrey didn't speak. He felt queasy, the heat from the fire and the rancid stink of the bedcovers overpowering. Edward should have been in the ground months ago. He had never before seen anyone so

near death cling so fiercely to life. The king's desire to see Robert
Bruce crushed seemed to be the only thing keeping him on the mortal
plain, as if his hatred of the man were something alive; a heartbeat
that pulsed within him, even as his skin sank on to his bones and all
the sweat and bile poured out of him. But what if his hatred wasn't
just due to Robert's treason? What if there was something else behind
it? Something more potent? More personal?

Edward's brow knotted as the silence lengthened. 'You may go,
Humphrey. Get some rest. You leave for Carrick at first light
tomorrow.'

Humphrey inclined his head. He made to leave, but as his eyes
caught on the chest again he switched back. 'My lord, can I ask why
you didn't tell me Aymer de Valence found the box that contained the
Last Prophecy when he took Kildrummy?' Humphrey saw a tic jump in
Edward's cheek. Some emotion flashed in the king's eyes, too quick
for him to discern what it was.

When Edward spoke his voice was low. 'I didn't want it made
public that the box was empty – that Bruce had taken the prophecy
from me.'

Humphrey hesitated, knowing he was walking out on to a frozen
lake that could crack beneath his feet at any moment, yet unable to
stop himself. There were things out in these depths that he didn't
understand. 'The attack on Robert in Ireland – you never explained
why you wanted me to uncover the details of it. I sensed there was
more to it than you were . . .' He searched for the right words:
'. . . willing to say at the time. Perhaps, my lord, such knowledge
would help me better predict our enemy's next move?'

Edward's voice was flint cold. 'I will tell you our enemy's next
move. He will attempt to raise sword and fire against us. He will seek
to break up the kingdom I have spent my reign uniting for the good of
us all and destroy everything we have laboured so long and bled so
hard to achieve. He will make a mockery of those he once called
brothers, the men of my Round Table, and a travesty of those who
sacrificed their lives for our cause. Men like your father. Do not forget
it was soldiers of Bruce's friend, William Wallace, who took his life at
Falkirk.' Edward nodded when Humphrey looked away. 'Bruce
betrayed you as much as he betrayed me. Worse, perhaps, for he used
you to get close to me, concealing his true nature in the false cloak of
friendship. The man is a liar, a murderer and a traitor, Humphrey. He

must be brought down at all costs. The survival of our kingdom depends on it.'

Prince Edward stood on the dockside, grasping Piers Gaveston's hands in his. 'This will not be for ever.'

Piers said nothing. His coal-black eyes flashed with sunlight as he glanced at the ship moored in Dover's harbour that was to bear him to France, banished by the king's order.

Edward clutched his friend's hands tighter, forcing the man to look at him. 'I swear it, Piers. When my father is dead I will send for you.'

'And what of your new wife, my lord prince? Will she bear my presence at your side?'

Edward's brow furrowed at his cold tone. 'She'll have no choice. Isabella will be my wife in name alone. My heart will always be yours.'

'My lord?'

Edward looked round to see his squire lingering uncertainly. Behind the young man the white cliffs were blinding in the March sunlight.

'The captain says he must leave, my lord. The tide turns.'

Edward reached for the purse that was tied to his belt. Unfastening it, he pushed it into Piers's hands. 'This should see you well until you reach Ponthieu.'

Piers stared at it. His jaw pulsed. 'I doubt it will last me a week.'

'Those aren't coins. They're jewels and gold – my rings, some brooches. All I could get my hands on.'

Piers's hand closed around the purse. After a pause he seemed to thaw. Reaching up, he touched Edward's face, a mess of browns and yellows where the king's fists had struck. The prince's head was covered by a hat, concealing the bald patches where his blond hair had been torn out.

Edward put his hand over the knight's, pressing it to his cheek. He felt anger and despair well up, threatening to overwhelm him. He'd spent so many years with Piers at his side, from the carefree days of boyhood, through the wild passion of adolescence to the slow-burning fire of love. He couldn't imagine him not being there. It was as if one of his limbs were being torn from him. Not caring that his men were waiting nearby, Edward leaned in and kissed him, aching at the soft fullness of his lips between the stubble of beard, the familiar perfume of his oil-scented hair, the warmth of his breath. 'You have my heart, Piers. Always.'

25

Barra, Scotland, 1307 AD

He felt as though God were tormenting him, sending him back to this island with the same heavy heart he'd borne that first voyage. How many more dead would he have to carry inside him before this war was over? His soul had become a graveyard.

Barra's rugged contours dominated Robert's vision, the sun descending in a blaze behind its hills, but all he could see were the faces of Thomas, Alexander and Lord Donough. He remembered, with aching detail, playing with his younger brothers, racing and fighting in Carrick's hills, back when they believed the earldom was the world and they were its masters. He remembered Thomas's trustworthiness and Alexander's sincerity. He remembered the way Donough's eyes would crinkle when he smiled and how his fosterfather's deep voice would fill his hall with the legends of Irish heroes. He stared into the sun, willing it to burn away the images, erasing the pain, the guilt, but they remained, haunting his thoughts. They had done since Cormac told him what had happened in Galloway. His foster-brother sat at the stern, wrapped in a blanket, his bruised face stained by the sun's dying light. Fionn lay at his feet, his head on his paws, eyes following the movements of the crew.

After crawling from that hollow they had stumbled through the woods for miles, Robert dragging Cormac alongside him, ignoring his anguished pleas to set him down and let him be. When they reached the shore, some miles north of Turnberry, Robert despaired, seeing the fleet out on the water nearing Arran, but adamant Edward and his men wouldn't leave without him, he had hauled Cormac along the cliffs to a hidden cove where he and his brothers often played as children. Vain hope blossomed into blessed relief when he saw the galley anchored in the shallows. As they staggered on to the beach, Edward and Nes came running to meet them, Fionn leaping excitedly around them in the waves.

Back on Arran, sombre at the failed invasion and the news from Galloway, Robert and his men had counted their losses, before seeking the sanctuary of the Outer Isles.

Robert's gaze moved from Cormac to the large figure who sat slumped against the mast, hands tied behind it. The attack, he reminded himself, hadn't been utterly fruitless. A sack had been placed over the captive's head, secured around his neck with rope. A few years ago Robert would never have treated a man of his stature with such dishonour, but things had changed. King Edward had seen to that. His eyes lingered on the captive, fingers itching to curl around his sword hilt and take his revenge in bloody strips from the man's body. Even with the knowledge that the prisoner was now perhaps his best hope, the urge was almost unbearable. Robert's attention was caught by a warning shout from one of the birlinns cresting the waves ahead of them.

Lachlan MacRuarie crossed the deck, looking to where the crewman was pointing. They were sailing into the mouth of Barra's harbour. The castle had appeared, rising from its island in the foreground.

'What is it?' Robert asked, standing.

'Unknown vessels,' murmured Lachlan, his gaze on the shore. 'Five of them.'

Robert shielded his eyes from the sun's brilliance. He could see them – five galleys lined up on the beach. They were smaller than Lachlan's, not quite as long or as sleek.

Edward moved up beside him. 'Who are they?'

Hearing a cry behind him, Robert turned sharply. It had come from James Douglas. The young man had leapt on to one of the benches, his face lit with elation. He was waving his arms over his head, his cheeks creased with a broad grin. Glancing back at the shore Robert saw figures running down the sand. He couldn't see their faces at this distance, but his eyes fixed on the bright yellow of their surcoats, all of which had a broad band across the middle. It was too far for him to pick out the detail, but, with a rush of joy, he knew they would be chequered blue and white. They were the colours of the High Steward of Scotland.

The sun had slipped behind the great hill and more people had appeared on the beach to welcome the men home by the time the first galleys ground ashore. Robert glimpsed Christiana among them, her hair flying like a banner in the breeze, but all his focus was on James Stewart, waiting in the shallows, his tall form draped by a fur-trimmed mantle that bore his crest. James smiled a rare smile as Robert jumped on to the sand and went to meet him. They embraced, laughing at the reunion, which neither man had expected to come.

Robert felt the wall of disagreement and resentment that had built up between them these past two years dissolve. There was only gladness, seeing his old friend alive, here with him at last. As he drew back, wondering where to begin, James Douglas approached, looking tentatively between them. Robert smiled and stepped aside, gesturing for him to greet his uncle and godfather. The young man started forward as if to embrace the steward, then halted and bowed respectfully instead.

The steward moved in and grasped the young man's shoulders. 'Your message was a prayer answered.'

Edward and Malcolm joined them, quickly followed by Gilbert de la Hay and Neil Campbell, all overjoyed at the sight of the steward; former adviser to King Alexander, once guardian of Scotland, and one of the most powerful lords in the kingdom.

After the greetings were exchanged and the first questions began, Robert held up his hand. 'There will be time to share stories later. Let me talk with James alone.'

Leaving his men to collect their gear, Robert led the high steward along the shoreline, away from the crowd. When they came to a stream that cut glimmering veins through the sand, he turned to him. 'When I found Malcolm he said he saw you ride from Methven Wood, but even then . . .' Robert shook his head. 'After everything that has happened, I didn't dare hope.'

'For my part, I had some hope to cling to,' James told him. 'Snatches of reports from men I sent out telling me you were alive. But I had to keep moving to avoid the English, who were hunting me in my lands, and the tidings became fewer as the months went by. By the time I got word from my nephew that you had found sanctuary here, faith had all but left me.'

'Do you know of the others? My family? Sir John? Christopher?'

'I heard Wishart and Lamberton were arrested and that John

MacDougall and the Black Comyn had raised an army against you, but other than that it was mostly fragments of rumour and hearsay, impossible to build a picture with.' James's tone was grave. 'I do know that Pope Clement has pronounced your excommunication.'

Robert thought he saw blame in the steward's brown eyes and perhaps a glint of anger. After a pause, he looked away, his gaze on the galleys still making their way in to shore, the black sails of the MacDonald vessels and the red of the MacRuaries' reflected in the calm waters of the harbour. His voice hushed with sorrow, he told James of the fate of his family at King Edward's hands and the black news Cormac had struggled his way from Galloway with. 'The dragon banner fulfilled its promise,' he finished quietly. 'Edward showed no mercy. I fear Alexander and Thomas will share the same fate as Niall.' He glanced at the steward, whose eyes were closed. Robert noticed his hair was greyer and the lines that creased his face deeper. He looked old, old and worn out.

Finally, James turned to him, his eyes moist in the twilight. 'I do not have words, Robert. I am so very sorry.'

'I sent them there, James. I sent my brothers to their deaths.' Robert sat on the beach, scooping up a fistful of white sand. 'I know Alexander didn't want to go. I ordered him from my side not because he would be of use in the fight, but because he wanted me to atone for Comyn's death. That's why I sent him away – for the sake of my own damn pride.' He let the sand trickle between his fingers, the grains scattering on the breeze. His voice hardened. 'I'll not let their deaths be in vain. I have to try again.'

James said nothing for a long moment. He looked over at the men and women crowded on the beach. Torches flamed in the gathering dusk. 'It is no mean feat to have won the allegiance of the MacDonalds and the lords of Garmoran. Malcolm, Gilbert, Neil and others would all lay down their lives for you. I myself will gather and arm as many of my tenants as I can.' His eyes flicked to Robert. 'But I do not believe this will be enough to fight a war on two fronts, not after what you say happened in Galloway and Turnberry.' James crouched down beside him. 'I beg you, my lord, make amends with those of your countrymen who stand against you. Your grandfather came to realise that only grief could be born in the hatred between him and the Comyns. That is why he stepped down after John Balliol was chosen as king. Maybe, for the sake of our realm, it is time for you to do the same? Time to atone?'

Robert thought back to that rainy day in Lochmaben; the day he had taken Carrick from his father and inherited their family's claim to the throne. He recalled his grandfather telling him then that the first duty of a king was to hold the realm together. But the man hadn't lived through these dark days. The war then had been gestating, unborn. Robert had heard this before from the high steward at Methven Wood and his coronation, but it was different hearing it now. He didn't feel anger or resentment. He felt calm in his discord. 'It is too late, James. None of us can wipe the slate clean. Too much blood has been spilled on it. The Comyns and their allies still believe John Balliol should sit on Scotland's throne. They will never accept me. Never pay homage to me. If I am to have any hope of rebuilding my kingdom they cannot be part of it. I know that now.'

'This is civil war, Robert. Blood against blood.'

'It became civil war when I killed John Comyn. There is only one way through it. One side must destroy the other if either is to survive. God willing, beyond it is civil peace.'

'You could wait – bide your time out here in safety? I do not believe King Edward is long for this world. From what you say, Aymer de Valence, Henry Percy and Dungal MacDouall have been running his campaign. That is not the Edward we know. I suspect this means he is too frail to make the journey himself. When his son takes the throne the landscape of this war will change, perhaps dramatically. Why not see how it lies then?'

'I cannot wait, James. Edward has defied death too many times. Who is to say his health will not improve – that we won't see him come north in the summer, under the dragon? I have to continue the fight. Every day the English in Scotland remain unchallenged, the stronger their dominion grows.'

'What of your family? What of Marjorie and Elizabeth? Edward may use them to punish you for continuing your war.'

Robert rose. 'I have someone who may help me with that. Come.'

He led the way back along the shore, retracing his footprints in the sand. The men were still unloading supplies from the vessels as more birlinns let down anchors in the bay, the crew using the lines of moored galleys as a bridge to clamber to the shore. Robert saw that the prisoner had been hauled off. He was kneeling in the sand, hands tied behind his back, the blood on his gold surcoat garish in the torch-light. Two of Lachlan's men were standing over him. The prisoner's head was moving frantically from side to side as if he were trying to work out where he was. Robert could hear his breaths.

'This is how I ensure my family's safety,' he said, turning to the steward. 'And, I believe, their freedom.'

The prisoner jerked round at his voice. 'Bruce! You bastard!' His voice was muffled through the hood. As he struggled to stand, one of Lachlan's men grabbed hold of the top of the sack, pushing him firmly back down.

James looked at Robert, shocked. 'Is that . . .?'

Robert smiled coldly. 'Henry Percy, Lord of Alnwick.'

'How?'

'Lachlan,' answered Robert, as deeply satisfied looking down on the humbled English lord now as he had been back on Arran when the captain had shown him his prize. Percy, who had cut a bloody swathe through the fleeing galloglass, hadn't seen the cliff edge in the mist and the chaos. His horse had gone straight over. He was only saved by being tossed from the saddle on to a ledge several feet below. His sword gone, he stood no chance against the tide of men pouring down to the beach.

'Release me,' Percy growled. 'Or your family will suffer.'

'My family are already suffering.' Robert kept his voice flat, matter-of-fact, careful not to reveal his emotions to the lord, who had been one of his brothers-in-arms when they were Knights of the Dragon. He didn't want the man to know his true feelings; didn't want him to be able to tell the king of his torment. He would not give Edward the satisfaction.

'Believe me, Bruce, it can be made worse for them.'

Robert gestured to Lachlan's men. 'Secure him.'

As they hauled the corpulent lord to his feet, Percy twisted towards Robert. 'My men will come for me, traitor, and when they do they will make you wish you were never born! You and all your bastard kin!'

Robert waited until they had led him away. 'I will offer to exchange him for my daughter, my wife and my sisters.' As he turned to the high steward to gauge his reaction, he caught sight of a man who had appeared on the edges of the crowd and was watching Percy being dragged up the beach. Robert stared at him, disbelieving what his eyes were telling him. There, standing on the beach was Alexander Seton.

James followed his gaze. He nodded. 'Alexander found me on Bute two months ago. He had been searching for you, as I had, without success. He elected to stay with me and wait for word.'

His surprise fading, Robert felt wariness creep in like a shadow. 'He deserted me, James, back in Aberdeen. I've not seen him since.'

'He told me. For what it is worth, he seems truly regretful of his actions.'

Alexander glanced round to see Robert staring at him. He seemed to stiffen, before coming forward, hesitantly. None of the other men, busy by the boats, had noticed him yet.

As he approached, Robert realised how much he had changed. Alexander's once broad, strong-boned face was thin. A beard, streaked with grey, covered his mouth and jaw. There was a new scar on his forehead and it looked as though his nose had been broken. The past year had clearly not been kind to him. Robert couldn't help but feel gratified.

Alexander dropped to his knees before him. 'My lord king.' He lowered his eyes. 'Forgive me.'

Robert looked down on him, strands of their long friendship tugging him in one direction, resentment and mistrust pulling him in another. 'Arise,' he said, after a moment. He watched Alexander get to his feet. 'Where have you been?'

'After Aberdeen I was in East Lothian for a time.' Alexander kept his eyes on the sand. 'I submitted to the English in the hope I would gain back my lands, but then I learned you were attacked in Lorn by John MacDougall's forces.' He raised his head. 'It was then that I realised the depth of my mistake. I couldn't bear not knowing what had happened – to you, to my friends, to Christopher – so I set out to find you.' He looked down at his hands. 'Hoping I could make amends.'

Robert wondered suddenly whether Alexander had heard what had happened to his cousin. He guessed he hadn't, since James hadn't known of it. He was thinking how to broach the subject, when he saw a woman approaching. It was Brigid, her bare feet sinking in the sand. Her expression caught his attention at once. He had seen that look on too many faces in recent months not to know what it meant.

The men and women wound their way down to the shore in the blue dusk, the flames of their torches gusting. Dark clouds tarnished the sky, casting shadows across the water. Waves whispered on the sand. When the procession came to the boat, raised up on a cradle of firewood near the water's edge, they spread out in a circle around it. Some glanced at one another for guidance, unsure, nervous even, of the unfamiliar ritual.

Robert was the first to approach the vessel. In one hand he held a piece of parchment, in the other the destiny Affraig had made for him. The brittle crown at the centre of the web swung on its thread. He paused at the side of the boat, a miniature version of the birlinns, no bigger than a coffin. Lifted from the sand on a dais of logs and tinder, it came up to his waist. He looked down at the body inside. Affraig looked tiny, wrapped in her shabby brown cloak, only her sunken, wrinkled face visible. Kindling and scraps of material had been stuffed in around her, making her look as though she were lying in a nest. She had died only three days ago, but even though the cold had helped preserve her, he caught the sweet stench of decay beneath the smell of freshly chopped wood and the herbs Brigid had placed around her.

After a pause, he placed the web of twigs on her chest. He remembered Affraig telling him his father had once come to her, drunk, demanding that she weave him his destiny; that he would be king. She had done so, but when one of his men assaulted her and the earl refused to give her justice, she had torn down that destiny and left it in pieces outside the castle walls. The curse had come to pass. His father had never been crowned king. The memory made him wonder if what he was doing here was right, but Brigid had told him this was what Affraig had commanded before she passed.

Tell him to burn it. Burn it with my body.

Robert stepped back into the crowd, still holding the parchment. He caught Brigid's eye and she inclined her head. Elena was beside her, clutching a spray of ferns. At a gentle push from her mother, the girl approached the vessel. She had to stand on tiptoe to place the ferns into the boat with the old woman's body. When she was done, she turned and hastened back to Brigid.

Christiana moved through the gathering to stand at Robert's side. 'My lord?'

Robert met her questioning gaze with a nod.

Christiana motioned to those of her men who bore torches. Together, they moved forward, surrounding the vessel with a ring of fire. One by one, they thrust the torches deep into the cradle of logs beneath the boat. As the pyre smouldered, tongues of fire flicking along the undersides of the vessel, the men moved back into the solemn crowd, watching as this rite from the old world was performed once again on their shores. No Christian burial for a witch. Affraig had wanted to burn. On Robert's request, Christiana had spoken to the elders among her people, those who had lived here under the Norse and remembered the ship burnings for the Viking dead.

'Thank you, my lady,' he murmured.

Christiana smiled, but said nothing, her green eyes filling with fire-light as the breeze fanned the flames and sent sparks swirling into the evening sky.

The fire grew quickly, engulfing the small boat and lighting the faces of the assembled gathering. Robert's gaze drifted over their silent ranks. Lachlan MacRuarie was standing nearby, a jewelled goblet clutched in his hand. A fresh wound carved through his cheek from the fight at Turnberry, a new scar for the collection on his face. The captain had lost fifty in the skirmish. Angus MacDonald three times that. The Lord of Islay was standing with his men, his eyes on the flames. Edward was there, with Nes and Neil Campbell, Cormac among them, his injuries still livid. Malcolm and Gilbert were behind, the Lord of Erroll towering over his companions, his face unusually sombre. James Douglas stood close beside his uncle. On the high steward's other side was Alexander Seton.

Seeing many heads bowed and eyes closed in prayer, Robert was surprised. He had asked them to join him in honouring Affraig, but none, apart from Brigid and Elena, had known the old woman. He realised, looking from Edward to Cormac, James to Angus, that each man was caught up in his own private grief. Affraig had become an embodiment of all their losses; a hundred deaths bound in her ancient body to be mourned as one. Looking back at the blaze, he thought of Niall, John of Atholl, Christopher Seton and Donough, holding each in his mind for a moment, before letting go.

Eternal rest grant them, O Lord, and let everlasting light shine upon them.

He thought of Marjorie and Elizabeth, Mary and his other three sisters, Robert Wishart and William Lamberton, his nephews, little Donald of Mar and young Thomas Randolph, Isabel Comyn: all locked up in English prisons for their loyalty to him. He thought of Thomas and Alexander, their fate unknown, but the worst feared. Tonight was for mourning the dead, but tomorrow was for the living. Whether with an army of ten, or ten thousand, he would liberate Scotland from his enemies and bring back his family.

There was a rush of heat as the flames caught Affraig's body, consuming flesh in a crackling roar and with it the crown of heather. As the web went up in smoke, Robert imagined his destiny being forged in the fire, taking life in its dazzling heart. He looked down at the parchment in his hand. Brigid had given it to him last night, shortly after his arrival on Barra. The soft, yellowed skin was covered with writing. It was surprisingly neat given Affraig's infirmity in her last days. His eyes lingered on three lines in the centre.

> And when the covetous king then dies
> The Britons, to reclaim their kingdom, shall rise.
> This is the truth, as spoken by the prophet Merlin.

Handing it to him, Brigid had told him her aunt's final words.

'She said, my lord, that you must embrace your ancient heritage. The blood of the old world flows in your veins, passed down from your mother and the kings of Ireland. Remember that, out here in the heartlands of the west. She said do not fight Edward with his own fire, but rather use it to light your beacon — your fiery cross. Speak to restless Ireland. Call on conquered Wales. King Arthur was ruler of the Britons. He is their champion, not Edward's. You must take him back.'

'My lord?'

Robert looked up from the parchment at the voice. He realised Alexander Seton had moved up beside him. While he had been reading Affraig's prophecy, the crowd had begun to strike up quiet conversations.

Alexander's face was cast in the shifting glow of the fire. 'Sir James told me you are planning to send a message to the English — offering to exchange Henry Percy for your family?'

Robert nodded.

'My lord, I beg you, let me take that message for you. Let me make amends.'

PART 4

1307 AD

Let their noble examples animate you; rouse up the spirit of the ancient Romans, and be not afraid to march out against our enemies that are lying in ambush for us in the valley, but boldly with your swords demand of them your just rights.

The History of the Kings of Britain, *Geoffrey of Monmouth*

26

Glen Trool, Scotland, 1307 AD

The rain swept in over the peaks, drenching the heather-clad slopes and falling in long, misty ribbons to the depths of the glen, which cut a great rift through the mountains. It needled the surface of the loch that filled the valley and drummed on the helms of the fifty men running fast along a narrow track that wound through the woods on the southern shore.

James Douglas, breathing hard, glanced over his shoulder, blinking rainwater and sweat from his eyes. Through the dark tunnel of trees he glimpsed riders in the distance behind him. The enemy was gaining. At Neil Campbell's warning shout, James twisted round to see a fallen tree looming up, blocking the path. He would have run straight into it. It looked as though it had collapsed recently, yet another victim of the spring storms. So far, such obstacles had aided the Scots, hampering the pursuit of the English cavalry, but the gap was closing. They couldn't outrun them much longer.

Throwing Neil a look of thanks, James clambered over the splintered trunk. Plunging down into the mud on the other side, he pushed himself up and sprinted on behind his companions, trying to ignore the throbbing ache in his legs and the burning in his lungs. There was nowhere to go but forward. To the right, the bank fell sharply into the deep waters of Loch Trool. To the left, the slopes climbed steeply through a dense forest of ash, holly and birch up into the craggy heights of the mountains.

Above the hammering rain and the harsh gasps of his own breaths, James heard the thud of hooves and the shouts of their pursuers, rough with triumph as they closed in on the Scots. In a sudden break in the trees to his right he caught a flash of fire away across the loch. The flaming arrow rose into the sky like a comet from the hills on the northern shore. At the sight of the signal, relief flooded through James, giving him an extra surge of speed. Moments later, he heard a faint rumbling sound. It began as a distant roll of thunder, echoing somewhere up in the heights. Ahead, his companions were slowing, turning now, as the rumbling swelled to fill the valley, along with a great wave of tearing and splintering sounds.

'Get down!' yelled Neil.

Reaching the others, James threw himself against the steep bank, just as a huge boulder came hurtling through the woods above the track. Hunkered down, hands over his head, he glimpsed the English, still some distance away, wheeling around, their horses rearing in panic. The boulder smashed straight through the first few lines, crushing one man and sweeping three more into the loch before it struck the surface with a great white rush. More rocks followed; scores of them, tumbling down the hillside in a flood of loose stones and felled trees, picked up by their momentum. The cavalry tried to spur their mounts out of the path of the danger, but there was nowhere for them to go. Cries of pain and terror rose as the rockslide thundered on top of them.

One boulder veered off course and came thumping down, dangerously close to James and his companions. Smashing through a tree above the Scots, scattering them with broken branches, it entered the loch in a plume of water. After it had gone, a strange silence descended, broken only by the mad chatter of birds and the faint cries of wounded men and horses. James stared up through the trees, listening intently. After a moment, a distant roar of voices sounded in the heights, building quickly to a crescendo.

Neil wrenched his sword from its scabbard. Eyes gleaming with fierce intent, he met James's gaze. 'For your father.'

James tugged free his own blade. 'For Wallace.'

Together, the fifty Scots raced back along the track towards the beleaguered English, their battle cries lifting to join with those of their countrymen, now pouring down the hillside in the wake of the boulders.

Ayr, Scotland, 1307 AD

As Humphrey opened the door, Aymer de Valence looked up, his face taut. The earl was standing over a table in the centre of the room, across the surface of which was scattered a confusion of maps and rolls of accounts. Chests and crates, as yet unpacked, lined one wall. Candles made a brave, but futile attempt at brightening the dingy chamber. The leaded windows were fogged with rain. There was a bucket in one corner, catching the overflow from a leak in the ceiling.

Aymer had a parchment in his fist. He raised it as Humphrey shut the door. 'Does the king not trust me?'

Humphrey frowned. 'What do you mean?'

Aymer came around the table towards him. 'You gave the impression Edward sent you here to aid me in my hunt for Bruce.'

'What is this about, Aymer?'

'I have just received word from the king. He demands to know why I haven't caught our enemy yet. He accuses me of being timid!' Aymer batted the parchment with the back of his hand. 'Lacking in decisiveness! Without any sense of urgency! Did Edward send you here to spy on me, Humphrey? To observe my methods and report back to him?' His eyes narrowed. 'Have you told him about Percy?'

'I haven't sent any reports to the king, not since I arrived. As for Percy, I am the one who counselled you to keep his capture quiet for the time being. I am still hopeful we may be able to retrieve him without the king needing to be troubled.'

A loud banging started up outside, the labourers returning to work after their midday meal. Humphrey's brow creased as the hammering reverberated through the chamber. He had arrived several weeks ago to find the town in chaos, carts congesting the streets, the English barracks bristling with scaffolding and piles of rubble everywhere. After Bruce's fleet had been repelled from Carrick, Aymer, fearing another attack, had returned to Ayr. Sending Ralph de Monthermer to man the garrison at Turnberry, he had remained to oversee the refortification of the town's defences. Ayr, razed during the course of the war by English and Scots forces alike, was still recovering from its last destruction.

Aymer stalked back to the table and tossed the parchment on to it. He took up a jug and poured himself some wine, lifting it questioningly at Humphrey, who shook his head. 'Damn that fat fool! How did

Percy let himself get taken?' Exhaling, Aymer sat heavily on a stool. 'It's almost a month since they took him. Do you think he is dead?'

'Robert isn't stupid. He will either ransom Percy for money, or else, if he knows of his family's imprisonment, exchange him for their freedom.'

'I was so close, Humphrey.' Aymer clenched his fist. 'So close to catching the bastard.'

Humphrey planted his hands on the table and stared down at the maps, his gaze drifting over Scotland's fractured west coast: long slits of sea lochs, barriers of mountains and tiny clusters of islands in vast expanses of parchment. *Where are you, Robert?*

The two men glanced round at a rap on the door. One of Aymer's knights looked in. 'Sir, there's a rabble at the gates, begging for food.'

'Get rid of them,' growled Aymer. 'And, next time, kill a few of them to show the rest you mean it.' He shook his head as the knight withdrew. 'I would have banished the entire population if I didn't need them to help me rebuild it.' He scowled. 'The whole stinking place is beset by vagrants, bleating about how their crops and live-stock were destroyed by Prince Edward and his men, leaving them destitute. I tell them to look to Bruce if they want someone to blame.'

'We could exploit that,' suggested Humphrey, his thoughts on the recent executions of Thomas and Alexander in Carlisle. His worry that the king's harsh justice would only inflame the Scots, making them more likely to rise under Bruce's banner, had been steadily growing. 'Right now, the people of Ayr are scared. They know better than most what an English army is capable of. That makes them compliant, yes. But perhaps, as more benevolent masters, we could begin to breed loyalty among them? Make them realise they cannot rely on Bruce to help them. Give them no reason to support him.'

'Do I look as though I have time to till the land in order to feed peasants?' Aymer's tone was acerbic. 'Our supply lines from the east are stretched thin enough as it is. We can barely maintain our own garrisons.' He drained his wine and got up to pour more, his voice rising as he continued. 'We have no idea where Bruce is or when the bastard will surface again. We do know he has strong support among the men of the Isles and added to that are these rumours James Stewart is alive and raising his vassals for war. I am one man, with limited resources at my disposal. The king may wish me to perform miracles, but I simply cannot rebuild Ayr, coddle these damn Scots *and* patrol every glen and loch in this godforsaken hole searching for that traitor!' With a vicious sweep of his arm, Aymer sent half the maps and rolls flying off the table.

Rarely had Humphrey seen the earl so agitated. He bent to pick up some of the fallen charts, keeping his voice calm to mollify the man. 'If the high steward is in his lands I have faith Robert Clifford will find him. Dungal MacDouall is patrolling Galloway with a host of our men. John MacDougall and the Black Comyn are out in force in Argyll and Lorn, and John of Menteith remains at Dunaverty Castle. When Bruce does surface we will be ready for him, Aymer.'

Just saying these words made Humphrey bristle with impatience. His need to find Robert had never been so acute. His last conversation with King Edward burned in his mind, inflaming his doubts and his growing suspicions. Where did truth end and the lie begin? He no longer knew – only that Robert might hold the key to unlocking the questions.

The door opened again and the knight reappeared.

Aymer glared at him. 'Blood and thunder, Matthew, just get rid of them!'

'It isn't the beggars, sir. Ralph de Monthermer has come. He's caught two of Bruce's men.'

Aymer and Humphrey met one another's eyes. In a moment, they both strode to the door.

The courtyard was chaotic, scattered with rubble and noisy with labourers working on the scaffolds. Following Aymer out of the building, Humphrey saw of a group of riders dismounting by the stables, the legs of their horses slathered with mud. Ralph de Monthermer was among them. The Earl of Gloucester's yellow mantle, emblazoned with a green eagle, was a splash of brightness in the dreary afternoon. Humphrey and Aymer crossed to him, pulling up the hoods of their cloaks against the rain, boots splashing through puddles.

Turning at their approach, Ralph's long, lean face, framed by a black beard, showed surprised pleasure. 'Sir Humphrey, I didn't know you would be here. Well met, brother,' he said, extending his hand.

As Humphrey clasped it, Aymer cut in, curt with impatience. 'What word from Turnberry, Sir Ralph?' He peered over the man's shoulder. 'You have prisoners?'

Humphrey noticed Ralph's expression cool, but the earl called to his company, five of whom approached, marching two men between them and leading a pack-horse. The animal had large sacks strapped to its sides, the sodden material straining with the weight of whatever was inside. Humphrey studied the two captives. One met his gaze, defiant despite the bruises on his face. The other, the younger of the two, kept his eyes on the ground, flinching as Ralph's men compelled him before Aymer. Humphrey didn't recognise either of them.

Evidently neither did Aymer, the dissatisfaction apparent in his tone. 'I was told they were Bruce's men?'

Ralph nodded to one of his knights, who tugged aside the defiant prisoner's threadbare cloak to reveal a tunic. Once white, it was covered in layers of blood and dirt. Humphrey's eyes alighted on the red chevron, just visible beneath the filth.

'One of my patrols caught them in southern Carrick. Show them,' Ralph said to the man leading the pack-horse.

The man complied, untying one of the sacks. The rain pummelled him as he worked. Humphrey glanced up, realising the sky had grown darker. Menacing clouds were flying fast and low overhead. As Ralph's man hefted the pack free with the aid of one of his comrades, both men struggling under the weight, the sack split. Humphrey and Aymer watched as a bright stream of silver gushed into the courtyard mud.

'I believe they've been collecting rents for Bruce,' said Ralph, turning to them as his men fought to stem the flow.

Aymer's expression had shifted to eagerness at the sight of the coins. 'Then they must know where he is based?' His eyes flicked to the prisoners. 'Tell me – where is your master? Where is Bruce?'

The older man met Aymer's baleful gaze, his own eyes narrowed with hatred. 'Your time is coming, English. Your doom draws near. When your covetous king dies we will reclaim our lands. The Britons will rise under King Robert, the Welsh and the Irish joining with us to push you back from our borders. This is the true prophecy of Merlin!'

Humphrey stared at the man, astonished by the vehement proclamation.

Ralph nodded grimly. 'He's been saying that since we caught him. But nothing more useful I'm afraid.' He grimaced, hunching up his shoulders as the rain became hail, pelting down around them, turning the ground white.

Servants, moving through the yard on errands, dashed for the shelter of the buildings. A loud rumble of thunder drowned the labourers' hammering. The black sky pulsed with lightning.

Aymer motioned to Matthew, raising his voice above the storm. 'Secure them for interrogation.' As the knight led Ralph's men towards the barracks, the two prisoners marched forcibly between them, Aymer turned back to the earl. 'My steward will show you where you can lodge for tonight.'

Humphrey cut in. 'I'll take him.'

Aymer frowned. 'You'll not help me question them?'

'I need something from my room. I'll join you shortly.'

'As you wish.' Turning on his heel, Aymer followed the prisoners into the barracks.

Ralph sighed with relief as Humphrey led him into the dry. 'It's like the end of days out there.' Pulling back his hood, he pushed a hand through his wet hair, rain dripping through his fingers. 'Aymer is becoming quite the lord of his little kingdom, isn't he? All that's missing is a crown.'

Humphrey looked round. Preoccupied by the prisoner's outburst, he realised he hadn't caught what Ralph had said. When his friend repeated himself, Humphrey laughed dryly. 'Indeed. But if anyone can make those men talk it is Aymer. You cannot fault his powers of persuasion.' He watched Ralph nod curtly, unsmiling.

There was little love lost between Ralph and Aymer. Three years ago, Aymer had told the king that Ralph was involved in an affair with the king's daughter, a revelation that had led to Ralph's imprisonment. His fortune had come good in the end for, on Joan's pleading, Edward eventually allowed them to marry and, by right of his wife, Ralph became Earl of Gloucester. But he'd never forgiven Aymer for the betrayal.

'Have you been here long?'

'A few weeks,' answered Humphrey, leading the way down a gloomy passage. A couple of servants hurried past, bobbing their heads at the two barons. 'The king sent me when he got word of Bruce's fleet.'

'Is my wife still with him at Lanercost?'

Humphrey nodded. 'Joan asked me to tell you that you're in her prayers.'

Ralph smiled. 'She is well?'

'She had a fever when I left, but she was in good spirits.'

'And my stepson? How is Gilbert?'

'He's been doing well in the prince's company,' Humphrey said carefully. No doubt Ralph would hear about the scandal that had swept through the royal court soon enough, but there was no need to fuel it with gossip. 'There has been some difficulty with Piers Gaveston, but I believe that is behind us now. Gilbert seems to have become firm friends with my nephew, Henry.'

'By God, when I think of those young bloods I feel old.' Ralph shook his head. 'It seems like an age since we were in their place – Knights of the Dragon.'

Humphrey halted outside a door. 'This should do you.'

Ralph paused, his face changing. 'Do you ever wonder, Humphrey, what our lives would now be like if Edward had allowed Robert to take the throne of Scotland when he was still loyal to us? Will Gilbert and Henry see peace in their lifetimes or will this become their war?' He pushed open the door, his brow furrowing. 'Where does it end?'

Humphrey didn't answer. He thought of the king in Lanercost, conducting this war from his deathbed, at each command from his lips another man strung up on a gallows, another mother's son cut down in a field. Where, indeed, did it end? 'I'll have wine and food brought.'

Leaving Ralph to settle in, Humphrey moved down the passage to his room. As he entered and closed the door, thunder boomed, rattling the window. The chamber was dark, the fire in the hearth burned to ash. He crossed to one of his chests, crouched and opened it. Rifling through the clothes inside, his fingers closed around a leather-bound book. As he pulled it out, the gold leaf writing gleamed.

The Prophecy of Merlin
Geoffrey of Monmouth

Humphrey knew the translation of the *Last Prophecy*, found by the king at Nefyn, off by heart, but although he'd read this book several times he was less familiar with those penned by Monmouth. Yet, as he stood scanning the pages, he knew in his heart he would not find the words the prisoner had uttered. He would have remembered such a prophecy. Was Robert using his knowledge of Merlin's visions, gleaned during his time as a Knight of the Dragon, to instil some new belief in his followers? Or was this something to do with the ancient text, missing from its vessel?

He heard the footsteps thudding fast across the chamber behind him, but before he could turn someone had grabbed him from behind. Humphrey stiffened as a blade pressed against his throat.

'Make a sound and I'll kill you.'

Burstwick Manor, England, 1307 AD

Elizabeth winced as the needle stabbed her. Holding up her finger she watched the drop of blood bead on the tip. Sucking it quickly, she continued threading the blue silk through the square of linen, fingers clumsy with lack of practice. The lettering was untidy, but she had no time to make it neat. Last week, after months of her pleading, they had finally allowed her to have tools for embroidery, once a week for an hour. That time was almost up. Her heart seemed to beat down the moments.

Time had taken on new meaning for Elizabeth these past six months in this cramped chamber. In the first weeks of her incarceration it had stretched endless before her, each day an eternity. The whitewashed walls of her prison, furnished with only a hard bed, a table and stool, seemed to contract until her mind felt as though it were collapsing in on itself. In those early days, when the fear she would be harmed left her and she came to realise she might sit in this room, alive and well, until she died, she had gone mad, throwing herself against the door, screaming and pounding her fists on it. Now, time was a single day, repeated over and over, with little variation except the slow changes of season she witnessed through the slats in the shuttered window that looked out over fields to distant woods.

Dipping the needle in and out through the cloth, Elizabeth thought of all the times when, as a girl, she had begged her father to allow her to enter a convent. She had been desperate for a life of silent prayer in the face of marriage to an elderly lord, whose last wife died giving birth to another of his children; so desperate she had run away with Robert, hoping he would lead her from that future. Fate was a cruel mistress. Not only had Elizabeth found herself locked in a loveless marriage, but now she finally had her wish – a life of solitary confinement, where all she had to occupy herself were prayers.

She finished the last two letters, cut the thread with her teeth and tied it in a knot. Turning the square of linen over, she read the stitched words.

Father, please help me. Your loving daughter.

Footsteps echoed in the passage. Elizabeth hastily tied the four corners of the cloth together. It wasn't much of a deterrent against prying eyes, but she hoped the gift she was sending it with would be enough to keep the bearer's silence, if not stay their curiosity.

As the footsteps stopped outside the door, Elizabeth tugged off her wedding ring, the gold band embedded with its glossy ruby. She remembered Marjorie once asking why women wore them on that finger and her answer that the vein there ran to the heart. Looking at it, lying in her palm, she felt a tinge of regret. She had always thought that vein ran cold in her, but now the ring was gone from her finger she felt its absence and thought of Robert. A key rattled in the lock. Elizabeth curled her hand around the ring and the cloth. She had to do this, despite the loss and the risk. Not just for her sake. Her prison might be bleak, but Marjorie, Mary and Isabel's ordeals must surely be unbearable. If she could, she would help them.

The door opened and a young woman appeared, carrying a tray. Elizabeth's fist tightened around the ring in relief. It was Lucy, not Maud. The maid closed the door behind her and balanced the tray on one hand while she locked it with a key, attached to her belt on a cord.

Lucy nodded to Elizabeth, a small smile lifting the corners of her mouth. 'My lady.'

Elizabeth counted each word, each hint of a smile from the young maid as a victory. Back at Lanercost she had begged King Edward to allow her servants, Lora and Judith among them, to remain with her, but the king decreed that the women who served her would be forbidden from smiling or even talking to her. Maud had followed the king's order to the letter, but Lucy, over the last few months, had begun to thaw in her bearing towards her prisoner.

'How are you today, Lucy?'

The maid shot her a nervous look, then dipped her head. 'I am well, my lady.'

Elizabeth watched as Lucy set down the tray, on which was a bowl

of brown stew, with a hunk of bread and a goblet of what she knew
would be watered-down wine. 'And your son? Is he better now?'

Lucy looked up, smiling despite herself. 'Oh, yes, my lady. Much
better.'

Elizabeth crossed the room slowly, moving towards the tray. At the
last moment, she turned to Lucy. Grabbing the maid's hand, she
thrust the crumpled linen and the ring into it. 'Lucy, I beg you, get
this to my father in Ireland.'

The maid stepped back, staring in alarm at the cloth and the ring
beside it, now nestled in her palm.

'The ring will be enough to pay for that cloth to be delivered to
Ballymote Castle and to compensate you handsomely for your trouble.
You only need find someone willing to take it. Someone you can trust.'

'My lady . . .'

'If your son sickens again you'll have money for medicine.' Elizabeth
pushed Lucy's fingers over the ring.

The maid looked at her apprehensively, but her fist remained
closed.

27

Glen Trool, Scotland, 1307 AD

The glen reverberated with sounds of battle. Distant screams rose above the clash of weapons. Robert stood listening to the echoes rising from the valley depths, trying to gauge what each discordant sound might mean.

The downpour had passed, leaving the rugged heights lost in a miasma of fog, as thick as soup. Before him, the hillside sloped away into the mists, the wet soil scarred with dark wounds where his men had levered out the boulders. Behind him, a banner was planted in the earth. The royal standard was long gone, left in Wishart's safekeeping, but before Robert had departed from Barra Christiana had given him this replacement. The cloth might be linen rather than silk, dyed yellow with saffron and emblazoned with a crudely sewn red lion, but it was still a powerful symbol with which to herald his return.

Landing on the Carrick coast a fortnight ago, Robert at once sent spies into Galloway, knowing if he didn't complete the task Donough and the men of Antrim had been sent to undertake his back would remain at threat the moment he turned his attention to the English in Turnberry and Ayr. The spies had returned with the unwelcome news that Dungal MacDouall had been joined by a strong English force. Leaving his fleet anchored off Arran under Lachlan's command and ordering trusted men to begin collecting rents from his vassals in Carrick, funds necessary to make a goodwill payment to the acquisitive captain, Robert had led the bulk of his army by hidden glens and high, snow-mottled passes, down into the lands of his enemy.

After the losses and injuries sustained at Turnberry, and without the full force of Lachlan's galloglass, he was down to six hundred men, all on foot. His spies had estimated MacDouall's force, bolstered by the English, at two thousand. An open confrontation seemed hopeless, but Galloway's wild landscape offered its own deadly arsenal in boulder-strewn mountains and wooded slopes. With his thoughts on the lightning attacks of the Welsh rebels in Snowdon and William Wallace's Forest ambushes, Robert had devised a plan, sending Neil Campbell and James Douglas to lure their enemies into his trap.

At his side, Fionn whined quietly, sensing his tension. Robert looked over at Edward, who was standing with Angus MacDonald and the small group of men who had stayed up here with him, all of them silent, waiting. Meeting his gaze, his brother headed across.

'I should be down there with them,' murmured Robert.

Edward said nothing for a moment, then shook his head. 'As Sir James said, you need to pick your battles from now on. Some you will have to lead, but others you must direct. You're too valuable for us to lose.'

Robert caught the stiffness in Edward's tone. He knew his brother, craving vengeance against MacDouall, dearly wanted to join the army sent into the glen in the wake of the boulders, but in just six months Robert had been bereaved of three brothers. He hadn't been able to bear the thought of losing Edward too. But now, listening to the battle rage below, he wondered uneasily whether he was following James Stewart's counsel to avoid the front lines because he agreed with it or whether, after his narrow escape at Turnberry, he'd lost his nerve. After all, he hadn't followed the rest of the high steward's advice.

Before leaving Barra to gather his vassals, James tried again to convince him to remain in the Isles until King Edward died. Robert refused, adamant the longer the English were allowed to stay in Scotland, the more entrenched they would become. His family could perhaps yet be freed by the ransom of Henry Percy, but the liberation of his kingdom would require strength of arms.

At the thought of Percy, Robert's mind shifted to Alexander Seton, and another decision he had been questioning himself over.

'Do you hear that?' Angus MacDonald moved up beside him, his shaggy black cloak beaded with rain.

'Yes,' Edward said suddenly.

Robert heard it too – a ragged cheer rising from the valley's depths. The faint sounds petered out and silence descended over Glen Trool.

The men looked at one another, but didn't speak, apprehension and anticipation battling within them.

Some time later, they heard the snap and rustle of undergrowth. Figures began to emerge from the fog. The company with the king had drawn their swords, but sheathed them on seeing their countrymen. Few soon became many, men panting with exhaustion as they appeared out of the murk, clothes soaked with blood and rain. A number held fistfuls of spears or swords and others clutched wine skins, cloaks and boots, stripped from the enemy. Some hauled wounded comrades. But all carried victory, borne in weary, but jubilant faces.

Robert saw Lachlan's brother, Ruarie, with a group of galloglass, his axe balanced over his broad shoulder, the blade dripping blood. There was Cormac, his face fierce with triumph, and James Douglas, bearing up a sandy-haired youth. Seeing Neil Campbell emerge with Gilbert de la Hay and Malcolm of Lennox, Robert went to meet them, relief flooding him.

'It is done, my lord,' Neil said, bowing before his king. 'The English have been vanquished.'

'Many were killed or unhorsed by the rocks,' said Gilbert, between breaths. 'We reckon we took half their number.' He grinned, wiping the sweat from his brow with his arm.

'MacDouall?' cut in Edward, appearing at Robert's side.

Malcolm of Lennox shook his head. 'The men of Galloway were still a fair way south down the glen, following the English on foot. My knights saw them fleeing.'

'The battle was fierce for a time, my lord,' Neil added. 'We had no chance to go after the Disinherited or the English who managed to escape.'

'We should follow,' said Edward at once, turning to Robert.

Cormac headed over, having heard the comment. He looked keenly at Robert, clearly hopeful of his king's agreement.

For a moment, Robert didn't speak, his own desire to seek vengeance for his brothers and Lord Donough wrestling with his need to stay clear in his command. 'No,' he said finally. 'If we follow MacDouall out of Glen Trool we will be in his territory – vulnerable. Even losing half their force our enemy still outnumbers us. But if we move now, while they're in disarray, we have a chance to attack the English in the north with the threat to our rear greatly reduced.'

'Brother—' began Edward.

Robert wasn't listening. He had caught sight of James Douglas, who had set down the sandy-haired youth he had been helping up the hill and was now standing over him, sword drawn. Robert realised with a jolt that the youth was his nephew, Thomas Randolph, captured a year ago at Methven Wood. Stunned, he started towards him.

Neil, following his gaze, caught his arm. 'My lord,' he murmured, 'your nephew was taken with a blade in his hand, fighting for the English.'

Robert's brow furrowed, but pushing past Neil he headed to where the youth was kneeling, clutching his side, his face clenched in pain.

Thomas raised his head as Robert approached. His expression filled with fear, before closing in on itself. He looked away.

James Douglas moved aside, but kept his blade trained on the young man.

'There is no need for such rough treatment, Master James,' Robert said sternly. 'He is my kin.'

James lowered the sword, but stood his ground. 'My lord, he admitted the English freed him on the promise he would serve their king.'

Robert stared at his nephew. 'A clever ruse, no doubt. To gain his freedom.'

Now, Thomas did look up. His face was ashen, except for two hectic points of colour in his cheeks. 'They told me you were hiding in the wilderness, too ashamed after what you did to John Comyn to show yourself. They said your countrymen had rejected you in their thousands – that God Himself had turned his face from you, unable to look upon a once cherished son who had murdered a man in cold blood!' Sweat dripped from Thomas's nose. 'All those months locked up in their prison, I refused to listen when they called you a coward. I told myself the English were lying when they said you were no better than a brigand, an outlaw, without the courage to face them on the open field. When I took up my sword for their king, I did so because I wanted to return home and prove them wrong. But now I see they were right!'

'Thomas, I—'

'I brought my father's men to fight for you at Methven – pledged myself to you. You left me there!' cried Thomas. 'I saw you ride right past me!' He clutched his side tighter, gasping with pain. 'Now, here you are in hiding, while your men fight your battle for you!'

Robert felt shame run hot through him as his sins and his secret fears poured from the mouth of his own nephew; damning him here on this hillside in front of his watching men. He thought of David of Atholl and all who had joined the ranks of his enemies. He thought of those who had died for him and those he had left behind. How many of them now cursed him from their prisons? For a moment, he quailed in the face of his own towering guilt, then he caught sight of Cormac, whose face still bore the scars of the assault in Stranraer.

'Did the king's men tell you what they did to my brothers?' he asked Thomas, his voice low. 'What they did to my wife and to your mother? Did they tell you they burned Turnberry to ash and put women and girls to the sword? That they imprisoned Robert Wishart and William Lamberton, men of the cloth, in irons?' His voice rose, hoarse with emotion. 'Did they tell you they hanged John of Atholl and strung up Niall, your uncle, only to cut him down alive so the mob could enjoy his terror as they put his neck on the block? Or how my foster-father knelt in mercy before Dungal MacDouall, who took his life in far colder blood than I took Comyn's? Did the English tell you that their king put my daughter in a cage like an animal? Answer me, damn you! Did they tell you this?'

Thomas averted his eyes from Robert's wrath. He bowed his head.

Robert stared down on him for a moment longer. 'Keep him under guard.' Turning, he strode back up the hill towards his banner, his men parting before him. 'Get ready. All of you. We march north.'

Ayr, Scotland, 1307 AD

Humphrey stood still, feeling the cold bite of the dagger against his neck. His instinct, after the shock had faded, was to fight, but whoever had hold of him was strong – he could feel that in the tautness of the arm around his chest. As lightning flared again, he caught sight of a reflection in the rain-stained window. He saw himself and, over his shoulder, a man in a hooded cloak, with a hard, desperate face. It was Alexander Seton. Humphrey had last seen the lord from East Lothian when Prince Edward's men took him from the battlefield in Lorn. 'What do you want with me, Alexander?'

The lord stiffened at the sound of his name, but when he spoke his voice was harsh, commanding. 'I know where Robert Bruce is.'

'Perhaps you should tell Sir Aymer. He is the one who had you released for this purpose.' Humphrey kept his voice calm, but his heart pulsed fiercely at the news. He wondered how Alexander had got in here, but the hammering outside reminded him the barracks were in chaos. It wasn't hard to imagine how someone might steal in unnoticed and get a servant to reveal where his lodgings were.

'I do not trust Aymer.'

'Very well. Tell me.'

'I will, when my cousin is released.'

At this, Humphrey realised Alexander didn't yet know about Christopher's execution. Did that mean Robert had no idea what had happened to his family – that King Edward's intention for him to suffer was as yet unfulfilled? 'That will take some time,' he began slowly. 'How will I know Robert won't have moved on before your cousin is set free?'

In the window's reflection, Alexander's eyes narrowed. 'I know where his base is – where he will retreat to when he leaves the main-land. Where his fleet is harboured. This is what I will tell you in return for my cousin's freedom.'

Humphrey's mind raced. So Robert was on the mainland now? 'How do you know this?'

'Because he sent me from there with a message.'

Humphrey wondered queasily whether this message might now be delivered by the blade at his throat.

'Robert has Henry Percy,' Alexander continued. 'He wanted me to tell you he is willing to exchange him for his wife, daughter and sisters. But I've not come here for that. All I want is my cousin.'

'I understand. As a sign of good faith, tell me where Robert is now.'

Alexander paused. 'Somewhere on the west coast. He was plan-ning an attack when I left, but I was only with him for one night – not long enough to hear the details.'

Humphrey's eyes alighted on the book on the floor at his feet where he'd dropped it. 'Have you heard tell of a prophecy – a vision of Merlin – in which the Welsh and Irish will rise with the Scots against us?'

Alexander didn't speak.

Humphrey could feel the man's heart beating fast against his back. 'Tell me,' he urged. 'And I'll give you what you want.'

'Yes,' said Alexander. 'I heard it from Robert himself. The night before I left he told his men it was the prophecy taken from Edward. He said the king kept it locked away because he didn't want anyone to know it predicted his death and that with that event the Britons would reclaim their lands. He is planning to send out messengers, proclaiming this to the Welsh and the Irish.'

Humphrey caught the cynicism in Alexander's tone. 'You do not believe it?'

'I remember what Robert said when he left Edward's service. He told those of us closest to him that the box he took from Westminster was empty – that there was no prophecy. Whatever he says now is for the benefit of his new followers. All those fools who have no idea he will lead them down into hell.'

Alexander's words ricocheted in Humphrey. A chill ran through him. He was brought back to focus by the sting of the blade.

'I've told you more than enough to prove myself. Now it is your turn. I want Christopher taken to my old estate in Seton. There's a chapel in the grounds where you will leave him in one week's time. You can send one of your men with him, but only one. When I see my cousin is unharmed I'll tell your man where Bruce is based.'

Thoughts swarmed in Humphrey's mind: he thought of the two prisoners, right now being prepared for interrogation, and of Aymer and Ralph, the king's cousin and his son-in-law, both steadfastly loyal without question. Maybe the prisoners would give up Robert's base and maybe they wouldn't, but, either way, Humphrey knew he wanted more than just a location now. He wanted the truth. 'I want you to play along with Bruce. Tell him I've agreed a parley to discuss an exchange of prisoners, to which he will bring Henry Percy. Tell him I—'

'You're not in a position to make demands,' growled Alexander. Grabbing Humphrey's hair, he pulled his head back, scoring his neck with the dagger until blood trickled. 'Don't think for a moment I'll not kill you and take my offer to another!'

There was a knock at the door. Alexander was distracted, only briefly, but it was all Humphrey needed. Grabbing the man's arm, he forced it from his throat, twisting Alexander's wrist until the man hissed and dropped the dagger. As the blade clattered to the floor, Humphrey kneed him in the stomach. Alexander dropped to his knees with a winded gasp, Humphrey pinning his arm at an excruciating angle.

'Sir Humphrey?' came a man's voice through the door. It was his squire, Hugh.

Grabbing the dagger from the floor, Humphrey thrust it at Alexander's throat. 'Agree to my offer,' he murmured, 'and you'll get what you want. Refuse and after I've killed you I swear, by God, I'll go straight to Berwick and take bloody retribution on your cousin.'

'Sir? Are you all right in there?'

Alexander looked up at Humphrey, his dark eyes filling with pain and desperation. He nodded once.

'I am fine, Hugh,' called Humphrey.

28

Loudoun Hill, Scotland, 1307 AD

From Glen Trool they moved north by way of lonely, windswept moors, following the winding courses of stony rivers, hidden by hills. All around them the land unfurled from the clutches of bitter winter, warmth burgeoning in the air and life springing in the earth, offering up new bounties in the woods and the fields. Around camp-fires at night, feasting on meat for the first time in weeks, the men relived their ambush of the English, buoyed up by their remarkable victory. Many spoke of Merlin's vision, believing their triumph against such overwhelming odds was proof of its veracity. Robert and those closest to him, who knew the truth of the prophecy and its origin, did not dissuade them from such speculation.

On the fringes of Carrick, deep in the forest beyond the Bruce castle at Loch Doon, held by the English, they camped for twelve nights while Robert sent messengers into his earldom to the places where those tasked with collecting the rents were due to gather and wait for word. They returned to him gradually, hauling handcarts filled with sacks of money and supplies or leading pack-horses weighed down with coins from tenants eager to hear word of their long-vanished lord. Some were even accompanied by young squires from the halls of Robert's vassals, keen to join the king's war-band, along with farmers, shepherds, drovers and fishermen. But not all that came out of Carrick was welcome.

Along with news of the loss of two of his men, caught by enemy soldiers near Turnberry, were reports of doors shut in the faces of the rent collectors and of widespread fear and suspicion among his tenantry. Many of those who had since returned to homes and settlements after fleeing the devastation caused by Prince Edward the year before were too scared of angering their English overlords to aid him. Others were deeply resentful of their absentee earl, who had left them without defence or aid, at the mercy of the invaders. This news, although not wholly unexpected, weighed heavily on Robert, whose mind lingered on Thomas Randolph's impassioned outburst on the slopes of Glen Trool. Although his nephew was misguided and hadn't been told all the facts by his gaolers, Robert knew the sentiment of his argument was based on an unpalatable truth. If it wasn't then so many of his countrymen – not just kinsmen of Comyn, but his own vassals and those, like David of Atholl, whom he had counted as friends – would not have turned against him.

A year ago, outside the walls of Perth, he had known he needed a victory over the English in order to inspire more men to join him and to help erase the stain on his reputation, tarnished by John Comyn's blood. He had failed, utterly, and all the months since, on the run, losing more followers, had only cemented that defeat and his failure as king and guardian of the people in the eyes of many of his subjects. His success in Glen Trool was a start, but a desperate ambush wasn't enough to serve as a foundation for his return to the throne. William Wallace only earned the full respect of the nobility of Scotland when he faced the English at Stirling on an open field, and won.

And so, when the last men joined them from Carrick with tidings that Aymer de Valence had gone to fortify Ayr, Robert led his ragged army north, coming out into the open barely twenty miles from the English-held garrison town. Here, in the shadow of Loudoun Hill, he waited, knowing it would not be long before the English got word of their presence.

The enemy was first spotted, a mile or so west of Loudoun Hill, by the glints on their spear-heads. Shielding their eyes from the morning sun, the Scots watched them come from their position on a broad meadow, where three wide ditches had been cut through the grass at intervals, one after another, with the middle trench overlapping the parallel lines made by the other two. The smell of up-cast soil, warmed by the May sunshine, was rich on the air. The meadow was bordered on either side by tracts of marshland, swamped by the spring rains. At the Scots' backs the slopes of Loudoun Hill, a great crag that thrust unexpectedly from the gentle landscape, rose steeply. A tough climb for men on foot, the cliff was impossible for horses to scale and offered a last-ditch refuge should they need it. Their supplies and the revenues from Carrick were stored on the summit under guard. It had seemed an ideal place for Robert to array his army, but for the meadow itself.

High and dry, it was perfect ground for the heavy cavalry Robert knew he would face. If his men weren't to be ridden down where they stood, he had to modify the terrain to his advantage. During a council with his commanders five nights ago, walking the field, he decided, based on the advice of Neil Campbell, who had fought with Wallace at Stirling, on using ditches to help funnel the English cavalry into smaller, less overwhelming groups. The trenches, dug laboriously over several days, his men using tools taken from nearby farmsteads, along with sticks and their bare hands, formed barriers both for the enemy to tackle and for the Scots to fall back behind.

Now, looking at the ditches, Robert found himself thinking these three holes in the earth were perhaps all that stood between him and utter annihilation. There was no time to dwell on the wisdom of his strategy, as away along the western road the vanguard of the English came into view. The confusion of colour and metal slowly divided into horses and men, trappers and surcoats. Pennons and banners flew above the lines of cavalry and infantry. There were different arms among them, but most at the head wore the blue and white of Pembroke. They filled the road as far as Robert could see, a great snake, winding inexorably towards him. He guessed there were two, maybe three thousand.

Swinging his shield from his shoulder, Robert forced his arm through the grips on the back. Unsheathing his sword, gifted to him by the high steward, the gold pommel flashing in the sun, he walked down the slope into the ranks of his waiting army, followed by his commanders. Wide-eyed farmhands clutching spears stood alongside thick-necked galloglass wielding their axes and veteran knights, swords in their mailed fists. Robert stood in their centre, turning in a circle to address them, his voice rising as he reminded them why they had come to this field.

He spoke of their families, their wives and children, mothers and fathers. He reminded them of their homes; the lands they worked and the land they loved. He conjured the ghosts of the men who had died deaths of heroes and martyrs, fighting those who would crush them beneath the fist of conquest. Andrew Moray, William Douglas, John of Atholl, Christopher Seton, Thomas Bruce, William Wallace. He told them these men were watching from the halls of heaven, watching them here on this field; they who were the inheritors of this long and bloody war, who carried within them the torch of those who had gone before. He told them this torch was a living flame of courage and honour, and that with it they would light a holy fire all along this hillside.

When he had finished, he walked down through their lines, beating the flat of his blade on the scarred surface of his shield. His commanders went with him, doing the same, until the meadow was clashing with sound. Robert halted in the gap between the first and second ditch, his men spreading out around him. There was James Douglas, determination clear in his face, here, so close to the lands of his father. Beside him was Malcolm of Lennox, his handsome face gaunt and drawn after the hardships of the past months, but no less resolved, his men arrayed around him. There were Gilbert de la Hay and Neil Campbell, Cormac and Angus MacDonald, surrounded by the doughty men of the Isles, wielding spears and lances, taken from the English dead at Glen Trool.

Ordering his spearmen to form a line, three men deep, from the edge of the first ditch to the second, Robert moved in behind them, pulling up the ventail of the mail coif he wore beneath his helm, covering his throat and jaw in the metal mesh. He had thrown James Stewart's cautions to the wind, along with his own fears. Thomas Randolph's accusations had awoken something fierce within him. Whatever met him here today, whether death or glory, no one would ever call him a coward again. Beside him was his brother, Edward, blue eyes glittering with the expectation of violence. Knights from Carrick and Annandale, who had served the brothers loyally for years, crowded close. Above them all, the banner given to Robert by Christiana was a vivid sweep of yellow against the spring sky, held aloft by Nes, his face lit with pride at the honour.

As the vanguard of the English reached the lower slopes of the meadow, they fanned out. The tension among the Scots rose. A few men peeled away to relieve themselves while they still could, others flexed necks and shoulders, swung weapons to loosen muscles, or rubbed slick palms on cloaks. Insects swarmed in the air. Robert fixed

on the distant banner of Aymer de Valence and felt a line of sweat
trickle down his cheek. A rabbit appeared on the meadow and sat
grazing, taking no notice of the tight mass of Scots at the high end of
the field, or the English forming up below. All at once a horn bellowed,
shattering the still. The rabbit bolted into its burrow and a flock of
birds cast from the trees on the crown of Loudoun Hill.

The cavalry came first in one long line, no breaks between, the
destriers moving from steady walk to trot, then at last to ground-
shuddering canter. To the Scots, they came as a great wave, rising to
meet them in a storm of billowing blue and white trappers, sunlight
flashing on hundreds of blades. Robert, feeling the earth quaking
beneath him, roared at his men to stand their ground. Those in the
front lines gripped their spears; a forest of barbs thrust outwards,
butts wedged against the ground. Others, clutching swords, dirks
and axes, pressed in around them. The horn sounded again from the
English cavalry, this time three blasts of warning as they crested
the slope and saw the ditches carving wide brown lines through the
meadow ahead. The outer flanks slowed and fell in behind the middle
section that now pushed forward in an arrow, aiming for the gap
between the first and second trenches, where the Scots crowded,
braced for impact.

The first wave of cavalry smashed into the heart of the Scottish
lines amid the baying of battle cries. The collision was brutal. The
front rows of Scots were forced back by the shock of it, men colliding
with comrades, some staggering, others falling, but the press behind
them wouldn't let them fall far. Screams sounded as horses were
impaled on the points of spears. Some riders were hurled over the
heads of the first ranks of Scots and sent tumbling into the mass
behind. Only their shrieks rose as they were savagely despatched by
dirks and stamping feet. The English knights, riding in behind the first
wave, had to pull their horses up short to avoid crashing into their
comrades, who had met, in the Scots, an immovable wall.

A destrier in front of Robert, skewered by two spears, was struggling to free itself, teeth gnashing, eyes rolling white. The two Islesmen
holding the spears, fought to keep their balance as the beast reared
up, blood streaming from its punctured neck. Robert lunged between
them, plunging his sword into the thigh of the knight astride it, clad
in the colours of Pembroke. The man's sharp cry was muffled by his
helm as the sword pierced his mail. Robert tugged the blade free,

hoisting his shield as the knight brought his sword swinging down at him. The blade smacked hard against the wood. Suddenly, the destrier collapsed, one of the spears snapping off in its neck. The knight toppled sideways. As he hung there for a moment, snared by the stirrup, Robert twisted his wrist and drove his blade through the slit in the man's helm. Blood erupted. The knight slid from the saddle, disappearing among a whirl of trappers and trampling legs.

All along the front lines horses bucked and thrashed, caught in the crush as the Scots pressed forward, stabbing with their spears, or hacking and chopping at the writhing barrier of beasts and men. Aymer de Valence's banner was lifted above the turmoil. Some English knights attempted to turn and break out of the deadlock, but found themselves hemmed in by those who had ridden in behind, channelled by the ditches. Others, on the edges, were knocked or jostled into the trenches. Horses tumbled into the furrows, riders crying out as they went down under the weight of their armoured steeds.

Robert yelled a command and, now, men clutching dirks, many of them galloglass, rushed between the spearmen and ducked in under the legs of the horses. With swift, brutal movements, they slit open the animals' stomachs. As the beasts buckled, entrails spilling, knights were dragged from saddles, their helms torn off like shells, the Scots eager to get at the vulnerable flesh beneath. The air was rent with screams and the thick squelch of mud, soaked in blood, urine and dung as horses voided their bowels in pain and terror. A sour stink choked the air. Men sweated and groaned, gasping as they pressed against one another in a vile orgy of death.

Even though their lines had withstood the ferocity of the first charge, the Scots, many of whom were more exposed than the mailed knights, weren't spared the slaughter. A squire from Carrick, fighting beside Robert, caught the hoof of a destrier in his face that caved in his jaw. Nearby, one of the galloglass had his head half severed by a knight's sweeping blade. His body remained upright, held by the crush, blood spewing in a hot red rain over his comrades. Others, trapped under collapsing horses, slowly suffocated as they were ground into the mud. Robert saw his brother only narrowly avoid a vicious strike from a knight in the Pembroke colours. Edward retaliated, roaring as he jammed his blade into the knight's side, puncturing mail and driving the broken rings into the man's flesh.

The bulk of the English infantry, led by small contingents of

cavalry, had split off in two divisions to attempt to outflank the
Scots, but both companies found themselves caught in the mire that
stretched away to either side of the meadow. Men, struggling in the
sucking mud, fought their way back to hard ground as the horns
blew, calling them to tackle the first of the ditches, beyond which
the Scots were arrayed. Breathing hard through his ventail, Robert
heard the horns blowing and saw the infantry approaching the
trench. Twisting to Nes, he yelled an instruction. The knight, still
gripping the royal banner, began waving it back and forth, the
yellow cloth streaming in the air above the heads of the front lines,
sending the signal to those behind.

Seeing the flag waving wildly, the first row of Scots along the edge
of the ditch crouched. Behind them archers rose, almost a hundred of
them, bows primed. Many were young men from Carrick and the
Isles, using their hunting bows, but some were veteran bowmen from
Selkirk, who had served under William Wallace. All at once, they let
fly a volley of arrows across the ditch, into the ranks of the infantry.
Men collapsed, struck by the missiles, others threw themselves to the
ground. As the foot soldiers picked themselves up and came on,
another volley tore through them.

The horns were blowing frantically now among the ranks of the
English cavalry. More horses and men were going down, the long axes
of the galloglass rising and falling like scythes through corn. In the
turmoil, Aymer de Valence's banner-bearer was pulled from his horse
and set upon by three of Angus MacDonald's men.

As the blue and white striped standard disappeared, sagging down
between the horses, Robert lifted his head and bellowed, 'On them!
On them now!'

The Scots pressed forward hard, scrabbling over the growing
wall of fallen horses and men to get at those behind. The English
line began to fall apart. Those trapped in the mêlée, their mounts at
the mercy of the ruthless galloglass, urged their horses around and
spurred them through the breaks now appearing in the crowd.
Others, seeing their comrades bearing down on them, wheeled
their mounts out of their path. More horses tumbled into the ditch
in the blind chaos of the retreat.

Aymer de Valence was bellowing orders, trying to pull his men
back to form up again and make another charge, but his banner had
gone and it was hard for his knights, encased in their great helms, to

pick their commander out of the mayhem. Now, the infantry, seeing the bulk of the cavalry riding towards them, with the Scots pressing in behind, began to falter. A few turned and ran back down the slope, thinking a general retreat had been sounded. Soon, more went with them, turning and fleeing. And, all at once, it became an avalanche.

The Scots sent up a roar that resounded across the hillside as they saw the English begin to rout, the cavalry riding pell-mell down the meadow, knocking aside their own foot soldiers in their haste. Robert led his army in their wake, shouting himself raw, sword aloft, slick with the blood of Aymer's knights. At last, the enemy had shown him their backs. At last, he had it – vengeance for Methven.

Burstwick Manor, England, 1307 AD

The key clicked in the lock. Elizabeth sat on the edge of the bed, toying with the ivory cross around her neck. As the door opened, she steeled herself to look up, not daring to hope, but unable to help herself. Maud entered, bearing a tray. The maid's face, as pale as uncooked dough, was as grim as ever. Elizabeth's hope was already sinking, but then she saw another woman following Maud. Her breath caught in her throat, until she realised she didn't know this second figure: an elderly woman with a pinched face and down-turned mouth.

Every day, after she had given Lucy her ring and the message, Elizabeth had tried to catch the young woman's eye as she delivered her food, hoping to see some sign that Lucy had done as she had bid. But the maid remained silent, refusing to meet her gaze. Then, nine days ago, she stopped coming altogether. Elizabeth tentatively asked Maud where Lucy had gone, but the woman hadn't answered. She tried to tell herself Lucy's son was ill again and she had been allowed home to tend to him, but as the days passed this had been replaced with other more tormenting imaginings – the message to her father fluttering on a midden heap and her wedding ring adorning Lucy's hand.

As Maud set down the tray, the new maid picked up the empty plate from the night before. The old woman glanced furtively, curiously, at the royal prisoner, sitting stiffly on the bed, before hurrying out, followed by Maud. Elizabeth watched them go. Just before the door was closed, she caught Maud's eye. The pasty-faced woman smiled, showing a mouthful of yellow teeth. Elizabeth started. She had never seen this expression on Maud's face. What had made her flinch, however, was not the smile, but the spitefulness behind it.

Elizabeth didn't know what it meant until she went to her tray. There, next to a bowl of grease-filmed stew, was a crumpled piece of linen. Picking it up, she opened it with shaking fingers to see a message in blue thread: her own words stitched in haste and hope, returned to her.

29

Barra, Scotland, 1307 AD

The rhythm of drums filled the air, a joyous heartbeat pulsing beneath the wild shouts and laughter. Bright fires burned all around the settlement, glowing in the faces of the men and women, who had drunk and danced and feasted their way through this midsummer's eve. Robert sat on a stool, nursing his wine and watching his men celebrate.

'Long live King Robert! Bane of the English!' roared Gilbert de la Hay, over the noise of the drums and the crowd. More calls echoed his and cups were lifted to the sky.

Robert raised his goblet to the lord and smiled.

Laughing, his face flushed with drink, Gilbert grabbed the hands of two young women and began dancing a boisterous jig. Others quickly joined in. Neil Campbell and Malcolm of Lennox looked over, grinning at Gilbert's enthusiasm. Nes had fallen asleep, slumped against Cormac's shoulder, the Irishman engaged in an animated debate with two galloglass. Brigid was sitting by one of the fires with some of the other women from the settlement, a soft smile on her face as she watched Elena race with her friends among the adults, skirts flying. Edward stepped aside good-naturedly as the band of children rushed past, then returned to his conversation with James Douglas. Another figure was with them, sipping nervously at his wine, his sandy hair the colour of straw in the firelight.

Thomas Randolph, under guard since he'd been taken at Glen Trool, had pleaded for an audience with Robert the night after the confrontation at Loudoun Hill. When the young man had gone down on his knees, begging his forgiveness, Robert had coolly asked his nephew why he'd changed in his opinion of him. Expecting the reason to be his triumph in the battle, he was surprised to hear Thomas say he'd been moved by the depth of the loyalty and love he had seen shown to Robert by his men. A week later, as they sailed from Scotland's shores, heading back to the Isles to regroup and gather more supplies, Robert had accepted his nephew's oath of fealty, along with pledges from more men who had flocked to his banner from across Carrick and Ayr, after news of his victory against Aymer de Valence spread throughout the earldom. Some had begun calling him a new King Arthur.

Robert's gaze moved to Lachlan, standing with his brother, Ruarie, and a group of their men. Catching his eye, Lachlan inclined his head, his crooked mouth twisting in a smile. With the revenues from Carrick, Robert had been able to pay the captain for his service; his fidelity secured. No longer was he treated as a foreigner in these Isles. He was their king and all due respect was paid to him. As the dancers whirled apart, James Stewart appeared briefly in the crowd. The high steward had been waiting on Barra when Robert returned, with fifteen ships filled with tenants from across his lands, come at his call to arms. Along with the new recruits, the galloglass and Angus MacDonald's men from Islay, Robert now had an army greater than the force he had commanded at Methven.

The war was far from over. King Edward and his men would retaliate, of that he had no doubt. Aymer, although beaten in battle, had not been crushed and remained in strength in Ayr. Worse, many of Robert's countrymen still stood against him, refusing to acknowledge his kingship. John MacDougall, Lord of Argyll, responsible for the attack that split Robert's forces in Lorn, dominated a swathe of the west coast with his army and his galleys, his blood-oath against the murderer of his cousin unfulfilled. There were rumours the Black Comyn had returned to the Comyn heartlands in the north-east – to Buchan and Badenoch – mustering more men for the fight, and Dungal MacDouall, the killer of Lord Donough, who had delivered Thomas and Alexander to King Edward, remained at large. No, the war wasn't over, and Robert knew he would soon have to abandon the safety of these Isles if he had any hope of securing his reign. But, for tonight at least, he could let his people celebrate.

His eyes moved across them – earls and lords, knights and mercenaries, blacksmiths, fishermen, cowherds, midwives and ale wives

– rejoicing as one. He had brought these men and women together, here on this tiny island in the middle of the Northern Ocean. Now, he must build them a kingdom.

Feeling someone move up beside him, Robert saw Christiana approaching. Behind her, his royal standard fluttered in the cool night breeze.

She offered up the glazed jug she held. 'Some more wine, my lord?'

Robert frowned into his empty goblet. He shook his head. 'I am done, my lady.'

Christiana smiled. 'Perhaps a walk?' Setting the jug down on the grass, she headed for the path that led out of the settlement.

Robert stared after her for a moment, then rose and followed, down the track towards the beach.

The midnight sky was a pale, pearlescent blue. Christiana's grey gown was gauzy in the half-light, slipping off one shoulder as she walked, her bare feet moving lightly through the sand. Her hair was piled up with silver pins and Robert's eyes lingered on the long curve of her neck, left bare. Soon, the sounds of revelry faded behind them and the rushing of the waves could be heard ahead. The grasses of the machair whispered as they made their way down on to the beach, past the glistening webs of nets and the dark hulks of fishing boats.

Christiana stood on the shore, looking out to sea, where the waves were laced with foam. 'You always look alone, my lord, even in a crowd.' Her voice was soft, thoughtful.

Robert looked at her, but she didn't meet his eyes. 'The curse of a king, perhaps.' When she didn't answer he followed her gaze out to sea. He could taste the salt of the breaking waves. 'As eldest son and heir to a throne you carry a burden of duty that never leaves you. It sets you apart from other men.' He shook his head, self-conscious. 'Unless you have borne it you cannot know what it is like.' Then, seeing her knowing smile, he laughed. 'Forgive me, my lady. I forgot to whom I was speaking.'

He closed his eyes, breathing in the sea air, content to be alone with her. After a moment, he felt Christiana's hand thread through his. Her fingers were cold. Robert's eyes remained closed, but now he was alert and fully aware of her presence as she moved in front of him. He felt her breath on his face, then her lips on his. The first kiss was soft, questioning. The second was demanding, her other hand coming up to grasp the back of his neck. His head swam with wine and the blood that raced through him as she opened her mouth to wetness, into which he sank his own. Desire flamed in him, a hotter, more urgent passion than he'd ever felt. Clutching her back, he forced her against him, bending to kiss her neck, now running his tongue up the hot curve of her skin, tasting wood-smoke and sweat. A sigh rushed from her lips.

At a stifled laugh somewhere nearby, Robert broke from her, aching. Two figures were lying entwined, a short distance up the beach. Christiana grasped his hand and led him back towards the track, their feet sinking in the sand.

Robert awoke to the milky light of dawn seeping through the shutters. Turning over in the bed, he saw Christiana lying beside him, her back to him. Her hair tumbled across the pillow. Reaching out, he took a strand of it between his fingers, twisting it gently to see its many colours – chestnut and auburn, copper and gold. For a moment, he thought of Elizabeth and a shadow passed across him, then Christiana stirred, the cover slipping down to her waist. His eyes travelled the smooth arc of her body, the swell of her hip, the light cast on her pale skin. He felt a spasm of desire, wanting to do what he had done to her last night here in the sober dawn where he could see her. But as he moved to touch her, there was a knock at the door.

Rising from the bed, he snatched his robe from the floor and pulled it over his nakedness. Opening the door, he saw Edward was outside. Beyond, the debris of the night's celebrations littered the settlement. Men slept, sprawled on the grass, shattered jugs and empty goblets strewn around them. Smells of stale smoke and vomit soured the crisp morning air. A few people were awake, stoking fires and taking buckets down to the stream for water.

'What is it?' Robert asked, seeing his brother's gaze flick past him, into the room where Christiana slept.

'Alexander Seton has returned. He has a message from Humphrey de Bohun.'

Lanercost Priory, England, 1307 AD

King Edward declined the hands of his pages as they reached out to help him rise. His legs shook beneath him and he had to grasp the bedpost. Sweat broke out all over his body, seeping through the freshly laundered shirt and hose his servants had dressed him in. His scarlet surcoat, which they had pulled gently over his underclothes, felt uncommonly thick. He had caught the worried glances exchanged by his pages on seeing how loose the garment had become on his gaunt frame. The belt they had looped around his waist, drawing in the folds of scarlet cloth, wrinkling the snarling faces of the three golden lions, had been punctured with two new holes by his tailor.

As one of his men came forward, holding his scarlet cloak, trimmed with ermine, Edward's eyes lingered on the worn creases in the leather further along the belt, from a time when his waist had been thick with muscle. He was vanishing. The thought made him clench his teeth against the discomfort as his page placed the heavy mantle around his shoulders. Across the chamber, Nicholas Tingewick stood watching, wringing his long-fingered hands. On the table beside the physician were his bowls and instruments, phials of ointment, herbs and leeches. Nicholas had come to make one last plea for him to reconsider, but Edward had rejected his counsel. He was finished with potions and prayers, done with bloodletting and bed-rest.

Steeling himself, he let go of the bedpost and crossed the room, light-headed and unsteady. The locked chest he kept at the end of his bed was gone, packed on a cart along with the rest of his belongings. The only things left in the chamber were the bed and his desk. As he shambled past the desk, his pages clustering nervously at his back, Edward's eyes alighted on one of the letters strewn on its surface, with the seal of Aymer de Valence attached. The parchment's yellowed edges had curled, dampened by the sweat of his fingers. The letter had come four weeks ago, the earl informing him of a skirmish against the forces of Robert Bruce at a place called Loudoun Hill. The gist of the battle was vague, Aymer glossing over his failure to capture the rebel king and speaking of an unfortunate and unavoidable loss of men, before writing at length on his renewed, unquestionable determination to crush their Scottish foe. But the earl's report wasn't the only one Edward had received.

Others told a different story. Messengers came with news of the massive defeats suffered by the English forces in Galloway and Loudoun Hill. They spoke of men flocking to Robert's banner from across Carrick, Ayrshire, Bute, Kyle Stewart and Renfrew, and of the rebel's command of an indomitable fleet that now controlled the waters. They spoke, too, of a prophecy sweeping Scotland: a prophecy that foretold his own death and augured the rise of Bruce as a new leader of the Britons. King Arthur reborn.

His men had failed him. His son, estranged from him in London, had disappointed him. No one else could be trusted to do what must be done. Edward knew that now. Sending missives into England and Wales, summoning the commissioners of array to call all able-bodied men to muster in Carlisle in three weeks' time, he had ordered his court to make ready to leave Lanercost Priory. He would meet his army in the city, then lead them to the Solway Firth where he would cross into Scotland and take the head of the traitor himself. He was Arthur – the Dragon King, ruler of all Britain. No one else would wear this mantle, least not Robert Bruce, the man who had threatened to undo his life's work and who now threatened his very legacy.

As Simon opened the door for him, eyes downcast, Edward moved slowly out into the passage, every part of his body protesting. He could barely breathe for the awful, solid pain in his bowels. He'd pissed black blood that morning. Outside, the June sunlight caused his eyes to water. He squinted against its glare as he made his way across the priory's lawn, away from the timber building that had been his dwelling all these months. He felt good to be leaving it, despite the agony of doing so. Too long had he stayed within its walls; too long had he relied on others to fulfil his last intent.

Carts piled with chests, sacks, coffers and barrels were lined up, grooms adjusting the harnesses, porters making last checks of the loads. The royal knights were waiting with their horses and squires. Queen Marguerite was there, mounted on a dappled palfrey, with his sons, Thomas and Edmund, and his infant daughter, Eleanor, swaddled against her wet nurse. His family would ride with him to Carlisle where he would leave them. Maids and cooks, tailors and clerics, all watched in silence as their once formidable, proud king, limped painfully across the grass to where Bayard stood. The warhorse was held by his squire, its scarlet trapper drifting in the wind. His men had prepared a litter for the journey, but Edward was determined he would ride into Scotland of his own volition; ride in as the warrior king he had always been. It was time to end this war, once and for all.

30

Near Ayr, Scotland, 1307 AD

'They're coming.'

Robert turned at his brother's voice. 'How many?'

Edward pushed through the trails of ivy that cloaked the chapel's entrance. The doorway was one of the only parts of the ancient structure still standing. The rest was a pale skeleton of weather-stained stone, ribs of arches and crumbling walls holding up a ceiling of sky. 'Ten,' answered Edward, joining him in the ruins. 'As promised.'

Robert nodded, but the tension didn't leave him. He glanced towards the cracked remains of the altar, where Gilbert and Neil stood over the kneeling form of Henry Percy. The lord's head was covered with a hood, his hands bound behind his back. He had lost weight during his captivity, although his stomach still bulged over his belt. When they hauled him from the galley that morning, up the cliff path to the ruins, Percy had cursed them, spitting threats through his hood. Now, he was silent, waiting. The fourth figure standing with them was Alexander Seton, his dark eyes fixed on the archway.

So far, everything was going as planned. Robert's men had been scouting the area these past three days for any sign this was a trap, as James Stewart and others had feared, but they had found nothing to indicate such. Now the English had arrived as expected with the number of men stipulated, a number matched by Robert's company. Alexander Seton's contrition and desire to make amends thus seemed proven, but he'd hardly said a word on the crossing from Barra and his reticence had begun to make Robert uneasy. He felt the man was keeping something from him. But, if so, he wasn't the only one.

Robert hadn't yet told Alexander about Christopher's execution and had ordered his men to keep quiet on the matter for the time being. He didn't want anything disrupting this parley, especially in light of David of Atholl's reaction to his father's death.

Hearing hoof-beats drumming outside, Robert looked back at the chapel's entrance to see a company come into view through the ivy-covered arch. They pulled their horses to a halt a short distance away, where knights from Carrick were waiting to greet them. Robert watched closely, his hand resting on his sword, as the ten men dismounted. In the cove below, Lachlan's galley waited, enabling him to beat a hasty retreat if necessary, but that was scant comfort now. If he was wrong in his judgement everything could be over for him in the next few moments.

There was a brief exchange and a figure stepped forward. He wore a blue surcoat, slashed with a white band, on either side of which were six golden lions. Unsheathing his sword, the man handed it to one of the knights, then began to walk towards the chapel, looking guardedly around him. Robert felt the blood pound in his temples as Humphrey de Bohun entered the ruin, his green eyes falling on him.

Humphrey had last seen Robert almost two years ago, when the man fled Westminster, his plan to take the throne in defiance of King Edward revealed in documents found on William Wallace. He was stunned by the change in his former friend. Robert, fresh-faced and handsome in youth, looked older than his thirty-three years. The glare of the midday sun beating down on the chapel's rubble-strewn aisle made a stark display of the scars on his cheeks and the lines that furrowed his brow. The stubble that shadowed his jaw was black, but his dark, shoulder-length hair had a few streaks of grey at the sides. Despite the fact he looked leaner in the waist he was still broad in the shoulders and clearly hadn't spent long without a sword in his hand. His surcoat displayed the red lion of Scotland, but the garment was damaged, crudely stitched in places.

After his surprise passed, Humphrey felt a tide of emotions sweep in. First came a spike of anticipation – the realisation that the quarry he'd been hunting all these months was now just within his reach. He thought briefly of Aymer, several miles away in Ayr, unaware that he was here, only paces from their mortal enemy. There was a heady moment where he wondered, if he killed Robert right now, whether the war would be ended, but as Humphrey's fingers drifted towards his hip he remembered he had given up his weapon. He noted Robert's hand curled around the hilt of his sheathed sword and felt at once vulnerable without his own. Beneath the urge to violence were older emotions – glimmers of friendship, shadows of regret and betrayal. But, as Humphrey came to a stop before Robert and Edward, one feeling lifted clear above the rest: hope that the man in front of him held the answers he needed.

Flies buzzed in the sticky air as the three men studied one another in silence. Humphrey saw only hostility in Edward Bruce's eyes, but there was something more thoughtful and pensive in Robert's. Beyond the king and his brother, down by the remains of an altar, three men, one of whom was Alexander Seton, stood over a kneeling, hooded figure, who, by the arms on surcoat and his girth, Humphrey knew was Henry Percy.

Robert followed his gaze with a nod. 'As you can see, I have what you want.' He looked back at Humphrey. His tone was stiff with cold formality. 'I want something in return.'

Humphrey studied him. If Robert felt anything about this dangerous reunion, he was keeping it well hidden. 'Sir Alexander told me – you want your family freed.'

'When they are released I will give you Sir Henry, unharmed. You have my word.'

Humphrey bit back the impulse to demand how he could be expected to trust the word of a traitor. 'May we speak alone?'

Edward Bruce cut in angrily. 'Say what you will. I am staying.'

Robert held Humphrey's gaze for a long moment, then nodded to Edward. 'Let me hear what he has to say.'

'Brother—'

'That's an order.'

Edward looked as if he were going to protest, but then he backed away and joined his comrades and their prisoner.

Humphrey waited until he was out of earshot. There were so many questions. He paused, then chose the first that came to mind – the easiest. 'Where is the Staff of Malachy?'

Robert let out a rough bark of laughter. 'You think I will answer that? This parley is for an exchange of prisoners – nothing more. I've not come here for an interrogation.'

'And I've not come to satisfy your wishes. I could have brought an army with me today – taken Percy by force and seized you. I haven't. But in return for that I want something for myself.'

'What?'

'I want answers, Robert.' When the man didn't respond, Humphrey continued. 'Why did you do it? Why take the staff, knowing what you knew?'

Robert turned away, shaking his head.

Humphrey stepped in front of him. 'Or did you never believe? Was it all a lie when you took the oath in Conwy? Did you join our brotherhood never intending to keep your vows? Did you always know you would betray me?' That last question bubbled up unexpectedly, the strength of feeling behind it surprising Humphrey. He realised, on asking it, that deep down, no matter Robert's deception, he had not been able to bring himself to believe that their friendship had been a lie. He could not square that with the man he had known all those years. 'I trusted you, Robert – fought alongside you in battle, laughed with you, confided in you. I bore your burdens, just as you bore mine. Did none of that mean anything? Please, tell me. I have to know.'

Robert didn't look as though he were going to answer. A gull landed on one of the fractured arches and called into his silence. 'It wasn't all a lie.'

His voice was so quiet Humphrey had to strain to hear him over the crying of the gull.

'I believed in the oaths I had taken and I believed in our friendship, until the night we rode into Scone.' Robert glanced behind him to where his men stood, some distance away. 'Until you forced me to take the Stone of Destiny.'

'It wasn't belief that turned in you then,' countered Humphrey, anger shooting through him. 'It was pride. You wouldn't give up your claim to the throne, even if it meant bringing both our kingdoms to ruin!'

'I swore an oath to my grandfather long before I swore my oath to Edward. I told him I would defend my family's right to the throne of Scotland. In that moment, I realised I could no longer serve two masters. I had to choose.' Robert met Humphrey's eyes. 'And now I know I made the right choice. Now I know the truth behind your king's so-called *Last Prophecy*.'

Humphrey felt his heart begin to thump. Now, he was nearing it – the question that had brought him here. 'What of your prophecy

– the death of the covetous king that will augur your rise to power as a new leader of the Britons? Will you try to tell me that is truth?'

'My prophecy is as true as men want it to be.' Robert smiled, but there was no humour in the expression. 'King Edward taught me well.'

'What does that mean?'

Robert shook his head. 'Let us do what we came here to do, Humphrey. Let us agree this exchange. My family for Percy. Yes?'

'Tell me. I want to know.'

As Robert studied him something shifted in his face, his expression changing from cold suspicion to faint surprise. 'When I took the box from Westminster it broke. When I looked inside there was no prophecy.'

Humphrey felt an icy tide wash through him, hearing Robert repeat what Alexander had told him in Ayr, but, still, he refused to accept it as truth. 'The text King Edward found at Nefyn was ancient. He had the *Last Prophecy* translated and kept the original locked in that box because he feared it could turn to dust. Maybe it had.'

'There was nothing, Humphrey. No trace of anything.'

'It predicted the death of King Alexander. It said he would die without issue. If the prophecy wasn't real, how is that possible?'

'That's what kept me doubting, even after I made my decision to fight for my kingdom – what kept me fearing I might bring Britain to ruin by my actions. Until this.' Reaching into the front of his surcoat, Robert pulled out the fragment of iron he wore around his neck on a worn leather thong. 'That night in my father's manor five years ago – the night we fought – I told you I didn't know the man who attacked me in Ireland. It wasn't a lie. I didn't know him. But James Stewart did.'

Humphrey listened, disquiet rising, as Robert spoke of the corpse in the cellar of Dunluce Castle and the high steward's shock as he recognised the dead man as Adam, a squire of King Alexander who had come from France in Queen Yolande's retinue and had escorted Alexander to his new bride at Kinghorn.

'This man,' continued Robert, 'who hunted me down in Ireland was with Alexander the night he died. That can be no mere coincidence. I was at Birgham, Humphrey. I heard Edward claim that Alexander had wanted to join their houses in marriage. He said our king had spoken of a possible union between Margaret of Norway and his infant son. If that marriage had gone ahead Edward would have taken control of Scotland through his son. But, then, Alexander chose Yolande for his new bride.'

Humphrey, seeing the abyss into which this conversation was heading – a far darker, deeper one than he had imagined – turned from Robert. But even as he did so he thought of Adam, commander of one of the king's crossbow regiments in Gascony and a member of the Knights of the Dragon. He hadn't seen the man in years. Edward had ordered him to question Robert on the identity of his attacker and whether the man was still alive. *Proof. He wanted to know if they had proof*. Humphrey had wondered himself about the king's possible involvement in Robert's attack, but had dismissed it as unthinkable. Now, a parade of the king's latest victims marched through his mind: John of Atholl, Christopher Seton, Alexander Bruce. He had seen, first-hand, what Edward was capable of. But the murder of his brother-in-law? Regicide? *He plotted against his father. After Evesham, he had the body of his own godfather, Simon de Montfort, mutilated. You saw what he did to his own son, just weeks ago.*

'Any children Alexander and Yolande had would have taken precedence over Margaret as heir to the throne of Scotland.'

'Stop,' murmured Humphrey. There was little force to the command.

'After Alexander died, Edward secured the pope's permission for his son to marry Margaret as planned. He would have got his wish had she not died on the voyage.'

Humphrey crossed to a stump of broken pillar and leaned against it. This was it – the spider at the centre of the web of secrets he had sensed spun between the king and Robert. It was, he knew, why he had felt so discomforted by the executions of Robert's brothers, why guilt had assailed him at the incarceration of the man's wife and family, and why his questions these past months had begun to shift in another, far more unpalatable, direction. His heart had known something his head had refused to accept: that Robert wasn't the only one who had lied to him. His wasn't the only betrayal.

Robert followed him, impassioned. 'I believe Edward ordered Alexander's murder so he could take control of Scotland, easily, without out a prolonged war. And I believe he invented the *Last Prophecy* to legitimise his conquest of Britain and keep his men faithful to his cause. The relics he took are powerful symbols of the sovereignty of each of our nations. In taking them for himself he claimed the very souls of our kingdoms. But he claimed you too, Humphrey. While he conquered my country with the sword, he conquered you with the power of prophecy. You fought for his lie because you believed you were saving Britain. You weren't. You were destroying it.'

Humphrey's mind filled with the slow decay he had seen in England these past years; rising poverty in the countryside and lawlessness growing in the towns. He thought of the reports coming in from beleaguered English settlers in Ireland, towns abandoned as the Irish pressed in on the borders. He had a fleeting thought of the king's sickness spreading to infect the realm, as if Edward himself had become the canker at the core of it. As he met Robert's gaze, he realised the man looked relieved, as if lifted of a burden. In turn, he felt as though all that weight were now crushing his own shoulders. 'Why have you said nothing before now?'

'Edward built this lie over years. Its foundations are deep and the defences he has raised around it – in the Knights of the Dragon and his Round Table – are mighty. It would take a lot more than my word to bring it crashing down. I had hoped to use the prophecy box against him somehow, but it was taken with my brother.'

'Have you told your men?'

'A small number know the box was empty. But Sir James asked me to keep my silence on my suspicions over Alexander's death. I wanted to find proof in London, but then Wallace was caught and . . .' Robert trailed off, shaking his head. 'In truth, I do not expect anything in telling you this, Humphrey. All I want now is my family. My daughter is in a cage, for Christ's sake!'

Humphrey pushed a gloved hand through his hair, closing his eyes. He couldn't take all this in – not yet – and he couldn't show any more weakness in front of Robert. The man was still his enemy. No matter what else this meeting had yielded that fact remained. He straightened, meeting Robert's eyes. 'Marjorie isn't in a cage. Edward passed the sentence upon her, yes, and she was taken to the Tower on his orders. But she never went into the cage. Queen Marguerite eventually managed to persuade him to house your daughter in a room there. Marjorie even has one of her own maids with her, I believe.'

'Aymer said otherwise. I heard him – when he was hunting for me. He taunted me, saying she was caged like an animal.'

'I expect he wanted you to suffer.' Humphrey saw Robert's face brighten and fill with hope. All at once, the grim, scarred man before him looked more like the youth he had known.

'Then, the others? Niall? John? Christopher? Is what I've been told untrue? Are they—'

'No,' said Humphrey. 'I'm afraid his leniency did not extend to your men.' He frowned. 'For whatever it is worth, I am sorry. Ralph de Monthermer and I petitioned the king to have mercy on them.' He looked down the aisle to where Henry Percy was kneeling. 'I can tell you now Edward will not agree to an exchange of prisoners. Sir Henry's life doesn't mean as much to him as your suffering does.'

'I don't believe that.'

'You should.' At the bluntness of the statement, Humphrey saw Robert's defiance falter. 'But if you release Henry into my custody and make me a promise I will do two things for you.'

'What things?'

'First – the promise. I want your word that you will keep your silence on what you believe happened to King Alexander.' As Robert went to speak, Humphrey cut in. 'Just as you feel it is your duty to protect your kingdom, I must defend mine. If Edward murdered his brother-in-law he will face judgement before God's tribunal. But I will not allow England to be tarnished by the accusation. Whatever the truth, Alexander's death must remain an accident.'

'You want me to give up my hostage and promise to protect the reputation of the man who hanged my brothers?' Robert's tone was blistering.

'The king is near death. Edward of Caernarfon will soon take the throne. You would do well to keep an ally in the royal court when that happens. He may be more open to negotiation than his father has been.'

'You cannot guarantee that.'

'No, but what I can assure you is that I will help your family. I will do whatever is in my power to ease their suffering. I could get your daughter moved from the Tower and make sure your wife has more agreeable lodgings in which to live out her days.'

'My sisters? Isabel Comyn?'

'I will do what I can.' Humphrey maintained his poise, as Robert searched his face.

'You said you would do two things for me,' said Robert, after a long silence.

'Give me Percy and I will tell you the second.'

Robert looked to where the prisoner knelt. He seemed to struggle with the decision, then gestured to Gilbert and Neil. 'Bring him,' he called, raising his voice.

The two men exchanged questioning looks, but they did as their king commanded. Henry Percy resisted as he was hauled to his feet.

The lord shouted through his hood as they marched him towards Humphrey. 'What are you doing with me? Where are you taking me? Tell me, God damn you!'

'Take him outside,' Robert told his men, when Humphrey nodded.

After Percy had been conveyed through the archway to the waiting company of knights, Humphrey turned back to Robert. He looked to the altar, where Edward Bruce and Alexander Seton stood frowning at these unexpected proceedings. 'You have a snake in your midst.'

Robert followed his gaze. 'What?'

'Seton told the Black Comyn of your intention to head to Islay. He is the reason John MacDougall of Argyll knew you were coming. I believe he was tortured for the information then, but when imprisoned in Berwick he freely offered to bring you in if we would spare his cousin the gallows.' Humphrey looked back at Robert, who had paled. 'When Seton came to me in Ayr it wasn't to deliver your message. He was going to tell me where your fleet was based in return for Christopher's release. He doesn't know he is already dead.'

'Why are you telling me this?'

'As I said – two pledges from me in return for two from you.' Humphrey took in the look of devastation on Robert's face, but could find no pleasure in it. 'Besides, I know what it's like to have a friend betray you.'

Burgh by Sands, England, 1307 AD

Humphrey rode into the English encampment, heading for the scarlet pavilion that loomed above the crowds of soldiers who filled the fields around the tiny settlement of Burgh by Sands, their upper arms adorned with bands of white cloth decorated with the cross of St George. The flanks of Humphrey's horse were foamy with sweat. He and his men had ridden hard from Carlisle, determined to reach the king before he crossed the water. Another ship was sailing into the vast, brown mouth of the Solway Firth to join the others moored there. Soon, there would be enough vessels to transport the king's army across the estuary to Scotland.

Humphrey drew his horse to a stamping halt outside the pavilion, his eyes on the ranks of the Galloway hills standing dark against the dun sky. A brisk wind hissed through the reeds of the nearby marshes. It was cold for early July.

Two royal knights were standing to either side of the pavilion's entrance. As Humphrey approached, one moved to bar his way. 'Sir Humphrey, I'm afraid the king is accepting no visitors.'

'It is urgent, Geoffrey. I must speak with the king at once.'

'I am sorry, sir.'

'As Constable of England, I order you to stand aside.'

Geoffrey faltered, glancing at his companion for help.

Humphrey didn't wait, but pushed past the man. As the knight stiffened and reached for his sword, he growled, 'Do not try me today.'

Entering the pavilion, Humphrey saw Nicholas Tingewick talking to several royal officials. They looked round, surprised, as he headed for the curtains that partitioned the king's bedchamber. Before they could stop him, he brushed aside the drapes and entered. He saw the bed erected in the centre of the large space, the womb-like red chamber unfurnished but for a black chest at the foot of the bed. At the head, obscuring Humphrey's view, stood the king's steward and his confessor. To the edges of the tent, pages clustered, pale and nervous. Seeing the priest was carrying a small, silver box, Humphrey's throat went dry. It was a pyx, for the bearing of the sacrament.

The steward looked round. 'Sir Humphrey—'

'Is the king dead?' Humphrey moved quickly to the bed.

Edward lay still, his legs and torso covered by a thin sheet, dampened by sweat. His body was wasted, his face as white and oily as melting tallow. His eyes were half-lidded and his mouth was open. Humphrey let out a sharp breath, seeing the king's chest rising and falling and a vein in his neck pulsing rapidly.

'He has been given the last rites,' the steward said quietly. 'We fear it will not be long now.'

Humphrey didn't take his eyes off the king. 'Leave us, would you please?'

'Sir, I . . .' The steward faltered into silence as Humphrey turned on him. Seeing the look in the earl's eyes, he nodded.

The steward and the priest retreated behind the curtains, followed by the worried pages.

Humphrey, left alone, stared down at the shrivelled form lying before him. The man they had called Longshanks, King of England, Duke of Gascony, Lord of Ireland and conqueror of Wales and Scotland, had become a withered cage of flesh and bone, from which his soul now strained to be free. Glistening streaks of oil had trickled through his white hair on to the pillow from the unction that had been applied to his temples. This man had been everything to him – he had given his life for him and his cause. Robert had exposed what he had feared for months, but Humphrey now wanted to hear it from Edward himself. The king owed him that much.

Humphrey thought of the questions Edward would have been asked as part of the rites. *Are you sorry for your sins? Do you desire to make amends and if God gave you more time, by His grace would you do so?* Sitting on the edge of the bed, he took hold of his father-in-law's hand. The king's eyelids flickered at the contact.

'My lord, can you hear me?'

Edward's eyes cracked open. His gaze came slowly into focus. 'Humphrey?'

'I am here.' Humphrey tightened his grip on the king's hand as his eyes slipped closed, waiting until his gaze was on him again. 'I have come to help you unburden yourself of your sins. It is time, my lord. Time to give your true confession.'

This time, Edward's eyes remained open.

An hour later, Humphrey left the king's chamber. The royal officials and servants, waiting beyond, all turned to him, their expressions shifting at the look on his face.

'The king is dead,' he confirmed into their silence.

Humphrey crossed to the steward, who had closed his eyes momentarily in prayer. 'We must keep this quiet as long as we can for the sake of our men still in Scotland. We cannot allow the Scots to know we are vulnerable, not until our new king has been proclaimed.'

The steward nodded slowly, but he looked uncertain at the task. 'I will do what I can, of course.' He let out a breath. 'I must send word to the prince and the queen at once.'

'I will deliver the message to the prince directly,' Humphrey told him. 'I have business in London.'

Leaving the steward to administer to the king's body, Humphrey headed for the tent's entrance. In their shock and grief, the pages and officials didn't notice the leather bag he now gripped tightly in his fist. As he pushed out of the tent into the grey afternoon, Humphrey realised his hands were shaking.

The Border, Scotland, 1307 AD

Alexander Seton was hauled unceremoniously from the horse. He stumbled as he landed on the uneven ground of the woods. As one of the men turned him roughly around and began cutting through the ropes that bound his hands behind his back, he met the gaze of Neil Campbell, who remained astride his horse. Alexander didn't speak, but after a long moment he averted his eyes from Campbell's cold stare.

'If King Robert or any of his men see you in Scotland again, your life is forfeit,' Neil reminded him.

'He made that very clear.' As his pack was slung at him, Alexander caught it. 'Robert need not worry. I'll not set foot in his kingdom again.' His voice hardened. 'There is nothing here for me now.' He headed for the edge of the trees, beyond which the road wound south through rolling hills – south to a life in exile. All he had sacrificed had been in vain. In the end, he had lost everything.

After a few paces Alexander looked back at the unsmiling faces of the men who had escorted him to the border. 'I did it for Christopher.'

When they didn't answer, he turned and walked out of the trees into the dusk, pulling up his hood against the mist of rain.

32

Burstwick Manor, England, 1307 AD

Elizabeth woke to the sound of voices. She sat up, disoriented. Golden light seeped through the shutters, but she couldn't tell if it was morning or evening. She had lain down to rest, not meaning to sleep. Perhaps another night had passed without her notice? The voices were louder, coming down the passage towards her. Other than distant calls that occasionally filtered in from outside she hadn't heard another human's voice in months. She felt herself flinching at the approaching sounds. As the key rattled in the lock, she pushed herself off the bed.

The first person she saw was Maud. The po-faced maid looked flushed and indignant.

Elizabeth started in surprise as a man moved into the chamber behind the woman. 'Humphrey,' she murmured, in one moment elated to see a familiar face, the next terrified he had come to execute some crueller punishment devised by the king.

'My lady.'

Elizabeth realised that Humphrey had changed, considerably, since she had last seen him almost a year ago. His physical appearance was little different; it was in his eyes and his bearing where the transformation had occurred. He had the look of a man in mourning. There was a haunting clarity in his green eyes.

'Are you fit to travel?'

'Why? Where are you taking me?'

'You're being moved to my manor in Essex. You will be well cared for there.'

Elizabeth took this in, not daring to hope it was true – that she might leave these walls, even for a moment; breathe fresh air. 'My father?' She suddenly wondered if she had imagined her message being returned to her, crumpled on the tray.

'The king decreed it, shortly before he died.'

'King Edward is dead?'

Humphrey's brow furrowed. He turned to the red-faced Maud. 'You did not tell her?'

'I was following the king's orders, sir,' said the maid sullenly. 'I wasn't to speak to her.'

Humphrey held out his hand. 'Come, my lady. My men are waiting to escort you. But, first, there is someone to see you. She is waiting outside.'

Feeling a heady mix of confusion, excitement and disbelief bubbling up inside her, Elizabeth stepped quickly forward and grasped Humphrey's hand. His skin was a warm shock after so long without contact, his grip firm as he led her past Maud, down the passage and out into the late August evening. The courtyard was filled with golden light, hazy with dust, disturbed by the horses and wagons. Elizabeth halted in the doorway for a moment, closing her eyes as the sun bathed her.

'Elizabeth!'

Her eyes snapped open at the voice. She saw a thin, dark-haired girl break free from the group by the wagons and race across the yard towards her. Elizabeth went to meet her, enfolding Marjorie tightly in her arms. Tears stung her eyes as she felt the girl's body begin to shake against her own. After a few moments, Elizabeth pulled back, smiling through her tears as she studied Marjorie, who had grown taller in the past year and looked less like a girl, more like a young woman. 'Dear God, but I thought I would never see you again.'

Marjorie looked at Humphrey, then back at Elizabeth. 'Where is my father? They will not tell me.'

'In Scotland,' answered Humphrey, his eyes moving to Elizabeth. 'Alive.'

'Will Marjorie be coming with me?' she asked him. 'To Essex?'

'No, my lady. But the king granted me permission to have her moved to Sixhills convent. She will be with her aunts there.'

'And Mary? Isabel?'

'It is all I can do. For now.' Turning, Humphrey motioned to his men. Two of his knights came forward, keeping close to the women. 'I have something to attend to, my lady.' His eyes flicked from Elizabeth to Marjorie. 'When I return we will be leaving.'

Elizabeth nodded, knowing he meant for them to savour this moment. 'Thank you,' she murmured.

Humphrey entered the chamber alone. Closing the door behind him, he leaned against it, letting his eyes take in the patterned rug, faded where the light came in, the hooded hearth, the pitted beams that crossed the ceiling, the table and chairs by the open windows, then, finally, the bed. This room was imprinted on his mind, indelible as a brand. It was the place where the souls of his wife and child had been released.

He had spent days in here after returning to the manor to find Bess had died in labour. Poisoned with drink and grief he remembered little of it – just flashes of rage and bright bursts of violence. He walked across the room, his footsteps hollow on the floor, and touched one of the posts of the bed, scarred by gashes. He had a memory of slashing at it with his sword. Moving around the bed, he put down the leather bag he had carried up from the courtyard and sat, breathing in the chamber's staleness, faint beneath the acrid smell of the logs blazing in the hearth. The flames were high and bright, the fire just lit by one of the servants, as ordered. Humphrey stayed there for a while, eyes closed, listening to two doves calling in the cote outside. Then, he turned to the bag beside him. Reaching inside, he pulled out a large, leather-bound book. Words shimmered in the burnished light of the setting sun flooding through the windows.

The Last Prophecy of Merlin

Humphrey turned the pages, his eyes following the delicate flow of the script, surrounded by margins filled with interlocking patterns of animals and flowers. He had been granted the king's permission to read this book the night of his initiation into the Round Table. Even though, by then, he knew the words within by heart, he had come to it in deep reverence, his breath quickening as he saw the sacred quest his king had charged him with set out before him. The soft skin of the pages had seemed almost alive to him then, decorated with whorls and trails of flowers, arched beasts and soaring birds that seemed to writhe on the parchment in the flicker of candlelight, the vivid colours of the inks, made from precious stones powdered down and mixed with wine, dazzling him. He had felt the words, rendered into Latin from old Welsh, calling down the years to him; grasping hold of something inside him, pulling him to follow their thread and surrender himself to their commands.

Now, looking down on the same pages, he couldn't believe how flat, how dead in his hands they were. The words, scribed in oak gall ink, were not ancient and had never been written in Welsh. They were younger than him. It was six weeks since the king had died, six weeks and yet still the truth was only just forming inside him, like a seed growing. Into what, Humphrey did not know. It was strange to have come to understand how much power there could be in nothing. He paused on a page with an image of a man standing before a fortress, behind which towered green mountains. The man held aloft a gold coronet: the Crown of Arthur, in the circle of which Humphrey now knew the lie had been born.

It was as a young prince, disgraced and exiled in Gascony, that Edward first learned of the crown. It had been raised, then, on the head of the warlord, Llywelyn ap Gruffudd, who, uniting the fractured kingdoms of Wales beneath him, had led a new uprising, burning and raiding lands granted to Edward by his father. On the dusty tournament grounds of Gascony, the prince had already come to understand the power of legends. Fighting under his new-made dragon banner, styling himself as King Arthur, men had begun to flock to his standard. He had seen how it empowered and inspired them, how loyal they were to something greater than themselves – something that lifted them above the mundane and delivered them into the realm of heroes. Edward knew, implicitly, that Llywelyn's achievement in unifying the disparate people of Wales lay in the power of that crown. And knew that to conquer his enemy he must take it from him.

It would be only after another twenty-two years and by great sacrifice of money and men that Edward finally vanquished Llywelyn, in which time he saw his father beaten, stripped of authority and dignity during the bitter civil war with his barons. On taking the throne, Edward had sworn an oath never to be so dishonoured by any man subject to him. To ensure this he began to expand his borders and consolidate his power, rewarding the faithful with gifts of land in the regions he conquered. In the conquest of Wales, his Round Table was formed and he wrapped his vassals – those whose strength he needed – in the mantles of champions: Gawain and Galahad, Mordred and Perceval, his men bound to him by vows more sacred than fealty, their loyalty fused in the table's endless circle. But what was once just a tournament guise had become something much greater for Edward. He didn't just want to be called by the name of a hero of old: he wanted to become the legend itself – Arthur, King of all Britain.

Edward had read Geoffrey of Monmouth's *History of the Kings of Britain* and the *Prophecies of Merlin*, of which the scholar said there were others yet to be translated. Claiming to have found one of these lost texts in a stronghold of his vanquished enemy, Llywelyn ap Gruffudd, the king presented it with great ceremony to the men of his newly fashioned Round Table, shortly after the birth of his son, Edward of Caernarfon. The *Last Prophecy* was his testimony, his ambition immortalised on parchment, and by it he would unite Britain beneath one crown. Prophecy would spur his men to further his intent, instilling in them a sense of the sacred, beyond the blood and sacrifice of war, the rising taxes and depleted fortunes. But the conflict in Gascony had rumbled on, becoming ever more unpopular, and Edward had seen his power start to slip. It was then that he established the Knights of the Dragon, an elite band of brothers formed of the young bloods at his court; those weaned on tales of Arthur and his knights, those more impressionable than their fathers.

Men, thought Humphrey, like him. He turned the pages of the book, his eyes passing over the images. There was Curtana, the broken sword a symbol of English royal authority, and the Staff of Malachy, the holy relic embodying the spirit of Irish nationhood. There, too, the Stone of Destiny, Scotland's kingmaker. As he turned to the last pages, he now saw the tiny variations in the stitching that bound them, where new pages had been added. Humphrey hadn't seen this when he looked that first time, blinded by the brightness of the lie. Reading the lines that predicted the death of King Alexander, he recalled Edward's breathless last words, there on his deathbed.

'*One life, Humphrey, may God forgive me. One life for the future of our kingdom, a kingdom united, bound in strength.*'

Slowly, carefully even, Humphrey tore the pages from the book, one by one. He ripped them into pieces, the words separating, the prophecy unravelling in his hands. When he was left with a heap of shredded parchment, he reached into the bag and pulled out a black box. While the sun's golden light had faded the glow of firelight had strengthened. It gleamed on the surface of the wood as Humphrey held it up, staring through the fracture in its side, in the depths of which Robert had first seen the truth. Gathering up the box and the torn pages, he crossed to the fire and crouched before it.

Here in this chamber, where his love had died, he fulfilled his promise to her father; the man to whom he had given half his life. He would keep his silence, even from the men of the Round Table who still believed in the lie. He would bear the king's burden alone. But it was the last thing he would do in his name. As he watched the pages flame and the box begin to smoulder, Humphrey felt it turn to ash inside him, but with this death came a strange feeling of freedom. Staring into the heart of the fire, he had a sense of his own destiny stretching before him.

33

Westminster Abbey, England, 1307 AD

It was late October, four days before the Feast of All Souls. Silvery morning sunlight slanted through the high windows of Westminster Abbey, shining on the pillars and arches, glowing in the stone faces of saints and angels. Hazy layers of incense and candle smoke shifted in the air over the heads of the host of earls and knights, countesses and clerks, bishops and squires, all cloaked in mourning black. Many had come from across England, from Cornwall and Lancaster, Pembroke and Lincoln. Others had journeyed further still, from Scotland, Ireland, Wales, France and the Low Countries. Above them, the great vault of Westminster Abbey soared, one hundred feet of echoing space filled with the rising voices of the choir.

Edward of Caernarfon watched in silence as three canons passed slowly around the ornate, wheeled hearse that had borne his father's body from St Paul's. As they sprinkled holy water across the coffin, which was draped with the dragon banner, Anthony Bek, the aged Bishop of Durham, intoned the Requiem Mass, his deep voice resounding across the silent multitude. Edward's gaze moved over the men and women crowded in around him. Humphrey de Bohun was there with his nephew, Henry. Close by were Aymer de Valence, Robert Clifford and Guy de Beauchamp, along with Ralph de Monthermer, still in mourning for the loss of his wife, Edward's eldest sister, Joan, who had succumbed to a summer fever. Ralph's stepson, Gilbert, stood stiffly at his side, recently made Earl of Gloucester in his place. Seeing many of the barons hanging their heads in respect or grief and the tears glistening on the cheeks of Queen

Marguerite and her ladies-in-waiting, Edward realised that he himself felt little, except relief.

In July, when Humphrey arrived with news of his father's passing, Edward had taken it in with cool acceptance. Heading north to claim his father's body, he was proclaimed king in Carlisle Castle, whereupon he had taken control of the army. After accepting the homage of loyalist Scottish barons and leaving the country in the hands of the English garrisons, Edward, Prince of Wales, Duke of Gascony and, now, King of England, led his men south in the wake of his father's corpse. Aymer de Valence and others had been incensed by his decision not to continue the campaign against Robert Bruce, but Edward refused to bow to their repeated requests. For the time being, he was done with the north – done with his father's endless war. There were other, more pressing things on his mind, in the form of his coronation and forthcoming marriage to Isabella of France, and, most crucially, the return of his love.

Edward glanced at Thomas of Lancaster, standing close by. While everyone else's attention was on the coffin or cast downward in prayer, his cousin was staring straight at him. For one disturbing moment, Edward saw, in the earl's grey eyes, some echo of his father, before the young man averted his gaze. Edward mollified himself by anticipating the look on Thomas's face when Piers Gaveston returned to the court. He had already sent for the knight, in exile in Gascony. Soon, he would be back at his side.

As Bishop Bek finished the Mass and a tide of amens flooded the abbey, Edward looked towards the screen that hid the shrine of the Confessor. There, in the place where the coronation chair that enclosed the Stone of Destiny stood ready for him, a tomb now awaited his father. Through gaps in the carved screen, he could just make it out. Surrounded by ornate gilt and bronze sepulchres, adorned with gleaming effigies, the open tomb was a great hulk of black marble, so dark it seemed to soak up all the light around it. It was his one commitment to his father's dying wishes.

Years ago, before he was born, his mother and father had reburied the bones of Arthur and Guinevere in an elaborate ceremony at Glastonbury Abbey. His father had ordered the remains of the once and future king to be interred in a plain black marble tomb, in the likeness of which he later fashioned the box for his precious *Last Prophecy*. Now, Edward Longshanks would be delivered into a resting place of the same design, where he would spend eternity. King Arthur, even in death.

Castle Tioram, Scotland, 1307 AD

Robert watched from the battlements as four more galleys sailed into the mouth of Loch Moidart to join the scores of vessels moored in a sheltered inlet, overlooked by Castle Tioram. The island on which the castle stood was linked to the shore by a causeway of rock and sand, only accessible at low tide. The banks beyond were crawling with men. Their numbers had been growing steadily through the autumn, as more answered his call to arms and made their way north to join him at Christiana MacRuarie's remote mainland stronghold. Many had come from the west coast, but in the past few weeks others had arrived from Wales and Ireland, word of his victory over the English at Loudoun Hill spreading far and wide.

With news of King Edward's death, received among Robert's men with relief and great jubilation, the prophecy had taken on a life of its own. What started as a murmur had become a shout. Now, with these last few galley-loads, his army would be almost three thousand strong. The war with England had paused, reports coming in over the summer that the king's men were packing up and moving south across the border. English garrisons still held the castles of Stirling, Edinburgh and Roxburgh, and occupied the towns of Perth, Dumfries, Aberdeen and Dundee, but it was clear their new king did not have the same drive as his father to continue the fight, as James Stewart had hoped and Humphrey de Bohun had implied. It was in this pause that Robert had turned his eye north.

The Comyns and their allies had made their continued aggression towards him clear with pledges of loyalty to King Edward II. Among their number was David of Atholl. The news, when it came, had been a blow to Robert, still stung by the revelation of Alexander Seton's betrayal, but it had helped him cement his decision. Food and supplies had been gathered from Rhum and Eigg, spears had been made, mail cleaned and blades whetted. He was ready. It was time to break out of the western strip of coast he had been confined to – time to confront his Scottish enemies, and clear the way for his return to the throne.

Hearing footsteps on the steps behind him, Robert looked round to see his brother appear on the walkway.

Edward was holding up a roll of parchment. 'One of our men has just come from Turnberry. He had this for you.'

Robert took it quickly, seeing the seal on the bottom. He had been expecting this for months. Unrolling it, he scanned the brief message inside. After a moment, he closed his eyes and murmured a prayer.

'Well?'

'It is done. Marjorie and Elizabeth are safe.'

Edward nodded. He grasped Robert's shoulder with a tight smile. 'It seems you were right about Humphrey. I am sorry I doubted you.'

Robert said nothing, his eyes catching on the last lines of the message.

I have kept my word. Now you must keep your silence.

Crumpling the parchment in his fist, Robert looked over at the men of his army, crowding along the banks, their encampment brightened by the colours of many banners. His gaze moved across the arms of Malcolm of Lennox, Neil Campbell, Thomas Randolph and Gilbert de la Hay, Angus MacDonald and Lachlan MacRuarie, all of them brought closer this past year, their brotherhood forged in loss and in victory. Raising his eyes beyond their ranks, over the wooded hills that blazed copper in the late autumn sun, Robert fixed on the ridges of the distant mountains, glazed white with snow. Beyond those peaks lay the Great Glen – doorway to the heartland of his enemies. Inside, he felt the wheel begin to shift, and turn.

PART 5

1308–1309 AD

Since then your kingdom was divided against itself; since the rage of civil discord, and the fumes of envy, have darkened your minds, since your pride would not suffer you to pay obedience to one king; you see therefore your kingdom made desolate . . . and your houses falling upon one another . . .

The History of the Kings of Britain, *Geoffrey of Monmouth*

34

Slioch, Scotland, 1308 AD

Robert sighed as Christiana kissed his neck. He felt the heat from her body as she lay on him, her weight pressing him into the powdery sand. Sweat ran down his cheeks into his ears and hair, prickling on his scalp. Eyes closed, he listened to her breaths against his skin, whispering like waves on the shore.

'*My lord.*'

At her voice he saw her staring down at him, her pale green eyes like two pools filled with liquid light. Twists of her copper hair tumbled over her shoulders to brush his face. She was laughing, but he didn't know why. Behind her, the sky was on fire. Turning his head, Robert saw droplets of red in the sand beside him. Blood. Alarm flooded him.

'*Christiana.*'

He tried to move her off him, but she was already gone. He could see her standing at the edge of the waves, looking out to sea, a small coffin raised up on a dais beside her, full of flickering fire. There was a figure inside it, but he couldn't see who. He struggled to sit. Although Christiana had gone, the weight of her remained. Sweat poured off him and he longed to plunge himself into the blue waters, but the blood caught his attention again. Now he saw it was a trail, leading away from him along the beach. Beyond, in the distance, the hills blushed in the sunset, their curves and swells like the forms of sleeping women. Robert followed the line of droplets, his feet crunching in the sand, which wasn't sand any more, but snow.

Ahead, a man was kneeling in the expanse of white, his back to him. He wore a red surcoat, which pooled around him like the blood. There was a shield in the snow beside him with three sheaves of wheat emblazoned on it. The man was John Comyn. The trail of blood now made a horrible sense. As Robert approached, foreboding rising in him, the man staggered to his feet and turned. There was a dagger protruding from his ribs. His hands rose to grasp at it. Then, as Robert's eyes moved up to the man's face, he realised it wasn't John Comyn standing there. It was his grandfather. The old lord thrust a finger towards him, his dark eyes filling with accusation.

Edward Bruce looked round as his brother cried out. Robert lay on a litter piled with blankets and furs, his head twisting from side to side. His face gleamed in the lantern's yellow glow, oily with sweat which tracked lines through the dirt and crusts of blood that had sealed over recent wounds. Nes crouched beside him.

Edward glanced to the opening of the makeshift tent, formed from sheets of waxed canvas strung up on the branches of the trees. 'Christ, if the men hear him like this . . . ?' He pushed a hand through his hair, which had been stuck to his scalp from the tight encasement of his coif and helm, rarely removed these past days. 'We cannot give any more of them cause to desert.' Edward's voice was thick with bitterness. Their campaign had begun in force and victory had opened her arms to them, eager and willing. Drunk on blood they had ravaged the lands of their enemies; a reckoning long sought. But then the sickness had come, stripping them of their strength and draining their resolve. The Black Comyn had seized upon their weakness, coming at them fierce and hard.

'We should withdraw,' suggested Gilbert. His face was drawn and dark circles shadowed his eyes. There was a cut along his left cheek, crudely stitched, where an arrow had grazed him during the attack on Inverness Castle weeks earlier. 'I say again, let us head south and find shelter until the king is well. Then we can return in strength.'

'There isn't time,' Neil Campbell told him flatly. 'Comyn will be on us before we can rouse the men. Many are still ailing. We cannot show the earl our backs. Not now.'

Edward nodded. 'We hold a strong position here. Comyn's cavalry couldn't breach our lines on the Christ Mass, when the sickness in our ranks was at its worst.'

'His infantry may have better luck,' warned Malcolm of Lennox, looking between Gilbert and Edward. 'And without our king to lead us?'

They all looked at Robert, sprawled on the litter, drifting in and out of consciousness. The strident blare of a horn rent the air outside.

Edward pushed his way out through the canvas sheets, followed by the others. The woods were crowded with men, splashes of colour from tunics and cloaks daubing the monochrome landscape of bare trees and snow. Many had risen at the horn's blast, donning helms and snatching up shields. Others, incapacitated from the fever that had swept through the army, while blizzards besieged them and lack of food debilitated them, lay prone by campfires, glancing anxiously around them as their comrades moved into action. The horn blared again, grooms soothing the horses tethered together in a clearing. The animals were part of the plunder they had taken from Inverness, before the castle was razed.

Edward saw Cormac, hastening towards him. His foster-brother's red hair was the only thing of colour about him, his face blanched by the cold. Thomas Randolph was at his side, his pale blue eyes wide with fear.

'They're coming!'

Edward set off through the trees. Gilbert and the others went with him. 'How many?'

'I'd say the scouts were right,' replied Cormac. 'Two thousand.'

Edward cursed. When the Black Comyn had challenged them a week ago he'd had less than half that number. With his cavalry unable to penetrate their position, well defended on a wooded knoll surrounded by boggy fields, the Earl of Buchan's archers had resorted to exchanging volleys with their own bowmen over the course of the Christ Mass. Each side had picked off only a few dozen of their opponents before the Black Comyn retreated from the field, leading his men back to Banff. There had been deep relief among Robert's forces at the enemy's withdrawal, the respite offering them and their king a chance to recover, but while many of the men had since shrugged off the sickness, Robert had only worsened. There were no healing herbs or roots to be found in the frozen wasteland and no amount of prayers had helped him. The mood among the men sank further when the scouts had ridden in two hours ago with word that their enemy was returning in strength.

The commanders came to the edge of the trees, boots splashing through the slush, breath misting the air. A few of the archers that formed a ring around the knoll nodded tautly in greeting. Most kept their eyes on the distance, bows ready in their hands. Edward followed their gazes.

Before him, the mound dipped down into a large, snow-covered plain, spiked with coarse grasses that thrust up from the underlying marsh. The mud was still churned in places where the enemy's cavalry had tilted futilely at their ranks, but in the plummeting temperatures of the last few days it had become crusted with a hard layer of ice. Here and there, the rigid limbs of horses and men stuck up out of the snow. Beyond the plain, about a mile to the north, a large column of men had appeared. At this distance they were just a dark mass against the white, but Edward had seen enough armies to know the scouts' estimates weren't wrong. Above him, the branches of the trees rattled like bones in the wind. It was picking up. The sullen sky augured another fall.

'Mostly infantry,' murmured Malcolm, his eyes narrowing on the approaching force. 'They'll not be so hindered by the marshes. They could break through our lines. Overrun us.'

'We have two score light horses at our disposal,' countered Neil, looking at Edward. 'The ground is frozen. We could charge them.'

Edward nodded slowly. 'We might be able to scatter them, keep them disorganised, before our own foot soldiers attack in strength.'

'I fear you overestimate the valour of our infantry, Sir Edward,' Gilbert cautioned. 'Our men have been without food or shelter for weeks. More importantly, they have been without their king. Just as Robert has weakened so has their courage. You've seen it as well as I have. I believe his absence, more than mere discomfort, is what caused so many of the cowards to slip away these past days.'

Edward looked back through the trees to where the men were gathering, hoisting weapons in frost-bitten fingers, shrugging shields over shoulders slumped with exhaustion. It was still a large force, but not as mighty as the one they had led out from Castle Tioram in the autumn, sickness, injury and, now, desertion stripping their ranks. It had been a source of great frustration for Edward to see how much of their will was bound up in Robert's own — that all their fates should be determined by him alone.

'King Robert is their champion,' finished Gilbert, unknowingly putting voice to Edward's thoughts. 'It was his valour at Loudoun Hill that inspired them – that caused so many of them to flock to his banner. We need him to lead them in the field again. To put fire in their hearts.'

'In that case, Sir Gilbert,' murmured Thomas Randolph, 'we need a miracle.'

Edward looked sharply at his nephew. Then, he was off and moving, hastening back through the trees.

'Edward!' Malcolm called after him.

But Edward didn't turn, sprinting towards the king's tent.

Earl John of Buchan, head of the Black Comyns and former Constable of Scotland, reined in his muscular roan courser and lifted his hand for his men to halt. His knights, dressed in black as he was, spread out around him, all eyes on the knoll that rose from the plain, knotted with trees. The enemy were clearly visible, their tunics bright against the white of the snow.

Comyn fixed on the distant figures hurriedly forming up between the trees at the sight of his army. His dark eyes glittered. Back in Banff, where he'd retreated to gather a force of foot soldiers, he had been tense, worried that in the pause Bruce and his men would move on, only to reappear outside another of his strongholds. But his apprehension had vanished earlier that morning when the scouts who remained in the area reported that not only had Bruce's army been here since the Christ Mass, but that the king himself was rumoured to be deathly ill, incapable even of rising. Several deserters caught slipping from Bruce's encampment confessed to the scouts that the king hadn't been seen in days. Some believed he was already dead. With this news, sweet music to his ears, Comyn had roused his troops, leading them with renewed resolve on the road to Slioch. Bruce's position, which had proven too indomitable for his cavalry, was now a prison in which Comyn would trap him. The scars that webbed the earl's hard face puckered with his smile. How long he had waited for this.

Bruce's ambitious toad of a father and his proud, stubborn grandfather had been thorns in the side of the Comyn family for years, but nothing had prepared the earl for the wounds inflicted by Robert himself: the brutal murder of his kinsman in Dumfries, the attack on his house and abduction of his weak-willed wife by Atholl; the crippling humiliation of Isabel's betrayal in crowning his hated enemy.

Bruce's seizing of the throne had toppled the Comyns from the seat of power they had held for decades. The Black Comyn had thought, after the routing of Bruce's forces at Methven and the ambush in Lorn by John MacDougall of Argyll, that they were finally gaining the upper hand. They'd had Bruce on the run, a wounded animal, beaten and surrounded. No one should have been able to come back from that. But, somehow, the bastard had.

In the autumn, his army swelled from the triumphs at Glen Trool and Loudoun Hill, freed from the threat of English assault by the recent exodus of the new king and his men, Bruce had swept north through the Great Glen like a storm surge, sudden, unexpected – devastating. Inverlochy, the great stronghold of the Red Comyns, had fallen first, assailed from land and water, the galleys of Lachlan MacRuarie and Angus MacDonald attacking from Loch Linnhe. When the castle fell the ships remained, forming a barrier that would prevent any attempt by John MacDougall to come to Buchan's aid. The path clear to the very heartland of the Comyns, Bruce had moved on. Next it was the turn of mighty Castle Urquhart, guardian of Loch Ness. Then Inverness. Then Nairn. The Earl of Ross, one of the Black Comyn's allies and the man responsible for the capture of Bruce's womenfolk, had been so overwhelmed the coward had offered the enemy a truce, before slinking away. This had left Comyn alone, standing between the rebel king and his total domination of the north-east of Scotland. Repelling Bruce's assaults on Elgin and Banff, he had set out to meet him.

Now, here on this plain under this bruised sky, with only an expanse of snow between him and his enemy, Comyn scented victory. Bruce's men, holed up in this frozen wilderness at the mercy of cold and hunger, were losing heart – that much was clear from the desertions. If the man himself could no longer lead them they would surely quail in the face of a determined assault. One push and this could all be over. The time was ripe. England no longer had a formidable king, or one who seemed bent on controlling Scottish affairs. John Balliol remained in exile in France, but if Bruce was crushed there was a chance Balliol could be returned to the throne. Then, the Comyn family would regain their place of power behind it.

The clink of weapons and the crunch of boots in snow filled the air as the infantry fanned out around the company of knights, readying themselves. The horses snorted, their breath pluming before them.

The afternoon sky was darkening. A raw wind flurried the drifts on the plain and snatched at the men's clothes. A few flakes began to fall. The earl rolled his shoulders, stiff under his hauberk and coat-of-plates, as he waited for the last men to move into position. He was now sixty and his muscles were less capable of bearing the weight of his armour, his formidable bulk having softened somewhat these past few years. But, inside, he felt as strong as he had in youth. His desire for vengeance was a potent force, pumping new life through him.

As the infantry formed up, the Black Comyn spurred his courser down their line, his harsh voice echoing across them as he told his men that their enemy lay dying in those trees, his men leaderless, faltering. Now was the time to destroy him and vanquish the rabble that had overrun their towns and plundered their lands. Now was the time to end Bruce, once and for all. Their earl's fierce words ringing in their ears, the men of Buchan set out across the frozen fields, grim of face and confident in step, hammers, maces and spears gripped in their fists. The Black Comyn urged his horse back to his knights, watching as the foot soldiers filled the plain before him, advancing on the wooded knoll. His infantry would breach the enemy's position, scatter Bruce's forces, then he and his sixty cavalry would ride them down.

The snow was falling faster, a storm of swirling white whipped by the wind. Arrows darted from the trees as the first lines of Comyn's soldiers came into range. Men ducked, those with shields raising them to protect themselves. A few screams sounded as barbs punched into flesh, but the mass of infantry moved on, quickening their pace over the ice-crusted marshes.

The cry of an eagle sounded somewhere above. Comyn glanced up, blinking into the blizzard. Just then, a roar resounded across the plain. One of his knights shouted in alarm. The earl looked sharply back as out of the trees came a host of riders. Forty, maybe fifty strong, they charged down from the knoll and on to the plain, heading for his infantry, snow gusting around them. Comyn's eyes widened as he saw, at their head, a yellow banner lifted, the red lion of Scotland rippling across it. Beneath it rode the king, his surcoat – emblazoned with the royal arms – unmistakable.

'Sir!' called one of his knights, his smile gone from his face. 'Is that Bruce? How is it possible? They said he was dying!'

The Black Comyn had no idea. Maybe the bastard had made a

miraculous recovery, or perhaps those deserters had lied to draw him
into a trap. Either way, it did not matter. Robert Bruce was clearly far
from death's door, riding fast and furious towards the faltering foot
soldiers. With him, their surcoats vivid against the snow, rode Gilbert
de la Hay, Malcolm of Lennox, Neil Campbell, Thomas Randolph and
the knights of Carrick and Annandale. Behind the cavalry Bruce's
infantry came pouring, hundreds upon hundreds of them, swarming
on to the plain.

Coming to his senses, the Black Comyn slammed his spurs into the
sides of his horse. The courser took off, thundering into a gallop. He
wrenched his sword from its scabbard as he rode, his men riding with
him. But it was too late. Bruce and his knights had already smashed
through the first lines of infantry.

Men were sent flying. Weapons thrashed and spun. The crack of
iron on steel resounded. Blood arced, black against the snow. With
the king's men cutting a swathe through them and his foot soldiers
coming rushing up behind, Comyn's men began to panic. As some,
caught up in the violence of the king's furious charge, scrambled to
get away from the stamping horses and plunging swords, those behind
started to flee. Now, the Black Comyn and his knights found themselves riding full tilt towards their own ranks. Comyn yelled at the
brigands to turn and fight, but all he saw were faces stretched with
fear and his men scattering before him.

Edward Bruce slid down from his sweat-soaked horse. His legs felt
weak, trembling from the exertion and the shock of the battle, but
inside he was soaring, triumph coursing through him. As he handed
his broadsword to a squire, he realised his gambeson and surcoat were
sodden with blood – none of it his own. Men were crowding around
him, more pushing in through the trees, their voices lifted in elation.
Others had been left on the plain to despatch the dying, overseen by
Gilbert de la Hay and Neil Campbell, but the battle itself was over.
The Black Comyn and his knights had fled the field, leaving hundreds
of foot soldiers to be butchered by Robert's forces.

'My lord.'

Edward turned to see a middle-aged man, gripping a blood-
streaked spear. His face was alight with adoration. He knelt in the
snow, bowing his head.

'My lord, never have I seen such valour in all my life.'

There were many calls of agreement.

'*Long live the king!*'

The lone shout was swiftly taken up by others. Knights, lords, squires and peasants, all began dropping to their knees around Edward. He viewed them through the eye-slits of his great helm, grinning as they cheered him, feeling a heady rush of pride. So distracted by their praise was he that it took him a moment to realise Nes had emerged from the crowd. The knight nodded subtly, tilting his head towards the king's tent. Punching his fist into the air and eliciting another loud cheer from the men, Edward turned and followed Nes through the trees.

Inside the makeshift tent, he saw Robert's head had been propped up on blankets. His eyes were open, focused for the first time in days, although his face was still deathly pale and slick with sweat. Robert's eyes narrowed in confusion at the sight of the man entering the tent, clad in the royal arms.

Now, concealed from the crowds, Edward removed his helm and crouched beside his brother. 'You're awake.'

Robert licked his cracked lips, his eyes lingering on the blood-stained surcoat. 'What happened?'

'I led us to victory. The Black Comyn's army was routed.'

'Comyn? Is he dead?'

'No. But we killed many of his men.'

Robert sank back, his eyes closing. His breathing was shallow. After a moment, he looked back at Edward. 'We cannot stop. We have to finish it.'

Edward nodded, his face uncompromising. 'I will, brother. I will.'

35

Westminster, England, 1308 AD

The council had been in session for two hours and tempers were starting to fray. As one of the pages hovering on the edges of the Painted Chamber came forward with a jug of wine to refill empty goblets, Humphrey de Bohun caught the man's eye and shook his head. With a nod, the page returned to his place, his bright silk tunic making him appear as though he had just stepped out of the gaudy mural on the wall behind him. Humphrey looked back at Aymer de Valence who was still speaking, his voice raised, face flushed. There was no need to add more fuel to this fire.

'This is the third such message we've received in as many weeks.' Aymer stabbed a finger at one of the pieces of parchment furled on the table. There were several of these letters scattered between the silver platters, littered with remnants of food. All bore seals of Scottish magnates – Earl John of Buchan, William of Ross, David of Atholl. 'It is clear our allies in Scotland are becoming increasingly desperate for aid in their struggle against Bruce. He is winning his war, damn it! We must act now, before it is too late. If he defeats his enemies in the north and east there will be nothing standing between him and our garrisons at Aberdeen, Perth, Edinburgh and Stirling. And if he takes those castles, what then?' Aymer looked around the table at Ralph de Monthermer, Robert Clifford and Guy de Beauchamp, the Earl of Warwick. 'He will turn his attention to England. That is what.' His eyes settled meaningfully on Henry Percy.

Percy nodded in support. 'We cannot allow Bruce to consolidate his position any more than he already has. I agree with Sir Aymer. We must strike while he is still vulnerable.'

Both men turned their attention on Piers Gaveston.

The young man, reclining in his high-backed chair at the head of the table, showed little reaction to their stares. His black eyes drifted to one of the platters of meat and cheese in front of him. He drew his knife from its sheath, the mother-of-pearl hilt glimmering in the jewelled light coming through the chamber's stained-glass windows. The dagger was a present from Edward, who had lavished gifts on Piers since his companion's return from exile, the most extravagant and unpopular of which had been the earldom of Cornwall. The ire among some of the older barons, simmering beneath the surface at the young man's rapid promotion, had boiled over last week when Edward, preparing to set sail for France to marry Isabella, had made Piers regent of the realm.

As Piers set the tip of the dagger on the table and began to twist it idly round, Henry Percy glared at him.

Aymer half rose from his chair, planting his palms on the table. 'We have received reports that Welsh and Irish recruits have been joining Bruce's army since the summer. He has been using the Prophecy of Merlin against us, saying that the king's death marks the dawning of a new age, and that the Britons will rise to take back their lands. They are calling him King Arthur for Christ's sake!' He swept a hand towards Guy de Beauchamp, Thomas of Lancaster and the others. 'We are knights of the Round Table. Bruce stole our precious relic and is now twisting our sacred prophecy for his own ends. He must pay for this!'

As Guy and some of the others nodded in agreement, Humphrey recalled, wryly, that Aymer had never been so committed to the beliefs of their brotherhood while the king was alive, focused on fighting the enemy with his sword rather than with prophecy. How strange, he thought, that it was him now sitting here in silence, unmoved by this impassioned speech. Only a year ago he would have been the one making it.

'Will we continue to do nothing while our enemies band together against us?' Aymer demanded. 'While Bruce lays waste to all we have laboured to achieve?'

Piers stabbed his dagger forcefully into a lump of cheese. 'The king was very clear, Sir Aymer. While he is in France I am to prepare the city for his coronation, not start a war.' He sat back with a shake of his head. 'Let the Scots fight among themselves. We will not waste any more of our resources on futile endeavours in the north.'

As Piers plucked the cheese from the tip and chewed it nonchalantly, Thomas, who until now had been sitting in stone-cold silence, slammed his fist on the table, upsetting several goblets and making Henry Percy start. 'How much have you taken from the royal coffers for your new tournament armour?' Thomas pushed the words through his teeth. 'Or that Arabian broodmare you bought at Smithfield? Or your attire for our king's coronation? Decked with a hundred pearls – so my squires tell me!' He stood abruptly, his grey eyes flashing in the prisms of light coming through the windows. 'And you have the gall to speak of wasting resources? You, Gaveston, are the greatest wastrel in our realm!'

For a long moment, Piers stared at Thomas, saying nothing. Silence swelled to engulf the chamber. Tossing the half-eaten wedge of cheese on to the table, the young man rose to meet the earl, his chair screeching on the tiled floor. 'The king was also very clear, Lancaster, about who held the authority in his absence.' Piers's voice was low. 'Be aware that by insulting me, his regent, you are insulting him.'

Humphrey cut in. 'My lords, the hour grows late. I believe we can achieve nothing more today. I suggest we retire.'

After a pause, Piers sheathed his dagger with a stab, his gaze still on Thomas. Turning, he swept out of the chamber, gesturing sharply at those of his followers who had accompanied him to the council.

Humphrey was disappointed to see his nephew, Henry, was one of the young knights who followed the Gascon automatically. As the rest of the council broke up, the barons murmuring among themselves, Humphrey headed out of the hall, seeking fresher air.

The perishing afternoon revived him. The Thames, swollen by January's storms, had broken its banks and the waters were lapping over the wharf, pooling outside Westminster Hall. A group of men worked in a line, hefting sacks of sand off a cart and piling them up along the river's edge. Humphrey watched them, thinking the flood would not be so easily held back.

'Humphrey.'

He turned to see Thomas of Lancaster crossing the damp cobbles towards him, tightening his cloak against the chill.

'We cannot let that arrogant son of a bitch treat us this way,' Thomas spat. 'I swear to God, I'll . . .' He trailed off, his jaw pulsing.

Humphrey gripped Thomas's shoulder, forcing the angry young man to meet his gaze. 'Our king returns in a fortnight. We can discuss plans for Scotland then. In the meantime, let us prepare for the coronation. When that is done there will be fewer things to distract Edward.'

Thomas shook his head, unwilling to be placated. 'I fear my cousin will always be distracted with that degenerate son of a whore filling his ear with poison.'

'It is possible, now both are married, that their wives will help to temper their passions.'

'Wives?' scoffed Thomas. 'My cousin's marriage was arranged by his father purely for political gain – Edward never wanted it for himself. And Piers and Margaret de Clare? The purpose of that wedding was merely to increase the bastard's power at court and put paid to the gossipmongers.' Thomas's tone was grim. 'Make no mistake, Humphrey, these women are no more than silks for our king and his lover to cloak their unholy liaisons in. Their passions must be tempered by other means.'

Pleshey Castle, England, 1308 AD

Thomas's words of warning stayed with Humphrey all through the next day as he travelled to Essex to prepare his household for the king's coronation. By the time he rode in through the gates of Pleshey Castle in the evening gloom, a heavy sense of foreboding had risen to shadow him.

His steward, Ranulf, met him outside the stables as the earl dismounted with his men beneath the motte. The tower on top of the high mound loomed above the buildings of the bailey, its whitewashed walls seeming to glow faintly against the gathering dark.

'Welcome, Sir Humphrey.'

'Good evening, Ranulf. You received my message?'

'Yes, my lord. The arrangements have all been made. Your retainers have been informed of when and where to assemble, and your tailors have almost completed the robes.'

Humphrey nodded tightly. The king had insisted that not only must all of London be decked out in finery, but his vassals, too, should be garbed to suit the occasion of his coronation in cloaks of gold samite.

Humphrey had borne the cost of fitting himself and his knights with new robes, but it was a reluctant hand he had put in his purse to do so. At a time when England was still suffering the aftermath of the long war with Scotland, poverty and disorder rife throughout the realm, it felt like an unnecessary expense.

'Have food brought to my chambers, Ranulf. I'll eat alone tonight.' As Humphrey started towards his lodgings his steward called after him.

'Sir, the lady has been asking when you might return. She has been rather — insistent.'

Humphrey looked back at Ranulf. He paused. 'I'll see her now.'

'My lord, I am sure it can wait until . . .'

But Humphrey was already heading for the guest quarters, a timber-framed building that overlooked the kitchen gardens. Nodding to a maid in the passage, who greeted him courteously, he approached the door at the end. After knocking, he slid back the bolt.

Elizabeth Bruce looked up in surprise as he entered. The queen was sitting reading at a table by the fire, its rosy flush painting her cheeks. The remains of a meal smeared a platter beside her. She looked healthier than she had when he first brought her to his manor last summer. Her face was fuller and the shadows were gone from her eyes.

'Sir Humphrey.'

The brightness of her smile gave him a pang of sorrow. Bess used to greet him with the same look of pleased relief whenever he returned home from a campaign. It was one of the things he had looked forward to, riding back to her. He greeted Elizabeth with a nod, closing the door behind him. 'My lady.'

Elizabeth had put down her book the moment he entered, but as she went to rise, he gestured for her to stay seated. He picked up a stool from beside the canopied bed and set it down in front of her.

'Is there news from Sixhills?' Elizabeth asked, before he had even sat.

'Marjorie is fine,' he assured her. 'And your nephew is doing well.'

Elizabeth smiled again, but sadly now. 'It is a shame Donald cannot meet his half-brother.'

Humphrey frowned, irritated. Elizabeth had asked before if he would petition King Edward to allow young Donald of Mar to live in the nunnery with Christian Bruce and her new child — Christopher

Seton's son. She had also pleaded for him to seek the release of Mary Bruce and Isabel Comyn from their cages. 'Earl Donald will remain in London as the king's ward, my lady,' he said firmly. 'As I have told you.'

She dropped her gaze with a brief nod.

Humphrey kept his eyes on her. After a moment, he laced his gloved fingers on the table and leaned forward. 'Did Robert ever speak to you about his intentions for his kingdom after his coronation?'

Elizabeth looked up, her expression shifting, becoming guarded. 'His intentions?'

'His plans. He knew his place on the throne wouldn't be secure until he overpowered the Scots who opposed him and defeated us.'

'Any plans my husband made ended at Methven Wood. I think you know that.'

'But if they hadn't – if his army hadn't been routed then – what would he have done? Would he have attacked England?'

Elizabeth sat back, brushing her fingers over the cover of the book she had been reading.

'You ask if Robert told me what he intended for the future of his kingdom?' She shook her head. 'He rarely told me what he was planning from one day to the next.'

Humphrey studied her, the hearth fire warm on the back of his neck. Elizabeth didn't meet his stare, but he saw only ghosts of regret in her downcast eyes, no sign of a lie. He thought of his meeting with Robert in the ruins of the chapel and the pact they had made: the safety of his wife and daughter in return for his silence on Edward's sins. But that was as far as their agreement had stretched – no peace between their kingdoms had been agreed.

At the time, Humphrey had discerned Robert's desire to return to his throne, although no sense the man would seek retribution against the English for the executions and incarceration of his family. But, judging by the desperate reports coming from across the border, he was systematically eradicating his enemies in the north. If Robert defeated the Comyns would he then turn his attention south, as Aymer believed he would? Would he follow in the bloody footsteps of William Wallace?

'The maids tell me the whole of London is preparing for King Edward's coronation,' Elizabeth said tentatively into his silence. 'I imagine there is great excitement at court?'

Humphrey didn't answer. His mind clouded with thoughts of the growing dissatisfaction among the barons. Their new king's reign had barely begun and already the court was divided. He flattened his palm on the surface of the table. Things would have to change when Edward returned from France. As earls it was their duty to ensure the safety of the kingdom. If that meant saving the king from himself, so be it. These days, he was not so awed by royal majesty. Edward Longshank's confession had seen to that. And what of Robert, should he turn his eye to England's borders? Humphrey looked at Elizabeth, who was staring at him, her eyes full of question. After a moment, he rose, unsmiling.

Elizabeth's brow furrowed. 'Humphrey?'

Humphrey nodded to the platter. 'I'll have the maids clear that.'

'Humphrey, please. Don't go!'

He paused, his hand on the door. Looking over his shoulder he saw the sadness in Elizabeth's face – the loneliness in her eyes. The chamber might be well-appointed, but it was still a prison. Steeling himself to pity, he headed out, closing the door and snapping the bolt in place. He was done being a pawn in other men's games. Elizabeth was an asset, a bargaining tool – nothing more. He would use her if he had to, for the sake of his kingdom.

Dundarg Castle, Scotland, 1308 AD

The flames surged into the sky, turning night to day. Their radiance was mirrored on the waters below the cliff-top castle. With a roar of timbers a section of the roof collapsed inward, sparks billowing. A cheer rose from the men around the castle's base, some of whom began to move back from the intensity of the heat. Outbuildings and barns, which they had set their torches to, were starting to smoulder, flames sparking to life and chasing one another up trailing thatch and through sheaves of straw.

From the saddle of his horse, Robert watched Dundarg burn, his eyes reflecting the flames. Smoke clouded the air. Its acrid odour had seeped into his clothes and hair after weeks of similar destruction. Sometimes at night – still feverish even though the worst of the sickness that nearly claimed his life had passed – he would wake with a start, the smell of burning thick in his throat. Looking east along the road they had travelled that day, Robert could see an orange pulse of fire from the mill they had put to the torch. All across Buchan and Badenoch, manors and castles, farms and stores had been set ablaze, leaving a landscape littered with charred ruins and blackened expanses of crops, the earth itself scorched of life.

After his army routed the forces of the Black Comyn on the plain at Slioch, Robert had begun a slow, painful recovery. Still weak, he had relied on his brother to take command of the men. Balvenie, one of Comyn's castles, had fallen early in the New Year. Tarradale, on the Black Isle, had followed. Men, quailing in the face of Robert's unstoppable advance, lay down arms and submitted. Others, inspired by his might, pledged their swords and joined his fight. Meanwhile, in the west, Lachlan MacRuarie and Angus MacDonald maintained a strong presence on the waters, hemming in the Lords of Argyll.

As spring thawed the snow on the mountain passes, reports filtered up from the south, where James Stewart and James Douglas had led a force into the Forest, young Douglas intent on regaining his father's lands from the now absent Robert Clifford. Already, their campaign had seen them take back a large swathe of the Border lands. In all these months, the English garrisons holed up in Stirling, Edinburgh, Roxburgh and Perth made no move to aid their Scottish allies. Nor was there any sign that the new King of England would come north to oppose Robert's offensive.

At last, when the snows cleared and flowers were festooning the meadows, Robert met the Black Comyn once again, this time on the road to Inverurie. There, in a fierce and bloody battle, he defeated him. The earl fled the field with his life, but little else. Many of his knights were killed and those who survived escaped south, leaving the earldom wide open, defenceless before Robert's forces.

There were more cheers as another section of Dundarg Castle collapsed and the barns began to blaze. Robert didn't join in. He took no pleasure in this. He'd thought he would have done, but these past months, lying on his litter with endless hours to think, he had come to realise it wasn't vengeance that now spurred him to rain down such destruction, but need. Pure, bitter need.

His grandfather had once warned him that the hatred between their family and the Comyns had the power to rip the kingdom apart. The old lord had been right. Robert hadn't known it at the time, but the dagger he brandished in the church of the Greyfriars had wounded him just as it had John Comyn, that dark deed setting in motion the events that followed, which had seen him stripped of everything. He had lost family and friends, his authority and dignity, and with his excommunication his soul remained at risk of eternal damnation. It had wounded their realm too. These lands were soaked in the blood of too many of Scotland's sons.

'Another one falls!'

At the harsh call, Robert saw Edward riding up the slope towards him. Others followed, rejoining the king and the rest of the army, voices lifting above the roar of the flames.

'Anything of value?' Robert asked, as his brother pulled his horse to a halt.

'The place was bare. They must have known we were coming.' Edward tossed the wine skin he was holding to Neil Campbell, who caught it deftly. 'I doubt we'll find much plunder anywhere now. Comyn is long gone, as are his people. It is time we moved on, brother. There are other targets to strike at.'

Robert knew Edward meant John MacDougall and Dungal MacDouall, the latter still at large after the skirmish at Glen Trool. His brother had become increasingly impatient to hunt down the man responsible for the capture of Thomas and Alexander, and the beheading of their foster-father. Cormac had strongly supported him in this. But Robert wanted to finish what he had started here. He never wanted to have to do this again.

'I'll move on when I'm done.'

Edward met his stare, his eyes narrowing. 'This war isn't over, brother,' he murmured. 'Not by a long way.'

'I am well aware of that.'

Drawing on the reins of the palfrey, taken from Balvenie's stables, Robert rode from the burning castle, followed by his men. As he went, he felt his brother's gaze on his back.

36

Cheapside, England, 1308 AD

It was the thud of drums that roused him from his delirium. Alexander Seton stirred to life, groggy and confused, his ale-addled dreams slow to fade as the world around him came into focus. The stink was the first thing to hit him – rancid vegetables and putrefied meat, night soil, sour vomit and dog faeces. He struggled to sit, swallowing back a fierce urge to retch. His movement startled several rats that had been burrowing in a refuse pile next to him, sending them scuttling behind a row of barrels stacked up outside a battered wooden door. Staring at the door, Alexander had a vague memory of being shoved out of it at some point during the night. Touching his jaw through the worn fingers of his gloves, it felt tender, bruised. There had been another fight.

His hand went quickly to his purse, tied to his belt beside his dirk. He let out a slow breath, feeling the weight of the coins inside, won in a cockfight yesterday. Whomever he'd fought with in the inn it had not been for money. Sitting upright, he pushed his hair out of his face and leaned against the damp stone wall, his breath fogging the air. His filthy cloak, trimmed with fur, and the faint warmth from the decomposing midden heap had saved him from freezing to death, but now he was awake the February chill was seeping into his skin. Far above him between the buildings, the upper storeys of which pressed in close on one another, was a slit of pristine blue sky. It seemed a long way away. The drumming was louder now, vying with the hollow clop of hooves on wet cobbles.

His head throbbing, Alexander stumbled down the alley, using the wall for purchase, his feet slipping in icy patches of slime. As he neared the mouth, he had to shield his eyes from the glare. Beyond the dim passage, Cheapside lay in full morning sun. Light gleamed in puddles on the wide street, flashed in the leaded windows of stores and glinted in the glass and silverware of the traders, who had set up their stalls outside. Gold flags had been strung in criss-crossing lines between the buildings, fluttering in the brisk air.

The decorations had been put up all over London for the coronation of the king, who had returned from France five days ago, making a procession through the city with his French bride. Alexander, caught unexpectedly in the press of crowds, had been forced to wait and watch while Edward and his retinue passed. It had been a grand display, the king surrounded by knights in brocaded mantles, wearing helms orna-mented with sprays of peacock feathers, or elaborate crests of wings and horns. The bridles of their horses had been strung with so many bells that the jingle could be heard even over the cheers of the crowd, all eager to catch a glimpse of their new queen, riding behind the king, accompanied by a host of dignitaries and ladies-in-waiting. Alexander hadn't waited to see her, but at a gap in the mob had slipped away down a side street. He had drunk himself into a daze that day, unable to get the images out of his mind, his bitterness curdling in him.

Below the flags adorning Cheapside's thoroughfare, men and women thronged the street, inspecting the stalls and bartering with traders. Some had congregated outside an inn, drinking from tankards and tucking into hot pies. Alexander's stomach, empty and bloated from last night's ale, ached at the sight. As the clamour of drums and hooves drew closer, people began to move out of the way. Following their gaze, Alexander saw a company riding down the street.

There were a dozen men on horseback, with four drummers on foot leading them. The riders wore cloaks of gold samite over their surcoats. Spurs and pommels of swords winked in the sunlight. A gaggle of children ran alongside. As Alexander watched, one of the men at the front reached into a purse and brought out a fistful of coins, which he scattered before the children, grinning as they shrieked and dived for them. Alexander's eyes remained fixed on the device on the knight's surcoat, revealed by the sweep of his arm. The blue silk was slashed with a white band, between which were six gold lions. Alexander's gaze darted across the others. There he was, riding in the midst of his men – Humphrey de Bohun.

At the sight of the man who had lied to him about Christopher's execution and who revealed his treachery to Robert, Alexander felt bile rise sour in his throat. He staggered back into the alley before Humphrey caught sight of him. Leaning against the damp stone wall, he closed his eyes as the company clattered past. In the inns, gambling dens and whorehouses of London, mixing with the drunk, the desperate and the anonymous, he could forget who he was, but these parades of nobility just served to remind him of where he had come from and how much he had lost in the fall.

After Neil Campbell escorted him to the border, Alexander had made his way to London, aiming to get as far away from Scotland as possible. But his ghosts had followed him here and he had come to realise the prison a man could make in his own mind was far worse than any dungeon. The hatred and anger of the early days was gone. All that was left was grief. In Scotland, living hand to mouth, an outlaw under Robert's command, he had thought himself stripped of everything.

He hadn't known that there would be so much more to lose.

Westminster Abbey, England, 1308 AD

The feast of St Matthias the Apostle dawned overcast and stormy. The crowds all along the route of the expected procession clasped cloaks tighter at their breasts and held on to their caps as the wind buffeted them. Odours of mud and sewage from the marshes that surrounded the Island of Thorney were strong on the air and the wheel of the nearby watermill clattered loudly in the fast flow of the Tyburn. It was soon drowned by the cheers that rose from outside the buildings of Westminster Palace.

People further down the route pressed in at the sound, leaning on one another's shoulders and hoisting children up to catch a glimpse of their king and queen. Royal soldiers hastened down their lines, pushing them back from the edges of the carpet that stretched from the palace halls to the soaring white edifice of Westminster Abbey. The host of clergy were the first to come into view, singing a solemn hymn. They were dressed in sumptuous ceremonial robes, the bishops bearing gold crosiers. The acolytes who followed swung censers that wafted clouds of frankincense over the onlookers. At the sight of Edward, walking in their wake, the crowds surged in.

At over six foot, the twenty-four-year-old king towered above most men in the crowd, his head erect as he trod the line of the carpet, which served to protect his feet, bare save for his black hose. In some places the carpet was soggy, having soaked up the water from the recent floods, in others his feet crunched over the heads of dried flowers, thrown before him by women and children. Edward's blond hair was blown wild by the wind, which snatched at the thin green robes clinging to his muscular frame. Following the king were the barons of the realm, clad in cloaks of shimmering samite and bearing the regalia.

First was Humphrey de Bohun, holding the royal sceptre surmounted by its jewelled cross. After him came the earls of Warwick and Lincoln, carrying two of the three ceremonial swords. The third, broken-bladed Curtana, the Sword of Mercy, was borne by Thomas of Lancaster. The king's cousin was tight-lipped, unsmiling. The earls of Arundel and Oxford followed, helping to carry a wooden board, on which were displayed the king's new robes, shoes and spurs. The men were forced to place their hands on the garments to stop them flying off in the gusts.

The last and most honoured position in the stately train was taken by Piers Gaveston, the newly made Earl of Cornwall. The Gascon strode in the wake of the other magnates, resplendent in a velvet doublet of imperial purple, festooned with pearls, the milky beads like a hundred gleaming eyes. He appeared the very picture of nobility; his black hair sleek with perfumed oil, his face handsome, his smile arrogant. In his hands he held the crown, the myriad gems flashing in the stormy light.

Behind, struggling through the spectators, came a host of dignitaries from France and England, the mayor of London and hundreds of courtiers. As they shuffled in through the abbey's arched doors, the crowds crushed in behind them, tracking mud across the tiled floor and elbowing one another to reach the best spot from which to watch the king's coronation. A scuffle broke out, royal soldiers fighting their way through to suppress it. More people were still pouring in as Edward reached the high altar.

There, the Bishop of Winchester, officiating on behalf of the bedridden Archbishop of Canterbury, performed the unction with holy oil and the consecration. After Edward took the oath of kingship the earls of England came forward, one by one, to dress him in his ceremonial garments. Aymer de Valence helped him put on one of his boots, after which Piers ornamented it with a golden spur. Once the scarlet mantle, trimmed with feather-soft ermine, had been placed around his shoulders, Edward was led to his throne.

The coronation chair, created by his father, was waiting for him, raised on a dais in front of the choir. The throne, painted in gilt with an image of a seated king surrounded by birds and flowers, contained in its base the Stone of Destiny, taken from Scone Abbey after the first invasion of Scotland. As the crown was placed upon Edward's head, Piers watched, a smile playing at the corners of his mouth. Oaths of fealty and acts of homage were then performed by the barons, before the queen was escorted in.

More brawls broke out in the nave, rough shouts punctuating the sweet rising voices of the choir that accompanied the twelve-year-old Isabella, daughter of the King of France. All eyes upon her, she lowered her gaze as she was guided to the altar, the long train of her red velvet gown sweeping the pavement of precious stones that lined the abbey floor. After her consecration she was led, her cheeks still glistening with tracks of holy oil, up to the dais, where she was seated beside the king on a small cushioned throne.

The barons led the cheers that reverberated through the abbey. The wave of sound drowned out the din of a wall collapsing in the older section of the abbey. Rubble cascaded in a shuddering rush on top of the heaving crowd. The first the king and queen knew of the disaster were the screams and the clouds of dust that billowed up into the nave. Edward half rose from his throne and Isabella pressed her hand to her mouth, before the Bishop of Winchester ushered them down from the dais and led them quickly out of a side door. The royal couple were followed by a stream of nobles, all hastening to the palace for the feast, leaving the soldiers and clergy to deal with the chaos.

Westminster Hall, England, 1308 AD

King Edward nursed his wine, watching in silence as his subjects celebrated the occasion of his crowning. Never before had he seen Westminster Hall so crowded. The vast chamber, two hundred and forty feet long, was lined with trestles that stretched in long rows from the raised platform that held his table. Dignitaries were stuffed into the benches, the silk and taffeta gowns of ladies crushed against the fur-trimmed mantles of lords. In spite of the grand congregation, here in honour of him, Edward felt utterly alone. Things had not gone well since his return from France and the tragedy in the abbey earlier that afternoon, in which one man had died, was a terrible omen for the start of his reign. How he longed for this day of disasters to be over. But it seemed God wanted to toy with him a little more yet.

A dozen arched windows on either side of the hall let in some light, but the day was drawing to a close and most of the illumination now came from scores of candles on the trestles. Most had melted to stubs, covering the linen cloths with pools of wax. Silver platters stood empty all along the tables, spoons resting on polished surfaces. Edward saw people craning their heads towards the servers and carvers who waited by the hall's doors. Others followed the flustered steward with their eyes as he hastened between the tables, checking the basins were being refilled with wine, which the pages had been ladling into goblets all afternoon in the absence of any food.

Varlets were traversing the hall with the animals from the Tower's royal menagerie that had welcomed people to the feast, in an effort to amuse the gathering. But the small black bear, being led around on chains, had snarled at a French countess, frightening her from the chamber, and the gyrfalcons had peppered several people's cloaks with droppings. The entertainment was rapidly growing stale and the flood of wine on empty stomachs was fraying tempers already worn thin. Many of the barons were livid that Piers had been chosen to bear the crown during the procession – an honour reserved for the highest noble in the realm – and Edward knew this fiasco with the food was just giving his men more reason to complain and the courtiers more chance to gossip. He could see them now, glancing up at his table, shaking heads, talking behind their hands.

Snapping his fingers at one of his pages, he ordered the man to the high gallery at the other end of the hall, where the minstrels were playing. After a moment, the music shifted in tempo, the pulse of drums inciting some of the younger men to get up and dance, taking the hands of the daughters of earls. Many of these knights, among them Henry de Bohun and Gilbert de Clare, the Earl of Gloucester, whom Edward had dubbed that morning, wore masks fashioned in the likeness of stags, boars and wolves. Older ladies and lords turned in their seats to watch as the young dancers threaded between one another.

Over the music, Edward heard a voice to his left. Glancing round, he saw Charles de Valois, one of Isabella's uncles, leaning closer to address him.

'I said I hear, my lord, that your men are concerned about the recent campaign of Robert Bruce in Scotland. Apparently, the territory captured by your father is all but lost?'

Edward felt himself pricked by the barb. He saw other dignitaries along the table staring at him. Among them were Isabella and his stepmother, Marguerite, the aunt of his new bride. Also there was Louis d'Evreux, another of the queen's uncles who had accompanied her from France. Edward smiled coolly at Charles. 'I can assure you, I am very much in command of my lands. Edinburgh, Perth, Stirling – and many other castles are under my control. Bruce may have had some minor successes against his countrymen in the far north of the region, but he will not find my garrisons so conquerable.'

Charles de Valois arched an eyebrow in response, but said nothing. Neither did Louis d'Evreux, who continued to study Edward coldly. Both men had been hostile towards him since they discovered he had sent all the wedding gifts, some of which had been from King Philippe himself, to Piers.

Just before the wedding, Edward had spent the Christ Mass with his lover. One night lying naked together by the fire, Margaret de Clare – Edward's niece and now Piers's wife – asleep in the next room, Piers had become inconsolable at the prospect of the marriage. His voice rising dangerously, referring to Isabella as *that French bitch*, he swore he would not be able to live if he lost Edward to the daughter of King Philippe, the man who had driven him and his father out of Gascony. Edward promised he would not, but to prove it had sent him those gifts. The act had been a reckless one, he had been aware of that at the time, but he needed Piers to know that though his bride might have his hand, she would never have his heart.

Edward looked at her now, sitting beside him. Isabella had changed from her coronation robes into a gown of green satin, the tight bodice of which pressed flat her barely budding breasts. A crown was perched on her head, her long, flaxen hair piled up around it with emerald-tipped pins. Isabella had a soft face, with full pink cheeks and a rosebud mouth. He had heard many people comment on her beauty, but he could not see it.

Although they had been married more than a month, they hadn't yet consummated their union. Edward knew her ladies-in-waiting and his squires had prepared, with much giggling and secrecy, the bed in the Painted Chamber, expecting this night would see the marriage blessed. In truth, the nervous girl beside him repulsed him. He knew what he must do to her – had done it when he was younger to the sister of one of his friends – but the thought made him feel sick to his stomach. Isabella would bring him and his kingdom benefits, both financial and political, and one day she would bear him the heirs he needed. But all she would ever be was a vessel, an egg.

His gaze moved to his love, seated along from him, a wolf mask perched on top of his head. Piers was seated beside his wife, but was turned away from her, watching the young men dance below, his fingers caressing the stem of his goblet. His face was cast in candle-light, his coal-black eyes gleaming. He had changed from his corona-tion outfit and now wore a green silk mantle, emblazoned with the six golden eagles of his coat of arms. Edward tried to catch his eye, but Piers was lost in thought. Instead, the king caught the intent gaze of Humphrey de Bohun, seated at the head of one of the trestles. The earl rose as if to come over, but just then the ring of trumpets announced the long-awaited feast, forcing him back down. Edward felt relieved – Humphrey had been keen to talk to him since he had arrived, no doubt about the damn Scots.

The pages entered to rowdy applause, ducking between the danc-ers to set down platters of venison scattered with wrinkled plums and boar surrounded by cinnamon-dusted apples. There was whale meat and roasted geese, pickled salmon, custards flavoured with spices and gingerbread.

After the young knights and ladies sat back down and the Bishop of London had said grace, Edward was the first to be served. As he put the venison in his mouth, he realised the meat was cold and greasy, sitting too long in its own fat. He swallowed with difficulty, but at his smile and nod, the nobles at once dug in heartily. Edward pushed his plate away. He could lose his temper at yet another debacle, but the man responsible for the celebrations was Piers – and he was the only one in this sorry gathering that he wanted to be with right now.

While everyone's attention was on the food, Edward rose, his white mantle, strung with emeralds, falling heavily around him. A few people got to their feet, but he waved them back down. His hand briefly brushing Piers's shoulder, he headed from the dais and out through a side door. Ignoring a man in a boar's mask, who had pressed a maid up against the passage wall and had a hand inside her gown, Edward hastened through the shadowy maze of corridors.

Inside the Painted Chamber, the warm light from the braziers glowed in the gold of the murals. Beneath a scene of Chastity conquering Lust, a firm hand pressing down the leering Vice, Edward halted, staring at the canopied bed. It had been decorated with scores of ribbons and bells, green leaves and fragrant herbs strewn across the covers – emblems of fertility. His hands clenched at his sides. He wanted to tear down the foolish garlands – burn them in the braziers' coals. Hearing a rap on the door, he turned.

Piers entered, his face hidden by the wolf mask. 'My lord king.'

Edward crossed the chamber in a few strides. After pushing the door shut, sliding the bolt in place, he shoved Piers against the wood, pulling up the mask so he could get at his mouth. He kissed the man hard. Piers drew back after a moment, his lips wet, surprise in his eyes at Edward's ardour. Then, he smiled.

They fell together on to the bed, the bells jingling madly, ribbons swirling down around them as they rolled across the covers. Edward wrenched off Piers's silk surcoat. Opening the man's shirt, he paused, devouring the sight: an expanse of muscle and smooth skin he had mapped so well with hands and tongue. This was what he wanted – this man he had loved since he had known how – not some pale, plump girl-child, who, like the war in Scotland, was just another product of his father's ambition. He leaned forward to kiss Piers's neck.

There was a knock on the door.

'Ignore it,' murmured Piers, reaching up to grasp his shoulders.

The knock came again, more insistent. Edward cursed. Jumping up, he drew one of the curtains around the bed, concealing Piers, then strode to the door. Pushing his hands through his hair, he opened it.

Humphrey was outside. The earl frowned on seeing him. 'My lord? Is everything all right? You left the feast.'

'I was feeling unwell,' Edward responded curtly.

'Do you need your physician?'

'No. Just a moment to rest. Alone.'

Humphrey's eyes flicked into the chamber.

Edward wondered if he had seen Piers leave. He moved to block Humphrey's view of the bed. 'I will return shortly.'

Humphrey put a hand out to the stop the door closing. 'My lord, I realise you have had much on your mind with the coronation, but we need to discuss the matter of Scotland as soon as possible. We need to make preparations – strengthen our garrisons in case Bruce attacks.'

'He doesn't have the strength to mount an assault on our castles.'

'Not yet perhaps, but soon he may have.' Humphrey's brow furrowed further. 'My lord, are you not concerned that you could lose lands your father fought so hard to win for you – lands on which so much silver and blood has already been sacrificed?'

Edward bristled at the comment, having just heard something similar from Charles de Valois. 'My father's obsession left England in a state of suffering, Humphrey. For now, the Scots pose no danger to us. Bruce is clearly intent on dealing with enemies among his own people. I will ensure that continues by negotiating a truce with him. When I am ready I will tackle him, but not until England is healed.'

'A truce?'

'Yes. I intend to send one of the prisoners with the offer, as soon as the celebrations are done.'

'Which prisoner, my lord?'

But Edward was already closing the door.

Portchester Castle, England, 1308 AD

'On your feet.'

William Lamberton, Bishop of St Andrews, stared up at the two guards who had entered. He shielded his eyes from the flame in the lantern held aloft by one of them. The chains around his wrists rattled. 'What do you want with me?' His voice, which had once boomed sermons around churches, had become a dry whisper after almost two years in this dank darkness.

'The king has a mission for you,' said the guard. 'Now, get up.'

Lamberton rose with difficulty. The irons that bound him to the wall of his cell allowed him some room to move, but not much. His muscles had grown weak from lack of use. He watched, his heart quickening, as the guard stooped to unlock his manacles.

As they led him, on trembling legs, down a foul-smelling passage, Lamberton glimpsed a figure, hunched in the shadows of a cell some distance from his. He knew who it was, even before the light from the lantern bled through the bars into the cell, briefly illuminating his old friend and mentor, the Bishop of Glasgow.

Robert Wishart's tonsure had grown out and his hair sprouted wild from his crown. His jaw was covered with a patchy beard and his skin was as wrinkled and yellow as old parchment. His eyes were open, staring in Lamberton's direction, but his once blue pupils were filmed with cataracts. The old man had gone blind during his incarceration.

'Brother!'

Wishart let out a surprised croak at Lamberton's call. 'William? Is that you?'

'It is me, old friend.'

'Come on,' the guard said roughly.

Lamberton twisted his head towards Wishart's cell as they marched him down the passage. 'Keep faith, brother!'

37

The Pass of Brander, Scotland, 1308 AD

The boulder smashed into the side of the mountain, pulverising the bedrock in a cloud of dust. The men, riding fast and furious along the narrow ridge below, lifted their shields as loose rock and earth cascaded down on them. A large chunk of stone struck Robert's shield, the impact knocking him off balance. As his boot slipped through his stirrup, he fell heavily against the pommel of his saddle, losing his grip on the shield, which tumbled away down the mountainside. His horse lurched, pitching him half from the seat, until he was hanging precariously out over the pass, his grip on the reins the only thing that saved him from plunging into the dark green waters of Loch Awe below.

'*My lord!*'

Robert barely heard the shout over the wind screaming through the visor of his helm. As he struggled to right himself, his horse galloping dangerously close to the edge, his mind flashed with a vision of King Alexander falling from the cliffs at Kinghorn. Then, someone rode up swiftly alongside him. He caught a glimpse of red hair as the rider bent forward, hand outstretched. With a lunge, Cormac caught hold of the bridle. Teeth clenched with the effort, he pulled the horse back on track, enabling Robert to haul himself upright and find his footing on the stirrup. The pass tapered ahead, curving out around an outcrop of rock. Cormac fell back, allowing the king to ride on.

Robert's heart thrummed in his chest as he manoeuvred the agitated horse around the tight turn, stones skittering out from under its hooves. The palfrey, seized from the Black Comyn's stables, was used to the rolling, fertile plains of Buchan, not this land of craggy peaks and thundering winds, where the heads of the mountains were cloaked in cloud and lochs were vast mirrors of ever changing sky. Sweat poured down his face stinging his eyes, the slit of world before him little more than a blur of motion and colour.

Another stone sailed up from one of the galleys, this time striking the ridge some feet below the pass. The crash of it echoed around the hillside. There were three ships on the water, where the expanse of Loch Awe narrowed to become a river flanked on one side by towering black cliffs and on the other by the hulking mass of Ben Cruachan, around the lower slopes of which the Pass of Brander wound. Each galley was mounted with a siege engine. Robert, risking a glance over the edge, caught sight of men rolling more stones across the decks. As the arms of the mangonels sprang up another two missiles were hurled towards the pass. They struck in rapid succession, but only succeeded in showering the riders with scree. This time, however, after the stones had bounced away down the hillside, the rumbling continued, growing louder.

For a moment, Robert thought it was an echo, but looking up he saw the cause. Three huge boulders were crashing down from the heights of Ben Cruachan, heading straight for the ridge. With a jolt of shock, he realised the enemy was going to try to do to him what he had done to the English at Glen Trool. Roaring a warning, his shout ringing around his helm, Robert wrenched his horse to a halt, forcing those behind to pull their own steeds up short. Many of his men had seen the danger and were stopping, faces tilted up the mountain, trying to determine the boulders' trajectory. A few rode on, oblivious.

Robert watched, helpless, as the rocks struck the pass, sweeping six men – Lennox's by their colours – out into the air. They screamed as they fell, their horses twisting and thrashing, to plunge into the dark loch. Robert's jaw clenched as he heard the faint cheers from the decks of the galleys – another victory for John MacDougall. The Lord of Argyll, he knew, was on one of those ships. MacDougall had been waiting for him to attempt the pass, the route to his chief seat and the very heart of his lordship. Knowing Robert aimed at Dunstaffnage Castle, he had set his trap here, hoping to prevent him from reaching it.

In the wake of the boulders, men appeared on the slopes above.

Many were barelegged, clad in the short woollen tunics favoured by Highlanders. One, a giant even at this distance, leapt on to an outcrop of rock and lifted his axe to the sky. His savage cry was taken up by others, who began to charge down the steep hillside. There were hundreds of them.

'Where the hell is Douglas?'

Robert recognised the voice behind him as Gilbert de la Hay's. He reached for his sword. Dear God, these men were going to force them off the mountain. There were too many. They would be over-run. More stones were flying up from the galleys, smashing into the ridge. One struck a knight from Carrick, killing him instantly. Another caved in the head of a horse. Mounts were panicking, rear-ing up.

All at once, the sky behind the incoming Argyllsmen darkened, fill-ing with arrows. Robert's eyes followed the feathered barbs as they arced upwards, before stabbing down at the running men. Many struck – punching into spines, necks and buttocks. Men fell in mid-stride, some flying head over heels down the slope, cracking skulls on rocks, breaking bones. The giant on the outcrop arched suddenly, dropping his axe as he tumbled into space. The huge man hit the pass just in front of Robert, his neck snapping.

After the storm of arrows came men, their own battle cries rever-berating. Inside his helm, Robert grinned in triumphant relief as James Douglas swept down on the Argyllsmen from the high slopes of Ben Cruachan, leading a host of men from his uncle's lordships. Turning in his saddle, Robert yelled an instruction at Nes, a few riders behind. The knight grabbed the hunting horn that hung from his baldric. Setting it to his lips, he blew three fast notes. Those further down the pass, hearing the signal, spurred their horses on.

John MacDougall's galleys let fly a desperate barrage of stones, but now the king's men were out of range and the cumbersome ships couldn't match the speed of the horses. The ridge descended, drop-ping close to the water as the river cut a course down to Loch Etive and, finally, the sea. In the far distance, a bridge appeared, spanning the rushing water. A few miles beyond lay the object of their race through the mountains – Dunstaffnage Castle.

Dunstaffnage Castle, Argyll, 1308 AD

Robert stood in the castle grounds, close to the chapel and its grave-yard. The evening light burnished the towers and turned the windows of the many outbuildings to molten gold. Lavender and rosemary perfumed the air, coming from the kitchen gardens. Birds chattered in the treetops on the edge of the promontory, beyond which the mouth of Loch Etive opened into the Firth of Lorn. In the distance, across the water, the sun was starting to set behind the mountains of Mull. It was a tranquil scene, very much at odds with the one just hours before, when Dunstaffnage had fallen to his company.

MacDougall's scouts, seeing Robert's men coming along the pass, had tried to burn the bridge in a desperate attempt to prevent them reaching the castle, but Robert's forces, led by Edward Bruce and Neil Campbell, had swept across, scattering the smouldering piles of logs and straw, riding down the fleeing men. Most of MacDougall's force had been with their lord on the loch or above the pass, leaving only a small garrison to defend the castle, which capitulated after a relentless two-day assault.

Lines of men, women and children were being led out through the gatehouse, across the drawbridge. Robert's soldiers escorted them, hauling anything of value to a pile of plunder in front of the chapel, where others sorted sacks of grain and barrels of meat from silver-ware and chests of money. Among them was James Douglas, who had joined them after leading the successful attack on the slopes of Ben Cruachan.

Douglas was quickly making a name for himself, having recently won back his father's lands in a daring assault on his castle, held by men in the pay of Robert Clifford. Thomas Randolph was with him, helping to separate the garrison, who were to be taken prisoner, from the women, children and servants. The two young men had become friends in recent months and Robert was pleased to see the influence James had over his nephew. Gone was the sullen youth who had fought for the English against him. Thomas was fast becoming a valuable member of his company.

Movement on the battlements caught his eye. Looking up, Robert saw the Argyll standard being pulled down. The black galley of the MacDougall arms folded in on itself as it was dragged from its pole. He felt grim satisfaction at the sight. Not only was MacDougall one of the greatest obstacles to his reign, but the ambush in the wilds of Lorn had caused the splitting of his company, which had led, ultimately, to the loss of his family. At long last, justice was served.

'Please! No!'

At the cry, Robert saw an adolescent girl trying to break from the crowd. She was reaching towards a young man being corralled into a group with the rest of the garrison, but was prevented from going any further by one of Angus MacDonald's men, who had hold of her arm.

The girl's face was taut with anguish. 'Let me stay with him – I beg you! He is my husband!'

The desperation in her voice was hard to hear. As Robert watched the soldier got tired of trying to pull her back and cuffed her across the face, sending her reeling. Her husband shouted in rage. Robert crossed quickly to the Islesman, who had raised his hand again, threatening to strike the girl as she cowered on the ground.

'Get up, bitch!' growled the soldier.

Robert grabbed the man's hand, twisting it until he cried out and buckled to his knees.

The soldier's face changed from anger to shock as he saw who had hold of him. 'My lord! I . . .' He trailed off in bewilderment, looking from Robert to the girl, who had scrabbled back and was staring wide-eyed at the king.

'Do that again and I'll see you hang. Do you understand me?'

The crowd had fallen into a hush, those directing the prisoners stopping what they were doing to watch. Many of the men looked surprised.

'I said, do you understand me?'

'Yes, my lord king,' murmured the Islesman, flame-faced.

The girl shrank back as Robert came towards her, but when he held out his hand to help her up she took it, glancing nervously at her husband, watching in stunned silence. Her cheek was red where she had been struck.

'Your husband will not be harmed in my custody,' Robert assured her. 'You have my word. When John MacDougall surrenders to me his men will be allowed to go free.'

Tears welled in her eyes. She bowed her head. 'Thank you, my lord.'

Robert addressed the rest of his troops. 'These men and women are sons and daughters of Scotland. They are under my protection. All of them.' His eyes raked them until he was satisfied to see many nodding in agreement.

Turning away, Robert caught the gaze of his brother. Edward was frowning in question, but Robert carried on past him, heading to inspect the pile of plunder. Things between him and his brother had been strained, ever since his sickness in winter had seen Edward take command of the army.

When Robert had returned to health, Edward seemed reluctant to relinquish that control – questioning his decisions, arguing against his strategies. Eventually, after the razing of Buchan, Robert had given his brother a mission of his own, in the hope this would temper his growing insubordination. While he marched on Aberdeen, intending to seize the port from the garrison left by Aymer de Valence, Edward was sent into Galloway to deal with the remainder of the Disinherited. He had returned a fortnight ago to join the attack on Argyll. Despite his failure to capture Dungal MacDouall, missing since Glen Trool, Edward had been victorious, bloodying the soil of Galloway with the slaughter of hundreds. The tales of his brutality had left a sour taste in Robert's mouth. The harrying of Buchan had been necessary, as was the campaign here in Argyll, but while his brother seemed to revel in the death and destruction, he himself had found he could take no pleasure in it.

The passing of King Edward, a year ago, had begun a change in Robert. For so long his war had been against the man; all his hatred, fear and rage directed at the ruthless king, who had taken so much from him. He had thought that to fight him he would have to become him, but now Edward was gone and the landscape of this conflict had changed, Robert realised he did not want to be the same. He knew all too well what it was to lose those he loved and had no desire to see that pain in others. The bitterness of this civil war in contrast to the devotion he had found among his followers had shown him that he didn't want to be a tyrant, who ruled with an iron fist. He didn't want to build his throne on the skulls of his enemies. He wanted his people to kneel before him of their own free will, out of honour and respect.

Robert turned at the sound of approaching hooves to see Neil Campbell riding into the castle grounds at the head of a company. He had sent the knight to track down and capture John MacDougall and his old and ailing father, thought to have been on the galley with his son. Neil had been only too keen, eager to hunt down the men responsible for the death of his father and his exile from his lands. Now, seeing a number of Campbell's men returning with prisoners on their mounts, hands tied to the pommels, Robert's anticipation rose.

Neil pulled his sweating horse to a halt and swung down from the saddle to greet the king. 'My lord.'

'MacDougall?' asked Robert, glancing past him to the crowd of horsemen.

'No, my lord,' answered Neil, pulling off his helm. 'He and his father fled to their castle on Loch Awe. I've left men on the banks to keep watch, but we're going to need ships to reach them.'

Robert was disappointed, but the news wasn't hopeless. Angus MacDonald's galleys had been following their progress down the coast and the lord was due to join them here any day now. They could use his ships to sail up from Loch Etive.

'We did find a few men hiding in the hills,' Neil went on.

'We'll hold them with the garrison, until the lords of Argyll have surrendered.' As Robert gestured for his soldiers to come and take the prisoners, Neil spoke up quickly.

'My lord, there is one who will be of great interest to you.' The knight called to two of his men, who came forward, marching someone between them.

Robert stopped dead at the sight of the prisoner. His cheeks were hollow from lack of food and his jaw was covered with a beard, but he was nonetheless immediately recognisable. It was Dungal MacDouall, former captain of the army of Galloway, leader of the Disinherited – the man responsible for the beheading of his foster-father and the capture of Thomas and Alexander. MacDouall's clothes were torn, the white lion of Galloway lost under layers of dirt. The scarred bulb of his wrist stuck out from under his gambeson, the hand taken by Robert in the chaos of that burning village five years ago. He met Robert's gaze, his eyes glacial, frozen with hatred.

Edward Bruce had seen him too. He pushed through the throng, his face filling with triumph at the sight of the hated enemy, who had evaded him in Galloway. Cormac appeared on the edge of the crowd, his axe in his fist. The Irishman stood motionless for a moment, staring at MacDouall. Then, he rushed at him with a strangled yell. Robert shouted at James Douglas, who lunged and grabbed hold of him. With Thomas Randolph's help he just managed to restrain the roaring Irishman.

Robert went to his struggling foster-brother. 'Enough!' He planted a hand on Cormac's heaving chest. 'I'll not give the devil another body. Not today. I have given him an army already.'

'I watched that bastard kill my father!'

'And he delivered my brothers to the gallows,' said Robert, not taking his eyes off Cormac's. 'But I killed John Comyn, his master, and my father killed his. So tell me, where does it end?'

Cormac let out a hoarse cry, but with the sound the fight seemed to go out of him. He slumped, his axe falling from his fingers. James and Thomas kept hold of his arms.

'We have won, Cormac,' murmured Robert. 'Now, the killing has to stop. Our kingdom must heal, or we'll be left with nothing. MacDouall will be tried for his crimes. You have my word. But justice will be served in my court. Not here.'

There were scattered shouts of alarm. Robert caught a rush of motion, but by the time he turned, Edward had launched himself at MacDouall. Robert roared at his brother, but it was too late. Edward took the captain's head with two brutal strokes of his broadsword.

38

St Andrews Cathedral, Scotland, 1309 AD

In mid-March, when spring lambs were growing bolder in the meadows and the snows were receding up the slopes of the mountains, leaving a land fresh and green in their wake, Robert held his first parliament.

The magnates and clergy of Scotland gathered in the chapter house of St Andrew's Cathedral, filling the hall in front of the dais, upon which their king was raised on a throne. Behind him, strung from wall to wall, was the royal banner of Scotland, the red lion rampant on gold. The banner, hidden by Bishop Wishart before his capture, had been brought by William Lamberton, who arrived in the autumn with the offer of a truce from King Edward II. Robert, overjoyed to see the formidable bishop returned to his circle, agreed the treaty with England, after which Lamberton had busied himself endeavouring to get Robert's excommunication, already dismissed by a council of the Scottish clergy, formally lifted by the pope.

Lamberton stood on the dais to Robert's left. To his right was James Stewart. Over the past months, while he led the campaign in Argyll, the high steward had been making preparations for the new government. Already, under his guidance, royal officials had been appointed and, slowly, the administration of the realm was coming back to life. Since Robert wrested Aberdeen from the English, trade had started to flourish with the Low Countries, the North Sea routes opened once more. Even more crucially, King Philippe of France — recalling the alliance the two countries had made at the start of the war — had recently recognised him as king.

There was a strange atmosphere in the hall, men struggling with a mixture of emotions. For many this was a moment of long-awaited celebration, but for others it was a time of mourning, their thoughts on those who weren't here to witness the fulfilment of thirteen years of struggle. For some, the assembly was the conclusion of their defeat, among them Earl William of Ross, the Earl of Sutherland and John of Menteith, all of whom had raised arms against Robert, but who had since surrendered.

A few men, Neil Campbell and Edward Bruce the most vocal, had been vehemently opposed to clemency for these barons — Ross had seized Robert's women at Tain and Menteith was responsible for the capture of William Wallace — but the king was adamant that any who now submitted would be accepted into his peace. Forgiveness, he told his men, would be the balm that healed the wounds of this war. But although his campaigns in Buchan and Argyll had seen the last real resistance against him crumble — the great houses of the Comyns and the MacDougalls falling after centuries in power — not all his foes were willing to accept his mercy. The Black Comyn had reputedly died in exile in England, but David, now the Earl of Atholl, Ingram de Umfraville and the earls of Angus and Dunbar remained at large, as did John MacDougall of Argyll, who, with his father, had fled his castle on Loch Awe.

Despite this, the parliament was an occasion for triumph, a day that Robert, in the dark months following the disasters in Methven Wood and Lorn, had not expected to see. The Wheel of Fortune had raised him up and now it was time to thank those who had helped him reach these heights.

One by one they came to him, those rewarded with lands and titles kneeling to perform the act of homage, clasping their hands and placing them between Robert's as they swore their undying loyalty. Some had been with him from the beginning: men like James Stewart, Nes and the knights of Carrick and Annandale. Others, many of whom fought for Wallace in the first days of the insurrection, had joined him along the way, pledging their swords and their hearts to him: Cormac of Antrim, Earl Malcolm of Lennox, Neil Campbell of Argyll, Gilbert de la Hay of Errol, Lord Angus MacDonald of Islay, Captain Lachlan MacRuarie, James Douglas, Thomas Randolph.

When the vows of homage and fealty were done, Robert was recognised — before all present and in the name of the community of the realm of Scotland – as the rightful king and true heir of Alexander III. By this declaration, John Balliol's reign was thus erased. On the smooth skin of the parchment it was as if the last seventeen years had never been. Under the skin of the land, countless bones told a different story.

After the parliament drew to a close, the men dispersing to prepare for the evening's feast, Robert walked the cathedral's cloisters with James Stewart.

'Still no word from Richard de Burgh?' the high steward asked him.

Robert shook his head. He had sent a message to the Earl of Ulster months ago, informing his father-in-law that he had secured Elizabeth's protection and appealing for him not to take up arms against him, should he be called upon to do so by the English. 'Could his silence be a good sign? It isn't a no, after all?'

When James didn't answer, Robert realised the steward had fallen back, unable to match his stride. He waited for him to catch up, noting again how old the man was looking. The high steward, once formidably tall, was rather stooped these days, his hair more grey than black. He repeated himself when James reached him.

'My brother-in-law will always do what is in his best interests. If it doesn't benefit him to join an English campaign against you he may well seek to avoid it. Edward Longshanks had to forgive Ulster his debts in order to encourage him to fight and the new king certainly doesn't have the kind of influence his father had.'

Robert nodded.

James tugged his mantle tighter as the wind whistled through the cloisters, carrying the bite of the sea. 'I couldn't help but notice today that things still seem troubled between you and your brother. It has been almost eight months, my lord.'

Robert felt a spike of anger at the man's measured tone. 'Edward openly defied me – in front of my men!'

'I am not saying Edward was right, doing what he did to MacDouall. He knows he wasn't. His wrath got the better of him. It can happen to us all.'

Robert wondered if James was alluding to that night in the church of the Greyfriars. 'It isn't just that,' he said tersely. 'I granted him the lordship of Galloway in the hope he would be satisfied with a command of his own, but it isn't enough for him. My brother wants me to break the truce with King Edward – lead a full-scale assault against the English with the aid of the Welsh and Irish. I know he has been going behind my back, seeking support for such a move.'

James said nothing.

Robert halted, staring at him. 'You agree?'

'The truce with King Edward is only temporary, on both your parts. Sooner or later it will have to be broken. You cannot allow the English to maintain their hold on the castles and towns they have in their possession. Edinburgh, Stirling, Perth, Dundee, Bothwell, Ayr, Jedburgh, Berwick, Dumfries, Caerlaverock, Lochmaben, Roxburgh.' The steward counted them off on his fingers. 'Through these, Scotland remains tied to the territories of the English crown and while Philippe of France may have recognised your legitimacy, King Edward most certainly has not. While he lays claim to any part of Scotland our kingdom will never be free. All this you know, my lord,' he finished quietly.

Robert let out a rough laugh. 'This – coming from you? The most cautious man in my kingdom?'

James averted his gaze. After a moment, he went and sat heavily on the low wall between the ribbed arches. 'You are right. I have been cautious.' The steward stared out over the square of windswept grass in the centre of the cloisters. 'I was cautious when your grandfather came, asking me to support his claim to the throne. I did so, but in secrecy, refusing to raise arms in his defence even though I believed he would make a finer king than John Balliol ever would, in thrall as he was to the Comyns. After pledging myself to your grandfather's cause, I simply walked away when Balliol was chosen.' He half closed his eyes. 'I still remember that day on the Moot Hill, the royal sceptre in my hands and Balliol's self-satisfied smile as I handed it to him.' He shook his head. 'When the war broke out, I supported the uprising of Wallace, my vassal, but again in secret, too scared of damaging my own position – too *cautious* – to come out openly for him.' He glanced at Robert. 'It was Bishop Wishart who finally persuaded me to step out from the shadows.' He smiled slightly at the memory. 'I never believed Wallace's peasant army could win. Not until Stirling.' The steward's smile faded. 'I followed him then, all the way to that godforsaken field at Falkirk, where I abandoned him. I fled that battle a coward, left my own brother and ten thousand men to die.'

Robert crossed to him. The steward's brown eyes were watery. He couldn't tell if it was from the wind. 'You would have been killed if you had stayed. All of you.'

'Would we?' James frowned up at him. 'Or would we have turned the tide? I set you on the path to the throne, Robert, ever pushing at you, but when I saw that chance slipping away, I forced you to England to beg King Edward's forgiveness. I sent you alone, into the fire, without aid or succour. I even stopped you seeking the truth of King Alexander's death. I was so obsessed with seeing you – my protégé – on the throne that I lost all sight of justice. It blinded me, too, to John Comyn's ambitions. I never should have persuaded you to make that pact with him. I should have known he would betray you. You once said Comyn's blood was on my hands as much as yours. If I hadn't convinced you to ally with him you wouldn't have gone to the Greyfriars that night and then, perhaps, none of this would have—'

'No,' Robert cut across him. He sat on the wall beside the high steward, forcing the older man to look at him. 'That sin is on me.'

'I helped to put you on the throne, but I didn't let you seize the power. I hid behind you, as I have always done – pulling the strings, watching from afar. It is no good excuse, but I grew to manhood in a court for the most part at peace with all but itself. My weapons were words, seals on parchments, spies in shadows, secret alliances.' The steward met his gaze. 'But you became a man in a kingdom riven by war. The sword has always been your weapon. I should have let you use it more.'

'It hasn't always served me well. After my coronation, all I could think of was forcing the English out of our lands, but then I went to Methven Wood.' Robert's voice became a murmur. 'I lost so much that day, James.'

The high steward turned towards him, his expression intent. 'You cannot let fear of loss rule you. Not like it has ruled me.'

'They have my child. My wife. My sisters. You yourself warned me of the danger of them being hurt while in English custody – used against me.'

'And you told me Humphrey de Bohun was concerned to keep the sins of King Edward secret? For now, you each have something dear to the other.' James tilted his head, making Robert look at him. 'But, in the end, a stalemate will achieve nothing. One of you has to make a move. The absence of your wife and daughter is yet another impediment to the security of the realm. Without Marjorie and Elizabeth you have no heirs.'

Robert turned his hand over, the gold of his wedding band gleaming in the dull light. He thought of Christiana MacRuarie, the woman who would share his bed tonight, as she had many times this past year. She had awoken in him a passion he had never known before, but although she had given him what he needed as a man, she couldn't give him what he required as king. He closed his eyes, remembering himself sitting hunched and hopeless in that hut on Barra, Affraig's words rasping in the darkness.

Your people have lost homes and livelihoods, sons and daughters. Do you know how they feel? Then you can stand with them – for them. Be their voice.

It wasn't just his own life, or his own family he had to protect. The declaration made in the parliament, confirming him as Scotland's rightful king, had reminded him of the oath taken on the Moot Hill three years ago, almost to the day, when the weight of this crown was cold and new. He had pledged, as guardian of the land, to defend their kingdom and, as shepherd, to defend his people. He had a duty to protect them all.

Robert stood. 'I think, after Longshanks's death, I fooled myself into believing that as long as I could quell my opponents in Scotland it would all be over.' He let out a humourless laugh. 'But the war is really just beginning, isn't it?' His laughter faded. 'How do I win my kingdom's freedom, James?'

The high steward got to his feet with a wince, using an arch to support himself. 'By throwing the cautions of an old man to the wind, my lord.' His brown eyes creased at the corners as he smiled. 'One castle at a time.'

PART 6

1312–1314 AD

O glorious youths, who now will stand by my side in arms, and with me repel the chieftains coming to harm me and the hosts rushing in upon me?

The Life of Merlin, *Geoffrey of Monmouth*

39

At the English royal court a storm was brewing. Clouds of a bitter conflict gathered, the atmosphere charged and volatile. Many could now feel it coming, but the first rumbles had begun four years ago, in the year of Edward's coronation.

After months watching the king bestow extravagant gifts upon Piers Gaveston, squandering money the realm could ill afford on sumptuous feasts and tournaments, the barons, led by the strident voice of Thomas of Lancaster, had finally risen in anger. With the full-throated support of the indomitable Archbishop of Canterbury and the threat of revoking their pledges of fealty, made in Westminster Abbey, the earls had forced their king to send his favourite back into exile. Edward, setting his seal to the writ, was wounded, resentful, but privately adamant the banishment would not last long. Appointing Piers as his lieutenant in Ireland and despatching him to Dublin to aid the Earl of Ulster in restoring English control, he at once set about currying favour with his opponents at court.

Flattery, bribery, promises of land and titles: Edward employed them all. Younger men such as his nephew, Gilbert de Clare, the Earl of Gloucester, were easy to win over. Humphrey de Bohun, ever the diplomat, eventually relented for the sake of peace. Others followed, not wanting to be at odds with their king – still so new to the throne – until, at last, Edward had the support he needed. Only twelve months after he had sealed the hateful writ, Piers was back at his side. But the king's victory was not absolute, for dissent lingered on in the shadows of his court, and the gaze of Lancaster remained fixed upon him.

Through these troubled days, with the war paused, but the air over Britain heavy with tension, England's enemy in the north was not idle. Using the truce to his advantage, Robert Bruce had busied himself re-establishing trade with the Low Countries. As the silver poured in, he opened up the sea routes to Ireland to buy grain and meat, weapons and armour for his growing war-band. Often in these months, MacRuarie and MacDonald galleys could be spied, riding the waves of the race. With Ulster preoccupied battling the Irish on his western borders, Edward turned to an old foe of Bruce's for help. John MacDougall, Lord of Argyll, had fled into England with his father following Bruce's invasion of his lands. Craving vengeance for the loss of his lordship, he was only too willing to offer his service to Edward, who made him captain of a fleet patrolling the waters between Dublin and Galloway in an attempt to disrupt Bruce's supply routes. But the MacDonalds and MacRuaries were masters of the sea and did not fall easily into enemy nets.

Meanwhile, Robert, breaking the terms of the truce, captured and razed several minor castles held by English garrisons, before launching, in a move feared by many, a series of raids across the border into Cumberland, Northumberland and Durham. Unlike the campaigns of William Wallace, these raids did not result in bloody slaughter, but rather in crippling blackmail. Landlords were offered the choice to pay up, or else see their crops destroyed, their livestock taken and their houses burned. Most submitted.

As reports flooded in from the beleaguered northern counties, cries to arms sounded at court, most vociferously from Aymer de Valence. Calls from the English nobility for the king to resume the war were joined in parliament by those of Scottish nobles, who, refusing to yield to Bruce, had sought refuge in England, among them David of Atholl, Ingram de Umfraville and the earls of Angus and Dunbar. With all these voices growing louder and more insistent, Edward was at last compelled to lead an army into Scotland. His campaign proved futile, Bruce and his men retreating beyond the Forth, leaving a land scorched and empty in their wake, no food to be found to supply men or horses.

The failed mission had done little except remind Edward of all he hated about this war. He had grown to manhood witness to this endless conflict and his father's obsession, which in the end consumed him. For Edward it had ended when he laid his father's body in that black marble tomb. Determined not to be dragged back into it, he now fixed on other means by which to deal with the Scots. Ignoring protests from his men, he sent messengers into Scotland with his own offer of tribute if Bruce ceased his raids and stopped his attacks on English-held castles. The offer was accepted and, once more, an uneasy peace was laid, like a thin sheet of ice, between the two nations. But no such peace could be formed in Edward's own court, where tempers ran hot and high.

The barons, led by Valence and others, fumed against the king for using money raised to fund a campaign to bribe their enemy. Scotland was growing stronger, while England was sinking deeper into poverty. Some in the Round Table believed the *Last Prophecy* was coming to pass – England slipping into ruin with the division of the relics. Others focused on the temporal, accusing the king of wasting his inheritance on luxuries, while letting the lands his father had fought and bled to win slip through his fingers. They told him he had let himself be guided by evil counsel and that, in fear for the future of England itself, they must insist he rid himself of the poison that had tainted his reign. They would neither bear arms for him nor honour their commitments, unless he agreed to a host of reforms cited in ordinances drawn up by a council of bishops, lords and earls. It was clear who the main target of these edicts was.

Once again, Edward found himself at the mercy of his own men, forced to send his lover away. And, once again, he determined this hateful act would not be long-lived, despite the growing darkness of the storm that even he could not now fail to see on the horizon.

Langley Manor, England, 1312 AD

Edward paced the bedchamber. He had been waiting all day and, still, there was no sign of him. Earlier, as the last light was leached by the January dusk, the drapes had been drawn by his page, but Edward had since gone to peer through them so often that finally he had pulled them back, affording himself a wide view over the manor's inner courtyard. The leaded windows were stippled with snow. There had been a fresh fall that afternoon, shrouding the rooftops, muffling the world in white.

The flames of the candles on the table guttered as he paced. Catching sight of himself in a looking-glass set beside the night lights, Edward saw his worry etched in lines on his brow and around his mouth. He had lost weight over the past year and these new creases in his face were more prominent now. In just a few months he would celebrate his twenty-eighth year.

Hearing voices outside, he hastened to the window. It was just two kitchen boys making their way to the bakehouse. One bent as if to adjust his shoe, leaving the other to walk on ahead. After a pause, the boy straightened, something in his fist. Raising his arm, he flung it at the other's back. The ball of snow hit with a thump. Shouting in protest, his companion crouched to scoop up his own, but the offender had already taken off across the yard laughing. Watching them, Edward was reminded of his youth, which was never far from his thoughts in this place.

King's Langley was a book, the story of his childhood written within its walls. The sound of his sisters' laughter, the stern voices of his tutors, the soft tones of his nurse: all echoed to him still in quiet passageways and empty rooms. It was here that he had first seen Piers – a black-haired youth, standing in the courtyard with an older man, eyes darting around, taking in the buildings and the people. Edward had watched from the window of this chamber as his father's steward had greeted the pair. His gaze had lingered on the boy with inquisitive eyes and skin warmed by a stronger sun than he knew.

As a child, Edward had often felt alone. His sisters were older, uninterested in him, his father and mother were frequently away, and, as heir to the throne, he was treated differently, even by his friends – all except Piers. At first, when the young Gascon squire was made a royal ward after the death of his father, Piers had been as a brother to Edward, both protective and teasing. Later, when he was appointed to the prince's household, the two of them had become inseparable friends. Later still, their friendship had changed into something else, something that frightened and exhilarated Edward. Over the years, they had spent many days in this manor together, the innocence of play turning, by brief looks and tentative gestures, half-smiles and lingering touches, into the growing awareness of love.

The first time he was forced to send Piers into exile, four years ago, Edward had come to realise just how strong that love was. Without the man at his side, he felt bereft. Those twelve months had seemed, then, the longest he had endured, but even they hadn't compared with these past three months of his lover's second banishment, made worse by his own increasing isolation at court.

In this time, the familiar loneliness of his childhood had swelled to engulf him.

The sound of hooves, muted by snow, echoed outside. Edward's breath misted the window as he leaned in to see a dozen or so riders enter the yard. He had come. The king returned to the mirror and brushed his hands through his hair, his expression now smiling back at him, the lines of worry gone. Footsteps sounded on the stairs. There was a knock and his steward opened the door. As Piers Gaveston entered, pushing back the hood of his snow-mottled cloak, the steward closed the door.

The moment they were alone, Edward embraced Piers. 'Thank God. I thought you would never come.' He smelled the damp on the man's cloak, the fresh sweat on his skin. He closed his eyes, savouring the solidity of Piers's body against his own.

Piers withdrew with a self-satisfied smile. 'I knew you would send for me before long. Those bastards be damned!'

Edward kept hold of his shoulders, but didn't return the smile. This greeting was merely a prelude to another farewell, albeit one of his own choosing. 'Piers, you cannot stay. I can't trust that your presence here will go unnoticed for long. My cousin has spies everywhere.'

'You're sending me away again?' Piers pulled from the king's clutches. 'Edward, I have been moving from place to place for weeks now, keeping out of their sight like a fox hiding from hounds. I will do it no longer. You are the king! Stand up to Lancaster and the others.'

'I will – when I am ready to.'

Piers shook his head and twisted away.

'My love, please listen, I have a plan.' Edward waited until the man looked back at him. 'I have gathered a company of men I trust. I am sending them with you to Scotland.'

'Scotland?'

'To Perth. I do not trust my cousin. In truth, I have begun to fear for your safety.'

'And so you plan to send me into the heart of the enemy's lands?'

'Perth is protected by my truce with the Scots.'

'The first truce didn't stop Bruce raiding England, or taking castles.'

'I wasn't paying him then. It isn't in Bruce's interests to attack Perth. Besides, he doesn't have the resources to do so – it is one of the most defensible towns in the realm. There, you will be able to stop running. What is more, your appointment as commander will prove to the barons that I am turning my attention to Scotland, as is their wish. They were appeased, were they not, when they saw your effectiveness in Ireland? I believe, this way, I will be able to win back their support.'

Piers said nothing, but neither did he turn away.

'I will follow you north as soon as I am able.' Taking the man's gloved hands in his, Edward met his dark, angry eyes. 'Your place is at my side, Piers. I swear on my crown you will be restored there before long.'

40

Pleshey Castle, England, 1312 AD

Elizabeth sat in the window seat, her knees drawn up to her chest, watching the snow swirl into view in the glow of a lantern outside the guest lodgings, illuminating a path that ran alongside the kitchen gardens. The first fall had arrived over a fortnight ago, in the last days of January. The year was now caught between the feasts of St Bridget and St Valentine and, still, the blizzards showed no signs of stopping. Earlier, she had watched the path being cleared by servants, but it was already mottled white again.

Her thoughts turned again to Humphrey. The earl had arrived at Pleshey three days ago – Constance, the maid who brought her meals, had told her so. Elizabeth was surprised he hadn't come to see her yet. He always did when he returned.

Sometimes, Humphrey's visits were brief; a mere greeting. At other times he stayed longer, playing chess with her and talking into the evening, although only ever about the safe and mundane: poor harvests and unseasonable weather, the celebrations in London for Queen Isabella's birthday. She never forced him beyond these bounds – she didn't need to, for it was Humphrey's silences and the things he did not speak of that told her the most. Gradually, in these past years, Elizabeth had watched him grow more and more preoccupied, secret worries weighing heavy on him. He was starting to look old, although at thirty-seven he was only nine years older than she was.

That afternoon, unable to curb her impatience, she had asked Constance whether Humphrey had left, but the maid assured her he was still in residence and that he was expecting guests, although she

didn't know whom. Watching the flakes dance around one another in
the lantern light, Elizabeth told herself Humphrey was occupied
entertaining some dignitary and that was why he hadn't visited her,
but a splinter of unease had lodged in her mind at his absence and she
couldn't get it out. It made her think of that night, several years ago,
when he had come asking what she knew of Robert's plans. The cold
determination in his green eyes had chilled her and for weeks after-
wards, when he didn't appear, she had feared for her safety. Nothing
had come of his questions and he never again asked her about Robert,
but the disquiet it had roused in her had been hard to forget.

Hearing the crunch of boots in snow, Elizabeth caught sight of a
tall, broad-shouldered man coming along the path. His face was shadowed by a hood, but as he passed by the lighted window, he glanced
inside. Elizabeth froze. So did the man. The two of them stared at one
another, only the pane of glass between them. The snow settled on
Aymer de Valence's shoulders as he stood there. His black eyes
gleamed in the lantern light, filled with the same unrelenting hatred
she had seen six years ago when he delivered her to Lanercost to face
the king's judgement.

After a long pause, the earl moved on, his footprints marking the
snow. Elizabeth's caught breath escaped in a rush. Moments later,
more footsteps sounded, along with voices. Jumping up, she blew
out the candles, plunging the chamber into darkness, save for the
glow of the hearth. Heart thumping, she pulled the curtains closed,
just as two more figures came into view. Peering through a gap in
the drapes, she watched them pass, recognising the larger of the
two as Henry Percy, the Lord of Alnwick. Both, like Aymer, were
dressed in dark riding cloaks, rather than their surcoats and mantles.
Somewhere out in the castle yard, she heard the clop of hooves and
the creak of wagon wheels.

Elizabeth sank on to her knees on the window seat, the splinter of
unease now a shard of fear. Why had these men come here under the
cover of snow and darkness? Was her fortune about to change?

As the last man entered, Humphrey nodded to his knights, who pulled
the doors shut. The two men would stand outside, ensuring no one
overheard this conversation.

It was stuffy in the chamber. The fire blazed, throwing its shifting
light across the faces of the seven men present. Those who had got to

Pleshey earlier had changed from their travelling clothes. Those who had just arrived smelled of the road – of snow and mud and haste.

Humphrey scanned them. Guy de Beauchamp, Earl of Warwick, leaned his rangy form up against the back wall, his brow prominent beneath the receding line of his red hair. Henry Percy, Lord of Alnwick, sat by the fireplace, his belly straining against his doublet, his blond hair dishevelled from the ride. Henry had only just arrived, his clothes sodden, his sword still hanging from the belt at his hip. Solemn-faced Robert Clifford was seated on the window seat close to where Aymer de Valence, Earl of Pembroke, stood, his eyes raking the room, judging, assessing. Ralph de Monthermer was present as was Thomas, Earl of Lancaster, younger than all of them, yet one of the most powerful barons in England, with five earldoms to his name.

They were men now, but Humphrey had known them all since boyhood; had learned to ride and to fight with them, had served the king's table as a page beside them. He had been at their initiations into the Knights of the Dragon and shared their excitement at the quest they had pledged to undertake; unaware of the lie behind it. They had been England's elite, ordained to follow in the footsteps of their fathers, destined for glory. Humphrey had been with them on the march to Wales and in the forests beneath Mount Snowdon, with snow and wolves and Welsh insurgents closing in. He had been with them on the long road to Scotland, in the stinking heat of Falkirk's bloody fields, in jubilant victory and sour defeat. He had stood beside them when they learned of Robert Bruce's betrayal, when they buried their king and raised up his son before God. All that and, now, it had come to this.

For a moment, he teetered on the brink, wondering if there was a way he could pull them back from this. But even as he thought it he knew the answer. Humphrey caught Thomas's eye and nodded.

At the look, Thomas rose and addressed the circle. 'My sources have confirmed it. Piers Gaveston has returned from exile.'

There were a few muttered curses at this news.

'Edward has sent him to command Perth. He left King's Langley a fortnight ago.'

'We should inform Archbishop Winchelsea at once,' said Clifford. 'According to the ordinances, Piers was forbidden from returning under pain of excommunication.'

'No,' Thomas said quickly. 'I do not believe the king will listen any longer, not even to Winchelsea. My spies tell me my cousin has sworn on God's soul not to heed the advice of any man on this matter, but to exercise his own judgement. As you know, he is moving his court to York. He has stated his intention is to deal with Scotland, but I believe he is placing himself between us and Gaveston.'

'What if it is true?' questioned Aymer. 'What if Gaveston has been sent north to make a move against Bruce – to prove his worth? A resumption of the war is what we have been demanding. We should let it play out.'

'Gaveston isn't in Perth to start a war against the Scots,' replied Thomas curtly. 'He is there because it is one of the few places my cousin knows we cannot reach him.'

'Then what do we do?' asked Guy, glancing from Thomas to Humphrey. 'Perth is a walled town, deep in enemy lands.' He shook his head. 'We'd need an army to take Piers from there.'

Humphrey and Thomas shared a look. Humphrey nodded at the younger man. 'Tell them.'

The room fell silent as Thomas spoke, outlining the plan. When he had finished, a mixture of emotions played on the men's faces. Humphrey saw surprise, doubt, thoughtful agreement and, on Aymer's, incredulous fury. He was the first to speak.

'You cannot be considering this?' Aymer demanded, challenging the others, before rounding on Humphrey and Thomas. His lips pulled back to reveal the wire on his front teeth. 'No! I'll not agree to it!'

'Not even for the good of our realm?' Thomas asked him.

'Not for anything. Do you hear me? I'd rather deal with a sodomite than that *serpent*!'

Henry Percy levelled Thomas with his blue eyes. 'I'll not ally with him either. The bastard took me prisoner.'

'Why do we even need his help?' questioned Robert Clifford. 'Why not send our own men into Perth to seize Gaveston?'

'Edward will doubtless have his guards on the alert not to open the gates to anyone they don't trust – whether Scot or Englishman,' responded Thomas. 'Gaveston has a large number of men with him. Gloucester has stayed loyal to the king, as have others.'

Humphrey pressed his lips together. Earlier, Thomas had delivered the bad news that Henry, his nephew, had gone north with Piers.

'He is well protected,' Thomas continued. 'As you said, Sir Guy, we would need a strong force to take him – a force that might then draw attack by Bruce's forces.'

'Even if we could take him,' Humphrey added, his eyes on Clifford, 'his abduction would be traced back to us. This way, we maintain our innocence.'

'This stone will kill two birds, Sir Aymer,' said Thomas, his eyes following the agitated earl. 'If Bruce agrees to this he will be breaking the terms of the truce. King Edward will have no choice but to turn his attention to Scotland then. The war will be resumed. We'll bear no more tributes paid out to our enemy.'

'But if this works, we lose Perth,' Henry Percy cut in.

Thomas nodded. 'A sacrifice, yes. But one I believe will benefit us in the long term.'

Ralph frowned. 'Why would Bruce do this, knowing he will break the truce and forfeit any more tributes?'

'We have things that will make it worth his while,' responded Humphrey. 'His family, for a start.'

'And if it works?' asked Guy, ignoring Aymer's glare. 'We all agreed we would take action if Piers returned from exile, but once he is in our custody – what then?'

'He'll be taken to France,' Thomas answered quickly. 'To be held in a foreign prison.'

Humphrey nodded. 'We know King Philippe is angry over Edward's treatment of his daughter, who has complained her husband is married to another. We believe he will help us.'

'Gaveston will be missing after the attack, assumed dead,' added Thomas. 'My cousin will mourn him and that will be that.'

Aymer turned on Humphrey, his eyes filling with accusation. 'Is this something you concocted in that secret meeting? You and Bruce?'

Humphrey met his gaze. 'This again? Christ, Aymer, how many times must I repeat myself?'

'Until the truth comes out!'

'The truth is that I met with Bruce that day in order to ensure Sir Henry's release.'

'Why did you keep it from me? Why did you not even attempt to capture him when you had the chance?'

Humphrey bristled, feeling the eyes of the others on him. 'I had no chance. I would have been dead before I drew a blade.'

'Henry said you were with Bruce for an age. What did two so-called mortal enemies have to talk about? Old times perhaps?' Before Humphrey could answer, Aymer continued. 'Maybe he was thanking you for helping him escape from Westminster.'

'How dare you accuse me of that!'

'Someone helped Bruce that day,' spat Aymer. 'Someone had to have warned him the king was about to arrest him.'

No one noticed Ralph de Monthermer tense and drop his gaze, all their attention on Aymer and Humphrey. The two earls stood a few feet from one another, drawn up to their full heights, facing off like stags in the rut.

'You are always the wronged one when it comes to Bruce, aren't you?' Humphrey struck his chest with his fist. 'I was his friend, God damn it, Aymer! I was the one he betrayed the most!'

Aymer didn't falter. 'You're right about one thing – we do have his family. I'll show you how we deal with Bruce.'

Before anyone could stop him, Aymer stormed out through the doors, pushing past the startled guards outside. Humphrey went after him with a shout, but was brought up short by Henry Percy. The large man stepped in front of him, drawing his sword.

'I am sorry, Humphrey,' Henry said, his voice low. 'But Aymer is right – when it comes to Bruce your judgement has never been clear.'

'Dear God, Henry,' murmured Ralph. 'You would threaten one of your brethren?'

Henry's cool blue eyes darted in his direction. He licked his lips, but kept the blade pointed at Humphrey's chest.

Humphrey's heart was pounding, but his fear wasn't for himself. Aymer's footsteps had receded down the passage. His knights hadn't gone after him. They were standing in the doorway, their own swords drawn, staring at the frozen tableau uncertain how to act.

Thomas walked slowly over to Henry and put his hand on the lord's blade. 'This wasn't Humphrey's plan, Henry. It was mine. If we do this we can save our realm from the blight that is Piers Gaveston. Then, united, we can concentrate our strength against Bruce. Our alliance with him will only be temporary. I swear it.'

Henry seemed to struggle with the decision. Finally, he lowered his blade.

Humphrey pushed past him. Snatching a sword from one of his knights, he raced from the building, out into the snow. His boots sank into the drifts as he followed the fresh prints made by Aymer, towards the guest lodgings. Barrelling inside, he almost fell over a maid, on her knees, picking up the fragments of a dropped jug. She cried out, startled, as he dashed past. Several doors were open along the passage, some still swinging. Up ahead, Humphrey heard a door bang back against a wall, followed by a woman's scream.

He reached Elizabeth's room in time to see Aymer hauling her off the window seat. The earl spun round, pinning her to him, an arm across her chest, his face cast in the red haze of the fire. Humphrey shouted as Aymer wrenched his dagger free and brought it to Elizabeth's throat. 'Stop!' He held up his free hand. 'Aymer, please. This is madness. She is a queen!'

'No queen I recognise.'

'She is Ulster's daughter then. That you cannot refute.'

'She is nothing but something to bargain with. An asset. You told me that yourself, Humphrey.'

Humphrey heard footsteps pounding down the passage. He didn't look to see who it was – didn't take his eyes off Elizabeth, who was staring at him, her cheeks drained of colour.

'I say we use her now,' continued Aymer intently. 'Let us take her and Bruce's daughter to the border and threaten to slit their throats unless he surrenders. Bruce is the real enemy. You – Thomas – you've both lost sight of that with this obsession with Gaveston.'

'It is the king's infatuation that has caused this, Aymer.' Thomas of Lancaster appeared in the doorway behind Humphrey. He moved into the chamber, his eyes on the furious earl. 'Don't let your hatred of Bruce blind you to that. Before we can deal with the Scots we must deal with the poison in our own realm.'

'I want him dead and buried, Thomas. Do you understand me? Bruce must pay for what he has done to us!'

'He will. By my oath, he will.'

Aymer took a long time to consider. At length, he lowered his dagger and released Elizabeth, pushing her roughly to the floor. Striding past Humphrey, he allowed Thomas to lead him from the chamber.

Humphrey waited until they had gone, then crossed to Elizabeth, who had her hand pressed against her mouth. Tears were streaming down her cheeks, but she made no sound. As his steward, alerted to the commotion, appeared in the doorway, Humphrey ordered him to bring wine. When he bent down to her, Elizabeth thrust out her hand as if to push him away. Humphrey ignored it. Helping her to her feet, he guided her to the window seat. His jaw tightened as he sat beside her and saw the livid line across her throat where Aymer's blade had cut her skin.

'I am sorry,' he murmured.

She turned on him, eyes flashing. 'And to think I was missing you! An asset, am I? Nothing more than something to bargain with? I thought you were my friend. I thought I could trust you.'

Humphrey said nothing, his mind stalling on her first words. After a moment, he drew her into his arms. 'You can trust me, Elizabeth. I'll not let any harm come to you.'

She stiffened, then slumped against him and began to weep. Feeling her breath warm on his neck, he stroked her hair to calm her. She tensed again, but now it seemed different than before. Her breaths slowed. He felt something change – felt it in her body and in his. She pulled back and looked up at him, searching his face. The fear was gone from her eyes. A question remained. Strands of her black hair were stuck to her face with tears. He reached out and pushed them away. Then, he was leaning in, his mouth opening over hers, knowing that she would accept.

41

Turnberry, Scotland, 1312 AD

Robert stood on the beach, watching the three galleys approach. The sand was littered with debris, thrown up by the violence of the March storms, but the sea was now as calm as a mill pond, impassive under a milk-white sky. Boys hunted along the shoreline, searching for treasures disgorged by the recent waves – dead fish to poke with sticks, maybe a rusted weapon lost in a battle. Robert wondered if the dragon shield he had tossed from Turnberry's battlements was among the flotsam, or whether the sea had kept that token for itself.

Beneath the billow of a sail, he picked out Christiana's halo of hair. He smiled. It had been almost six months since he had seen her last. The Lady of Garmoran had returned to Barra in the autumn with Lachlan and Ruarie to train a new season of galloglass and arrange for more galleys to be sent to Ireland to gather supplies for his army. Angus MacDonald had done the same, the ending of Scotland's bitter civil war and the pause in the conflict with England giving them all the chance to rebuild their lives.

As the galleys entered the shallows, Robert sent Nes and the other men waiting with him to help haul the boats on to the sand. Christiana was escorted out of the first, picking up the skirts of her pale blue gown as she made her way towards him. She wore a woollen cloak of the same colour, trimmed with the cloud-soft fur of mountain hares. She was followed by Brigid and Elena. Grown tall like her mother, Elena looked more like a young woman than a girl now. One half of her face was strikingly beautiful, the other scarred by the fire that had almost claimed her life.

Christiana came to him with a smile. Taking his hands in hers, she bowed her head. 'My lord king.'

Robert drew her close, breathing in the salt scent of her hair as he kissed her.

At first they had tried to be discreet, but the proximity in which they had all lived these past years had made such effort futile and, in the end, they stopped hiding their affection. Still, there remained between them the knowledge, unspoken but clear, that Robert was fighting to bring his family back to his side and, whenever that day came, Christiana would lose her place there.

Robert released her. 'How was your journey?'

'Uneventful. We waited out the storm on Islay. Lord Angus sends you his good wishes. He has had fishermen making the ladders you requested through the winter. He told me to tell you he will deliver them shortly – says they'll be stronger than lobster pots.'

Robert's brief smile faded. 'They will need to be for the task ahead.'

Leaving his men to help secure the vessels, he escorted Christiana up the beach, motioning for Brigid and Elena, lingering at a respect-ful distance, to follow. He looked back at Brigid as they climbed the dunes. 'There's something I think you'll be glad to see.'

Ahead, the thud of hammers could be heard. Striding up on to the bluffs, Robert led the three women into a bustle of activity. Outside Turnberry's walls, a new village was slowly going up, in place of the one the English had burned to the ground. He and his men had taken the castle last year from the garrison left there by King Edward. He had since been rebuilding the village with funds from the king's trib-ute and from what he had collected in raids on northern England – the enemy thus paying for what they had destroyed.

A few houses were almost complete, labourers clambering over the structures, covering thatch with stone-weighted nets. The rest were only half built, men hauling timber and stone from carts, others hammering in nails, or mixing up mud for the daubing. A smell of freshly sawn wood filled the air. As their king walked through their midst, men paused in their labours to bow or call out a greeting. It had been a slow process, but after many years absent from his earldom, he was finally regaining the trust and respect of the people of Carrick.

'The villagers have returned?'

Robert glanced round at Brigid's question. She had paused on the edge of the building work, a strange expression on her face. He saw she was holding her daughter's hand.

'Some.' *The ones who survived*, he thought, but did not say.

Robert realised the look on Brigid's face was sadness. He had assumed she would be happy to see the new village resurrected from the ashes of the old.

She seemed to read his thoughts, for she forced a smile. 'Affraig would be glad.' She paused. 'My lord, would you give us leave for a while? I should like to visit my aunt's old home.'

'Of course. Wait here and I'll have my men escort you.'

As Brigid nodded her thanks, Elena slipped from her side and went to a cluster of primroses growing on the edge of the dunes. Crouching, the young woman picked the flowers, arranging them into a bunch in her hand. As she lifted them with a smile to show her mother, the scars on her face crinkled. All at once, Robert felt he knew the cause of Brigid's sadness. He had started to rebuild what had been destroyed in the war, but there were some things that could never be healed. Not even with time. The scars, in his people and in the land, would remain.

Christiana threaded her fingers through his. 'What is it?'

Robert realised he had been frowning. 'Sometimes it feels as though the war is over. Then I remember there is still so much to be done – so many battles yet to be won.' His hand in hers, he led Christiana towards the castle, which towered over the half-built village.

The sense of normality here – the men busy at work and the children at play – was part illusion. Turnberry's cellars were stockpiled with food to outwait a siege and the men on the battlements had horns and beacons, ready to sound the alert. Carrick was back in his possession, but further south and to the east the English still had dominion over the royal burghs and great castles of his realm: Edinburgh and Perth, Dumfries and Berwick, Roxburgh and, most vital of all, Stirling. The enemy was a shadow, always there, even when the sun was shining.

'Sir James told me I must win back my kingdom one castle at a time. He just didn't tell me how.'

'You miss him.'

It wasn't a question, but Robert nodded, James Stewart's face conjured in his mind. The high steward had died several months after the parliament at St Andrews. His surviving son, Walter, a young man barely out of boyhood, had taken on his mantle. Yes, he missed James – missed him dearly.

'The ladders you have Lord Angus's men making? They will surely be of use?'

'For some strongholds, yes.' Robert shook his head. 'But grappling ladders and battering rams will not be enough for others. Without siege engines and skilled engineers . . .?' He motioned to Turnberry's scarred walls. 'This was a victory hard won and it has nothing like the defences of Stirling. I watched Longshanks batter that castle for months with his engines and his Greek Fire. In the end, Stirling's garrison were the ones who opened the gates.' He exhaled sharply. 'I feel I am nibbling at the extremities of some enormous beast.'

The two of them entered the castle's bailey, the guards standing sentry at the gates nodding in greeting. Robert called two others in the guardhouse to gather a party to escort Brigid and Elena. There was more activity here, stables and other outbuildings being erected along the walls. Smoke drifted from campfires. There was a heap of rubbish piled in one corner, left over from the English occupation. Most of it was useless, his men having picked through it for anything of value – weapons and clothing, rope and firewood. Up on the battlements the royal banner of Scotland hung limp in the lifeless afternoon air.

'Go for its eye.'

Robert glanced at Christiana as they walked across the courtyard. 'Its eye?'

'Go for the beast's eye, or whatever is vulnerable. Then, maybe, you can bring it down.'

'I'm not sure any part of this beast is vulnerable,' Robert answered, leading her into the castle.

A few hours later, as dusk was falling and the wind was picking up, driving rain across from the mountains of Arran, Robert, lying awake in his chamber, heard a horn sound on the battlements, signalling the approach of someone. Leaving Christiana asleep in his bed, he shrugged on his robe and made his way down to the courtyard. The gates, shut for the evening, were being hauled open and a company was riding up. Robert smiled, seeing the banner raised in the hand of one rider – three white stars on blue – the arms of James Douglas. The young man had been busy fortifying his lands, since taken from the English.

James dismounted in the courtyard, then took something from the bag strapped to his horse's saddle and crossed to Robert. 'My lord king.'

'It is good to see you, James. What word from the south?'

'All is quiet for the most part, my lord. Sir Edward and Sir Neil are patrolling the border, but there has been no sign of reinforcements coming north to relieve English garrisons. Five days ago, Sir Gilbert seized six supply wagons from Edinburgh, headed for Dumfries.'

Robert nodded, pleased. He might not be able to tackle the larger castles directly, but he could disrupt their supply lines; eventually starve them into submission.

'There is one thing, though, that has come from England, my lord.' James raised the object he had taken from the bag. It was a leather scroll-case. 'A man carrying this was caught by our scouts trying to cross the border near Annandale. When questioned, he insisted it was delivered directly to you. He said it would be in your interest to receive it – that it was from an old friend. The scouts brought him to me.'

Robert took the case. 'Do you know what it is?'

'No, my lord. It wasn't for me to read.'

Robert nodded with a half-smile. He put his fingers in the top of the opening and pulled out the rolled parchment inside. Opening it, his eyes went first to the seal on the bottom. It was one he recognised, but hadn't seen in years: a winged serpent stamped in red wax. It was the seal of the Knights of the Dragon. His brow furrowing in uneasy surprise, Robert read the message. 'The enemy wants to make an exchange,' he murmured.

'An exchange?' James stared at him. 'An exchange for what, my lord?'

Roxburgh Castle, Scotland, 1312 AD

Mary Bruce started from a fitful sleep. Moonlight slanted in through the tower's slit of a window, gleaming on the iron bars of her cage. A raw April wind moaned through the aperture, bringing with it a mist of rain. Thinking it was the cold that had woken her, Mary pulled her thin blanket tighter around her body. The thing was teeming with lice, but these past six years she had learned to live with them crawling on her skin and in her hair; learned to live with her cramped confinement and the offerings of watery porridge and gristly stews, in the early days sometimes flavoured with a glob of spit from the guards. She had learned to live with it all by pushing everything that was good and light deep down inside herself – by burying hope. Now, she was numb, moving mechanically through the same routine, day in, day out.

There were sounds outside the cell door: a deep grunt followed by something heavy hitting the door. Mary sat bolt upright, the blanket falling back. The moonlight faded as rain began to hammer on the roof of the tower. She listened, tense, over the sound of the downpour. Once, three summers ago, a guard had come in the night. Pinning her down on the boards of the cage, one hand around her throat, he had pulled up her dress and tried to force himself on her. She had fought like a wild thing, twisting and scratching, screaming hoarsely until another guard had come in and hauled him out. She hadn't seen the man again, but night sounds always woke her now.

After a pause, Mary heard the rattle of a key in the lock. She scuttled into the far corner of her cage, where a cloth was strung up to conceal her bucket. Her spine banged painfully against the bars as the door opened. A figure entered. She could see his silhouette through the cloth. Her bladder felt full, heavy. She felt a fierce urge to void it, but was desperate not to for shame. She bit her lip hard. The cage door creaked as it was opened.

'Come out.' It was the voice of Sim, one of her night guards. Of all of them, he had always been the least unpleasant. 'Quick now.'

Mary stayed where she was, uncomprehending.

After a moment, Sim entered with a curse. Bent almost double, he made his way over to her. Taking her by the arms, he pulled her from the cage. 'Hush now,' he urged as she cried out. His eyes were wide in the gloom. 'I'm not going to hurt you. Understand?'

Mary shook her head, frozen in confusion, but she didn't struggle as he led her through the cell door. She gasped as her foot caught on something. Looking down, she saw a figure slumped against the wall. It was Osbert, her other night guard. Down through the tower, her legs trembling from fear and lack of use, Mary stumbled on the steep steps, but Sim kept a firm grip on her and didn't let her fall. At the bottom, he shrugged off his cloak and threw it around her shoulders.

'It's cold out.'

Mary stood shivering under the weight of the garment, staring at Sim in bewilderment as he unbolted the tower door, then checked outside.

She sucked in a breath as he ushered her out, the rain striking her like needles. Sim hastened her across the yard, her bare feet splashing through puddles. The moon had vanished, obscured by clouds. Through the bailey, past the stables, the black hulks of towers rising all around, he led her to a small gate in the walls. The rain pelting them, he unbolted it.

Beyond, a path wound down the steep mound on which the castle was built, between two rivers. Sim didn't take the path, but headed instead alongside the curtain walls. Mary's feet slipped in mud, threatening to tumble her down the bank. There was a foul stink as they passed a latrine chute where the ground was slimy. As the wall ended, the mound sloped down to the broad waters of the Tweed. Sim paused, glancing up at the battlements, then took her hand and guided her down the bank. In the rain-soaked gloom, Mary saw the outline of a boat, moored among the reeds. There were two figures inside.

She tried to resist Sim's pull on her arm as she saw them, but he compelled her forward. As one of the figures in the boat stood and reached out his hand, Mary looked over her shoulder at Roxburgh's walls, towering behind her. If she screamed, the guards on patrol would surely be alerted. But, then, they would just put her back in the cage. As the hand grabbed hers, she didn't fight, but allowed the men to help her into the boat. She sat on a bench at the prow, shivering madly inside the wet cloak, as Sim pushed the boat off and jumped in behind her. The splash of oars was drowned by the bubbling of rain on the water. The men didn't speak until they reached the north bank of the Tweed, at the edge of woods. One jumped out and pulled the boat in, allowing the others to disembark.

Under the shelter of the trees, Sim took his cloak from Mary's shoulders. 'You'll go with them now.'

'Where?' she asked him, her voice quavering with cold and fear.

Sim didn't answer, but turned to the men. 'My payment?'

One of them had a bag over his shoulder. He held it out to Sim, but kept hold of it when the guard reached for it. 'This buys your silence.'

Mary felt a new rush of fear as she caught his English. Most of her guards had been Scots.

'You have my word.'

Taking the bag, Sim ducked off through the trees and disappeared. As the two Englishmen led her through the woods, Mary heard the whinny of a horse. Waiting in the darkness was a small company of five or so riders. After she was hoisted into a saddle in front of one of them, the man dug in his spurs and the horse took off along a track.

Mary clung to the pommel. 'Where are you taking me?' she asked. But her voice was a whisper that the wind and the rain and the pummelling hooves snatched away without answer.

Some time later, after several miles, they came to a halt by the banks of a fast-flowing burn. The rain had ceased and the moon, sailing out from behind the clouds, turned the waters silver. Mary, chilled to her bones, realised it was a ford. She was expecting the men to cross, but instead, the one she had ridden with dismounted and helped her down.

'Go,' he said.

She shook her head, not understanding.

'You're free,' he told her, digging his foot in the stirrup and swinging into the saddle.

She stayed where she was, not trusting his words. What cruel trick were they playing? Hoof-beats approached. More riders appeared on the other side of the ford, steam pluming from the mouths of their horses. Mary stepped back from the water, terrified by the sight of yet more men coming for her out of the darkness.

One jumped down from his horse. 'Mary!'

At that voice she felt hope – the bright thing she had buried all these years – come bursting up through the layers of desolation and despair. She cried out with the strength of it, almost sinking to her knees. The man ran across the ford, his feet splashing through the water. His hood was back and she could see his face in the moonlight. It was him. It was her brother.

Edward took Mary in his arms, holding her tightly as she wept.

42

Perth, Scotland, 1312 AD

The walls of Perth towered over the moat, a mass of solid darkness against the midnight sky. The black waters were still, except for the occasional bubble or ripple as things moved below. Mist curled off the surface like smoke. It was a murky night with only a thin waxing moon to light it, and cold for May.

Robert crouched on the banks where the reeds grew tall. He heard a croak, followed by a splash, as a frog leapt to safety from the men crawling up to the water's edge. There were hundreds of men, concealed by the reeds and made one with the shadows by their dark clothes and mud-smeared skin. Robert's gaze travelled up the smooth stone face of the town walls to the battlements above. He caught the flicker of torchlight, but some distance along the walkway, towards the west gate. He thought of the message that had come to him in Turnberry, the image of the dragon stamped in wax still vivid in his mind. It seemed the information given about the town watch was right. So far, so good.

He glanced at his brother, hunkered beside him. Edward's face was daubed with mud, leaving only his eyes to glint in the gloom. His brother hadn't wanted them to come here – had protested vehemently against it in council and, when overruled, warned Robert in private that he was foolish even to consider acting on their enemy's proposal. Now they had Mary back, Edward believed they should simply renege on the deal, but Robert had no doubt his daughter, his wife and his other sisters would suffer the consequences of such betrayal. William Lamberton had spoken of the harsh conditions he and Bishop Wishart had been kept in and the change in his sister Mary told him all he needed to know of her terrible ordeal. He wouldn't risk the comfort Humphrey had promised him Marjorie and Elizabeth were being kept in. Besides, there was another, more critical, reason to act.

To the English, Perth was an artery, by which supplies could be channelled to other strongholds in their dominion, most notably Stirling. As a walled town its defences were impressive. The River Tay that ran through it allowed supplies in by sea and an escape route out. It was well garrisoned by English soldiers and by Scots loyal to them. Christiana had told him to go for the vulnerable part of his enemy and, by their own hand, the English earls involved in this conspiracy had weakened Perth – giving him information not only on the town watch, but also numbers of the garrison and where they were stationed. This deal with the devil offered the opportunity he had been waiting for.

Yet still, as he studied the walls before him, Robert couldn't help but think of that summer's evening, six years ago, when he had looked down on Perth from the fringes of Methven Wood. The English had drawn him here then, too. Was his brother right – was he making a mistake? Was the wheel about to shift again? Robert looked over his shoulder into the shadows, picking out the gleam of many eyes. Over the past years, his force had grown from a few hundred war-weary men to several thousand. He had led them all here to this place, through fire and battle, desperation and fear, hunger and heartache. It was time for one last push; time to throw caution to the wind and take back his kingdom.

Rising into a crouch, Robert moved forward, hefting the rope ladder, made by Islay's fishermen, over his shoulder. The iron grappling hook attached to the end bumped against his back. Slowly, he made his way down the bank, into the black water. The ooze beneath him shelved suddenly, but he kept his balance and kept going. He had sent a lone man across earlier to check the depth. At its deepest point the moat only came up to the chin of a medium-sized man. It was, however, freezing, snatching his breath as it washed up over his waist. He was dressed, like his foot soldiers, in hose and hide boots, with only a leather aketon for armour. All of them had forgone mail, too heavy for their task tonight.

Robert checked behind to see his men following – lords and earls, knights and peasants – moving slow and silent through the moat in the wake of their king, most up to their necks in blackness. If anyone looked down from the battlements now, he thought, they would see a tide of heads gliding towards the walls. Robert halted a few feet from the jutting base of the defences. Something switched past his thigh – an eel or a fish. The others who carried rope ladders fanned out to either side of him. He had made them practise this for days, back in Turnberry. It would be harder here, in water, but the movement was the same.

Eight rope ladders were hurled up, one after the other, over the walls. The grappling hooks made dull clinks as they struck the stone walkway beyond. Robert waited, holding his breath. No shouts of alarm sounded, no bells, no running footsteps. He pulled on the ladder, testing it was secure. The three-pronged hook held fast. Carefully, his muscles straining with the effort, the ropes twisting and creaking under his weight, Robert began to climb. His men followed, placing dirks between their teeth, swords, hammers and axes dangling from straps and sheaths. With water trickling from them, their hands and faces black with mud, it was as if the moat itself had come to life and was crawling up the walls of Perth.

Piers Gaveston pulled his hauberk over his gambeson, while his squire struggled to attach the greaves to his shins. The bell of St John's was clanging, echoed by other bells around Perth's walls, but their ringing was gradually being drowned out by the approaching roar of many men and the clash of weapons, interspersed by screams. Piers cursed and kicked out at his squire, still fumbling with the buckles of the greaves.

'They'll have overrun the town before you finish, you fat-fingered fool! Go! Saddle my horse!'

The squire fled.

As he swung his green mantle, emblazoned with six golden eagles, around his shoulders, Piers heard shouts outside, much closer now. He crossed to the window. The two-storey hall, one of several commandeered by him and his men on their arrival in Perth, looked out over the market square, partially lit by the ghostly glow of lanterns. Piers fixed on the scores of men flooding in from the main street behind a fleeing rabble of citizens, caught outside their homes. Shock jolted through him as he saw the black faces of the invaders, before he realised they were smeared with something. His own men, Henry de Bohun among them, were racing on foot to engage, joined by Scots, whose loyalty proved in no doubt as they cut their way savagely through the first few attackers. But Piers could see the enemy greatly outnumbered Perth's garrison.

Snatching up his sword, he hastened down through the building, barking at pages and servants lingering in the passages to take up any weapon to hand and follow him. Outside, there was no sign of his squire, or his horse. Piers caught sight of Henry de Bohun by the stables, engaged with a knot of black-faced attackers. There was no time to think or plan. The enemy were pouring in from all sides, fierce fighting breaking out across the square. With a roar, Piers, Earl of Cornwall and champion of countless tournaments, set off towards the incoming horde, entering the fray like a lion.

Henry de Bohun sat hunched against the stable wall, his breaths coming fast and shallow. The battle was over, but the cries of wounded men and the rough shouts of the enemy continued. Henry clenched his teeth as he pressed down on his thigh, torn open by a sword stroke. He had to staunch the bleeding. His eyes flicked to the corpse lying in the entrance. The dead man was Piers Gaveston's squire. Blood, black in the gloom, was still pumping from the man's opened scalp, cleaved by an axe Henry guessed.

Using his hands, he pushed himself across the dusty floor, sweat trickling down his cheeks. Pausing at the edge of the stable's entrance, he glanced outside. His English comrades were being rounded up, relieved of their weapons and marched down the main street. The loyalist Scots were among them, hands tied behind their backs. It appeared those of the garrison who had survived were being escorted out of Perth, allowed to leave with their lives, but nothing more. How had this happened? They were supposed to be safe here – the king had told them so.

The coast clear, Henry edged his way to the corpse. Removing the belt from around the squire's waist, he slid back out of sight and wrapped the length of leather around his thigh, buckling it with a grunt of pain. Risking another glance outside, he was wrestling with the question of whether to stay hidden or give himself up when he saw a company heading towards the stables, marching a cloaked man between them.

Henry crawled into one of the stalls and pushed the door to as the company hastened into the stables.

'Did anyone see you?'

'No.'

'You are certain? They cannot know he was taken alive.'

Henry frowned. These men were speaking French, not Scots. What was more – he had heard that last voice before.

'I am certain, my lord.'

Henry pressed his face to the crack in the stall door. He could see men moving outside. His breath caught as he saw the face of one of them. It was dark and the man's cheeks were coated in mud, but Henry knew him. It was the rebel leader himself. Robert Bruce.

There was a snort behind him. Henry looked round as a black destrier loomed out of the shadows. As the beast lowered its head and nudged at him, Henry pushed its nose away. The warhorse belonged to Piers.

The voices came again.

'Here, put this on him.'

Henry returned to the crack. The cloaked figure he had seen being marched between these men was now in view. His hood had been pulled back and Henry saw a length of cloth tied around his mouth. One of his eyes was badly swollen and blood spattered the side of his face, but the man was still recognisable. Piers Gaveston. The Gascon struggled as they tugged off the cloak that had been thrown over his shoulders and removed his mantle and surcoat, both of which displayed his arms. Holding him fast, they pulled a plain tunic over his hauberk, before wrapping the cloak back around him and pulling up the hood.

While this was being done, four of the men split off, moving into the stalls on the other side of the stables. As they led out four horses, Henry heard Robert's voice again.

'Take him straight to the border. Don't stop for anyone.'

When the first horse was ready, Piers was hauled into the saddle by two of the men. As his hands were tied to the pommel, sounds of protest came through his gag.

Robert clutched the arm of one of the men, who moved to climb up behind the Gascon. His voice was low, but Henry caught the words. 'Neil, make sure he is delivered to Lancaster himself. I don't want any misunderstanding.'

'Yes, my lord.'

The clatter of hooves drowned out all other sounds as the men rode out of the stables, Piers, hooded and gagged, among them. After they had gone, Henry leaned back against the stall door, trying to make sense of what he had just witnessed. The pain in his leg had dulled to a throb. He looked round as the destrier snorted again. Teeth gritted, Henry pushed himself upright and reached for the bridle, hanging on the stall door.

43

York Castle, England, 1312 AD

Dawn was breaking, spilling scarlet light between purple towers of cloud. Aymer de Valence stood in the window, watching the sky change. The clouds looked like thunderheads, their bruised shadows reflected in the waters of the King's Fishpool and the River Foss. It had been a humid night, without a breath of breeze, the air thick with the cloying scent of overripe fruit from the orchards. Scooping water from the basin in front of him, Aymer splashed his face. He had been awake for hours, staring at the ceiling as the sweat trickled off him to soak the sheets. So far, everything had gone to plan, but he didn't think he would be able to rest now until the deed was done.

He had been at the border with Thomas of Lancaster and Guy de Beauchamp when Piers had been brought to them by the Scots. Aymer half hoped Bruce might deliver him himself, at which point, he had decided privately, he would take action. But the man hadn't been so foolish. After Neil Campbell made the exchange, Lancaster and Warwick headed south with Piers, planning to take him to Dover where Humphrey de Bohun had arranged a ship to spirit him to France. Aymer, meanwhile, had gone to York, it being agreed one of them should be with the king when word came of Piers's disappearance, to keep the finger of blame pointed at the Scots. He had been only too happy to volunteer; keen this dangerous business would soon be over and they could return their attention to the downfall of Robert Bruce.

When Aymer arrived in York, Edward had been furious about the reported disappearance of Mary Bruce from her cage in Roxburgh

Castle. The king had already ordered the removal of Isabel Comyn from her prison at Berwick, afraid she might be liberated next. The countess was to be placed in the custody of one of the king's trusted companions, the French knight, Henry Beaumont. Mary's disappearance, however, had soon paled into insignificance when word came of the fall of Perth to Bruce's forces, along with news that several high-ranking nobles were missing in the wake of the attack, among them Henry de Bohun and Piers Gaveston. Edward, beside himself, had at once sent messengers into Scotland, offering a generous reward for the safe return of Piers. Only silence came back.

Aymer had settled down to wait for the news that Piers was on his way to France. Soon now, the king's grief would turn to rage and the Scots, God willing, would feel the full force of England's wrath.

Hearing footsteps in the passage, Aymer turned from the window. The surprised voice of his squire was followed by the gruff tones of someone else. After a moment, there was a loud banging on the door. Before Aymer could respond, it opened. The king's steward stood there, flanked by four royal soldiers.

'Sir, the king wishes to speak to you.'

Aymer's pulse quickened at this abrupt announcement, but he offered the steward a frown and a quizzical smile. 'At this hour?'

'Right away, sir.'

'Then, you must excuse me while I dress more appropriately for such an audience.'

'Now, Sir Aymer. The king insists.'

Aymer bristled, his face flushing, but seeing the tight expression on the steward's face and the hands of the soldiers on the pommels of their swords, he realised he had no choice but to obey. His smile gone, he strode to the door, pausing to grab his robe from the clothes perch. Pulling the garment on over his undershirt and hose, he followed the steward out of the guest lodgings towards the king's quarters, beyond which the walls of the keep on its high mound, were stained with the dawn's stormy light.

King Edward was waiting for him. He turned abruptly as the steward ushered Aymer inside his chamber. Aymer was at once struck by the change in the king. These past few days Edward had been feverish in his anxiety over Piers's disappearance, alternating between begging his men to track down Piers, praying fervently for his safe return and castigating himself for sending him to Perth in the first place. Now, however, despite his bloodshot eyes and dishevelled appearance, Edward looked poised. Dangerous. Aymer thought the young man had never looked so much like his father. His unease swelled.

'Where is he?' The king's voice crackled with suppressed emotion.

'My lord?'

'Piers? Where is Piers?'

'I'm not sure I understand what—'

'*By God, Aymer, don't you play the fool with me!*' As Edward roared this, he raised his fists and started towards the earl.

Aymer stepped back.

'Henry de Bohun saw you!' Spittle flecked from Edward's mouth. 'He saw you with Thomas and Guy – saw you take Piers from the Scots. Henry arrived last night, half dead from his wounds, barely able to stay in the saddle, but determined I should know the traitors in my midst!'

At the word *traitor*, fear flooded Aymer, bringing with it images of William Wallace on the executioner's slab, John of Atholl hauled up on that high gallows and Niall Bruce's neck being pressed down on the block. He knew he was caught. There was only one thing to do. Aymer collapsed on his knees before the furious king, clasping his hands together in pleading prayer. 'My lord king, I beg your forgiveness. I never should have gone along with their plan. I thought they were acting in the best interests of the realm – but they were wrong. I see that now.'

'Whose plan? Tell me!'

As Aymer gave up the names of the men who had met in Humphrey de Bohun's castle, Edward's face changed from livid red to ashen white. He stumbled back, raising a hand to his brow. 'Dear God. You are all against me?'

'My lord, we—'

'Where were they taking him?' Edward said, rounding on him. 'Henry followed them, but lost them on the road.'

'To France. Lancaster arranged for him to be placed in custody there.'

'This was my cousin's plan? He is at the heart of this?' Edward stared down at Aymer. 'My God, what have you done?' Before the earl could answer, the king was shouting for his steward.

Blacklow Hill, England, 1312 AD

They rode north, leaving Warwick Castle behind them. The distant torchlight on the walls flickered faintly through the rushing darkness of the woods. As the ground rose, snatches of sky appeared between the breaks in the canopy. A sliver of moon hung in the blackness like a torn fingernail. Catching a flash of pale wings, Thomas of Lancaster looked up to see an owl swoop over him. He felt the knot of tension in his body coil tighter.

All the way from the border, Thomas had felt as though he were being watched. On the journey, he insisted their company sleep outside, not wanting to risk being seen in inns or monasteries, even though they were unknown in the towns and none of them wore anything to identify them. Guy de Beauchamp had mocked him for his caution, but had gone along with him – well aware of the risk they were taking. It hadn't been a hardship, the June nights mild and dry, but the men had been glad to reach Warwick that afternoon, with its promise of soft beds and warm food. Their prisoner secured, they had feasted well, Thomas making sure the pages kept Guy's goblet filled. The inebriated earl and his men had retired early, giving Thomas the chance he had been waiting for since they left the border.

The horses slowed, their heads bowing with the effort of the climb as they neared the crest of the hill. The men leaned forward in the saddles to make it easier for them.

'Sir?'

Thomas looked round as one of his knights called to him. The man was leading a palfrey on which sat their prisoner, his head covered with a hood, hands tied to the pommel.

'Let us be done with it,' the knight urged in a low voice. 'We're far enough from the castle, surely?'

Thomas could hear the unease in the man's voice. He had to do this now, before any of them backed out. Or, indeed, before he did. He had planned to do the deed beyond the town walls, where it would not be interrupted or witnessed, but although that had been the case for the past mile he had kept on going. The moment he halted his horse, the moment he would have to commit to what he had decided to do months ago. That night in Humphrey de Bohun's castle, the others had all gone along with his plan, trusting his word. They hadn't known he never intended to keep it.

Ahead, the ground levelled.

'Here,' said Thomas, reining in his horse.

The crown of the hill was cast in the moon's spectral light. Trees surrounded them in a ring, surging in the breeze. Dismounting, Thomas watched as his men untied the prisoner and hauled him from the saddle. Two of them forced him to his knees.

Thomas walked towards the kneeling man, the weight of his sword hanging heavy from his hip. Earlier, he'd had his squire whet the blade. It scraped against the leather as he drew it from the scabbard. 'Take off his hood.'

Piers Gaveston shook his head wildly as the hood came away, desperate to see where he had been brought, and by whom. He was gagged, but his eyes spoke volumes as they fixed on Thomas. He went still, seeing the sword in the earl's hand. After a pause, Piers tried to speak, but the words, muted by the gag, were incomprehensible.

Thomas stared at him, feeling the tension tighten every sinew in his body. Despite his disgust and his hatred of this man, this wasn't the same as facing an enemy on the field of battle, where death was roaring and eager. Death, here, was silent, reluctant – went by the name of murder.

The plan Guy, Aymer, Humphrey and the others had agreed to – sentencing the king's lover to perpetual imprisonment – Thomas had never believed in himself. Edward would find out; some day he would find out and Piers would be brought back to his side. He was certain of it. Thomas gripped the hilt of his sword. Sweat broke out on his brow. There was only one way to deal with this disease at the heart of their realm. The corruption must be excised, once and for all.

Piers struggled madly as Thomas stepped towards him, but the two knights held him firm. Somewhere in the woods surrounding Blacklow Hill an owl screeched, covering the muted cry as Piers Gaveston, Earl of Cornwall, was run through.

44

Lochmaben, Scotland, 1313 AD

The keep was a fractured finger of stone, pointing skyward. Charred remains of buildings lay scattered around the base of the motte; blackened timbers of barns sticking up like the ribs of some great corpse that weather and time had stripped of flesh. Robert stood in the ruins, staring at what was left of the castle that had once been the heart of the lordship of Annandale, stronghold of his grandfather and the place where he had left behind boyhood and become a hunter, a fighter, a man – the place where he made a promise to his grandfather to uphold their claim to the throne, and where this journey had begun.

The Bruce family had moved their chief castle to Lochmaben almost two centuries ago, after the river swallowed their fortress at Annan, the waters said to have risen at the command of St Malachy, in vengeance for the lord's betrayal. Now, looking at the devastation wrought by the English in more recent times, Robert thought of the Irish saint's curse echoing down the years. Had that one treacherous act of his ancestor been as a stone in a pool? Were these still the ripples of that? And what of his own sins: his lies and betrayals, the spilling of John Comyn's blood at the altar? How far and how wide would those yet spread?

There was a rustle of undergrowth and Fionn appeared. The hound trotted over, strands of reeds caught in his shaggy coat. Robert guessed he had been hunting by the loch. It was midsummer and the evening sky was a washed-out blue. The twilight cast the ruins in an eerie glow, making them seem even more forlorn. He wondered if he would ever see this place whole again; wasn't even sure he wanted to. To build over this corpse of a castle seemed somehow disrespectful. It had become a monument, a tombstone for his family – a reminder both of what had been lost and what he had yet to regain.

'My lord.'

Robert turned as Nes approached through the broken line of what had been the castle palisade.

'Sir Gilbert de la Hay has come, my lord. He has word from the siege camp at Stirling.'

Robert felt a jolt of anticipation. 'It has fallen?'

'The messenger didn't say, my lord – only that Sir Gilbert must speak with you urgently. Our man was on his way to Dumfries to alert you when he saw us here.'

Robert set off across the debris-strewn ground, back to his horse and the men who had accompanied him from Dumfries, where he had been accepting pledges of fealty from local landowners. Dumfries had fallen to him in the spring, its garrison finally starved out. Soon after, he had taken the Isle of Man with the aid of Lachlan MacRuarie and Angus MacDonald. Caerlaverock and Lochmaben had followed, along with Buittle, once chief stronghold of John Balliol. Now, the entire south-western approach to Scotland was under his control. The English had lost the Solway Firth.

All these victories had been made possible by the English themselves, deeply embroiled in their own internal struggles this past year, following the unprecedented execution of Piers Gaveston. It was an outcome Robert hadn't foreseen when making the secret pact with the former Knights of the Dragon, but one that had favoured him greatly. With risk of retaliation a distant threat – the barons and their king at war with one another – he had used England's turmoil to his advantage, finally fixing his sights on one of the great eastern castles: mighty Stirling, the key to the kingdom.

When Perth fell to his forces, he had razed it, the royal burgh too vital a staging ground to be allowed to remain. Its destruction left Stirling isolated. The cliff-top fortress, under the command of Sir Philip Moubray, a Scottish knight loyal to the English king, had become an island, cut off from aid. In the spring, Robert sent his brother to surround it; his intent, to starve Stirling's garrison into submission.

As he approached his men, waiting for him beyond the castle ruins, Robert felt his anticipation build. If Stirling had indeed fallen, then the struggle to reclaim his kingdom was almost won. Of the other chief strongholds in enemy hands, only Edinburgh, Roxburgh and Berwick remained. When they fell the realm would be in his control and, then, he could concentrate on freeing his family. He now felt satisfied he had made the right choice in appointing his brother as commander of the siege. Edward, whom he had made Earl of Carrick and Lord of Galloway, had become increasingly impulsive, determined to fight this conflict his own way. Head of a growing war-band of his own, he had made several unauthorised assaults on secondary fortresses, one of which almost ended in disaster. Robert had sent him to Stirling to keep him fixed on one target. Now, it appeared, he was justified in that decision.

By the time he and his party rode in through the gates of Lochmaben's New Castle, the first stars were splinters of light in the eastern sky. The compound, built by Edward Longshanks using material from the old castle, was surrounded by earthen ramparts topped with a palisade. A wooden fort stood at the centre. Robert had been using it as a base to store supplies and the plunder taken from Dumfries and elsewhere. He saw some of Gilbert de la Hay's men outside talking to the garrison. They greeted their king with respectful nods as he entered the fort.

Gilbert de la Hay was waiting for him in the main chamber, along with Thomas Randolph, who Robert had left in charge in his absence. His half-nephew had changed out of all recognition these past few years and had become one of his most trusted captains. For his loyal service, Robert had made him Earl of Moray, a new earldom created out of the lands of Buchan and Badenoch.

Thomas and Gilbert both looked concerned and Robert's anticipation of good news from Stirling curdled at their expressions.

'My lord king,' Gilbert greeted, rising from the table he had been sitting at. The late June sun had turned his mop of hair white and burned his nose an angry red.

'What is it, Gilbert?' Robert asked sharply.

'Sir Edward has agreed terms of surrender with Stirling's commander.'

Robert frowned. 'But this is good news. Dear God, Gilbert, by your face I thought—'

'He made a deal, my lord,' Gilbert cut in quickly.

'A deal?'

'Perhaps challenge would be the better term. Sir Philip Moubray sent an envoy to your brother's camp, begging him to lift the siege. Moubray asked for a respite in which to seek the aid of King Edward. He swore, if the English king did not come north to relieve him, he would surrender Stirling without a fight.'

'Tell me my brother turned him down?' said Robert in a low voice.

'My lord, I'm afraid he agreed. In fact, he told Moubray to tell the English they have until next Midsummer's Day. A full year. If they fail to appear before the walls of Stirling Castle to lay claim to it by then, Moubray and the garrison will give themselves up to you.'

'He called them out?' murmured Robert. He crossed to the table, which was covered in maps and charts, marked with the castles and territories he had captured these past four years. He went to sit, then changed his mind and remained standing, fists balled on the table.

Thomas glanced at Gilbert, then spoke into the silence. 'My lord, the English are surely too involved in their own struggles to agree to Moubray's request for aid?'

Robert said nothing. He stared down at the maps beneath his hands. He'd had men patrolling the border all these years, watching for sign of the enemy. Had King Edward marched north against him he would have done what he had during the last campaign: scorch the earth and retreat beyond the Forth. His victory over Aymer de Valence's forces at Loudoun Hill had been remarkable, as Wallace's triumph at Stirling Bridge had been. But other than that one pitched battle, in which God and fortune had blessed him, his war had been fought by skirmish and ambush, sea raid and night attack. No matter his strength of arms, no matter the loyalty of his men, Robert knew his army could not compare with the force of England. Battles that pitched foot soldiers against the iron might of their heavy cavalry were doomed to fail. Wallace and ten thousand Scots had learned that lesson – it was written in blood in the fields of Falkirk.

'My lord?'

Robert looked at his nephew, who repeated his question. He shook his head in response. No matter how divided their enemy was, this, he knew, was something that could unite them. By this deal, made in his name, his brother had effectively gone to the border and challenged the English to a duel. To ignore it would render King Edward a coward. The king's honour was now at stake.

'No,' Robert murmured. 'They will come.'

Pleshey Castle, England, 1313 AD

'Welcome home, my lord.'

Humphrey nodded to his steward as the man crossed the yard to greet him. 'Thank you, Ranulf.' Around him, his men dismounted, removing caps and gulping at wine skins. It was warm for late September and they had ridden many miles that day.

'How fared you in Westminster, sir?'

Humphrey noted the apprehension in Ranulf's voice. Such anxiety had become characteristic of his staff over the past year, all of them fearing what the outcome of the rift between their lord and their king might be. There had been times – England teetering on the brink of civil war – when not only their livelihoods, but their lives had been in danger. He smiled to reassure the older man. 'Do not worry, Ranulf. I have made my peace with the king.' Humphrey slid off his gloves. 'He still needs my service against the Scots.'

Ranulf nodded. 'When will the muster take place?'

'In the spring. We'll receive the summons in the next few weeks.' Humphrey handed his dust-stained gloves to the steward. 'Is Lady Elizabeth in her chambers?'

'I believe she is in the garden. Shall I have her brought to you?'

'No, thank you.'

Leaving his steward to see to the rest of the company, Humphrey headed across the yard, through the arched door in the wall that surrounded the kitchen gardens. Stooping beneath trailing strands of ivy, he saw a guard loitering on the pathway that ran around the beds of flowers that bordered a lawn dotted with pear and plum trees. The guard had his thumbs hooked in his belt and appeared to be enjoying the sunshine. Some distance away, his charge was sitting on a bench reading.

'My lord.' The guard straightened as he saw Humphrey.

Humphrey nodded to him. 'You may go, Nicolas.'

As the guard ducked through the door, closing it behind him, the figure on the bench looked up from her book.

Elizabeth smiled as Humphrey headed over, but her expression held the same uneasy question as Ranulf's. She went to rise as he approached, but he gestured for her to stay, acutely aware this dance between them was still so faltering. Elizabeth was a queen, but she was his prisoner. She was his enemy, yet she was his lover. He sat on the bench beside her. The air was sweetened by fennel and sage.

Elizabeth studied him. After a moment she nodded, as if he had answered a question. 'It is happening, isn't it? You are going to war?'

'Yes.'

'When?'

Humphrey paused. A year ago he never would have spoken to her about such matters, but many things had changed in that time. Her hand was splayed on the bench beside him. Reaching down, he threaded his fingers through hers. 'Next spring – before the truce made for Stirling runs out.'

Elizabeth shook her head. 'I thought, with the Earl of Lancaster against him, that the king would not—'

'Sir Thomas and Sir Guy have been accepted into the king's peace.'

Humphrey took in her surprise. There had been similar reactions at court when the king had made the announcement. For a time, it had seemed such a thing would not be possible, despite all the mediations and negotiations that had taken place over the past sixteen months since the execution of Piers Gaveston.

The bloody demise of the Earl of Cornwall, whose gored and beheaded body had been found by four shoemakers on Blacklow Hill, had sent shock waves throughout England. Aymer de Valence, throwing himself on the king's mercy, had revealed the identities of those involved in the conspiracy to abduct Piers, which ended in the man's murder. Edward, mad with grief and rage, pointed the finger of blame directly at Lancaster and Warwick. Guy de Beauchamp vehemently denied any part in it, but the king was out for blood and was determined that all who had plotted against him be punished severely.

In little doubt the deed had been done at Lancaster's hand, Humphrey and the other barons had been furious at being taken for fools, but nonetheless had stood firm against the king, refusing to relinquish their lands or their freedom for what they maintained had been done in the best interests of the realm.

For a time, civil war seemed inevitable, but then the first steps towards peace had been brokered by King Philippe of France and Edward's nephew, the young Earl of Gloucester, Gilbert de Clare. The reconciliation between the king and the barons had been finalised at the autumn parliament, but Humphrey knew it was a fragile peace at best – made only for the sake of the war to which the king had been forced, by the challenge of the Scots, to turn his attention. There was hatred between Edward and Lancaster that Humphrey believed would not now be satisfied, except with blood.

Elizabeth shook her head. 'I cannot believe he forgave his cousin.'

'We all have a common enemy now.'

Elizabeth looked at him, her eyes sharp. 'My husband, you mean.' She removed her hand from his. 'Will you be leading the army? It is your honour as constable, is it not?'

'It is.' Humphrey looked out over the gardens. 'But I'm not certain of my place yet. I may have earned the king's forgiveness. His trust will be harder won.'

'So you will prove yourself in battle against Robert? Win back your spurs?'

Elizabeth's voice was tight. Without waiting for an answer, she stood and walked over to the flower beds. Plump red roses decorated the thorny bushes. Bees were busy among them, gathering the last of the pollen before the flowers withered with autumn's chill.

Humphrey went to her and put his hands on her shoulders, feeling the tension in her body. 'This war is inescapable,' he murmured. 'Sooner or later, we knew we would be going back.'

Elizabeth turned, looking up at him. 'It is you I am afraid for, Humphrey. But what does that make me?' She raised a hand to her head, laughed humourlessly. 'My husband made me a rebel and you have made me an adulteress.'

Humphrey wrapped his arms around her. He'd been beset by his own demons of guilt and castigation since their affair began, but he had ignored them for the sake of the miraculous feeling of his soul's reawakening, after the long night of grief caused by Bess's death.

'And if you win?' she murmured, reaching up to grasp his arm. 'What happens to Marjorie and my sisters-in-law? What happens to Robert? To me?'

'I do not know,' he answered truthfully. 'Let us not speak of it. Not yet. It is months away. We still have the winter.'

Humphrey closed his eyes, the sun warm on his face. If only they could stay in this garden. If only this was another time, another place – where his destiny and hers weren't entwined with that of a man who had once been his friend; a man he was now duty-bound to meet with a sword in his hand.

45

The Torwood, Scotland, 1314 AD

A round a circle of fire in the heart of the ancient forest a host of men were gathered. The flames lit their faces as they talked among themselves, passing around wine skins and bowls of oat-thickened stew, with the ease of men who have known one another for years. Above them, branches of trees formed a tangled ceiling.

For Robert, seated with them, a tree stump for his throne, the forest was just another hall. He had taken counsel and broken bread with these men in many such places these past eight years since his enthronement – in the ruins of sea-girt fortresses, on lonely, heather-clad moors, in the snow-wreathed heights of mountains, on wave-dashed beaches under a vault of stars. He had sat with them in prayer and mourning, in defeat and triumph, in sorrow and exultation, their union bound by the bonds of this war.

As he nursed his wine, his gaze moved over them: Earl Malcolm of Lennox and Sir Neil Campbell, Lord Gilbert de la Hay, Nes and Cormac, Walter Stewart with the mantle of the kingdom on his young shoulders, and William Lamberton with those keen eyes, one ice-blue the other pearl white, that seemed able to see into men's souls. There, too, were the heroes of the hour, Thomas Randolph and James Douglas, fresh from daring assaults on Edinburgh and Roxburgh castles, won in the spring by extraordinary feats of courage and cunning. Tales of their bravery were being lauded far and wide, Douglas's use of a herd of cows to conceal him and his men from Roxburgh's garrison leading to jokes that Scotland's cattle were being employed in the fight against the English. Robert hadn't thought it possible, but now, of all the great strongholds that had been in enemy hands, only Stirling remained.

Robert looked at his brother, whose challenge last summer at the gates of the castle had brought them all here. After learning of the pact, he had reprimanded Edward severely, but the two of them had since settled into a tense truce. Even with his impetuousness, Edward, his only surviving brother, was still one of his most competent captains. Often, in recent years, Robert had seen a hungry, discontented look in his brother's eyes, as though he were a man searching for something to satisfy him, but not knowing what would. Now, that look was gone. Edward had wanted this confrontation.

'My lord.'

Robert looked round as one of his knights leaned in to speak with him.

'More have arrived.'

Seeing a company of men heading through the trees, Robert rose to meet them. The other men around the campfire halted their conversations, turning with calls of joy as Angus MacDonald approached. The Lord of Islay was swathed in a black cloak that swung from his broad shoulders. His bright blue eyes gleamed in the flames of the torches carried by his men.

Angus dropped to one knee before Robert. 'My lord king.'

Grinning broadly, Robert raised him up and embraced him. 'It is good to see you, my friend.' Looking beyond the lord, he saw more figures appearing in the forest gloom, scores of them, some leading mules with packs strapped to their sides. 'And you come with an army it seems.'

'Four hundred from Kintyre and Islay. Some from Argyll too.' Angus smiled. 'And I am not the only lord come from the Isles.'

Now, among the men, Robert saw a motley crowd of scarred, muscular figures, clad in leather aketons and short tunics, many bare-legged and all with great axes hanging from straps on their backs. The galloglass had come. As he looked for sign of their captain, his gaze fell on a slender figure emerging through the trees, her red hair flaming in the torchlight.

Christiana smiled at his surprise, coming forward to kneel and kiss his hand.

Robert saw that Kerald was with her, with others he recognised from his months out in the Western Isles.

'My brothers bid you well, my lord. They send these gifts.' Turning, Christiana motioned to Kerald.

The man's Gaelic rang through the trees as he called the men leading the mules to come forward. Removing the sacks from the animals, they laid them on the ground. As one was opened, Robert saw it was filled with short swords, most of them cleaver-like falchions, the blade of each bound in cloth to stop them scything through the sack. Edward Bruce and Neil Campbell moved closer to inspect them.

'Arms and armour,' Christiana told them. 'English made.'

Robert nodded his gratitude. It was, he knew, as much as he could hope for from Lachlan MacRuarie. Unless it suited him personally, the captain would rarely join a fight on land.

'This is from me.' Taking an object from Kerald, Christiana handed it to him.

Unwrapping the cloth, Robert exposed a short-handled axe. It was a beautiful weapon, its crescent blade of gleaming steel inscribed with the runes he had seen carved on Viking graves on Barra. The wooden shaft was bone-smooth. It looked old, but well-cared for.

'My father's,' Christiana explained. 'It was a gift from the King of Norway.' She motioned to the runes. 'It is called the Blade of the Isles.'

'Thank you.' Robert met her gaze. 'You have given me so much else already.' He hoped she knew the depth of his words.

Christiana kept her green eyes on him for a long moment, seeming to understand. But then her smile faded. 'My lord, I bear something else from my brother – a word of warning from the waters. The fleet under command of John MacDougall of Argyll has been ferrying large numbers of men from Dublin to England since the spring. Lachlan has learned that Irish chieftains in the west have even received missives, summoning them to join King Edward's army.'

Robert ignored the voices of concern among his men at the news. Cormac, he saw, had stepped forward. 'What was their response?'

'As a lady, I cannot repeat it. Suffice to say, the Irish will not serve the English king.'

A few gruff laughs sounded. Robert didn't share his men's amusement. 'What of Sir Richard de Burgh?'

'I am sorry to say the galleys of Ulster have been seen among the fleet.'

Robert let this sink in. He had hoped, fervently, that the letters he had sent to his father-in-law would have prevented such action. The formidable earl could bring a substantial number of men to the fight, as well as the necessary supplies of grain with which to provision King Edward's army. Gilbert and the others were cutting in now, asking more questions of Angus and Christiana, turning to one another to discuss the implications of these tidings.

Robert had presided over many such counsels these past days, but now he felt the need to walk and think. He passed the axe to Nes, who took it carefully. 'See our guests are given whatever they need.' He clasped Angus's hand. 'We will talk later, my friend.' Turning to Christiana, Robert motioned through the trees. 'Walk with me, my lady?'

Moving out of the glade, he led her through the vast camp that had sprung up in the forest these past weeks. The Torwood, through which the Roman road from Edinburgh cut its arrow-straight path to Stirling, was the point of muster for his army. Sentries murmured greetings as he passed. He had scores of them stationed all around the edges of the camp and along the road itself.

It was mid-May and the evenings were light and mild, but beneath the dense canopy the gloom of night was thick. Campfires flickered off through the trees, will-o'-the-wisps of flame, against which the figures of men were silhouettes. Smells of leaves and earth mingled with the sharp odour of wood-smoke and the pungency of food and dung. Latrine pits had been dug and screened with hanging cloths. Carcasses of venison and bunches of skinned coneys hung from branches, the flesh drying brown. Horses were pastured in leafy clearings, bags of oats and bundles of hay stacked close by. There were five hundred of the animals, a mixture of palfreys, coursers, hobbies and rounceys under the command of the marshal, Sir Robert Keith, who had joined Robert's company several years ago and had been recommended to him by James Stewart. There were a few tents, here and there, but most of the shelters were of latticed twigs covered with leaves. A number of women moved among the shelters – mistresses and wives, maids and laundresses – but for the most part the camp was filled with men.

There were young fishermen and cowherds, as thin as saplings, who had not yet seen battle, but were eager to prove themselves. There were muscled carters, ploughmen and sure-legged drovers, butchers and blacksmiths, burgesses and squires – men who had been crushed by the fist of Edward Longshanks, only to struggle through the bitter war that followed, pitting Scot against Scot. There were archers from Selkirk Forest, who had fought under William Wallace; men with fire in their bellies. There were men from Ireland and Wales who had come to fulfil the promise of the prophecy and to fight under him, their new Arthur, his legend reclaimed from a covetous English king. There were earls and knights: scarred veterans of the war that had begun eighteen years earlier.

The fiery cross, sent out in the spring, had called them all to this place and, by the thousand, they had come – all the strata of his realm, from the highest to the lowest. Robert had kept Affraig's counsel close to his heart these past years and now he stood among his people; a man who had fought and lost with them. He wasn't a distant ruler, shut up in a glittering tower. Truly, he was one of them – King of all Scots.

'How many men do you have?' Christiana asked, halting on the edge of a glade, which had become a makeshift armoury. Men sat knitting links of mail and fixing flights to arrows. More were busy fitting iron spear tips to twelve-foot shafts. There was a huge pile of these weapons nearby.

'With Lord Angus? Over six thousand foot. Five hundred light horse.'

Her eyes narrowed in question as she looked at him. 'So, you plan to fight?'

Robert led her away, out of earshot of the men working on the weapons. He paused by an outcrop of mossy rocks, through which a burn bubbled. 'My brother, Thomas and James, Neil, others – all wish it.' She waited for him to continue. 'I do not doubt the courage of my men – that has been proven beyond measure – or their skill, for I've trained them mercilessly these past months. But infantry cannot stand for long against heavy cavalry, no matter how brave their hearts and the strength of their arms. King Edward's army will be far greater than mine. If I had any doubt of that before, your tidings that Ulster will join him put paid to it.' He shook his head.

'You told me William Wallace only had foot soldiers when he fought them beneath Stirling Castle and you bested Aymer de Valence at Loudoun Hill without a horse among your army.'

'But against those two victories I can set a dozen defeats. None worse than Falkirk.' Robert leaned against one of the rocks, the damp stone cooling his back. 'Ten thousand men lost their lives only a few miles from where we now stand. That battle broke Wallace. After that loss, he couldn't command the respect of the realm. I have spent eight years fighting for just that. I cannot throw it away, all to satisfy the reckless word of my brother.'

'What will you do? They are coming for you regardless.'

'I will lure them to an ambush; use my forces to pick off as many of their number as I can, then withdraw. The English will find themselves deep in my lands with Stirling their only base. I have razed every other castle they could take and my people have scorched the land and driven cattle into the mountains. The enemy will soon be forced back south to find food. When they are gone, I will lay siege to Stirling until it yields. This time, there will be no pact.'

As he spoke the words, Robert realised the conviction of his decision. James Stewart may have counselled him to throw caution to the wind, but that did not mean he should throw sense there too. He would not undo all his careful strategy in one heroic, doomed clash of arms. Reaching out, he took Christiana's hands in his. 'But I am done with talk tonight.'

He drew her to him and kissed her, gratefully losing himself in the soft wetness of her mouth and the warmth of her body, pressed to his. They stayed entwined like this for some time, before he drew back and kissed her brow. Closing his eyes, Robert exhaled and rested his forehead on her shoulder.

Christiana moved in against him, holding him.

Edinburgh, Scotland, 1314 AD

Humphrey came awake to see his squire clutching his shoulder. He sat, wincing at the pain that flared through his body. 'What is it, Hugh?'

'Sir Gilbert is leaving, sir.'

'What?' Humphrey pushed himself to his feet, bent under the low dome of the tent. 'How late is the hour?'

'It is dawn, sir.'

'Halt him.'

With a nod, Hugh ducked out through the tent flaps.

Humphrey thrust his hands roughly through his sweat-slick hair, gathering himself. He'd only had a few hours' rest, having spent most of the night in a war council with the king. Yesterday, he had shaved and washed for the first time in weeks, but his mouth felt gritty with road dust and his skin was sore, burned by the late June sun. It was two days from midsummer – two days from the deadline and still more than thirty miles between them and Stirling. Crouching to grab his cloak from the pile of his armour, Humphrey disturbed a scrap of blue silk. Elizabeth had tied it around his arm as they said goodbye in the courtyard of Pleshey Castle. He reached out and touched the favour, before rising, his jaw tight. Heading out of the tent, he swung the cloak over his undershirt and hose.

Dawn was breaking across Edinburgh. The sky, which had barely got dark, was a cloudless turquoise and augured another gruelling march in the heat of the coming day. The first rays of sun gleamed on the crags of the rock on which the castle perched. The fortress, high above him, was a ruin, its towers and walls broken and blackened by fire. Crows crowded the fractured battlements, picking over what was left of the bodies of those who had fallen in the Scots' attack. It was yet another totem of destruction.

The English had seen many such sights on their way north, marching through lands blighted by Bruce's raids. In Northumberland they found whole settlements deserted, but for a few starving desperates who begged aid from the great train of men and wagons rumbling through, some falling to their knees at the sight of the baggage train, carrying cages of poultry, casks of wine, sacks of oats, wheat and barley, along with tents and rugs, armour and lances. A few joined the army: skinny boys looking for pay as infantrymen, women selling their bodies to road-weary soldiers, pardoners and healers offering up more dubious services. These followers now clustered around the edges of the vast English camp, like scavengers hoping for scraps.

Humphrey strode through the camp, spread out on meadows around the royal burgh, cast in the gauzy light of the rising sun. Wagons, horses and men, punctuated here and there by the tents of the barons and shrouded with a fog of smoke, stretched as far as the eye could see, almost to the docks at Leith, where the masts of many ships were just visible. While the king had marched up the Great North Road from Westminster, these vessels had followed by sea, carrying more supplies.

Across the camp, hundreds of standards displayed the arms of the nobles who had come to fight. A swathe of blue and white stripes

marked the retinue of Aymer de Valence, who had recently been reap-
pointed Lieutenant of Scotland. Black lions were dotted about the
enclave of Richard de Burgh, the Earl of Ulster, joined by a large contingent from his lands in Ireland. There were also a number of Scottish
banners here, bearing the devices of Ingram de Umfraville, a former
guardian of Scotland, the Earl of Angus and young John Comyn, Lord
of Badenoch, son of the man murdered by Robert Bruce.

The like of this army, formed of three thousand cavalry and over
fifteen thousand infantry, hadn't been seen in Scotland for years, but
by all accounts it needed to be, for reports from those Scots still loyal
to King Edward informed them that Robert Bruce had been gathering large numbers of men in the woods south of Stirling. Edward
hadn't come just to answer the challenge of the Scots and save the
castle: he had come to destroy the enemy and their rebel leader once
and for all. The king needed this victory. Despite the peace made with
his barons at the autumn parliament, the rifts in his realm remained,
starkly evident in the absence of many of his earls from the field.
Thomas of Lancaster, Guy de Beauchamp and Henry Percy, along
with Arundel, Surrey and Oxford, had sent the obligatory number of
men, but no more. They themselves had not come.

Humphrey, with Aymer de Valence, Robert Clifford and Ralph de
Monthermer, was one of the few involved in the conspiracy against
Gaveston who had joined this campaign. Despite everything that had
happened – despite the lies Longshanks had told him and the weakness of his son – he felt duty-bound to serve. He had devoted his life
to the crown and his father had died honourably in service to it. For
him, the call to arms had been one he hadn't been able to ignore.
Even so, he had still borne the brunt of the king's anger.

The king's lack of faith in him – or perhaps venom towards him –
had been made clear in his decision to appoint Gilbert de Clare
commander of the vanguard and, worse, joint constable of the army,
a role that was Humphrey's hereditary right, passed down from his
father. Swallowing his pride, he had tried his best to work with the
king's nephew, but the arrogant young earl was making that task
increasingly difficult.

Approaching Gloucester's camp, through crowds of infantry
slumped around low-burning fires, Humphrey saw it had already
been dismantled, Gloucester's servants strapping bags on pack-horses
and kicking earth on the fires. Half the earl's knights were mounted

on their caparisoned destriers, armed in bulky coats-of-plates, mail hauberks, greaves and gauntlets. Their shields, slung over their backs, were painted with their lord's arms – three scarlet chevrons on gold. Squires would bear their helms and lances. There were other companies here too, all part of the vanguard, formed of four hundred mounted men. Among them, Humphrey caught sight of Gilbert's stepfather, Ralph de Monthermer, and his own nephew, Henry de Bohun, one of Gloucester's closest friends.

Feeling a fresh spike of anger, he marched the last few yards to where Gilbert de Clare was mounted on his warhorse, a tan stallion from Andalusia. Hugh was there talking to the earl, who seemed focused on getting his squire to adjust his horse's girth strap.

'Sir Gilbert.'

The young man turned at Humphrey's curt call. He feigned a smile that didn't reach his eyes. 'Sir Humphrey.' He looked him up and down, appraising the state of his dress. 'Will you not be joining us?'

'I wasn't aware we were leaving,' said Humphrey, trying to keep his tone measured.

'The king wanted us to set off as soon as the light broke. We must make haste if we are to relieve Stirling's garrison in time. Were you not told? I swear I sent messengers to all the men of the vanguard.'

'Mine must have gone astray.'

Gilbert shifted in the saddle and glanced at his squire. 'That will do.' He shortened the reins, pulling the horse's head up sharply. 'I would advise you to hurry, Sir Humphrey, we cannot wait for stragglers.' His lip curled. 'Not when there's a slaughter of Scots to be had.'

Pricking his spurs at the warhorse's sides, Gloucester urged the animal into a trot. Those already mounted followed him, others swung up into their saddles. As Humphrey moved back out of the way, he caught the gaze of his nephew, but Henry rode on past him without word. They had barely spoken since his part in the plot against Piers had been discovered.

Calling for Hugh to follow him, Humphrey, fuming, strode back to his own camp, passing scores of infantry, who were slowly rising with the dawn, the toll the forced marches were taking plain in their haggard faces.

From behind the cover of a cart, Alexander Seton watched Humphrey de Bohun stride past, the earl's face like thunder. It had been years since they had seen one another, but he didn't doubt the man would recognise him. It was, he knew, hard to forget the face of someone who has threatened to kill you. Up until now, the vanguard, middle-guard and rearguard of the cavalry had been so many miles ahead of the columns of infantry there had been little risk of being spotted.

Alexander watched Humphrey pass by the camp of Aymer de Valence. Last night, when his company had arrived and he had seen those blue and white stripes, it had taken a fierce effort of will not to go looking for Pembroke – the man who reneged on his word and executed his cousin. Alexander waited until Humphrey was gone, before returning to his fellow soldiers.

'Looking for something good to break your fast with?' asked Luke. The burly miller from Kent held up a crust of bread in question as Alexander squatted down by the fire.

'Just having a piss.'

Luke tore off half the bread and handed it to him. 'The rats in my mill eat better fare.'

'We'll be grateful for it later,' murmured Nigel, a spindly-armed mercer's apprentice from Suffolk. 'I heard our good captain saying we'll be marching twenty miles today.' Nigel's eyes darted to the captain who led their company of one hundred men, shouting from the comfort of his saddle for them to move their damn legs.

Alexander, chewing on the dry crust of bread, heard several of the others curse bitterly at this. The forced marches through the hot days had made their muscles sing with pain and cut their feet, clad for the most part in soft hide shoes, to bloody ribbons. Most men on this campaign had been pressed into service by their local sheriffs. Those who could afford it had bribed their way out, leaving the poorest and weakest of their districts to make up the numbers required by the king's summons. When asked, Alexander had told Luke and the others that he too had been forced, but the truth was that when the commis-sioners of array came to the market cross at Cheapside he had been one of the first to volunteer.

Using coins won in a cockfight he bought himself a sword, his own having gone years ago to pay his debtors. It was a falchion – the sword of an infantryman – and one of inferior quality at that, but it was more than many of these men had. Some, it was true, were skilled fighters, such as the corps of crossbowmen from Bristol, the spear-men from Ireland and the longbowmen from south Wales. But most

– called up from Kent and Sussex, Yorkshire and Devon – were untrained and untried. Only a few had armour, just the odd stained gambeson or ill-fitting helm among them. The one thing all of them did have was a white band of cloth, emblazoned with the red cross of St George, tied around their upper arms and worn with pride and reverence; as if this emblem would somehow protect them against the enemy, in place of armour or a weapon. Alexander had one too. It bound his arm, always in his vision.

'Do you think the rumours about the Scots are true?'

Alexander glanced round at the question to see one of the younger men staring at him. 'Rumours?'

'That they're savages.'

Alexander laughed dryly. 'No more than you or me.' His smile faded quickly. When asked about his strange English, he had told these men he was from France. It hadn't been hard to fool them – as a nobleman he'd spoken French rather than Scots.

'I hear they eat the dead and their leader converses with the devil,' piped up another.

Luke patted the red cross on his arm. 'St George will soon put the fear of God in Bruce and his men.'

Alexander said nothing. As the sun poured golden light over the sprawling encampment, his eyes drifted to the broken battlements of Edinburgh Castle. Despite the ruinous state of the place, his heart sang to be back in these lands, where once he had been lord of a rich estate and a warrior in a band of brothers.

46

Bannock, Scotland, 1314 AD

Robert's company crowded among the trees on the edge of the New Park. The hunting reserve, established years earlier by Alexander III and formed of well-spaced woods and open ground, lay two miles south of Stirling Castle. Before them, the ground sloped down to the Bannock Burn, a wide stream, through which the Roman road from Edinburgh ran. The burn, about half a mile distant, was a line of glimmering gold in late afternoon sun. The wheel of a mill, downstream from the ford near the village of Bannock, was just visible, churning slowly in the water.

The men were so quiet the birds had started chattering in the tree-tops again. All the men were fixed on the road, sweat beading their faces. It was midsummer's eve and the air was close, even under the cool canopy. Insects swarmed in hazy beams of light, which slanted through the branches to glint on helms and spear-heads.

Robert, seated astride a dappled grey palfrey, glanced round as Angus MacDonald handed him a water skin. The steel plates on his mail gloves flexed as he took it. The spring water flooded his parched throat. No wine today and no food other than bread – all of them fasting for tomorrow's feast of St John the Baptist. As Robert passed the skin back to Angus, the hand axe Christiana had given to him shifted against his side. Reaching down, he slid the weapon from the loop of leather that secured it to his belt, opposite his broadsword. The blade flashed in the sunlight as he swung it loosely in his hand, testing its weight. There were scars in the smooth handle and in the steel edge. He wondered whose blood it had been christened with.

Yesterday, as he drew his army back from the camp in the Torwood, Christiana had retreated to the safety of a nearby hill, along with the other women and camp followers. They had taken the general supplies with them, although the stockpiles of grain and meat that would provision his troops were secured under guard in nearby Cambuskenneth Abbey. Robert and his captains had taken up positions in the New Park. Split into four companies, each made up of around fifteen hundred men, the majority on foot and armed with twelve-foot-long spears, they were spaced out through the woods, set for retreat.

Furthest to the north, in the shadow of St Ninian's kirk, Thomas Randolph had command of the vanguard, made up of men from his earldom of Moray. Young Walter Stewart and his cousin, James Douglas, held joint command of the second company, composed of men from Douglas's lands and the Stewart lordships of Renfrew, Bute and Kyle Stewart. The third, not far from Robert's, was captained by his brother, Edward, near to where the marshal, Robert Keith, was stationed with the five hundred light horsemen. Robert himself commanded the rearguard, joined by Islesmen under Angus MacDonald and men of Lennox under Earl Malcolm, along with a large number of Carrick knights.

To the west, the land rose into hills and moors. To the north and east lay a boggy plain known as the Pows: a labyrinth of streams and tidal pools bordered by great loops of the River Forth. This left only two viable routes by which the English could attempt to reach Stirling Castle: the Roman road through New Park, or a longer more circuitous path that led through crop-fields to St Ninian's kirk. Thus, Robert's company would most likely be the first to encounter the army that, any moment, would rear its monstrous head on that sunlit road.

Earlier that day, he had sent James Douglas on a reconnaissance to check on the approach of the enemy and their numbers. James had returned some hours ago looking grim. In private, he described to Robert the huge host that was coming their way – filling the road for miles, so it seemed the whole horizon was a creeping forest of lances, ablaze with banners. Robert, disquieted by the news, ordered the young man to keep it to himself, not wanting to sow seeds of panic among the company.

As he twisted the axe in his hands, rolling his shoulder muscles, stiff from the weight of his hauberk, Robert's eyes drifted over the verge to either side of the road. The smooth-seeming land there was a lie. His men had spent yesterday afternoon digging scores of small pits, which now pocked the area, each hole filled with a sharpened spike then covered over with leaves and twigs. These snares, which would seriously injure horse or man, would hamper the English army's ability to fan out in their deadly cavalry charge and, instead, keep them bunched in a tight formation that would funnel them straight to him. He and his men would lead a lightning strike against them, doing as much damage as possible, before retreating north. His trap was laid. Now, to draw them in.

Robert's grip tightened on the axe as he heard the distant, but unmistakable thudding of hooves, like a heartbeat in the earth.

The Road to Stirling, Scotland, 1314 AD

The steady clop of many hooves and the ringing of bridles vied with the snorts of horses and the murmured voices of the men. Dirt rose from the road in choking yellow clouds. It had been a dry start to the summer and there had been no rain for days. Dust covered the silk trappers of the knights' destriers and the surcoats and mantles of the men, clogged the links of their mail coats and powdered the steel plates of greaves and vambraces, and the domes of their crested helms. The mouths of the horses were foaming around their bits. The beasts, Humphrey knew, would need watering soon. He glanced left and right, looking for signs of a stream, but the tangled sprawl of trees disappeared in a leafy gloom through which he could see little.

The vanguard had entered the ancient Torwood that morning, having followed the Roman road from Edinburgh, the route taken by Edward Longshanks sixteen years earlier when he marched on the Scots at Falkirk. Humphrey remembered that journey well, riding in the retinue of his father. It had been a different atmosphere then: the knights filled with a grim resolve to punish the Scots under their leader, William Wallace, who had so gravely humiliated them on the field at Stirling. That determination was still there, but in veterans like him it was now tempered with caution. These past years they had learned not to underestimate their enemy. The growing tension wasn't helped by the breathless air or the oppressiveness of these endless woods. This was favoured ground for the Scots – the perfect territory for ambush. A bird flickering through the canopy would turn the heads of many and have them reaching for their swords. But not all the men of the vanguard were quite so guarded.

A short while ago, the middle-guard, captained by Robert Clifford and Henry Beaumont, had split off from the road, taking another route to Stirling, as determined in council with the king. The two forces would form a pincer movement, approaching the castle from different directions. King Edward had given Beaumont the title Earl of Buchan and had promised he could claim this Scottish earldom if he was victorious, engendering in some of the men the sense that this was a race. It was a race Gilbert de Clare seemed determined to win.

The earl had pressed the vanguard on hard through the afternoon leaving the rearguard, commanded by the king, many miles behind, the tramping columns of infantry and the baggage train stretching even further back towards Falkirk. The head of the formidable snake they had formed had broken from the body and was now isolated. Humphrey had tried to impress upon Gloucester and his young comrades the danger they were in, but Gilbert, whose retinue outnumbered Humphrey's, refused to curtail their speed, saying the deadline set by the Scots for the relief of Stirling was tomorrow and time was running short. When Humphrey reminded him the king had put them in joint command, Gilbert rudely retorted that was merely a concession. The king wanted new blood on this campaign and men he could trust in charge of it. Humphrey, incensed, but unwilling to divide their force when it was at its most vulnerable, relented, allowing the earl to lead them on.

Up ahead, men's voices lifted as the trees began to thin. Humphrey squinted at the brightness as the afternoon sun stabbed down through the breaks in the branches. The woods gave way to a patchwork of fields interspersed with blackened expanses where crops had been burned to stubble. There was no sign anywhere of either humans or livestock. The men didn't comment on the desolation, used to such sights in the march from the Borders. Further along, the road dipped down towards a wide stream, beyond which it rose again and disappeared into more woods. Suddenly, there was a shout from one of the men at the front. Humphrey rose quickly in his stirrups to see what had alerted them. As the sun filled his vision, he raised his hand to shield his eyes. There, in the shade of the distant trees, were figures

– hundreds of them. It was hard to tell with the distance and the sunlight, but it appeared as though they were scattering.

Gilbert clearly thought so, for he let out an excited yell, 'The Scots! The Scots! They're fleeing! *On them!*' Snatching his lance from his squire, the Earl of Gloucester spurred his warhorse along the road, followed by his men, among them Henry de Bohun.

Humphrey yelled a warning, but the din of hooves drowned it out. Spitting a curse, he snapped down his visor and wrenched free his broadsword. '*With me!*' he roared at his knights and squires, kicking hard at the sides of his horse.

As he charged with the rest of the vanguard, through the rising plumes of dust, stones skittering off his helm, kicked up by the destriers in front, Humphrey fixed on the figures beneath the trees. There was one man on a grey horse out in front of the others. He caught a flash of red on his yellow surcoat and the gold gleam of a crown mounted on his helm.

Robert.

St Ninian's Kirk, Scotland, 1314 AD

The tower of St Ninian's rose from the green shroud of the woods, its stone walls blushing in the sun. The fifteen hundred men of Thomas Randolph's company sat on the grass in its cool shadow. Earlier all of them had been poised and ready, spears in their hands and helms on their heads, but as the day wore on the heat and the wait had taken their toll. Now, most of them had removed their helms and had set down their spears. Some talked, while others dozed.

Thomas Randolph leaned against the low wall that ringed the church's cemetery and took another draught from his water skin. Bees thrummed in the long grass that had grown up either side of the track that led to the church. In front of him, the land sloped into a broad meadow, dappled pink with orchids. Beyond, woodland rose. A heat haze rippled over the trees, distorting the air. Swilling the water around his mouth, Thomas glanced behind him at the resting men. He'd heard several of them muse that the English wouldn't show themselves today and, if they did, it would be the king's force that encountered them. While proud to be the commander of one of the king's companies, Thomas couldn't help but feel restless, wanting to be in the fight with his uncle. His victory at Edinburgh had given him a taste of fame that he didn't want to see fade in the face of other men's glory.

There was a sound somewhere off in the woods to the south – it sounded like a cheer. Thomas pushed himself from the wall, frowning as he listened over the hum of bees and the murmured conversation of his men.

'Quiet,' he said sharply, turning to those nearest to him.

Suddenly, the sky over the woods darkened. The air filled with harsh caws as a huge flock of crows flew over. The men stopped talking, watching as the birds surged overhead. A few crossed themselves at the ill omen. After they had gone, Thomas heard more sounds: distant shouts and the shuddering echo of arms. He was turning to alert his men when two figures burst out of the woods and came sprinting across the meadow. They were his scouts, set to watch the track further down.

'Sir!' panted one, racing up the slope. 'The English!'

Beyond the meadow, from out of the fringes of the wood, came a mounted troop of men, five hundred or more strong.

As Thomas tossed aside his water skin and yelled at his men, they began jumping to their feet, snatching up spears and pulling on helms. Swiftly, eyes wide, but focused, they moved into the formation they had been drilled in every day for the past five months.

Where moments before they had been scattered across the grass in the shadow of the church, the company now became a giant crescent, six men deep, their twelve-foot-long spears balanced on shoulders and gripped, two-handed, so as to be effectively manoeuvred; jabbed and thrust when needed. Such formations of spearmen, known as schiltroms, had been employed at Falkirk by William Wallace, but unlike Wallace's stationary rings, Randolph's schiltrom was a movable hedge of iron-tipped death, capable of advancing in its crescent, then closing round into a ring to protect itself.

At Thomas's order, the fifteen hundred men began to move as one down the slope on to the meadow to meet the incoming cavalry, over the heads of which the banners of Robert Clifford and Henry Beaumont soared.

Bannock, Scotland, 1314 AD

Robert, shouting at his company to form up among the trees, saw the English vanguard break. Splitting from the main body, a pack of men came charging along the road, lances raised. As they plunged through the ford over the Bannock Burn, the hooves of their destriers kicked up plumes of water that glittered with fractured sunlight. They were about half a mile away, but gaining quickly, the powerful horses eating up the distance. He realised, as they powered their mounts up the road, that they weren't going to fall foul of his traps. Rather than forming into a long line, as expected, they were coming in a fragmented column, with little sense of order. No matter. They would fall the same on to the points of his spears.

Spurring his grey palfrey along his rapidly forming crescent of men, Robert urged them out of the trees in their schiltrom, spears forward, ready to shatter the cavalry's charge. He bellowed that the might of St Andrew was in their arms and the blessing of God upon their souls. Angus MacDonald and the fifty other mounted men with their king, among them Malcolm of Lennox, Nes and Cormac, had ridden out of the cover of the woods, hefting shields into place and drawing swords, maces and war-hammers. The approaching hooves of the English were a wild drumming, filling the air. Battle cries were tearing from throats. Lances were levelling, couched for impact.

'*My lord king!*'

Robert, bellowing at his troops, twisted in his saddle at Angus MacDonald's yell. The Lord of Islay had thrust his finger towards the road. One knight had split off from the others and was thundering towards him, up the grassy bank. Robert caught a wave of blue silk, the man's mantle billowing as he came, lance levelled. Instinct took over, firing through Robert. Raking his spurs across the palfrey's sides, he sent the animal plunging down the slope towards the incoming knight. In his hand, he still had the axe Christiana had given him. He tightened his grip on the shaft. Some of his men were crying out in fear and warning. He paid them no heed.

The Scottish king and the English knight came together on the hillside in a shuddering rush of limbs and metal. The lance was thrust towards Robert. At the last moment, he swerved, pulling his body out of its lethal path. Its iron tip sliced on past him, missing him by inches. At the same time, he rose in his stirrups. With an almighty roar, Robert swung the axe, bringing it carving round towards the knight's helmed head. The Blade of the Isles struck with such force it sliced through the helm, the padded coif and the skull beneath, all the way down through the brain. There was a wrench in Robert's arm and a snapping sensation, then he was powering on past, the momentum of the charge carrying him some distance, before he was able to wheel his horse around. In his hand was a splintered stump of shaft. The axe blade had vanished, buried in the skull of his opponent.

Behind him, an immense cheer rose, sending a flock of crows scattering into the sky from the woods. Turning, Robert saw the knight crumpled on the grass. His horse had bolted. The rest of the English had slowed their advance at the sight of their fallen comrade. Spurring his horse back up the slope, Robert saw six golden lions on the blue of the man's mantle. Something cold went through him. The man's head had been split like a nut, his face carved open and a fractured stub of wood sticking out obscenely. The gleam of the blade was visible in the grey sludge of brain. Although the face was ruined, Robert knew it wasn't Humphrey. He felt an unexpected sense of relief as he kicked his horse back to his cheering men, drawing his broadsword as he went.

Now, shouting at them to keep in good order, he led them surging down the hillside towards the faltering English vanguard, which had split itself into a ragged mess with the impetuous charge of the knights.

Most of the English at the head were clad in gold surcoats emblazoned with three red chevrons – the arms of the Earl of Gloucester. The earl was visible among them, his helm crested with a spray of goose feathers dyed red. He was yelling, rousing his men to form up and charge the incoming Scots. Behind them, plunging along the road, the rest of the vanguard rode to aid their comrades.

The first clash was brutal, Robert and the fifty horsemen with him crashing straight through the front lines of knights. Robert hacked his broadsword into the neck of a rearing horse, spattering himself and the beast's rider in a hot spray of blood. The knight dropped his lance, but raised his shield to block as Robert swung the sword at him. The steel blade smacked into the wood with a resounding crack. As his horse, blood pumping from the deep wound, buckled under him, the knight fell forward. His free hand flew up instinctively, but was no defence for Robert's sword that came arcing in at his neck.

Close by, Malcolm of Lennox was clashing with another of Gloucester's knights, the red roses on his surcoat livid in the sunlight. Grabbing his opponent's bridle, Malcolm hauled the man in closer and rammed his sword into his side. The knight doubled over, retching blood that gushed beneath his helm. Beside them, another English knight, shouting furiously, carved the head off one of Malcolm's men. Angus MacDonald was hacking through the front rows of the enemy. Having felled two squires, he cuffed a knight's lance aside with his shield, then battered the man's head with a furious chop of his sword. The man's helm dented, the eye-slit crushed along the bridge of his nose. He tried to wheel his horse out of the mêlée, but his horse was cut out from under him by the spearmen of the king's schiltrom, who now surged in.

Destriers reared up, hooves striking at the men in front of them. Others gnashed at their tormentors. One beast bucked so violently its back hooves propelled the spearman it struck into two men behind him, knocking them flying. More English knights were ploughing into the fight, but they had lost any momentum and their horses were slowed by exhaustion after the day's march. A number of them tried to form up in a line to charge the flanks of the crescent of spearmen, but as they spread out from the road they found themselves at the mercy of the hidden pits dug by the Scots. Beasts screamed piteously as they staggered into the holes, spikes puncturing hooves, laming them instantly.

A roar came swelling through the trees of the New Park. The men of the beleaguered English vanguard twisted round, eyes widening in horror as hundreds upon hundreds of spearmen cascaded down from the woods. They were led by two score horsemen. At the front, sword raised, was Edward Bruce.

Gilbert de Clare had been knocked from his warhorse and was fighting furiously on foot. A ring of Scottish spearmen were closing in on the earl, but he was making short work of them, clouting aside their spears with his broadsword and stabbing savagely at necks and thighs, unprotected by armour. Now, seeing this new host come to aid their king, he thrust his sword into the face of a young man in front of him, then turned and barrelled his way through the press. His retainers moved in at his back, fending off blows while he grabbed the reins of a riderless horse. Jabbing his mailed boot into the stirrup he hauled himself into the saddle and spurred his way out through the mass of men.

Humphrey roared at the others to withdraw, before kicking his destrier out of danger, battering aside several spearmen as they lunged at him. Many of the English were doing the same, those who could breaking from the fight and charging down the road, back the way they had come. As the vanguard scattered, fleeing across the Bannock Burn, many Scots howled in triumph and raced to follow, but Robert, panting hard and soaked in sweat, bellowed at them to stay. He had seen too many men charge a fleeing army in blind exultation, only to find themselves cut off and cut down.

The dust on the road was clotted with blood, the ground around it littered with bodies of horses and men. Robert wiped the sweat from his eyes and did a quick reckoning. He had lost maybe a score, although a fair number were also injured, some badly so from the cries and groans as their comrades tried to help them. The English, however, had suffered far worse casualties. Casting around, Robert counted more than sixty dead or wounded men, many in the colours of Gloucester or Hereford. Ordering Angus MacDonald and Malcolm Lennox to take those left alive prisoner, he turned to meet his brother, who was riding towards him.

Edward shook his head with a grin as he pulled his horse to a stamping halt by his brother. 'You left none for me.'

'There will be more,' said Robert, between breaths, thinking of the host James Douglas had described to him. He looked in the direction of the fleeing knights, who had crossed the Bannock Burn and were already disappearing in the shadow of the Torwood. Although their faces were covered by helms, he was certain Humphrey de Bohun had been among them. He wondered what on earth the earl had been doing. It seemed unthinkable that Humphrey would have headed such a disorganised charge. 'They might as well have thrown themselves on our spears,' he murmured.

'My lord king!'

Turning, Robert saw Cormac approaching. His foster-brother's axe was dripping blood and his horse was snorting and agitated. He was escorting another rider, whose blood-drenched surcoat was decorated with three white stars. It was Thomas Randolph.

The earl's face was flushed and sweat soaked his cheeks, but he was grinning broadly. 'My lord, we defeated Robert Clifford's company! They tried to come at us through St Ninian's, but my men sent them into a rout.'

Cormac, too, was grinning. Malcolm and Angus, having caught wind of this victory, were riding over, calling questions, their faces filling with exultant disbelief.

Somewhere in Robert, a flame sparked to life, but he kept his calm, unwilling to let it burn out of control. This wasn't over. Not yet. 'Gather the prisoners and tend to the wounded,' he told his men. 'We make camp.'

47

Near Stirling, Scotland, 1314 AD

It was late in the day when the main host of the English army crossed the Bannock Burn. Scouts sent south from Clifford's company, vanquished by the spears of Thomas Randolph's men, had warned King Edward the Scots held the New Park and they would not be able to ford the stream by the Roman road. At this news, the vast train of men headed by the king and his rearguard diverted from the road and moved across open country, following the prints of hooves gouged in the track by Clifford and Beaumont's knights. Endless lines of weary infantry limped in their wake, followed by the baggage train, the wheels of two hundred wagons groaning round in the dust.

East of the ford, the Bannock Burn twisted its way through a wooded gorge, flanked by steep banks, as sheer as cliffs in places, trees and bushes clinging to the muddy sides. Where the gorge opened out the track descended into the wide burn. The muscular destriers of Clifford's company had waded easily enough through these waters earlier, but it was a different challenge for thousands of infantry, let alone the supply wagons. A halt was called, men sent off to find materials with which to bridge the stream. They returned gradually, carrying doors and roof timbers from houses at the nearby settlement of Bannock, as dusk lit the land in a crimson haze.

Once across the water, a copse of trees gave way to a great plain, sheltered on one side by an escarpment, the ridge of which was shrouded with the darkness of the New Park woods. To the north-west, Stirling Castle was now visible, towering on its crag of rock. For the English, their target was now tormentingly close, but cut off by the waters of another burn, the Pelstream. In the twilight of the midsummer's eve, the flat plain seemed an inviting place to camp, tufted with sweet-smelling heathers, but as the cavalry struck out across it they soon discovered the long grasses concealed a riddle of streams and pools that stretched all the way to the mighty River Forth, a looping silver ribbon to the north. It was here — men floundering in this honeycombed mire, cursing as the ground gave way suddenly beneath them and swatting uselessly at the midges that swarmed up around them — that the vanguard finally found them.

Gilbert de Clare and Humphrey de Bohun urged their spent horses through the vast crowds, who were trying as best they could to set up camp, the hooves of horses making a black soup of the soft peat. Men stopped what they were doing, eyes lingering on the blood-soaked trappers and mantles of the knights of the vanguard riding through their midst. A few were slumped in their saddles, wounded, squires leading their horses. Humphrey and the others ignored the men's anxious, questioning looks, winding their way through the tortuous labyrinth of streams towards the king's company, marked by his royal standard.

The Earl of Gloucester rode in sullen silence, mounted on a palfrey several hands shorter than his magnificent Andalusian destrier, left for dead on the road by the ford. Humphrey too was silent. A cold fury had been welling in him these past few miles at the actions of his co-commander, whose recklessness had led to the deaths of many of their men, including his own nephew. The sight of the army hunkering down in this insect-plagued quagmire did little to temper his mood. The infantry were exhausted, the cavalry demoralised; all of them disheartened by the prospect of an uncomfortable night ahead after the day's long march. Glancing over his shoulder, up the escarpment to the distant trees, Humphrey thought about Robert and the strategy the rebel leader had favoured these past years. If the Scots attacked tonight, they would be in dire straits.

Clustered around the king and his household knights were the barons, among them Aymer de Valence, Richard de Burgh and Ralph de Monthermer. They were clearly involved in a council. Torches, thrust into the ground, illuminated their backs. As the vanguard approached, Ralph, standing on the outer edges of the circle, was the first to spot them.

Moving to greet them, his expression changed from relief to shock. 'What happened?' he asked, crossing straight to Humphrey.

'We were repelled by Bruce's forces at the ford.'

'Dear God. How?'

'Ask your stepson.'

Gilbert de Clare, hearing Humphrey's sharp remark, jumped down from his horse. He had removed his helm and his face was contorted with anger. 'We might have won had you not hung back like a damn coward!'

Humphrey felt the fury close over him, numbing any sense of restraint. 'You useless fool,' he breathed, striding towards Gloucester, grabbing for his sword as he went.

He was stopped short by Ralph, who planted a warning hand on his chest. 'Easy, my friend.'

Humphrey forced back his rage with effort. Blame and reprisals would do no good right now. There would be time for those later. Releasing his grip on his sword hilt, Humphrey thrust a finger at Gloucester. 'Just know that the blood of my nephew – of all our men – is on your hands.'

'What the hell happened?'

The harsh voice belonged to Aymer de Valence, who had broken from the king's company and was heading over. His boots and mail hose were caked with mud. More smeared the plates of his greaves. The men of the vanguard were dismounting, some helping wounded comrades, calling for water and wine.

Aymer and Ralph listened, tight-lipped, as Humphrey recounted the skirmish, his tone terse.

'Sir Robert and Sir Henry suffered similar losses,' said Ralph, when he'd finished.

Following his gaze, Humphrey saw Robert Clifford nearby. The knight was talking to Henry Beaumont. He had a cut on his forehead that was trickling blood down his face. Every so often, he would wipe at it with the back of his arm. There were wounded men there too, laid out on blankets, servants and priests hovering around them.

'Four score men dead,' said Ralph. 'Eight knights.'

Aymer turned and spat. 'Curse Bruce and his dogs.'

'The night isn't over,' Ralph reminded them. 'David of Atholl should be in place by now. We'll sour the Scots' victory before daybreak.'

Humphrey nodded after a pause. 'What does the king plan to do?'

'We move against them at dawn, in force,' answered Aymer. 'Let the whoresons taste our blades.' He nodded towards the circle of men gathered around the royal standard. 'Come. He will want to hear your report.'

Looking round, Humphrey realised Gilbert de Clare had already moved off in the direction of the king. His jaw tightened. He would be damned if he'd let Gloucester use him as a scapegoat. Leaving Hugh to deal with his weary horse, Humphrey headed with Aymer and Ralph over the uneven ground towards Edward. As he approached, an infantryman, marked by the cross of St George, peeled from the outer edges of the assembly, where he was lingering, holding a bucket. In his haste, the man almost knocked into Aymer de Valence.

'Careful, you oaf,' growled the earl.

As the man murmured an apology, Humphrey caught a glimpse of a bearded face, lit briefly by the glow of a torch. Feeling a tug of recognition, he paused, staring after the man, who was hurrying away. Humphrey went to move after him, trying to get a better look at his face, certain he knew him.

'Humphrey.'

Turning at Ralph's call, seeing the king had risen and was looking in his direction, Gloucester at his side, Humphrey continued on. Before he reached Edward, he glanced back with a frown, but the infantryman had disappeared, swallowed up in the great mass of men and horses that covered the plain beyond the Bannock Burn.

The New Park, Scotland, 1314 AD

The Scottish captains gathered in the gloom of a glade. The circle of sky above them was still light despite the lateness of the hour. There was an atmosphere of taut excitement, men talking eagerly among themselves; some leaning in to grasp Thomas Randolph's shoulder and praise his victory against Clifford's forces, more shaking in their heads in admiration as they listened to another telling of their king's heroic duel with an English knight. The weapons of those involved in the fighting had been cleaned and wounds dressed, but the copper odour of the enemy's blood, soaked into surcoats and mail, was sharp on the mild night air.

With the war leaders were three high-ranking clergymen. William Lamberton stood alongside the Bishop of Arbroath Abbey and Abbot

Maurice of Inchaffray, who years before had aided Robert's flight through the wilderness, along the old pilgrim road to St Fillan's shrine.

Robert stood before them all. He had removed his helm and mail coif. Only his gold crown now encircled his head. As he raised his hand, the hum of voices died away and all eyes turned to him. 'Your grace, will you say a prayer for the fallen?'

As Lamberton spoke, commending to God the souls of those who had died, his strident voice softened by the solemnity of the prayer, the men around the glade bowed their heads. When the bishop had finished, a rush of heartfelt amens rose from the company, many of those present caught in the uneasy conflict of guilt and relief that followed survival of a battle.

'And a cheer for our king,' called Thomas Randolph, 'for letting the English know fear today!'

Loud applause followed the earl's call, lightness spreading through the company in the wake of the prayers.

'*Long live King Robert!*'

Robert noticed Angus MacDonald glance over at him. The lord didn't join in the cheers. After the English vanguard had been repelled across the ford, the older man had quietly cautioned his rashness in charging the English knight. He reminded Robert that he was their head, as well as their heart. Without him, the body of their army would collapse. They needed him now more than ever. He had to protect himself. Robert had brushed off his concern, saying he was more worried what Christiana would say about her father's broken axe. But, privately, he knew the lord was right. Despite the day's triumphs, they remained in great peril.

'We have all shown valour here today,' Robert said, addressing the men. 'We stung the enemy badly – with wounds they will not soon forget. What is more, we now have a number of noble prisoners.' This, for Robert, had been the real boon of the day. The capture of English knights would perhaps give him the bargaining power he needed to release more members of his family. Such hope had never been far from his thoughts, even more so since Mary's liberation. 'My scouts have told me the main host of the enemy is now camped on the Pows. Tomorrow is midsummer – the last day they have to reach Stirling before Sir Philip Moubray surrenders the castle. My guess is they will attempt to move on it at first light.'

'The Pows?' said Gilbert de la Hay. He let out a snort. 'They couldn't have chosen a worse place to spend the night, unless they picked the Forth itself.'

A few men chuckled.

'We should take advantage of their folly,' said Edward Bruce, turning to Robert. 'Let us attack them tonight, before they have a chance to move against us.'

Thomas Randolph, Neil Campbell and others added their agreement.

Robert cut in across their keenness. 'We faced only two companies today. Against both, we had the advantage of a good position and the element of surprise. The Pows, at night, would prove as much bad ground for us as for them.'

'My lord,' said Malcolm of Lennox, 'I share your caution, but I believe Sir Edward may be right – we have a chance, now, to damage them badly.'

Robert said nothing for a moment, watching the determined nods among the company. He wanted to believe them – to agree with them; the flame that had sparked in him after the battle still fluttered inside him. But he knew something they didn't. 'I kept something from you all today – something I thought would lead to panic if it was known.' He glanced at James Douglas. 'Master James, will you tell them the truth of what you saw today.'

As James spoke, describing the vastness of the army he had seen coming down the road from Falkirk – the cavalry in their thousands, the endless columns of infantry too numerous to guess at – the men in the clearing fell silent.

Robert saw the accusation in Edward's eyes, his brother clearly wanting to know why he hadn't shared this with him. He scanned the rest of them. 'I share your wish to destroy the enemy, but we have half their number, maybe even less than that. Yes, we won today. But we were tested against only four of their captains. King Edward will have many more with him. Pembroke, Gloucester, Essex and Ulster we know are here. No doubt the earls of Lancaster and Warwick, Surrey and Arundel are also among his retinue.'

Thomas Randolph's brow had furrowed at the revelation, but he shook his head, not willing to relinquish his hope for further victory. 'His grace has brought the Brecbennoch to the field, my lord.' He gestured to the Bishop of Arbroath, who had carried the sacred relic casket of St Columba with him, to imbue the Scottish army with holy fire for the fight. 'No matter the strength of their force, my lord, we have God and St Andrew on our side.'

Edward nodded. 'If we do not try now, we will face them all again another day.'

'My lord king!'

At the shout, the men in the clearing looked round.

Robert saw Nes, striding his way through the undergrowth. Behind him came two Carrick knights. They were bearing up another man between them. As they approached, Robert saw a wash of blood staining the man's surcoat, ripped open across his chest. The blood gleamed wetly in the twilight, as did the man's face, which was clenched in pain. It was one of those he'd left on guard over the army's supplies at Cambuskenneth Abbey.

'What happened?' he said, crossing to the man, followed by Lamberton, who called for someone to bring water and cloth.

'Forgive me, lord king,' breathed the scout, grimacing. 'We tried to fight. They were too many.'

'Who?' demanded Robert. 'English?'

The man shook his head weakly. 'Scots. Wearing the colours of Atholl. They attacked us in strength at the abbey.'

'David,' murmured Robert, his heart sinking.

'Our supplies?' Edward asked the man, coming in beside his brother.

'They took what they could and burned the rest. It's all gone, my lord.'

Two servants hastened into the clearing, bearing the water Lamberton had asked for. The scout's head lolled back on his shoulders. The knights laid him carefully on the ground, while the bishop crouched beside him, placing a gentle hand on the man's slick forehead.

Robert turned away, his jaw tightening. He had hoped time might have diminished David's hatred of him, but clearly, the man still wished him nothing but ill. It was yet another bitter legacy of this war. He looked around at the faces of his men. Where there had been determination, he now saw shock and doubt. He felt the faint flame within him flicker out. It was not so long ago that he had stood in another forest clearing with these men and had let his own urge for victory drive them all into disaster. The ghost of Methven Wood haunted him still. He would not make the same mistake again.

Edward seemed to see the change in him, for he stepped towards him. 'My lord, I—'

'No,' Robert cut across him. 'This settles it. I cannot keep an army in the field without supplies. We will withdraw north at first light. Sir Malcolm's lands will provide cover and food for our men.'

Malcolm nodded.

'They can have Stirling. For now,' Robert added, looking meaning-fully at his brother. 'We need to regain the advantage.'

Edward didn't respond. He was staring at a point over Robert's shoulder, his face registering disbelief. 'Is that . . .?'

Robert turned, following his gaze. More figures were approaching through the undergrowth, two of them Malcolm of Lennox's men. They, too, held a figure between them, but in force rather than support, their faces grim as they marched the man towards the camp. Robert stared at the figure, gripped between them. He was tall, with a thick beard and dark unkempt hair. There was a white band of cloth around his upper arm, decorated with the red cross of St George. As the party came closer, emerging from the shadows of the trees, the man's face became clear. Although he was greatly changed – new scars on his skin, grey streaks in his hair, his once powerful body gaunt and stooped – Robert knew him. It was Alexander Seton.

Others were turning to the captive in surprise and anger.

'Traitor!' shouted someone.

Neil Campbell crossed to Robert, his eyes on Alexander. 'I watched him cross the border, my lord. I warned him if he returned it would be on pain of death.'

'My lord king,' murmured Alexander, bowing his head before Robert.

Robert's eyes narrowed. 'I am not your king,' he said sharply, gesturing at the band of cloth on his arm. 'You gave that allegiance to another.'

'In body, yes,' replied Alexander. 'Not in heart.'

Robert's anger rose, hot. 'And when you betrayed me? When you told my enemies my plans? When you led the wolves to my door? Was that just in body?'

Alexander hung his head.

The man looked like he had been through hell in the years since he had last seen him, but Robert barred the door to pity.

After a moment, Alexander looked up at him. 'You are right, my lord. I betrayed you.' His gaze flicked to Edward, Neil and the others, who had formed a protective ring around their king. 'I betrayed you all. But I have come to make amends.' He looked back at Robert. 'Ask your men. I walked freely into your camp.'

One of Sir Malcolm's knights, gripping Alexander's arm nodded. 'That is true, my lord. He surrendered his weapon and told us he had vital information about the enemy.'

'What information?' Edward asked quickly.

'The English are camped down on the Pows.'

'This we know,' Neil answered roughly.

Robert motioned for the knight to quiet. 'Go on,' he ordered Alexander.

'To reach Stirling by the date agreed for the surrender, the king had to lead us in forced marches from the border. The men are already exhausted and disheartened. They now face a long night with little prospect of sleep. More than that, King Edward seems unwilling to put faith in some of his most experienced commanders – those who fought his father's war for years. He has made Gilbert de Clare constable alongside Humphrey de Bohun. I have witnessed first-hand the resentment this has caused.'

Robert thought of the disorder of the English charge that afternoon. Now, it made sense. 'What of Lancaster and the other veterans?'

'Lancaster isn't here. He sent men for the campaign, but by no means many. There are others, too, who refused to serve. Warwick, Surrey, Arundel.'

A few of the men began talking at this, their excitement building.

Robert ignored them. 'I've seen how large their force is. No matter who serves him, King Edward's army still outnumbers mine.'

'The greatest army is useless without a strong commander to lead it.'

'William Wallace showed us that not two miles from here,' agreed Edward, his eyes on Robert, 'when he destroyed the English under the Earl of Surrey.'

Robert's jaw tightened. He kept his gaze fixed on Alexander, trying to read the man's face. 'Why are you telling me this? What do you hope to achieve?'

'As I said, I want to make amends.' Alexander paused. 'And perhaps there is some small retribution for Christopher – vengeance for his death at their hands.'

'Or it's a trap,' said Neil. He glanced at Robert. 'My lord, we cannot trust anything he says.'

Alexander didn't take his eyes off Robert. 'What I have told you is the truth, on the blood of my cousin and on my own life, which I place freely in your hands.'

Robert stared back at the man who had been his friend for many years, who had been with him when he first joined the rebellion and had fought alongside him. In many ways Alexander reminded him of himself. They had both been led by ambition and pride, and they had both had suffered for that – crushed by Fortune's Wheel. After a moment, he turned away. Neil and Malcolm began speaking, but he held up his hand. 'I need to think.'

Robert walked from their circle. Heading between the trees, he left behind the encampment – all the questions and opinions. The ground rose gently. He climbed with it, lost in thought, until he came to another break in the trees. Here, he paused, lifting his face to the sky. A few stars glittered faintly. He could see the castle, crowning its spur of rock. Here, in this place, Stirling to the north and Falkirk to the south, he stood between Scotland's greatest victory and its worst defeat.

Closing his eyes, Robert summoned the dead. They crowded around him in the shadows of his mind: James Stewart and John of Atholl, men who had been like fathers to him; Christopher Seton with his quick laugh; Lord Donough with his wise eyes and stories of ancient heroes; rough-tongued Affraig, weaver of men's destinies; his mother, the Countess of Carrick, a tall silhouette, fainter than the others, yet still with the power to provoke a deep longing in his soul; the fleeting ghost of his father; his brothers, loyal Niall and grave Alexander, steadfast Thomas; then William Wallace, an omen both of good and ill, casting his great shadow from Smithfield's gallows; then, at the last, his grandfather, an old lion of a man, with his mane of white hair and his fierce eyes.

'*What would you do?*'

'Brother?'

Robert turned to see Edward emerging from the trees. He hadn't heard him approach.

'It isn't safe out here,' cautioned Edward, coming to stand beside him.

Robert gave a short laugh.

Edward grinned and shook his head. 'I suppose that was stating the obvious.' His smile faded as he looked towards Stirling Castle. 'I know you blame me for forcing you to come here.' His tone was softer now.

Robert glanced at him. For so many years Edward had been his mirror, both the same and opposite. He was a month from his fortieth birthday, Edward a year. The threads of silver in his brother's dark hair were in his too. Battle-scarred, hard-bitten – they were sons of this war, half their lives expended in its struggle.

Edward met his gaze. 'But in truth, Robert, you are the one who brought us to this place. You are the one whose banner rallied our men, whose victories inspired them, whose call to arms summoned them. You have brought them here. What for, if not for victory? Or – at least – the chance to fight for it?'

'You believe Seton?'

'I believe in you. We all do.'

Robert nodded after a moment. Reaching out, he grasped his brother's shoulder.

Edward gripped his hand in answer, then walked away down the hillside.

When he had gone, Robert felt the dead gather back around him, thickening the shadows. So long as Scotland remained in the grip of his enemy their ghosts would not rest easy – and neither would he. He remembered the words of James Stewart spoken in the cloister of St Andrew's, on the day of his first parliament. *You cannot let fear of loss rule you.*

Now, as he cast his eyes to the sky, he caught the faint glimmer of Mars, smouldering in the heavens.

48

Near Stirling, Scotland, 1314 AD

Beyond the scarred ridges of the Ochil Hills, midsummer's day was breaking, the new dawn pouring molten light across the meadows and marshes, blazing gold along the battlements of the castle and setting fire to the waters of the Forth. To the north reared Ben Lomond. Behind its dome, the mountains of the Highlands marched into blue distance.

Smoke hung in veils over Stirling, drifting in ribbons from campfires and pluming dark from the ruins of Cambuskenneth Abbey, which had burned throughout the night. Beneath its shifting layers, the vast plain around the castle rock seemed to be moving, alive with horses and men. In a slow tide they came, almost twenty thousand strong, advancing on the slope that had sheltered them through the night. Up on that ridge the trees of the New Park were a soft green mantle, gilded by the rising sun.

At the head of the host was King Edward, mounted on his piebald warhorse, riding in the shadow of his scarlet standard, across which the three gold lions glimmered. With him were three thousand cavalry, made up of barons and knights, squires and men-at-arms. Among them were the English lords on their armoured destriers: Humphrey de Bohun, Aymer de Valence, Gilbert de Clare, Robert Clifford, Henry Beaumont and Ralph de Monthermer, all with crested helms on their heads and shields on their arms, displaying the devices of their mighty houses.

There were Scottish nobles such as Ingram de Umfraville, David of Atholl and young John Comyn. While, around the king, were thrusting young tourney champions like Giles d'Argentan, who had fought under Aymer de Valence at Methven. Others were leather-faced veterans like Marmaduke Tweng, who had battled William Wallace on this plain seventeen years ago and was one of the few Englishmen to ride from that fight with his life and honour intact. All carried lances, the fourteen-foot poles of ash barbed with iron. They were carried vertically, pennons and favours fluttering from their lengths, so it seemed as if the cavalry rode within a forest.

The infantry were at the rear, crowding the plain behind rows upon rows of horses, the marshy ground heaped with dung. The soldiers were sore and aching from their long march here, but nonetheless determined, roused by the prayers of the priests and by the promise of their commanders: that this would be a day of victory against the hated Scots; that they would return to their towns and families with pride at the honour they had won for their kingdom. They gripped spears and bows, clubs and hammers.

Edward and his men ascended the slope, riding up on to firmer, flatter ground. Their horses were confident now, ploughing forward, goaded by spurs. To the south and east, the land fell sharply into the gorge cut by the Bannock Burn. Ahead, rose the New Park. Now, they saw the enemy.

The Scots were coming down out of the woods, thousands of spear-heads catching the dawn light, as if a glittering sea were pouring from the trees. They moved in four companies, one behind the other. With them were several hundred cavalry on small, sturdy horses, led by Robert Bruce, riding beneath his standard, the red lion rampant on a sweep of gold. The English knights appraised them as they approached. Many were surprised – not expecting the Scots to have chosen to meet them openly on the field. Others were grimly satisfied by the inferior numbers of these common foot soldiers, to whom they – the flower of English chivalry – would now teach a lesson in blood.

As the Scots fanned out in their companies, forming four great crescents on the hillside, Edward scanned them from the height of his destrier. He hadn't wanted to come – to cross the border and resume his father's war. But now he was here he would prove himself, to the Scots who had challenged him to this duel and to the barons who had betrayed him. On his mantle, which bore the royal arms of England, he wore a silver stag's head brooch. Piers had given it to him on the night of his coronation. It had taken over a year, but finally he had laid his love to rest in the chapel at King's Langley. His rage had melted in the cold tide of his grief. Now, grief had frozen into resolve. He would slake his thirst for vengeance on these men before him, then let him return, his sword stained with Scottish blood; let him return victorious to look down upon those who had refused to follow him here. Let the craven curs be humbled by his triumph, none more so than Lancaster, his hateful cousin.

Ahead, as one, the Scots knelt, the sea of glittering spears falling in a wave of darkness as the weapons were laid on the ground. The king and his men heard the words of the Lord's Prayer come whispering across the grass towards them.

Edward laughed in surprise. 'So, they kneel to ask for my mercy?'

Beside him, Aymer de Valence's lip curled. A few of the other lords joined in the laughter.

Ingram de Umfraville, a former guardian of Scotland, shook his head. He didn't laugh. 'They ask for mercy,' he murmured, his eyes on the kneeling lines of his countrymen, 'but from God, my lord, not you.'

The mirth faded among the lords.

Edward's eyes narrowed. 'Then let us send them to Him.' He turned in his saddle. '*Archers!*'

Arrows stabbed down around the Scottish lines. The men remained crouched where they had knelt in prayer, ducking from the steady rain. Most didn't have shields and many no real armour, so where missiles struck they struck hard. Men collapsed as bolts punched into throats and shoulders. Others hunkered down behind dead or dying comrades, using them as shields. At Robert's command, the Scottish archers, many of them the green-clad men of Selkirk, answered the English with volleys of their own, but they weren't a match for the scores of Welsh longbowmen or the one hundred crossbowmen King Edward had called from Bristol and their own barbs, for the most part, clattered harmlessly off the steel- and iron-clad ranks of knights.

Another barrage was exchanged, but this time the rain from the English lines was lighter. Horns were sounding. Robert, watching from the saddle of his palfrey, some distance behind his companies of spearmen, guessed that not all of the English archers had yet been called up from behind the tight rows of cavalry. The deep gorge of the

Bannock Burn, which lay to the left of the English position, was causing them to funnel up from the plain, bunching into knots as they
emerged on the field. More cavalry were coming up, visible by their
lances, but until the front rows moved they had nowhere to go,
neither did the infantry.

Now, as the hail of arrows diminished, Robert knew it was his
chance. As he raised his fist, a horn sounded among his own troops,
its deep voice echoing along the ridge. At the signal, the fifteen
hundred Scots of the first schiltrom – under the command of Edward
Bruce – began to advance.

The points of their spears went first, a slow-moving wall of iron-
spiked death. The front two lines of the schiltrom walked shoulder to
shoulder, no gaps between. Behind, three more rows gathered in
tight, most of the men armed with axes and dirks. Edward and his
knights, among them Neil Campbell and Gilbert de la Hay, rode at
the back of this shield of spikes, which fanned out as it advanced
towards the English lines. Yelling orders, they kept it in good formation, shouting at the men to close any gaps that appeared, roaring
battle cries to goad them on.

Again, Robert raised his fist and, again, the horn echoed. Now, the
schiltrom led by his nephew, Thomas Randolph, set out, the earl's
men eager, blooded by yesterday's victory. Another blast and the third
schiltrom, commanded by James Douglas and Walter Stewart
followed. That morning, as William Lamberton blessed the troops,
Robert had dubbed several young men in his army, among them James
and Walter. The cousins, newly knighted, rode proudly together
behind the ranks of their spearmen, both keen to win their spurs this
day. Now, the three huge crescents were moving in one great phalanx,
advancing steadily on the enemy, still forming up, some distance away.

Robert's own schiltrom remained with him. Angus, Malcolm, Nes
and Cormac were mounted around him, the sun illuminating their
faces beneath the rims of helms and the mesh of mail. Before him, the
men of Islay, Kintyre and Lennox waited, augmented by the galloglass, axes brandished. Close by was the marshal, Robert Keith, with
the horsemen. Robert would keep his troops back for now; wait to
see where they were needed. Beside him, his royal banner had been
planted in the earth, fixing his position and his resolve.

That morning, breaking bread with his men, he had set aside all
doubts. Addressing them, he had spoken of the eight years of struggle

that had led them from the Moot Hill here to this place at the heart of their realm. He spoke of the flame of hope that had been faint in the darkness and threatened by the winds around it, but never truly extinguished. He spoke of freedom, the first love of all people, for which they and so many before them had poured forth their blood. Freedom – for the hope of which St Andrew and St Thomas, and all the saints of Scotland, would ride with them into battle.

A distant cry rippled across the field. Robert's eyes darted towards the source. He saw a group of knights at the front of the English ranks suddenly break from the lines and urge their horses towards his brother's schiltrom. They were led by Gilbert de Clare of Gloucester, visible by his red-crested helm at the front of a band of gold-clad knights. His arms were joined by those of Robert Clifford, Ralph de Monthermer, the Red Comyns and David of Atholl. No horn had been sounded and the attack seemed rushed and ragged; not the usual steady advance of knights, from walk, to trot, to gallop. But it was still the thunderous charge of heavy cavalry; a sweeping tide of death made of muscle and bone, determination and arrogance, all sheathed in tons of iron and steel, now hurtling towards the advancing foot soldiers. The ground shook with their coming. Lances that had been raised swung level. Robert rose up in his stirrups, as his brother's spearmen braced for impact.

The clash of Gloucester's cavalry meeting the schiltrom resounded across the hillside. The air was rent with splintering cracks as lances and spears shattered. Men and horses were run through, flesh torn and sliced and punctured. Others were sent flying; knights pitched from saddles, spearmen hurled back against their comrades. But it held. The schiltrom held. Even as his men slipped and tumbled, others surged in to take their places, jabbing at the knights and their mounts, pressing in along their lines. His brother was riding along the back rows, bellowing at them to stand fast. A knight in Gloucester's red and gold hurled a war-hammer across the knotted ranks towards him, but Edward swerved out of its path.

Their lances broken, or else tossed aside, the knights drew swords to strike out at the front rows of Scots, but the twelve-foot spears that gouged at their horses kept them at bay. Although some managed to cuff aside the poles and hack at those wielding them, more Scots pushed in to stab at them from the sides. Horses, pierced by multiple spears, screamed and writhed. Those caught in the thick of the line, unable to break free, buckled in agony, bringing their riders down to the level of the Scots and exposing them to the spikes of maces and the curved blades of axes.

Horns were blaring wildly among King Edward's ranks, the cavalry still emerging from the plain. It was a tight battleground, without the space for the cavalry to deploy with the full force of an ordered line. More knights were forming up, preparing to storm the incoming schiltroms of Thomas Randolph and James Douglas and Walter Stewart, but for those caught in the chaos of the first charge, it was too late. With Edward Bruce's orders cried at their backs, the schiltrom pressed forward, pushing hard against the enemy. The ragged line of English and Scottish knights began to break. Knots of coloured surcoats came undone like a huge patchwork cloth being torn apart as men were cut off, divided from their comrades. Injured horses were collapsing under the determined onslaught of spears and men, spilling blood over the grass, already soaked red.

Those who could were now wheeling their mounts around, trying to ride from the chaos. Young John Comyn was one of them, but as he turned, his horse was killed under him. Beast and man fell together, disappearing beneath the hedge of Scottish spears. Close by, another horse reared, its hooves striking out. Its rider was Gilbert de Clare, who had led the charge, the red goose feathers on his helm waving madly. The earl let out a fierce cry and swung his blood-wet blade at the men pressing in on him. He felled two, before his horse stumbled, pitching him out of the saddle. The Earl of Gloucester went down, the weight of his armoured destrier collapsing on top of him.

Gloucester's fall was as a pebble in a pond, the shock of it rippling out in waves, from his knights and the men around him, all the way down to the English lines.

King Edward, his visor raised as he urged more knights forward, ready for another charge, saw it happen. His eyes widened in horror as his nephew sank beneath the heaving tide of men. 'Dear God! Gilbert!'

Beside him, Aymer de Valence's hard face was livid at the sight of their men being torn apart on the spears of the Scots. He turned to the king. 'Archers, my lord!' he snarled, over the din of horns and the clash of the battle. 'We need them here! *Now!*' He thrust his finger at the other two approaching schiltroms. 'Let those curs have a volley! We'll rip them apart and ride them down!'

Tearing his gaze from the place where his nephew had fallen, Edward swallowed thickly and shouted the order to his captains.

As the horns continued to bellow, more archers struggled up the escarpment to join the others already there, notching arrows to bows or loading quarrels in crossbows, preparing to let fly another barrage.

At a shout from Malcolm of Lennox, Robert saw the English and Welsh archers priming their bows. There were more of them now, aiming at the schiltroms of Thomas Randolph and James and Walter. The first missiles were launched, soaring over the ground, now rapidly closing between the enemy and his men. Robert gritted his teeth as the storm swept through the two schiltroms. Men, struck, reeled and arched, dropping their spears to clutch at the barbs embedded in thighs and stomachs. The crossbow bolts proved especially lethal, punching into men with terrible force.

Screams sounded and the lines broke, here and there, as the injured went down, but the formations held, men stepping in to fill the breaches, others dragging wounded or dead comrades behind them, so they didn't clog up the ground. The schiltroms kept on moving, closer now to the English, but the bowmen were loosing more missiles. Robert knew it was the archers that had been Wallace's downfall at Falkirk, his spear rings unable to withstand the onslaught. He was ready for this.

At his signal, Sir Robert Keith and the five hundred horsemen now swept down from the brow of the hill, cantering swiftly to where the field levelled out. The archers, clustered on the outer flanks of the English cavalry, saw them coming. Some shifted round, aiming arrows at the incoming charge. Some horses, hit, plunged to the ground in clouds of dust, but many more kept on going. The company of archers began to break, then scattered as the horsemen came hurtling towards them. Within moments they were in a rout, fleeing for safety, ignoring the commands being shouted by their leaders.

The men in Robert's company let out a cheer. A few of them broke ranks, starting forward a few paces, champing at the bit to join the fight.

'My God, they have made themselves sheep in a pen!' shouted Angus, turning to Robert in astonishment, as the English cavalry struggled on the slope, no real room to manoeuvre – lest they fall foul of the Bannock Burn gorge which fell away on their left flank. Rows of knights were starting to sweep in waves towards the other two schiltroms, but there was little ground left to give them momentum as they dashed themselves upon the walls of Scottish spears.

This was it. Robert could feel it. Promise of victory charged the air, crackling through him. He drew his broadsword, given to him by James Stewart at his coronation. The gold pommel flashed like a star in the morning sun. He called for his banner-bearer to hoist the royal standard, then, with a yell, urged the men of his company forth into the fray. As he rode, the dawn light in his eyes, his men beside him roaring his name, Robert felt that familiar song of war sing its violence through his limbs, drumming his heart against his chest. He would throw himself out over the abyss of this battle; let death or glory rush to claim him.

49

Near Stirling, Scotland, 1314 AD

The battle was dour and vicious. The sun had risen higher, throwing garish light over the great swathes of men locked together all across the field. Dust filled the air in choking clouds, kicked up by the hooves of the horses. The spearmen of the schiltroms choked and panted, blinking away the salt sting of the sweat pouring into their eyes. Many moved sluggishly now, pressed in against comrades and enemies alike, propping one another up as they toiled for blood.

The red of it was everywhere: splattered brightly on surcoats and across faces, slimed dark along blades, clotted in hair and beards. More was on the ground, congealing in a swampy, stinking soup of spilled bowels and entrails, severed limbs, vomit and horse dung. The mêlée was so densely packed that if a man collapsed and went down among that foul stew he would never get up again. Many were trampled by hooves, or had the breath crushed out of them.

Those who had lost lances and swords used shields to shatter jaws and faces. Spearmen, wedged in at close quarters, resorted to dirks to stab at groins or the bellies of horses. Others used their bare hands, falling on one another, gasping, pressing eyes into skulls with their thumbs, wrapping hands around throats. Guttural cries and strangled shrieks rose; a dreadful clamouring chorus. It was as if the earth had split and hell itself had come bubbling up through the rift. Soldiers, wild-eyed and slathered in blood, screamed shrilly as they hacked their enemies apart. In the craze of battle men were unravelled, undone.

Knights and squires, slumped dead in their saddles, mail punctured and slashed, were carried on the currents of fighting. Other beasts stampeded through the chaos, a danger to English and Scot alike. There were ebbs and flows of fighting still, but for the most part the English cavalry had become pools on a strip of sand, isolated from one another and from their infantry, at the mercy of the incoming tide of Scots. The knights hurled swords and war-hammers at their ranks in desperation, trying to break them, to no avail. The Scottish schiltroms had joined to form an almost unbroken line, forcing the English back towards the slope they had ascended, back down on top of their infantry, struggling and failing to reach the beleaguered knights, despite the desperate ringing of the horns.

Edward Bruce had been unhorsed and fought on foot alongside his spearmen, scores of knights and squires from Carrick and Annandale packed in around him. Edward was exhausted, but he fought like a savage, battering his blade at another of Gloucester's knights, still fighting furiously to avenge their fallen lord. Close by, Gilbert de la Hay chopped his way through the enemy, alongside Neil Campbell, whose teeth were bared as he thrust his sword into the meat of another man's face.

James Douglas, still mounted, was duelling with one of Humphrey de Bohun's knights, his sword whip-quick in his hand, slivers of red-hot metal sparking from both their blades. His cousin, Walter Stewart, was surrounded by his father's men, fiercely protective of the young steward, who was nonetheless holding his own against a knot of men-at-arms in the colours of Ingram de Umfraville. Some distance away, Thomas Randolph smacked aside a sword strike with his shield and lunged at the man who had delivered it, thrusting his blade through layers of padding, into the muscle beneath. He snarled as he withdrew the sword with a vicious twist of his wrist.

In the heart of the king's company, Cormac of Antrim hefted his axe, two-handed, and swung it into the chest of a squire who had just tried to run him through. The Irishman's face was feverish, sweat streaming down his cheeks. His two front teeth had been kicked out by a horse and his top lip was a bloody mess. Not far away was Robert himself, his surcoat misted with blood, the gold crown on his head flashing as he cut and thrust from the saddle of his palfrey. Angus MacDonald fought alongside him, roaring the battle cry of Islay. Nearby were Nes and Malcolm of Lennox, the earl's handsome face smeared red. There, too, was Alexander Seton, fighting on foot with his falchion. The cross of St George was gone from his arm. That

morning he had begged Robert to allow him to fight and the king had
finally agreed. Alexander was pushing forward, his eyes on the white
and blue stripes of Pembroke around King Edward, visible beneath
his banner, beyond the shifting battle lines. In his mind, his cousin's
face burned like a beacon. Close by was a riderless horse, caught in
the fray, stamping and tossing its head. It wore a trapper in the colours
of Gloucester. Snarling with effort, Alexander propelled himself
towards it.

At the ferocity of these captains and their king, the English cavalry
were falling back, closer to the slope; back, closer to the mass of
infantry still trying to surge forward. Suddenly, from behind the Scots
came a clamour of cries.

The camp followers, watching the battle from the safety of a hill
beyond the woods, had seen their countrymen winning and now,
spurred by jubilation and the chance for glory, they rushed to join
them – cooks wielding pans and knives, grooms brandishing hay
forks, servants and carters with sticks and rocks.

Humphrey de Bohun was caught in the core of the fighting when he
saw this new host swarming down the field towards them. They were
too far for him to tell whose men they might be, but his heart quailed
at the sight of fresh forces, come to join the ranks of the enemy.
Gloucester had fallen, as had Robert Clifford. So, too, had many of
his own knights. Humphrey glimpsed Ralph de Monthermer nearby,
surrounded, fighting grimly for his life, but he couldn't get to him.

As Humphrey battered aside another spear and stabbed at the man
who held it, the muscles in his shoulders screamed with pain. The
favour Elizabeth had given to him was still tied around his arm, but
the blue silk was now sodden with blood. His horse was wild-eyed
and bleeding from several cuts, but the mail skirt beneath its trapper
had saved the beast from mortal wounds. Jostled and shoved in the
crush, it was all he could do to stay in the saddle. His helm had been
dented by an axe blow. The visor had broken and was hanging by its
hinge. Up in his saddle, he could see the full extent of the chaos.
Everywhere was a sea of helmed heads and a tangle of spears. The
Scottish schiltroms were pushing in, relentless. He could hear his
own men panting, struggling for breath, but the Scots were starting
to shout, their voices lifting in triumph. He knew they could smell
victory – just as he could taste defeat. They were coming on too hard,

too fast. He could feel his horse staggering backwards under the onslaught. All around, men were falling on top of one another, a wall of bodies building. In Humphrey's mind flashed a memory: his father going down at Falkirk, sinking in the mire, his side pierced by a Scottish spear.

There were more shouts from the Scots.

'*On them! On them! They fail!*'

Humphrey cried out as the tip of a spear grazed past his cheek, slicing open skin. He swerved from the worst of it, then struck at the man wielding it, almost severing his arm at the elbow. The man reeled away, but another stepped in to take his place. Some knights, those who could, were wheeling their horses around, tearing free from the crush. To his left, Humphrey saw a gap in the crowds. In desperation, he jerked on the reins and kicked his way towards it.

All of a sudden, the English lines broke.

Aymer de Valence was with the king when they witnessed the avalanche begin. It was just a few men at first, peeling from the lines, then more followed, until everywhere horses and men were fleeing, surging towards them. Aymer, who had raised his visor to get a better view of the battle, realised the peril. They were trapped – caught between the advancing spiked wall of Scots and the thousands of their own men on the slope behind them. To the left was the defile of the Bannock Burn. The only way out was right, along the edge of the escarpment towards Stirling Castle.

'My lord!' He twisted round to the king, who was yelling hoarsely at his impotent captains to send in the infantry. 'We must go! *Now!*'

Edward jerked round, staring at the earl aghast. 'Give up the battle?'

'We've no choice!' Aymer's eyes flicked to the raging flood of men, almost upon them. He swung his shield from his back and drew his sword. 'If you're captured we lose this *war!*' Turning, he shouted at Giles d'Argentan and Marmaduke Tweng. 'Get the king to safety.' He pointed his sword along the ridge.

The two veterans didn't need telling twice. Giles spurred his horse through the fray, clearing a path, while Marmaduke grabbed the king's bridle and, kicking at its sides, forced Edward's piebald destrier along with him. Aymer moved to follow, shouting at those of his men still around him to withdraw. The royal standard-bearer galloped hard after the king, the retreating banner signalling many more knights and squires to follow their leader.

All at once, a horse came hurtling towards Aymer, a gold trapper flying behind it. For a moment he thought it was one of Gloucester's men, then he realised the man astride it looked nothing like a knight – dressed in the poor, mismatched clothing of an infantryman. The man's bloody face was lit with furious intent. Aymer knew him. Alexander Seton. The Scottish lord rose in his stirrups, the short sword in his hand swinging towards him. Aymer lifted his shield to block the blow. At the same time, he brought his own sword slicing in.

First, there was the concussion in his arm as Seton's sword struck. The blade scored across the edge of the shield, then skidded off. Aymer felt its sting as the tip slashed across his face, partly exposed by his raised visor. In the same moment, there was the impact in his sword arm as his own blade connected with Alexander's chest. The man flew back, hurled from the saddle, and disappeared among the hooves and feet of those now trying to follow their king. Aymer, gritting his teeth at the searing pain in his cheek, wheeled his horse around. Taking one last look behind him, the earl's eyes fixed on the royal banner of Scotland, closer now, the red lion clearly visible, rearing triumphant. With a bitter cry, Aymer de Valence kicked his destrier after his fleeing king.

When King Edward fled the field, the English forces knew the battle was lost and the Scots under Robert knew they had won. As the Scots poured down the hillside on top of the stampeding enemy, disorderly rout turned into disaster.

The English cavalry, bearing down on the infantry, began a great, tumultuous exodus. Men knocked down in the press found themselves suffocated by the hundreds who crawled on over them, burying them in the churned earth. Those near the back, still spread out across the boggy plain, pushed north, stumbling over the stream-riven ground. Many threw themselves into the deep waters of the Forth. Those who could swim made it to the far banks, but many more were dragged under the broad river's current. Thousands of others floundered on the plain, twisting into the sudden dips and pools, easy targets for the hordes of Scots swarming to engulf them. Horses careered, knocking men down. Porters and grooms around the baggage train, some distance from the fighting, jumped from the wagons and fled, wading back through the Bannock Burn.

Up on the ridge, in the blind chaos of the rout, knights and squires, trapped between the Scots and their own infantry, urged their horses into the woods to their left, many unaware of the defile that opened beyond. The animals plunged through the trees only to hurtle off the edge of the cliff-like banks. Men and beasts screamed as they fell, the destriers breaking trees and branches on their tumbling downward course. Water and mud burst up from the wide stream as they plummeted into its depths. Others crashed down on top of them, forcing those struggling in the weight of their mail beneath the surface. Hundreds met their fate here. Others, gasping, fought their way over this bridge of writhing flesh to get to the other side. The waters of the Bannock Burn were churned brown with the flailing limbs of drowning men.

50

Near Stirling, Scotland, 1314 AD

It was over, a little more than two hours after it had begun. The battleground, a vast, ruined canvas, was daubed all over with the blood of the fallen. The stink was horrific. Men staggered about, retching, stomachs turned as they waded through the mess of burst and broken corpses. Already, scores of crows were circling in the sky, drawn by the promise of a feast. Others settled in the trees, hunched like black gargoyles.

Cries and groans, whimpers and pleas rose all around, cut through by triumphant yells and cheers. Some Scots punched fists into the air, wide-eyed and battle-drunk, some sat in silence, numb with exhaustion. Many leaned on the shoulders of comrades, laughing and crying with relief, gulping at skins of water and wine. Others crouched beside injured friends, trying to comfort them in their last moments of life. Hundreds of the remaining English nobles, those who hadn't fled or been killed, were being rounded up, taken prisoner.

Robert was up on the ridge with his captains, overseeing the aftermath of the battle. He had dismounted from his horse and had handed his helm and shield to his squire. His muscles felt as though they were on fire, but victory animated him, pumping the blood hot through his veins. His heart still hammered in his chest, as if it didn't know the fight was over. As Nes passed him a skin, he pulled off his padded arming cap and upended the skin over his head, closing his eyes as the water poured on to his scalp and down his face. It stung as it trickled through the deep wound over his left eye, where a stray sword strike had carved skin to the bone. Later he would have his physician stitch it closed, but for now he was needed here. His commanders were returning to give reports from different parts of the battleground and receive new orders.

James Douglas rode up with Walter Stewart, both men, along with a host of knights, having pursued King Edward along the ridge.

'My lord,' greeted James, breathless. 'The king has fled south.'

'He didn't make it to the castle?' asked Robert, surprised.

'He did,' answered Walter Stewart. A faint grin flickered at the corner of the youth's mouth. 'But Sir Philip Moubray refused him entry. He was forced to turn back.'

'The king was seen riding with Aymer de Valence, through the Bannock Burn,' finished James. 'Our men reckon he had around five hundred knights with him.'

'I want you to follow, as far as you can,' Robert told the two young men. 'Take as many of them as possible, but take them alive. I want prisoners – not more dead to bury.'

As James inclined his head and turned his horse, Robert saw his brother approaching. Edward had removed his helm. His face was streaked with sweat that had tracked lines through the blood. Behind him came a company of Carrick knights, hauling more bodies to add to the rows already being set out on a cleared stretch of grass. These dead men were nobles, whose bodies would be respected as befitted their rank. For the common soldiers, a mass grave would be their resting place.

Edward's knights had to step carefully on the ground, slippery with blood and covered in the debris of broken lances, discarded swords, dead horses and men. One of the corpses already laid out there was Gilbert de Clare, the Earl of Gloucester, his face a mess of livid cuts and bruises, eyes wide and bloodshot. Beside him, the men placed the first of the bodies they were carrying. Robert recognised the arms. The dead man was Giles d'Argentan.

Edward halted beside his brother, his eyes on the English knight, whose armour had been rent in numerous places. 'Sir Neil says he saw him taking King Edward to safety. He must have ridden back into the battle once he got the king out.' He shook his head, wiping his forehead with the back of his arm. 'It took three of my knights to bring him down.'

Robert caught the admiration in his brother's tone. He nodded. 'He will be returned to his family with the others. Make sure no one plunders their—' He fell silent, catching sight of another of the corpses being brought down. This one was even more familiar. It was Robert Clifford, royal knight, veteran of the war, and once his brother in the Knights of the Dragon. Clifford's body was utterly broken, his head lolling back as they hauled him to the row. 'Careful,' Robert called sharply.

His eyes lingered on this growing line of bodies of knights, earls and lords. Truly, the flower of English chivalry had been plucked.

'My lord.'

Turning, Robert saw Thomas Randolph escorting two prisoners. One, held up by two squires, face pale, teeth clenched in pain, was Ralph de Monthermer. The other, walking unaided, his hands tied behind his back, was Humphrey de Bohun.

As they came closer, Robert locked gazes with Humphrey. He saw the devastation reflected in the earl's eyes – the horror, the humiliation, the bitterness of this defeat. Such a thing, he knew, could undo a man. Robert felt no joy, no triumph in the knowledge. Instead, he felt pity. Old threads of friendship pulled inside him. But for the countries in which they had both been born, but for their destinies that had diverged on two different roads, they would have still been friends.

Nes appeared at his side. 'My lord, there is someone asking for you. I think you should come.'

'Have my physician tend to him,' Robert told Thomas, motioning to Ralph. His eyes flicked back to Humphrey, briefly, then he turned away and followed Nes down the field to the edge of the slope, where the dead were thickly clustered. 'Who is it?'

'Alexander Seton.' Nes glanced at him. 'He is badly injured, my lord.'

Robert had to climb over the bodies to reach Alexander. He was lying on his back, one of his legs trapped under a dead horse, his arms splayed out to either side of him. His face was marble white. Sweat soaked his hair. Robert's eyes moved to the wide red slash across his chest, which had torn through his gambeson and the flesh beneath, clearly made by the mighty stroke of a sword. He could see the splintered bones of ribs, beneath the raw mess of muscle.

Alexander's eyes went to Robert as he crouched beside him. He licked his lips. 'Aymer de Valence.'

Robert's jaw tightened.

'But I gave him a mark of my own.' Alexander tried to laugh, but his lips just twitched. 'Something to remember me by.'

'You and me both then,' said Robert, with a grim smile.

Alexander stared at him. 'I didn't just betray you to the English, Robert. Katherine, your first wife's maid – I made it so she lay with that man in Ayr, made it so you found them. I wanted her gone so you would have nothing to distract you from the throne. But in helping you fulfil your own ambition I merely wanted to satisfy my own.' He closed his eyes with a grimace, then opened them again. 'I have no right to ask it, but, still, I beg your forgiveness. For all of it.'

Robert took a moment to answer. 'You have it.' He grasped Alexander's shoulder, felt the man shuddering beneath his hand. 'Christian had a son in Sixhills. I have heard he looks like his father.'

Alexander reached up and gripped Robert's wrist. 'Get her out, my lord,' he murmured. 'Get them all out.'

Robert glanced back up the hill to where the noble dead were being laid out and the prisoners corralled; all of them worth their weight in ransoms. 'I will,' he murmured. Feeling the hand around his wrist release, he looked back.

Alexander Seton died with his eyes open, staring at the midsummer sky.

Rising, Robert moved off. He stood for a moment, surveying the carnage of the battlefield. Both the cost and the value of this victory were visible on every inch of ground. The implications of what he had achieved here today were starting to form, nebulous, in his mind. To the north, the walls of Stirling Castle blazed gold in the morning sunlight. He lifted his face to heaven, closed his eyes.

Lochmaben, Scotland, 1314 AD

In the autumn, when the trees that encircled Castle Loch had changed their colours, their reflections gilding the waters like the gold borders of a mirror, Robert returned to Lochmaben. He came with a large company of men, including some of his captains, Thomas Randolph, James Douglas, Walter Stewart and Edward. Their sister, Mary, accompanied them, as did William Lamberton.

Others of his men, Angus MacDonald, Gilbert de la Hay, Neil Campbell and Malcolm of Lennox among them, had returned for the

time being to their estates, some of which had been recently gifted to
them. Christiana MacRuarie had gone too, sailing back to Barra. In
the final days of summer, they had spent their last night together on
the wild Carrick coast. The next day, Robert had stood on the sands
of Turnberry, watching her war galley pull out into the waves.
Christiana had stood at the stern, the sail filling with wind behind her,
the divide of the sea growing between them.

Standing with Robert and his men, at the crossroads where the
road led west to Dumfries and south to Carlisle, was a prisoner.
Humphrey de Bohun was clean-shaven, dressed in a black doublet and
hose, a cloak around his shoulders. His own clothes, ruined, had been
burned after the battle. The wounds on his face were mostly healed,
although the scars stood out starkly in the afternoon sunlight. It was
three months since the battle on the plain by the Bannock Burn.

King Edward and his knights, pursued relentlessly by James
Douglas's company, had made it as far as Dunbar, where the king
boarded a ship and set sail for Berwick. Sir Philip Moubray, the
Scottish commander who had held Stirling for the English, had
surrendered the castle to Robert and had since come into his peace.
Many of the dead, too numerous to count, were thrown into a grave
by the banks of the River Forth. The bodies of the nobles were
returned to their families for burial. Of those who survived and had
been taken prisoner, some had already been exchanged for ransoms.
Others, Robert had released without penalty, among them Ralph de
Monthermer, his old friend in the Knights of the Dragon, who had
saved him from Longshanks's wrath with a pair of spurs. Now, only
Humphrey remained in his custody. The earl, Constable of England,
had been his greatest prize.

Fionn's barking alerted the men to the approach of someone.
Robert heard the hooves before he saw the company, coming along
the road from Carlisle. A group of knights rode at the head in front of
two covered wagons. They wore the livery of King Edward. Some of
Robert's men shifted their stances, hands near weapons. Their victory
over the enemy, although overwhelming, hadn't yet ended the war.
Robert, however, was confident that it would be a long time before
the English king would be able to send another force north to engage
him. Edward's reputation, tarnished before the battle, had been
severely damaged by the catastrophic defeat. The riders halted a short
distance away. Some of them dismounted, staring down the road at

the waiting Scots. Others moved to the back of the wagons, from which they escorted a number of figures.

Robert stepped forward, shielding his eyes from the sunlight. He felt a strange mixture of hope and dread at the sight of them. Did they blame him for these lost years? Would they even know one another now? As the figures began walking towards him, watched over by the English knights, he fixed on one at the front: a tall, slender young woman, in a plain black gown, a white coif on her head. For a moment, he didn't recognise her, then he realised, with a stab of emotion, that she was his daughter.

He had last seen her, eight years ago, when he had thrust her, weeping and begging him to stay, into Elizabeth's arms during their desperate parting in the woods beyond St Fillan's shrine. Marjorie wasn't a girl any more. The years they had lost were all too visible in her face and body: those of a woman's. With Marjorie walked his sister, Christian, hand in hand with a young boy, who looked so much like Christopher Seton Robert felt the sort of joy he imagined he would feel if he saw the man himself again. Behind came his youngest sister, Matilda, and his half-sister, Margaret, grey-haired and stooped.

Unable to contain herself, Mary ran to greet her sisters, crying out with grief and joy as they embraced one another. At his side, Robert saw Edward's blue eyes were shining. Thomas Randolph was the next to break from the company, hastening to his mother. At the last, came Elizabeth, Robert's wife and queen, arm in arm with a shuffling, bent old man. It was Robert Wishart, the Bishop of Glasgow. William Lamberton murmured a prayer at the sight of his friend.

All of them were the price of an earl's ransom.

Robert turned to Humphrey, watching the company approach in silence. The earl's eyes held a sorrow he couldn't fathom.

Humphrey met his gaze. 'Am I free?'

'Yes.'

Humphrey hesitated, seeming about to say something further, but he merely inclined his head.

Robert understood. There was nothing more either of them could say.

He watched Humphrey walk away, along the road towards the waiting English knights. The earl paused as he passed Elizabeth. Leaving Wishart – once the leader of the insurrection, now an old blind man – to be guided by Bishop Lamberton, she turned to him.

Robert couldn't hear what they said, but he saw her look at the ground and shake her head and saw Humphrey's hand move, as if to reach towards her, then stop.

Whatever question was forming in his mind was vanquished as Marjorie ran towards him. Robert went to meet his daughter, drawing her into his arms. He pulled back after a long moment, smiling as he brushed away her tears with his thumb. 'My God, you look like your grandmother.'

Marjorie returned his smile with a laugh. 'That is what Christian says.' Her eyes searched him as she spoke, as if familiarising herself with this new face of his – all its unfamiliar scars and lines; stories she did not know.

Robert looked over at Christian, who was hugging Matilda and Mary, her young son standing close by. He realised there was someone absent from this company. He knew about Isabel Comyn, having been informed during negotiations for the exchange of prisoners that the countess, delivered into the custody of Henry Beaumont, had died, much to his grief and his guilt for not being able to release her sooner. But he was expecting his nephew, Donald of Mar, Christian's son by her first marriage. 'Where is Donald?'

'He chose to stay in England, in the king's household,' Marjorie told him quietly, her eyes on Christian. 'He said he felt at home there.'

'My lord king.'

Robert looked round to see Elizabeth approaching. Marjorie moved aside, allowing them to greet one another. Robert inclined his head to her. 'My lady.' As they lapsed into silence, unsure of one another, unsure of what to say, Robert held out his hand. Elizabeth took it, glancing up at him as his fingers closed over hers.

After more greetings were exchanged, Robert led his family over to where their horses and the rest of his men were waiting. The English had already gone, dust settling on the road in their wake. After calling for the squires to bring horses for his wife and daughter, Robert paused, looking up at the broken keep of his grandfather's castle. Ivy had trailed up the sides, covering over the ruin. Below, an oak tree that he remembered climbing as a youth had grown tall, its branches reaching almost to the crown of the motte.

He thought of the tree in Turnberry that had held the web Affraig had made for him in the fire-bruised dark of her hovel, a lifetime ago. When he took the throne and the web didn't fall he had doubted its power. Now, he felt he understood. Affraig's belief in him had carried his prayer all the way to Barra and there, burned up in the funeral boat with the old woman, his destiny had been fulfilled not by a fall but by a rise; of smoke and sparks on the night air and of his people's faith in him, their king. It was in that moment, surrounded by men and women of his realm, that his hope had been rekindled and his war had risen from the ashes.

His gaze lingered on the ruins of the keep. Twenty-two years ago, he had made a promise in the shadow of those walls – a promise to uphold his family's claim to the throne.

In the end, he had done so much more than that. In the end, he had upheld his nation's claim to their kingdom.

EPILOGUE

1329 AD

Dumfries, Scotland

1329 AD

*R*obert made his way slowly down the aisle, his footsteps hollow on the floor of the empty church. A smell of incense lingered in the air. He paused for breath, placing a hand on one of the pillars that flanked the nave, his eyes on the rood screen at the end. Behind that screen was the high altar. He felt a tightness in his chest; more so than the usual pressure he'd been beset with this past year as the debilitating sickness enveloped him. Steeling himself to it, Robert passed the screen and entered the choir.

At the sight of the altar, his mind flashed with memory — himself and John Comyn, struggling, eye to eye, his hand thrusting the dirk into the man's ribs, blood, wine-dark, flowing. He let the ghosts come; let them fight their ancient battle once again, in silence in his mind. When the memory faded, he crossed to a row of candles, set alight by the monks in preparation for the afternoon office. As promised, they had left one unlit. Robert picked it up, the wax cold and smooth in his hand. He had come to say a prayer for one man, but now he was here so many more dead crowded around him, wanting a flame for themselves. Turning the candle over in his hand, he thought what an impossible task this pallid length of beeswax would have, were he to light it for the souls of all who had gone before.

Almost fifteen years had passed since the battle by the Bannock Burn. That battle had taken the lives of many, but the years that followed had claimed more. Despite his great victory that day, the war with England had rumbled on, the two nations biting at one another; skirmishes and raids, sieges and bursts of violence interspersed with brief truces and fruitless negotiations, neither side willing to yield to the other's terms. Then, nine years ago, he had sought the aid of the papacy in recognition of Scotland's freedom and its independence from England. To this end a letter was sent to the pope from Arbroath Abbey, in the name of the community of the realm and set with the seals of numerous Scottish noblemen. Four years later, the papacy had recognised him as King of Scotland and a long-lasting truce was established with England. But the war had one final convulsion to make, which had shaken both countries to their foundations.

Two years ago, King Edward had been deposed in a rebellion led by his wife, Isabella of France, and her lover, Roger Mortimer. The king was imprisoned and his young son set upon the throne as Edward III. It was rumoured Isabella had ordered the murder of her incarcerated husband by way of a hot poker inserted into his bowels. Robert, fearing the intentions of the new king, who was guided by the powerful forces around him, moved to meet him in force. The campaign ended in young Edward's resounding defeat at Stanhope Park, at the hands of James Douglas and Thomas Randolph and, finally, last year, resumed negotiations resulted in the Treaty of Edinburgh, which had seen Scotland granted its sovereignty and the end of the war begun thirty-two years earlier by Edward Longshanks.

Fortune had turned many revolutions, in him and in his kingdom; their fates entwined. He had achieved much, in both the wheel's rising and its downward courses, but victory and honour had not come without cost. Now, as he felt death's pull in his wasted body, Robert wanted one more chance to atone for the sin that had seen his reign born in blood.

Taking the candle, he held the wick to one of the other flames. As the fire fluttered to life, he cupped his palm around it, lest it gutter and wink out. Setting it down carefully, he closed his eyes and said a prayer for John Comyn's soul.

When it was done, he said a prayer too for the others: for Marjorie, his daughter, who'd had less than three years of life beyond her release, dying in a fall from her horse and leaving behind a son, born to her husband, Walter Stewart. He said a prayer for Elizabeth, his dutiful wife and queen, who had passed last year and who, despite the coolness of their marriage, had given him four children. David, his only surviving son, was now his heir. Robert said a prayer for Neil Campbell, his brother-in-law by the knight's marriage to his sister Mary, which had lasted only a year before Neil's death. He said another for his brother, Edward, who, unable to live a life in his shadow, had embarked on a campaign to Ireland to aid the Irish in their struggles. He had crowned himself High King of Ireland, but the expedition had ended in disaster and Edward, his last surviving brother, was captured and beheaded, just four years after the battle at the Bannock Burn. Lastly, and after a pause, Robert said a prayer for Humphrey de Bohun, killed along with Thomas of Lancaster seven years ago by King Edward's forces, the king finally taking his revenge, long-sought, for the murder of Piers Gaveston.

Opening his eyes, Robert lingered for a moment on the candle, its flame fluttering in the cool air of the Greyfriars Church. Then, he turned and headed back down the aisle and out into the spring sunlight, where his men were waiting for him: faithful Nes and Thomas Randolph, Gilbert de la Hay and Sir James Douglas, nicknamed the Black by the English, who had learned to fear him.

Now he had lit that candle, which he had paid the monks to keep alight through the years to come, Robert had one last journey to make before he travelled the long dark road all men must take – a journey west across the sea, to a distant isle.

AUTHOR'S NOTE

Voltaire is thought to have said, *history is the lie commonly agreed upon*, and when dealing with the life of Robert Bruce that statement often seems to ring true. This part of Robert's career – from the rout at Methven to midsummer's eve at Bannockburn – is, in terms of the recorded facts, frequently ambiguous and, on occasion, downright impenetrable.

When Robert disappears from Dunaverty Castle on the Mull of Kintyre in September 1306, we have no idea where he went or what he did for more than four months before he reappears in Carrick early the following year. The island of Rathlin off Ireland was cited as Robert's hiding place by John Barbour in his epic poem, *The Bruce*, written c.1375. But others have suggested Ireland or one of the Western Isles, even Orkney or Norway. I went with Rathlin, the most common theory and somewhere I was relatively easily able to get to for research (albeit on a vessel nicknamed the *Vomit Comet*). I also placed him on Barra in the Outer Hebrides, which has a strong natural harbour and is believed, at this time, to have been in the possession of Christiana MacRuarie, who was said to have aided Robert.

There are many other gaps in our understanding of the rebel king and the band of men who 'took to the heather' with him on the long march to Bannockburn and the struggle for independence. As is often the case with medieval armies it is difficult, sometimes impossible, to pin down numbers of troops. A letter written to Edward II in around 1308 by John MacDougall claims Robert was then menacing Argyll with a force of ten to fifteen thousand, but at Loudoun Hill in 1307 Barbour puts his army at six hundred fighting men and perhaps as many 'rabble', while modern historians suggest he commanded only around seven thousand in 1314 at Bannockburn.

Dates, too, prove problematic. We don't know exactly when the Battle of Inverurie against the Black Comyn was fought and we don't know whether Robert's campaign in Argyll against John MacDougall took place in 1308 or 1309. The Battle of Glen Trool is afforded only a fleeting, rather confused mention in the records, but has swelled over the centuries to become one of Robert's greatest victories, now complete, at its atmospheric setting, with information boards that neatly set out the battle's location, along with a date, troop numbers and sequence of events, none of which is actually known – as I discovered after hiking up there with the historian, Edward J. Cowan.

Other, even more important, locations confound us. The site of the Battle of Bannockburn has been pitting historian against historian for years without conclusion. Most historians, including Fiona Watson who was kind enough to give me access to her report on the subject, favour what is known as the Dryfield (now the site of the Bannockburn High School playing fields) as the place where the main battle was fought. Although some, including Scott McMaster who showed me around the battle-site, give compelling arguments for the Carse (a lower-lying area formerly known as the Pows or *Les Polles*), where the English were thought to have camped on the night of 23 June. Two other sites: the Borestone and an area of the Carse nearer to the Forth, have also been mooted, although these are now afforded less credibility. In the end, I opted for the Dryfield, but until more archaeological evidence is found the argument will no doubt continue.

Likewise, many myths have sprung up around Robert and his contemporaries over the centuries, perhaps the most famous of which is the spider. The earliest reference we have for the now legendary arachnid appears in a posthumous edition of David Hume of Godscroft's *The History of the House of Douglas*, published in the mid-seventeenth century, in which it is James Douglas who witnesses the creature trying and trying again to spin its web. Sir Walter Scott, writing his *Tales of a Grandfather* in the nineteenth century, attributed this story to Robert Bruce. Of course, the allegory fits Robert perfectly – the man who, despite all the losses suffered, refused to give in and forced himself on to succeed finally. But, for me, there could be no actual spider in the narrative. Instead, I used Affraig and her webs of destiny, partly drawing on medieval magical practices and partly echoing Ariadne and her thread, to capture the spirit of this enduring myth.

It is both a blessing and a curse that so much and yet so little is known about the life and times of Robert Bruce. The gaps in our knowledge offer exciting opportunities for the historical novelist, but it is often a challenge to join up this fragmented narrative when there are so many contradictions, repetitions and holes in the accounts. Also, as I've noted in the previous novels, while we may sometimes know what someone was doing, and where and when they were doing it, we very rarely know *why*. The novelist, unlike the historian, is always required to make a decision as to a character's motivations.

It is a challenge I relish, but I'm always aware that even when fictionalising events – whether for the sake of plot or pace, to fill in a blank, or to turn a complex, drawn-out episode into something more thrilling and readable – I want it to be at least plausible and since the history is what inspired me in the first place I want to respect it, even within the boundless imaginings of fiction. To this end, what follows is a breakdown of the significant alterations I've made to the history, such as it is known. For those wishing to know more about the period please refer to the bibliography.

Alexander III and the succession

Rather than duplicating what I've written about at length in the previous author's notes, I'll just say briefly that chroniclers of the time and modern historians regard the death of Alexander III – separated from his escort on the road to Kinghorn and found dead the next morning – as an accident. The murder is pure fiction. It was the fact Alexander was thought to have mooted the possibility of a union between his granddaughter and Edward's son and heir in 1284, and that when the king married Yolande any offspring they produced would have rendered this proposition meaningless, that led me down the *what if* route.

Also, Robert acquired the earldom of Carrick in 1292 shortly after John Balliol was appointed king by Edward, but it was his father who inherited the family's claim to the throne. However, Robert was accused of aiming at the crown as early as 1297 and so I chose to have the legacy passed directly from his grandfather to him. The Bruce family were at Norham, not Lochmaben as I have it, when Edward announced his decision to choose Balliol as king.

Aymer de Valence and the Battle of Methven

Throughout this trilogy I've been rather mean to Aymer de Valence, who is considered to be one of the more honourable figures in the English royal court at this time, but as Robert's main opponent from Methven on he fitted well in the role of antagonist. Although he did occupy Perth in 1306, I have fictionalised his brutal treatment of the townsfolk. That said, the hanging of insurgents and enemy garrisons was becoming increasingly common at this point in the war.

I've slightly altered events leading up to the skirmish in Methven Wood, so as to simplify what is a convoluted and occasionally unbelievable sequence, but the battle itself and the outcome remain the same. Essentially, after approaching Perth to challenge Valence, Robert's army was ambushed in Methven Wood and sent into a rout. This may well, as noted by G.W.S. Barrow in *Robert Bruce and the Community of the Realm of Scotland*, have been Robert's saving grace, for had he won at Methven, 'he would almost certainly have met the English king in the field in a major pitched battle, eight years before he was ready for it.'

Robert's brother, Niall, is thought, at this time, to have been looking after the king's wife and daughter and the other women, rather than taking part in the battle, but I wanted to keep him in the narrative until the point when he escorts the women to Kildrummy. We do not know the exact chronology of events following Robert's flight from Methven. We don't know for certain what routes he took, or even when, exactly, the attack in Lorn by John MacDougall occurred. But I have, for the most part, followed Robert's escape as it appears in Barbour's poem.

Edward I

After appointing Aymer de Valence Lieutenant of Scotland and instructing him to 'raise the dragon', i.e. show no mercy towards Robert and his supporters, Edward I made what was clearly a long and painful journey north, hoping to take command of the campaign against his adversary. We do not know what he was dying of, although at the time it was said to be dysentery. We do know he had to be carried in a litter and that when he arrived at Lanercost Priory provision was made, in the form of quarters built for him and his queen, for what was to become a lengthy stay.

I have Prince Edward in his father's camp at the beginning of the novel, but in fact the king had already sent his son into Scotland, in command of a strong contingent of newly made knights, who raided Robert's lands in Carrick.

Alexander Seton

Much of Alexander Seton's role has been fictionalised in order to fill in considerable gaps in the records, but I've tried to follow, as much as possible, his actual trajectory. He isn't thought to have been related to Christopher Seton, but it worked well for my purposes to have them as cousins. We do know that Alexander, a lord from East Lothian, was captured in 1306 by English forces, but was subsequently released by Edward I, in contrast to many of his comrades. His part in revealing Robert's plans to the Black Comyn is fiction, but Aymer de Valence's march on Kildrummy, where John of Atholl and Niall Bruce had sought sanctuary for the women, has made some question whether there might have been a spy in the ranks.

In 1308 Alexander was said to have made a pact along with Neil Campbell to 'hold together in defence of their king', but after 1310 he went over to the English. Crucially, he returned to Robert on the night of 23 June 1314 to inform him of the demoralised state of the English camp and to tell him he could win. Alexander didn't die at Bannockburn, but went on to serve Robert for many years and was well rewarded for his loyalty.

Robert vs John MacDougall

As noted, we do not know the exact chronology of what happened after Methven, but it seems Robert may have been aided by the Abbot of Inchaffray and passed through St Fillan's shrine to a place known as Dail Righ where he was ambushed by MacDougall, although it isn't clear when this battle was fought.

At this point in the novel, I have the abbot talk about absolution, but in reality Robert had already been absolved for the murder of John Comyn by Robert Wishart in Glasgow. Also, Christopher Seton and Christian Bruce were already married.

Prince Edward

Prince Edward was in the west at this time, raiding Bruce's lands, soon after which he, along with Piers Gaveston and other young knights, ended up in trouble with the king for heading off on tournaments rather than focusing on the campaign against the Scots.

Wanting to keep Humphrey de Bohun prominent in the narrative, I have him sent to meet the prince in Carrick and, from there, attempt to join up with MacDougall in Argyll. In reality, the prince went directly from Carrick to meet Aymer de Valence's forces at Kildrummy.

It was John of Menteith who commanded the siege against Dunaverty, which fell only to reveal that Robert had fled, but, again, to keep Prince Edward and Humphrey in the story, I have them take part in the assault.

The violent argument between the prince and his father is based on the account of English chronicler Walter of Guisborough. Piers Gaveston was banished after Edward asked the king if he could grant the Gascon the county of Ponthieu. There has been much speculation, and opinions remain divided, over Prince Edward's sexuality and whether or not he had a physical relationship with Piers Gaveston. There is, however, no doubt that their close bond, whatever it was based on, led to a disastrous division in the royal court, which began between Edward and his father, and eventually took England to the brink of civil war.

The fate of Robert's family

Kildrummy was said to have fallen to the English by the treachery of a blacksmith. Niall Bruce was taken from here and executed in Berwick. Bishops Robert Wishart and William Lamberton were captured and imprisoned in England, but slightly earlier than portrayed. Lamberton was indeed later released to negotiate with Robert on behalf of Edward II. John of Atholl and the women, possibly attempting to escape to Orkney or Norway (where Robert's sister was queen), were taken at Tain.

Queen Elizabeth was placed under house arrest at Burstwick Manor, in the care of two old women who were forbidden from talking to her. She was later moved around, including to Barking Abbey in Essex. Her affair with Humphrey de Bohun (whose wife, Elizabeth, was still alive at this time) is fiction. Marjorie Bruce was initially sentenced to imprisonment in a cage in the Tower of London, but Edward relented and sent her instead to a Yorkshire nunnery.

For her part in Robert's coronation, Isabel Comyn was imprisoned in a cage in Berwick Castle, apparently fashioned in the shape of a crown. Some reports indicate this was open to public view, others that it was inside a tower. She was released in 1312 and sent to a nunnery and, from there, placed in the custody of Henry Beaumont. Beyond that, her fate is unclear. Mary Bruce, for reasons unknown, was also put in a cage, at Roxburgh Castle. She appears to have been released around 1310, but was kept in English custody until she was exchanged, either in 1312 or 1314. Of all the Bruce women, Christian Bruce got off lightest: sent to a nunnery in Lincolnshire. Her husband, Christopher Seton, however, was hanged and beheaded, but at Dumfries (site of the murder of John Comyn, which he'd been involved in) not Berwick as I have it in the novel. John of Atholl was hanged in London – the first earl to be executed in England for two hundred and thirty years.

Alexander and Thomas Bruce were captured in Galloway, along with an Irish magnate and a large contingent of Irishmen, by Dungal MacDouall. The Irish magnate was beheaded by MacDouall and the brothers were executed by Edward. As noted in the previous novels, Lord Donough is fictitious as is Cormac, although it is has been suggested that Robert and Edward Bruce were possibly fostered to an Irish lord in youth, Robert owned lands in Antrim and there is mention of a foster-brother on the run with him in Carrick. Again, it is all a question of connecting the dots between what is known and what is unknown.

The survivors of Edward's brutal punishments, including Elizabeth, Marjorie and Wishart, were exchanged for Humphrey de Bohun after the Battle of Bannockburn. But Robert's nephew, Donald of Mar, when offered the chance to return to Scotland, did choose to remain in the court of Edward II.

MacRuaries and MacDonalds

As noted, we don't know where Robert spent the winter of 1306, but we do know he had some help from the Isles, in the form of Angus MacDonald, Christiana and Lachlan MacRuarie. Lachlan, in particular, is a fascinating, but slippery character, who flits in and out of the records, appearing briefly on one side of the conflict before vanishing and reappearing on the other. Our information for the Western Isles at this time is patchy at best, so I've had to invent much of it, but still in line, where possible, with what we know.

The role of Thomas and Alexander Bruce on Islay is fiction, as is Robert's time on Barra, although the English accused him of being Christiana's lover, which is entirely possible given his illegitimate children. James Stewart's appearance on Barra and his dealings with Robert at this point are my invention, as is the capture of Henry Percy, although Robert did assault Turnberry and in Barbour's narrative we find the fire that summoned him and his men prematurely from Arran and Aymer using one of Robert's hounds to attempt to track him down.

David of Atholl

As with Alexander Seton, David, Earl of Atholl after his father's execution, had a volatile relationship with Robert, switching sides several times during the conflict. He left Robert's company sooner than I've portrayed – shortly after the murder of John Comyn, whose daughter he was married to. With so many characters and so much allegiance-swapping going on, I was forced to simplify his role in the novel. In reality, David fought for the English until 1312, when he came into Robert's peace and was made Constable of Scotland. Edward Bruce then seduced his sister, Isabel of Atholl, causing David to switch back to the English. He destroyed the Scots' supplies stored at Cambuskenneth Abbey on the eve of the Battle of Bannockburn.

The Prophecies of Merlin

I've written about the veracity of the prophecies, the relics, King Edward's Round Table and his obsession with all things Arthurian in my previous author's notes. Here, I will just say that a new prophecy of Merlin was said to be sweeping Scotland in 1307, proclaimed by 'false preachers' of Robert Bruce, predicting that upon the death of the 'covetous king' the Scots and the Welsh would band together and reclaim their lands.

Robert's return

As mentioned, we know only scant details about Robert's triumph at Glen Trool. Here I have Thomas Randolph taken fighting for the English and returned to Robert's company. This did happen, but slightly later than portrayed.

It was the Battle of Loudoun Hill that changed everything for Robert, with one English ally commenting that he never enjoyed such support among the Scots as he did after this victory against Aymer's forces.

Robert's campaign against the Comyns and their supporters started two months earlier than depicted. Again, as mentioned, the exact timeline of events is unknown, although Robert was said to have fallen gravely ill and had to be carried on a litter before the forces of the Black Comyn, whom he finally bested in a running battle on the road to Inverurie. The Black Comyn was aided at this time by several other Scottish barons, including David of Atholl.

We do not know whether Robert's campaign in Argyll, which culminated in the Battle at the Pass of Brander and the fall of Dunstaffnage, occurred in 1308 or 1309, but I have tried to follow what we know of the events. The execution of Dungal MacDouall by Edward Bruce is, however, pure fiction. MacDouall's story is far more complex – and thus emotionally unsatisfying – than I had chance to portray. After fleeing Edward Bruce's raid on Galloway in 1308, he surrendered himself and the town of Dumfries to Robert in 1313. Robert allowed him to go free and MacDouall went to Man in his service, but switched to the English once more and was then captured again by Robert. This time, when released, he remained with the English, dying in 1327.

Edward II and Piers Gaveston

Edward I died at Burgh by Sands in July 1307. His death was kept secret for a fortnight while his son, then in London, was informed.

After a lacklustre attempt to hunt down Robert, the new king – to all intents and purposes – gave up his father's war and followed his body back to Westminster. He at once had Piers returned to his side and although he was wed to Isabella of France, it was commented upon that he seemed more married to his childhood friend.

Humphrey de Bohun and Aymer de Valence were attending the wedding in France in January 1308, but Piers was indeed made regent in Edward's absence. He was also made Earl of Cornwall, but a few months earlier than portrayed. The coronation at Westminster is relayed much as described in the chronicles, including the collapse of a wall in the abbey.

The chronology of events portrayed in chapters 39–43 comprises perhaps the most fictionalised section of the novel. The conflict between Edward II and the barons from 1308 to 1312, while fascinating in and of itself, is simply too drawn out to do justice to here, especially when the narrative is counting down to Bannockburn.

Instead, I have taken several key events – Piers's command of Perth (which occurred in 1311), Robert's attack on Perth (which took place in January 1313), Mary's release from English custody (which happened in either 1312 or 1314), Piers's return from exile, his capture and subsequent execution (in 1312) – and amalgamated them into a connected sequence, the outcome of which is ultimately the same as it was in history. Robert didn't make any such pact with Thomas of Lancaster at this time, neither did he capture Piers at Perth and deliver him to the barons. In 1321, however, Thomas was said to be negotiating with Robert against Edward II and in this correspondence was referred to as King Arthur.

In reality, when it was discovered, in either late 1311 or early 1312, that Piers Gaveston had returned in secrecy from exile, into which he had been forced by the ordinances of the reformist Lords Ordainers, he and Edward fled to York. One chronicle states that Thomas of Lancaster, Aymer de Valence, Humphrey de Bohun, Guy de Beauchamp and the Earl of Arundel now formulated a secret plan to capture Gaveston. Lancaster was said to have openly demanded the Gascon be sent back into exile. The barons then moved north against the king and his favourite and besieged Scarborough Castle, which Piers was in command of. Piers eventually surrendered to Aymer de Valence, on the basis he would not be harmed. Valence took him to Oxfordshire, but it seems he was duped by his fellow conspirators, among them Lancaster, Warwick and Hereford, for Gaveston was wrested from him and taken to Blacklow Hill in Warwickshire, where he was executed.

The finger of blame for this act – which was actually performed by two Welsh foot soldiers – has been pointed variously at Thomas of Lancaster, Guy de Beauchamp and Aymer de Valence. After Piers's death, England came close to civil war. It took a year before a tentative peace was made between the king and the barons involved, although, as portrayed in the novel, many of them refused to fight for him at Bannockburn, which proved Edward's undoing. Piers Gaveston was laid to rest in King's Langley in 1315.

Bannockburn

As mentioned, I've gone with the Dryfield site for the main battle. Another point worth noting is that some historians now think the schiltrom under the command of James Douglas and Walter Stewart was invented by John Barbour in order to bolster Douglas's reputation. Also, some believe the so-called 'challenge of Stirling' Edward Bruce offered to Philip Moubray was made only a matter of months before the battle itself, not a full year. Moubray was apparently offered safe passage to ride out to Edward II and inform him of the situation in Stirling and the position of the Scots in the New Park.

After the battle, Humphrey de Bohun wasn't taken from the field, but from Bothwell Castle, where he fled with Ingram de Umfraville.

Robert's death

After securing Scotland's independence from England in 1328, Robert died in Cardross the following year, aged fifty-five. He was believed to have been suffering with a disease for several years prior to his death, which some chroniclers said was leprosy, although this has never been proven.

He asked for his heart to be taken to the Holy Sepulchre in Jerusalem, a crusade undertaken by James Douglas, who carried it as far as Spain, where he died in battle against the Moors. James's body was brought back to Scotland and Robert's heart was buried at Melrose Abbey. It is believed it lies there still.

Robyn Young
Brighton
March 2014

CHARACTER LIST

(* Indicates fictitious characters, relationships or groups)

*ADAM: Gascon commander in a crossbow regiment of Edward I

*AFFRAIG: wise woman from Turnberry

*AGNES: laundress to Marjorie, Countess of Carrick

*ALAN: squire of Gilbert de la Hay

*ALAN: scout in Robert's army

ALEXANDER III: King of Scotland (1249–86), brother-in-law of Edward I by his first marriage, died in 1286

ALEXANDER BRUCE: brother of Robert and Dean of Glasgow

ALEXANDER MACDOUGALL: father of John MacDougall, Lord of Argyll and Lorn

ALEXANDER SETON: lord from East Lothian and *cousin of Christopher Seton

ANGUS OG MACDONALD: Lord of Islay

ANTHONY BEK: Bishop of Durham

AYMER DE VALENCE: Earl of Pembroke, cousin of Edward I and brother-in-law of John Comyn III

BLACK COMYN (THE): Earl of Buchan and head of the Black Comyns

*BRICE: one of Neil Campbell's men

*BRIGID: niece of Affraig

CHARLES DE VALOIS: French noble, uncle of Isabella

CHRISTIAN BRUCE: sister of Robert

CHRISTIANA MACRUARIE: Lady of Garmoran

CHRISTOPHER SETON: son of an English knight from Yorkshire and *cousin of Alexander Seton, married to Christian Bruce

CLEMENT V: pope

*COL: serving boy at Aberdeen Castle

*CONSTANCE: maid to Elizabeth at Pleshey Castle

*CORMAC: son of Lord Donough and foster-brother of Robert

DAVID OF ATHOLL: son of John of Atholl

DONALD OF MAR: son of Christian Bruce and Gartnait of Mar, Robert's nephew

*DONOUGH: Robert's foster-father and lord of the Bruce estates in Antrim

DUNGAL MACDOUALL: former captain of the army of Galloway

EDMUND: son of Edward I and Marguerite of France

EDWARD I: King of England (1272–1307)

EDWARD BRUCE: brother of Robert

EDWARD OF CAERNARFON: son and heir of Edward I, King of England (1307–1327)

*EDWIN: steward of Robert's father in Writtle

ELEANOR OF CASTILE: first wife of Edward I, mother of Edward II

*ELENA: daughter of Brigid

ELIZABETH (BESS): daughter of Edward I and Eleanor of Castile, wife of Humphrey de Bohun

ELIZABETH BRUCE: daughter of the Earl of Ulster, Robert's second wife and Queen of Scotland

*EWEN: knight of Alexander Seton

*FERGUS: soldier in Robert's army

GARTNAIT OF MAR: Earl of Mar, first husband of Christian Bruce, father of Donald

*GEOFFREY: royal knight

*GIL: prisoner at Berwick Castle

GILBERT DE CLARE: Earl of Gloucester

GILBERT DE LA HAY: Lord of Erroll

GILES D'ARGENTAN: English knight

*GILLEPATRICK: one of Angus MacDonald's men on Islay

GUY DE BEAUCHAMP: Earl of Warwick

HENRY III: King of England (1216–72), Edward I's father

HENRY BEAUMONT: knight in the court of Edward II

HENRY DE BOHUN: Humphrey's nephew

HENRY PERCY: Lord of Alnwick

*HUGH: squire of Humphrey de Bohun

HUMPHREY DE BOHUN: Earl of Hereford and Essex, and Constable of England

INGRAM DE UMFRAVILLE: former guardian of Scotland

ISABEL OF ATHOLL: daughter of John of Atholl and his wife, the countess

ISABEL BRUCE: sister of Robert, marries Eric II and becomes Queen of Norway

ISABEL COMYN: Countess of Buchan, wife of the Black Comyn

ISABELLA OF FRANCE: daughter of King Philippe IV, wife of Edward II and Queen of England

ISOBEL OF MAR: a daughter of the Earl of Mar, Robert's first wife and mother of Marjorie Bruce

JAMES DOUGLAS: son and heir of William Douglas, nephew and godson of James Stewart

JAMES STEWART: High Steward of Scotland

JOAN OF ACRE: daughter of Edward I and Eleanor of Castile, wife of Ralph de Monthermer

JOAN DE VALENCE: sister of Aymer de Valence and wife of John Comyn III

JOHN OF ATHOLL: Earl of Atholl and Sheriff of Aberdeen, married to a daughter of the Earl of Mar, making him Robert's brother-in-law

JOHN BALLIOL II: Lord of Galloway and King of Scotland (1292–96), deposed by Edward I in 1296

JOHN COMYN III: Lord of Badenoch, head of the Red Comyns, married to Joan de Valence, killed by Robert in 1306

JOHN COMYN IV: son of the man killed by Robert

JOHN MACDOUGALL: Lord of Argyll and Lorn, cousin of John Comyn

JOHN OF MENTEITH: son of the Earl of Menteith

*JUDITH: maid to Marjorie Bruce

*KERALD: one of Christiana's men on Barra

LACHLAN MACRUARIE: captain of the galloglass, half-brother of Christiana

LLYWELYN AP GRUFFUDD: Prince of Wales, killed during the 1282–84 conquest

*LORA: maid to Elizabeth Bruce

LOUIS D'EVREUX: French noble, uncle of Isabella

*LUCY: maid to Elizabeth in Burstwick Manor

*LUKE: infantryman in the army of Edward II

MALACHY (ST): Archbishop of Armagh (1132–37), canonised in 1199

MALCOLM: Earl of Lennox

MALCOLM III (CANMORE): King of Scotland (1058–93)

MARGARET: half-sister of Robert from his mother's first marriage, mother of Thomas Randolph

MARGARET (THE MAID OF NORWAY): granddaughter and heir of

Alexander III, named Queen of Scotland after his death, but died on the voyage from Norway

MARGARET DE CLARE: *sister of Gilbert, niece of Edward II, wife of Piers Gaveston*

MARGUERITE OF FRANCE: *sister of Philippe IV, second wife of Edward I and Queen of England*

MARJORIE BRUCE: *daughter of Robert and Isobel of Mar*

MARJORIE OF CARRICK: *Countess of Carrick, Robert's mother, died in 1292*

MARMADUKE TWENG: *English knight*

MARY BRUCE: *sister of Robert*

MATILDA BRUCE: *sister of Robert*

*MATTHEW: *knight of Aymer de Valence*

*MAUD: *maid to Elizabeth in Burstwick Manor*

MAURICE: *Abbot of Inchaffray*

NEIL CAMPBELL: *a knight from Argyll*

*NES: *former squire to Robert, made a knight*

NIALL BRUCE: *brother of Robert*

NICHOLAS TINGEWICK: *royal physician to Edward I*

*NICOLAS: *guard at Pleshey Castle*

*NIGEL: *infantryman in the army of Edward II*

*OSBERT: *guard at Roxburgh Castle*

OSBOURNE: *blacksmith at Kildrummy Castle*

*PATRICK: *one of Angus MacDonald's men*

*PATRICK: *Robert's servant*

PHILIP MOUBRAY: *commander of Stirling Castle*

PHILIPPE IV: *King of France (1286–1314), father of Isabella, cousin of Edward I*

PIERS GAVESTON: a Gascon knight in Prince Edward's household, made Earl of Cornwall

RALPH DE MONTHERMER: royal knight in the court of Edward I, married to the king's daughter Joan, stepfather of Gilbert de Clare

*RANULF: steward of Humphrey de Bohun at Pleshey Castle

RICHARD DE BURGH: Earl of Ulster and Lord of Connacht, father of Elizabeth

ROBERT BRUCE V: grandfather of Robert, competed for the throne of Scotland, died in 1295

ROBERT BRUCE VI: father of Robert, former Earl of Carrick

ROBERT BRUCE VII: Earl of Carrick, Lord of Annandale on his father's death and King of Scotland (1306–29)

ROBERT CLIFFORD: royal knight

ROBERT KEITH: royal marshal in Robert's court

ROBERT WINCHELSEA: Archbishop of Canterbury

ROBERT WISHART: Bishop of Glasgow

*ROLAND: soldier at Kildrummy Castle

RUARIE MACRUARIE: half-brother of Christiana

*SIM: guard at Roxburgh Castle

*SIMON: doorward of Edward I

SIMON FRASER: Scottish nobleman and rebel

SIMON DE MONTFORT: Earl of Leicester, led a rebellion against Henry III, died in battle with Edward, his godson, in 1265

THOMAS OF BROTHERTON: son of Edward I and Marguerite of France

THOMAS BRUCE: brother of Robert

THOMAS OF LANCASTER: Earl of Lancaster and nephew of Edward I, cousin of Edward II

THOMAS RANDOLPH: son of Margaret Bruce, Robert's half-nephew

*TOM: squire of Alexander Seton

WALTER STEWART: son of James Stewart

*WILL: knight of Alexander Seton

WILLIAM LAMBERTON: Bishop of St Andrews

WILLIAM OF ROSS: Earl of Ross

WILLIAM WALLACE: leader of the Scottish rebellion against Edward I in 1297, executed in 1305

YOLANDE OF DREUX: second wife of Alexander III and Queen of Scotland

GLOSSARY

BASINET: a close-fitting helmet, sometimes worn with a visor.

BRAIES: undergarments worn by men.

COAT-OF-PLATES: a cloth or leather garment with metal plates riveted to it, worn under the surcoat.

COIF: a tight-fitting cloth cap worn by men and women, it could also be made of mail and worn by soldiers under or instead of a helm.

CROWN OF ARTHUR: a coronet worn by the princes of Gwynedd, most notably Llywelyn ap Gruffudd who styled himself Prince of Wales. Edward I seized the crown along with other important Welsh relics during the 1282–84 invasion and sent it to Westminster Abbey.

CURTANA: also known as the Sword of Mercy because of its symbolically broken tip, it was thought to have belonged to St Edward the Confessor and became part of the English regalia used in coronations.

DESTRIER: a warhorse.

DIRK: Scots for dagger.

FALCHION: a short sword with a curved edge.

FOSSE: a ditch or moat.

GAMBESON: a padded coat worn by soldiers, often made of quilted cloth, stuffed with felt or straw.

GEOFFREY OF MONMOUTH: thought to have been a Welshman or Breton by birth, Monmouth resided in Oxford during the twelfth century, where he was possibly a canon of St George's College. Later, he became Bishop of St Asaph. He wrote three known works during his life, the most famous being *The History of the Kings of Britain* of which the *Prophecies of Merlin* became part, followed by *The Life of Merlin*. Despite mixing established British history with romantic fiction, Monmouth presented his writings as fact and many readers of his works took them as such, accepting King Arthur and Merlin as historical figures. Monmouth's works, although criticised by some of his contemporaries, were hugely popular during the medieval period and from his *The History of the Kings of Britain* sprang the immense canon of Arthurian literature that graced Europe over the following centuries. Chrétien de Troyes, Malory, Shakespeare and Tennyson were all influenced by his work.

HAUBERK: a shirt or coat of mail with long sleeves.

HUKE: a hooded cloak.

MAGNATE: a high-ranking noble.

MOTTE: a castle or keep built on a mound, often surrounded by a bailey.

PALFREY: a light horse used for everyday riding.

PROPHECIES OF MERLIN: written by Geoffrey of Monmouth during the twelfth century. Originally composed as a separate volume, the *Prophecies* were later incorporated into his *The History of the Kings of Britain*. According to Monmouth he was translating the work into Latin from an older text. Monmouth has been credited as being the creator of Merlin, but it is now believed he derived this enigmatic figure from earlier Welsh sources.

QUARREL: an arrow for a crossbow.

SCHILTROM: a shield ring usually composed of spearmen.

STAFF OF MALACHY: also known as the Staff of Jesus, it was a wooden crosier covered with gold. It was believed to have belonged to St Patrick, who is said to have received it from Jesus. Highly revered by the Irish, it became connected with Malachy, Archbishop of Armagh, when he was forced to pay off the leader of the secular clan who had possession of the staff and control of St Patrick's Cathedral and its diocese. According to popular law, only when Malachy had the staff could he claim to be the rightful archbishop. The staff was taken to Dublin in the late twelfth century, where it was burned as a superstitious relic in the sixteenth century.

STONE OF DESTINY: also called the Stone of Scone, it was the ancient seat used in Scottish coronations. Thought to have been brought to Scone in the ninth century by Scotland's king, Kenneth mac Alpin, its origins are unknown. It was seized by Edward I during the 1296 invasion and taken to Westminster Abbey where it was set in a specially designed throne and became part of the English coronation ceremony. It remained here until 1950 when four students stole it and returned it to Scotland. It was later sent back to England, before being officially presented to Edinburgh Castle in 1996, where it remains on display. It will be returned to Westminster for future coronations.

SURCOAT: a long sleeveless garment usually worn over armour.

VAMBRACE: armour for the lower arm.

VASSAL: a retainer subject to a feudal superior, who holds land in return for homage and services.

VENTAIL: a flap of mail that can be pulled up and secured to protect the lower half of the face during combat.

Succession to the Scottish Throne

DAVID I
1124–1153

EARL HENRY
(d. 1152)

MALCOLM IV
(1153–1165)

WILLIAM THE LION
(1165–1214)

MARGARET

ADA & FLORENCE III OF HOLLAND

DAVID EARL OF HUNTINGDON
(d. 1219)

ALEXANDER II
(1214–1249)

ALEXANDER III
(1249–1286)

ALEXANDER
(d. 1284)

DAVID
(d. 1281)

MARGARET
(d. 1283)
& ERIC II OF NORWAY

MARGARET
(THE MAID OF NORWAY)
(d. 1290)

FLORENCE V OF HOLLAND
Competitor

MARGARET

DERVORGUILLA & JOHN BALLIOL

JOHN BALLIOL
Competitor

ISABEL & ROBERT BRUCE

ROBERT BRUCE LORD OF ANNANDALE
Competitor

ROBERT BRUCE EARL OF CARRICK

ROBERT BRUCE

ADA

HENRY HASTINGS

JOHN HASTINGS
Competitor

JOHN

BIBLIOGRAPHY

Armstrong, Pete, *Bannockburn 1314, Robert Bruce's Great Victory*, Osprey, 2002

Baker, Timothy, *Medieval London*, Cassell, 1970

Barbour, John, *The Bruce* (trans. A.A.M. Duncan), Canongate Classics, 1997

Barrell, A.D.M., *Medieval Scotland*, Cambridge University Press, 2000

Barrow, G.W.S., *Robert Bruce and the Community of the Realm of Scotland*, Edinburgh University Press, 1988

Barrow, G.W.S., *The Kingdom of the Scots*, Edinburgh University Press, 2003

Beam, Amanda, *The Balliol Dynasty 1210–1364*, John Donald, 2008

Branigan, Keith, *Ancient Barra, Exploring the Archaeology of the Outer Hebrides*, Comhairle nan Eilean Siar, 2007

Brown, James, *Carrick, Scotland, Beyond the Tourist Guides*, Carrick Community Councils' Forum, 2009

Cannan, Fergus, *Galloglass 1250–1600*, Osprey, 2010

Chancellor, John, *The Life and Times of Edward I*, Weidenfeld & Nicolson, 1981

Clairvaux, St. Bernard of, *Life of St. Malachy of Armagh* (trans. H.J. Lawlor), Dodo Press, 1920

Cornell, David, *Bannockburn, the Triumph of Robert the Bruce*, Yale University Press, 2009

Cowan, Edward J., *For Freedom Alone: The Declaration of Arbroath, 1320*, Birlinn, 2008

Cowan, Edward J. and Henderson, Lizanne (eds.), *A History of Everyday Life in Medieval Scotland, 1000–1600*, Edinburgh University Press, 2011

Cummins, John, *The Hound and the Hawk, the Art of Medieval Hunting*, Phoenix Press, 2001

Daniell, Christopher, *Death and Burial in Medieval England 1066–1550*, Routledge, 1997

Davis, I.M., *The Black Douglas*, Routledge & Kegan Paul, 1974

Dean, Gareth, *Medieval York*, History Press, 2008

Duffy, Seán, *Ireland in the Middle Ages*, Macmillan Press, 1997

Edge, David and Paddock, John M., *Arms and Armour of the Medieval Knight*, Bison Group, 1988

Fawcett, Richard, *Stirling Castle (Official Guide)*, Historic Scotland, 1999

Frame, Robin, *Ireland and Britain 1170–1450*, Hambledon Press, 1998

France, John, *Western Warfare in the Age of the Crusades 1000–1300*, UCL Press, 1999

Given-Wilson, Chris, Kettle, Ann and Scales, Len (eds.), *War, Government and Aristocracy in the British Isles c.1150–1500*, Boydell Press, 2008

Gravett, Christopher, *Knights at Tournament*, Osprey Publishing, 1988

Gravett, Christopher, *English Medieval Knight 1300–1400*, Osprey Publishing, 2002

Grove, Doreen and Yeoman, Peter, *Caerlaverock Castle (Official Guide)*, Historic Scotland, 2006

Haines, Roy Martin, *King Edward II, His Life His Reign and its Aftermath 1284–1330*, McGill-Queen's University Press, 2003

Houston, Mary G., *Medieval Costume in England and France*, Dover Publications, 1996

Hyland, Ann, *The Horse in the Middle Ages*, Sutton Publishing, 1999

Impey, Edward and Parnell, Geoffrey, *The Tower of London (Official Illustrated History)*, Merrell, 2006

Kieckhefer, Richard, *Magic in the Middle Ages*, Cambridge University Press, 2000

Leyser, Henrietta, *Medieval Women, a Social History of Women in England 450–1500*, Phoenix, 1996

Lindsay, Maurice, *The Castles of Scotland*, Constable, 1995

Lynch, Michael, *Scotland, a New History*, Pimlico, 1991

McDonald, Andrew R., *The Kingdom of the Isles, Scotland's Western Seaboard c.1100–c.1336*, Tuckwell Press, 1997

McNair Scott, Ronald, *Robert the Bruce, King of Scots*, Canongate, 1988

McNamee, Colm, *Robert Bruce, Our Most Valiant Prince, King and Lord*, Birlinn, 2006

Moffat, Alistair, *The Sea Kingdoms, the History of Celtic Britain and Ireland*, Birlinn, 2011

Monmouth, Geoffrey of, *The History of the Kings of Britain* (trans. Lewis Thorpe), Penguin Classics, 1966

Monmouth, Geoffrey of, *The Vita Merlini* (trans. John Jay Parry), BiblioBazaar, 2008

Morris, J.E., *The Welsh Wars of Edward I*, Sutton Publishing, 1998

Morris, Marc, *A Great and Terrible King, Edward I and the Forging of Britain*, Hutchinson, 2008

Nicolle, David, *The History of Medieval Life*, Chancellor Press, 2000

Oram, Richard, *The Kings and Queens of Scotland*, Tempus, 2004

Reese, Peter, *Bannockburn, Scotland's Greatest Victory*, Canongate, 2000

Rixson, Denis, *The West Highland Galley*, Birlinn, 1998

Rixson, Denis, *The Small Isles, Canna, Rum, Eigg and Muck*, Birlinn, 2011

Spufford, Peter, *Power and Profit, the Merchant in Medieval Europe*, Thames and Hudson, 2002

Tabraham, Chris, *Scotland's Castles*, Historic Scotland, B.T. Batsford, 2005

Tabraham, Chris (ed.), *Edinburgh Castle (Official Guide)*, Historic Scotland, 2003

Talbot, C.H., *Medicine in Medieval England*, Oldbourne, 1967

Watson, Fiona, *Under the Hammer, Edward I & Scotland 1286–1307*, Tuckwell Press, 1998

Weir, Alison, *Isabella, She-Wolf of France, Queen of England*, Pimlico, 2006

Wilkinson, James and Knighton, C.S., *Crown and Cloister, the Royal Story of Westminster Abbey*, Scala, 2010

Williams, Ronald, *The Lords of the Isles, the Clan Donald and the Early Kingdom of the Scots*, House of Lochar, 2000

Yeoman, Peter, *Medieval Scotland*, Historic Scotland, B.T. Batsford, 1995

Young, Alan, *Robert the Bruce's Rivals: The Comyns, 1212–1314*, Tuckwell Press, 1997

Zacour, Norman, *An Introduction to Medieval Institutions*, St James Press, 1977

Excerpts used as epigraphs on part titles taken from:

The Vita Merlini, Geoffrey of Monmouth (trans. John Jay Parry), BiblioBazaar, 2008

The British History of Geoffrey of Monmouth (trans. A. Thompson, revised edn J. A. Giles), William Stevens (printer), London, 1842